Grant S... ...y and brought up in rural we... Au...ia. ...ter studying at the London School of Economics he worked as a money broker with Exco in Sydney. He now lives in Oxfordshire with his wife and children, and is the author of one previous thrille *Due Diligence*.

Also by Grant Sutherland

Due Diligence

East of
the City

Grant Sutherland

HEADLINE
FEATURE

First published in 1998
by HEADLINE BOOK PUBLISHING

First published in paperback in 1999
by HEADLINE BOOK PUBLISHING

A HEADLINE FEATURE paperback

10 9 8 7 6 5 4 3 2 1

ISBN 0 7472 5694 2

Typeset by
Letterpart Limited, Reigate, Surrey

Printed and bound in Great Britain by
Mackays of Chatham PLC, Chatham, Kent

HEADLINE BOOK PUBLISHING
A division of Hodder Headline PLC
338 Euston Road
London NW1 3BH

www.headline.co.uk
www.hodderheadline.com

Thanks to Toby Stubbs and Bill Wood for their generous assistance during my research for this book.

1

1

'You still want it?'

When I didn't answer her little joke, Ms Kerry Anne Lammar, the senior sales agent on the Cooper's Dock development, went on down the hall and turned right.

'I don't think you've seen the kitchen,' she said.

I let my fingers trail along the wall as I followed her. They'd painted the walls, and laid the carpet too, since the last time I'd been to see it. In the kitchen I found Kerry Anne striking a pose by the fridge. She was smiling.

'You like?' she asked me.

Every surface gleamed. The woodwork was mahogany, and the cupboards looked big enough to get lost in. There was a built-in cooker and microwave, and other gadgets I didn't even recognize. God knows what Mum would have made of it.

But when all I said, was, 'It's okay,' Kerry Anne's smile just froze.

She turned away from me then, started opening and closing cupboard doors, telling me what was what. She wasn't exactly rude, but you could tell she wasn't happy either. Kerry Anne was in her mid-forties, and when I'd first rolled up in her office and asked for the penthouse details, she'd treated me like dirt. Since then I'd put down the hundred grand deposit, and now she didn't treat me like dirt any more, but she still thought of me that way. It was the trace of my old accent, I guess. And my age. She just couldn't accept that a thirty-three-year-old East End boy deserved forty thousand pounds' worth of kitchen inside a million pounds' worth of penthouse.

She was still explaining the fancy ventilation system as I wandered off to check out the other rooms. They'd all been carpeted too, and painted, and most of the light fittings were done. In one of the back bedrooms, I paused a moment and looked out of the window, between the buildings, to the flat where I lived. My kid sister Katy would still be in bed. I'd lived there nearly six years, and every morning of the past two I'd go out onto the balcony, drink my coffee, and watch the workmen scramble around the building site that had gradually turned into the flashest apartment block on the Thames.

And now I was standing in it. Cooper's Dock.

'Mr Collier?'

Kerry Anne, she just couldn't keep that pissed-off tone out of her voice. And she was searching for me in the wrong direction.

'Mr Collier, I wanted to show you . . . Mr Collier?' Her voice drifted away as she went on with the search.

I wandered through the second bathroom into another bedroom, then out into the lounge. Light. It came pouring in through the wall of glass that separated the lounge from the balcony. I slid the door open and stepped outside.

The morning breeze was cold coming up off the river. I did up my coat and rested my forearms on the railing. The view was a stunner. East to Docklands, West to the bridges, and the whole South Bank laid out in front. Six months earlier, when my parents died, I'd thought about reclaiming my deposit and letting the penthouse go. It was too late for that now. I was locked in under the terms of my contract. If I didn't produce the rest of the money by the following weekend, I'd forfeit five thousand quid of my deposit weekly. Five grand a week until they found another purchaser for the penthouse. Or until my hundred grand deposit, which I'd borrowed against my flat, was gone. Rocking forward on the balls of my feet now, I wondered how far out I'd land if I jumped.

There was a sound behind me. I turned to find Kerry

Anne rapping her knuckles on the plate-glass. She pointed at her watch, and shouted, 'Another appointment,' the words barely reaching me outside. She disappeared, and I leant back against the railing and considered my uncompleted purchase.

The penthouse was huge, and now that it had been fitted out it really looked like a million quid, maybe more. Back when I'd paid the deposit, they hadn't even finished this floor; I only had the plans to go on, but I'd always hoped it might turn out to be something special. And that's what had happened; the finished article was a cracker, even better than I'd hoped.

Did I still want it? Oh yeah, I still wanted it. It was everything I wanted, the security and respectability, the whole bit.

All I had to do now was get my promotion at work confirmed. Once I'd done that I could sell my flat, then my bank manager would stump up the rest of the cash for the penthouse. But my promotion. There, if I could bear to look at it, was my problem. The promotion I'd been promised, the reason a normally cautious man like me had put a hundred grand on the line, just hadn't happened. Showed no sign of happening. A little fact I'd neglected to tell Ms Kerry Anne Lammar.

Now I hurled a quid coin way out into the river, just for luck. When I got in to work, I was going to have to speak with my boss.

2

The Lloyd's Room isn't a room, it's the first three floors of the Lloyd's Building. Each floor is shaped like a square doughnut, open-side facing inward to the atrium. The atrium goes up past the glassed-in offices till it reaches the top floors where the Lloyd's Chairman and the Council hold court. But the Room is the heart of the place, that's where the business of Lloyd's gets done. It had been my place of work for twelve years, ever since my big bust-up with Dad.

'Morning, Ian.'

'Morning,' I said, not really recognizing the bloke. One of the brokers. He stepped off the escalator ahead of me and veered left.

I went right, making my way down to the Mortlake boxes, the cluster of desks where me and the other Mortlake underwriters spent our working day. Passing through the Room I got a few nods, but only a few; it was shaping up to be a busy morning in the market. For nine months a year the brokers drifted in and out, the underwriters sauntered around the Room arranging mid-week games of golf, and half the market disappeared on freebies to the States. Sometimes, occasionally, a policy got written. Then from November through February the place came alive. Brokers you hadn't seen for twelve months were suddenly queuing at the box, their folders bulging with 'slips', the various policy renewals for the coming year. And that's how it was that morning. Brokers going from box to box, underwriters referring to their PCs, talking to the brokers and studying the slips, the whole market earning its keep. Angela Mortlake, my boss, was busy.

I slid into my chair.

'Good night at the dogs?'

I looked over the PC at my least favourite colleague, Frazer Burnett-Adams. My father used to be a bookie at the dogs. Frazer's father was a baronet. He found some way of reminding me of these two facts several times each week.

'That crack wasn't even funny the first time you made it, Frazer.' I glanced at the files on my desk. 'And the first time you made it was five fucking years ago.'

While he told me I had no sense of humour, I scrolled through the overnight e-mail. A few notes on the Ottoman Air case – a disputed claim currently in court – from our solicitor, but nothing vital. I looked over at Angela again. She was still busy.

'I hear there's no chance Ottoman are going to settle. Must be a worry for you.'

'Give it a rest, Frazer.'

He put up his hands, all innocence. Just asking, he said.

Then his attention was diverted by a broker, but I knew it was only a short-term reprieve. Frazer was forty years old. He'd been underwriting at Lloyd's for fifteen years, the last five of those with us on Syndicate 486. When Angela Mortlake went into hospital for her mastectomy six months back, and I replaced her temporarily, Frazer went ballistic. He'd calmed down a bit since she'd come back, but I knew he was still doing everything he could to shaft me. I wasn't the only one who wanted Angela's job. Now when I saw she was free I got up and went over to join her.

'Did you hear about Sebastian's place?' she asked me.

'Hear what?'

'Last night,' she said as I pulled up a chair. 'It burnt down.'

My head jerked round.

'Everyone's talking about it,' she told me.

Three yards away from us, a queue of brokers had

formed; they were waiting to show us their slips, the policies they were touting around the Room. Angela signalled one of them over. It was Nigel Chambers from WardSure. Sebastian Ward, whose house had burnt down, was his employer. He confirmed what Angela had told me, but he didn't seem to know anything more about it. He cracked some joke about hoping Sebastian was fully insured. Ignoring that, Angela pointed to his folder.

'The satellite?' she said, and he sat down and pulled out a slip.

Sebastian's house had burnt down. While I waited for that one to hit me, Angela started into the routine, the last haggle with the broker, the final push and shove before she signed. Even now, after the mastectomy that had knocked her so badly, Angela was still one of the best. She had insurance in her blood. She was a Gastonville before she married Allen Mortlake, and the Gastonvilles have provided Lloyd's with quite a few Chairmen, one or two a century, and at Lloyd's that kind of thing matters. If you listened to the talk, the name was half the reason Allen Mortlake married her. Instant connections. Anyway, between them they knew the market inside-out.

Now she picked up her stamp and banged it down on the slip. It left a row of squares, and above these the syndicate title, MOR 486.

'Fifteen,' she told Nigel.

She put numbers in the squares, then wrote '15%' and her scratch, 'A. Mortlake', the A and M big and looping. She'd just insured fifteen per cent of a thirty million-pound satellite launch in Guyana. Then Nigel Chambers pulled another slip from his folder.

'CAT risk in the sunny isles?' Catastrophe insurance, he meant, in the Caribbean.

Angela stood and stretched. 'Not interested,' she said.

He shuffled his papers together and moved on. Angela glanced back at the queue of brokers waiting to deliver their pitch.

I said, 'How do they think it happened? Sebastian's place.'

'No idea.' She said she'd only just heard herself an hour ago.

'Have you spoken to him?'

Shaking her head, she looked at me. It was a pretty weird moment; I could see what she was thinking. Three months earlier, sitting at my desk on the 486 box, I'd come completely and spectacularly unstuck.

I'd been running a set of stats through my PC when one of the brokers came and put a fire policy down in front of me. It was straightforward, a good premium, a nice piece of business for the syndicate. He started talking it up, telling me what a blind man could see, how attractive it looked, and the next thing I knew I was floating. A disembodied state, that's what the psychiatrist called it, involuntary withdrawal. Suddenly I'd slipped back three months, back to the night my parents died. I could see flames flaring out the top windows and black smoke going up past the moon. I could smell it too, just like on that night, and taste it. That's what finished me, the sour taste of ash. The broker was still trying to sell me on the policy as I slid to my knees choking. I really couldn't breathe. A few moments later I blacked out.

When I came round Angela was kneeling beside me, a crowd of gawkers gathering.

I'm all right, I'd told her.

Ahha. Don't tell me, Ian, she'd said. You just felt like a good lie-down.

Later on she spoke to the broker. How my parents died was no secret, and when the broker told her about the fire policy I guess she just put two and two together. The next day she sent me to a shrink. I only saw him the once; he was useless.

'Anyway,' she said now, turning back to her desk, 'we've got enough on our plate here.'

'Angela, can I have two minutes?'

She glanced up at me. 'I don't know any more about it, Ian, honestly. Just that it burnt down.'

'My promotion,' I said.

She took a second with that. The one and only time

we'd discussed this freely was back last year before she'd gone into hospital for the mastectomy. Back then she'd told me the job was mine if I wanted it, but when she came out of hospital she didn't do what she'd said she'd do, and retire. She came back to the Room. Just a temporary thing, she'd told me, while Allen, her husband, sorted out the merger he was putting together.

But now when she looked over at Frazer, I was sure it wasn't the merger she was thinking of, but me. She didn't know if I was up to the job she'd once offered me.

'Angela, this is pretty important to me, I've made some commitments—'

'You'll have to speak with Allen.'

'But you said—'

'I don't want an argument,' she said, smiling through clenched teeth at the brokers who were standing just out of earshot. 'If you want to discuss it, Ian, go upstairs and see Allen. But don't take all day, we're getting busy.'

She beckoned a broker forward from the queue. A tight knot formed in my stomach as I headed upstairs.

On the top floors of the Lloyd's Building you've got the offices of the Chairman and his Deputy and their staff. The Adam Room is up there too, Floor 11, used for Council meetings and ceremonial occasions. Between these top floors and the Room down below it's all offices, solicitors and brokers, that kind of thing. Most of the Managing Agents moved out to cheaper places a long while ago, but not Allen Mortlake. I'd heard him say he'd be damned if he was going to walk half a mile just to get to the Room, but I knew there was more to it than that; there usually was with Allen. He wanted a seat on the Lloyd's Council to top off his career, and here, right near the centre of power, was the best location from which to run a discreet campaign.

When I went into his office I found him at the window, hands resting on the plate-glass, looking down. The window overlooked the atrium and from where he stood he could see into the Room. Behind his desk sat his daughter – another colleague of mine on the 486 box – Justine.

'Like beetles on a dunghill,' he said turning. 'Think things might firm up?'

'Good chance,' I told him.

'No way,' Justine said.

She didn't even bother to look up from the magazine she was reading – sometimes I really could have slapped her. But all Allen did was raise an eyebrow at me and smile.

Justine was Allen and Angela's only child. Down on the box Angela kept a pretty firm rein on her, but in private they both spoilt her like crazy. She was one of the lucky people, that kind who take it for granted that the world is made for them. She was good looking in a plastic kind of way, and the only worry she ever seemed to have was how to spend her money.

'This one,' she said now, circling something in the magazine as she handed it up to her father.

He gave it the once-over, then nodded.

I said, 'Have you heard from Sebastian?'

'I've left a message for him to call me,' Allen said. Apart from Sebastian's company putting a lot of business the Mortlake Group's way, Sebastian Ward was a Mortlake family friend. But Allen being Allen, that didn't stop him from looking up at me now and asking, 'Do we know who wrote the lead on his house?'

'Not us,' I told him cheerfully. I told him the only personal business we'd written on Sebastian was the kidnap and ransom policy, the K and R. A promotional stunt we'd cooked up with Sebastian to announce our entry into that market. 'But whoever did his house will be bleeding.'

'Good,' he said, and he shot me a smile.

Glancing at Justine, who was flicking through the magazine, I said, 'Allen, can we have a quick word?'

When he turned to her she kept flicking. He was a big man, imposing, and it wasn't just his size either. He'd started his career at Lloyd's in the claims department of one of the marine syndicates, then worked his way onto their box. He'd gone from deputy underwriter to underwriter in seven years, married Angela, then formed his own Managing Agency. You wouldn't say he was liked, he wasn't the chummy kind, but he was respected, and I think he probably preferred it that way. His wife Angela never treated him as casually as Justine did, but even with his daughter there were limits.

'Go on,' he told her now. 'If you find something else, tell me tonight.'

She frowned, and circled something else saying, 'This one too.'

'Good God,' he murmured, looking at the magazine over her shoulder. I craned over and caught a glimpse of the dress she'd circled in red ink. The name at the top of the page was Valentino.

Laughing, Justine got up and strolled out, telling me she'd see me down on the box later.

Allen rolled his eyes at me, like saying, Daughters. What can you do?

I wondered how I was going to put my problem to him. Sack your wife, I need the job?

But there wasn't going to be a better time, so I took a breath and said, 'Allen, I wanted to have a word about the situation on the 86 box.'

He cocked his head. 'Situation?'

'Angela's retirement.'

He gave me a direct look, as if he was weighing something up. Then his private line rang, and he answered it. It was Angela.

While they talked, I wandered across to the window and looked down at the Room. Down there the world's risk was being traded and spread. From every part of the globe the brokers' agents had gathered policies – insurance against crop damage in Australia, flood risk in the Caribbean, earthquakes in Bangkok, fire in the American mid-West – and now the brokers had brought them on to us, Lloyd's of London. There were display cabinets downstairs full of silver plates, model ships made of ivory, and all sorts of other presents from various underwriters to historic figures like Nelson who'd saved British ships and cargo from going down. The Lutine Bell and all that. This same business had been going on for centuries, about as establishment as you get; I'd come a hell of a long way from the dog tracks. And now when I was all set to top the past thirteen years of my life off with a promotion and a penthouse, Sebastian Ward, the man who'd first opened the door to me at Lloyd's, had lost his house in a fire. What were the odds on that?

When Allen hung up the phone, I turned.

'I really think it should be settled,' I said. 'The delay's not helping, even the brokers are starting to ask what's going on.'

He didn't respond. I was all set to give him the works, why I deserved the job, and why I deserved it right now. But the look on his face stopped me cold.

I asked, 'Bad news?'

'The fire at Sebastian's,' he said, staring at the phone.

Something fluttered in my throat. 'Is he all right?'

'No,' Allen said, 'he's not all right.' His hands went to his face again and his voice came out muffled. 'Angela's coming up. She's got Max with her.' Max was Sebastian Ward's son.

I said, 'What happened?'

Allen didn't move, he kept his hands to his face. I felt a prickling sensation up my neck.

'Is he dead?'

It was a few seconds before he lowered his hands. He looked straight at me. 'No, not dead.' His face was flushed now. I thought it was shock at first, but then I realized it was something more like anger. 'The stupid bastard,' he said, 'has been kidnapped.'

3

For a while I just stood there not saying a word. Allen pushed his hand up through his hair again.

'Bastard,' he said. 'The stupid bastard.'

He got up from his desk and went to the atrium window. His face was pink now, turning pale.

'Are they sure?' I said. 'What is it, some rumour?'

He gave a quick shake of the head. 'There's a note. Max got it at the office.' Max Ward, Sebastian's son, was the deputy manager of WardSure. Allen explained that Max had brought the note straight over to the Room and shown Angela; it was definitely a kidnap and ransom, a K and R. Now Angela was on her way up with Max. 'Bastard,' Allen whispered again, but he didn't mean Sebastian now, it was the whole situation. He dropped his hand. 'What are the chances, Ian?'

I stared at him, dazed. I suggested, hopefully, that it might be a hoax.

'Hoax,' he said like grabbing at a lifeline. Then he pulled a face. 'What about the house?' He slapped the plate-glass. 'First time up. Can you believe it?'

I couldn't, not really, or maybe I just didn't want to. And maybe I should have been thinking a bit more about Sebastian just then too, but I wasn't, not at first. What I was thinking was that if this really was a K and R, and we had to pay out, I could forget about my promotion. It was me who had talked Allen and Angela into writing K and R business in the first place; so far Sebastian Ward was our one and only policy. Five million quid. I was starting to feel quite sick.

15

Then Angela burst in with Max just behind; she gave the note to Allen.

'What now?' Max said, turning a frantic half-circle. 'It's your responsibility, isn't it?'

Allen told him to settle down.

Max threw up a hand. 'He's been kidnapped, for fucksake. Settle down'

'When did you get the note?'

'Just now.' Max turned left then right. 'Fifteen minutes, I don't know. I came straight over.'

'No phone call?'

'Just the note.'

Angela asked her husband if he'd called Bill Tyler yet. He went to his desk and made the call. Max kept asking stupid questions; I thought Angela was going to hit him.

I backed over to a chair by the wall and sat down. I bent forward, elbows on my knees, head in hands, and stared at the little red triangles in the carpet. Bill Tyler. Not just our security expert on the Ottoman case, he ran the specialist K and R rescue team, the guys we'd told him we were never going to need. And now we needed them.

'Ian?'

I lifted my head. The three of them were looking at me now.

'Take the note to Tyler,' Allen said, hanging up. 'He needs to see it.'

I went over and got the note.

'He's leaving his office right now,' Allen said. 'He'll meet you at the other place.'

I glanced up from the note. Allen saw I was lost.

'Snap out of it, Ian. The safe-house.'

'Allen—'

'What?' he barked.

No, I thought. This definitely was not the time.

Shaking my head, I told him, Nothing, then I headed for the door.

Max said, 'I'll come too.'

I glanced back at Allen. He screwed up his face then gave a quick flick of the hand.

'Take him with you,' he said. 'Get going.'

Sebastian Ward was a real face in the market. There are plenty who think they are, and even more who want to be, but Sebastian was it, the real thing. When he came into the Room people noticed; after ten minutes there'd be a cluster of senior underwriters around him, Sebastian chatting and smiling and generally charming the pants off the lot of them. Partly it was business, his company WardSure was a fair-sized broker so he could send plenty of premiums their way, but it wasn't just that. He had boxes at the opera and Ascot, he entertained on a grand scale, but it wasn't even that either. Allen Mortlake used to call these underwriters Sebastian's 'free caviar' friends, but that wasn't true; Sebastian was honestly liked. As a broker you don't go from being a one-man-band to owning and managing a company like WardSure without having some special gift. And Sebastian's gift was this charm, an instinct for putting people at ease, somehow making even acquaintances think of themselves as his friends. I sometimes wondered if Allen didn't envy Sebastian that. They were both big men at Lloyd's, but whenever I saw them walk into the Room together it was Allen Mortlake who ended up standing on the edge of the group that formed. It wasn't Allen's opinions on the market anybody wanted to hear, not while Sebastian was delivering the latest jokes he'd picked up from God knows where.

And even before Sebastian got seriously rich he had the charm. I know that, because I was there. It was Sebastian I had to thank for rescuing me from the dogs and my old man. But now Sebastian Ward had been kidnapped and his house had burnt down, it was a bloody strange turn.

The safe-house was in that no-man's-land between Docklands and the City; the taxi dropped us in the next street. Max tagged along beside me, we turned into a lane, walked fifty yards, then turned again. He kept asking who Bill Tyler was.

'You'll see.'

17

'But what's he do? What's this safe-house bit?'

When the Mortlake Group put Bill Tyler's company on a retainer and a secrecy agreement was signed, it cut both ways. If we ever had to use their services, no third parties were to be informed. I wasn't sure yet where Max fitted into that arrangement.

I said, 'Ask Tyler.'

'I'm asking you, Ian.'

When I didn't answer him, he gave me a pissed-off look.

In a vague kind of way I'd known Max for more than twenty years. He used to trail around after Sebastian at the dogs, a pimply-faced kid three years older than me who always had his hands in his pockets. Sebastian bet with my old man quite a lot. He sometimes brought Max down the Gallon Club of a Monday night – that's when the bookies and a few big punters did their settle-up for the week. I'd be sitting in the corner drinking my Coke and Max'd be perched up at the bar near the men. He'd say Hi to me, but that was all. I guess when you're fifteen a twelve-year-old isn't someone you want to be seen with, but I only understood that later. When I was twelve, I thought Max was a prick.

When we got of the safe-house I hit the buzzer, wondering how I was going to explain Max to Bill.

After a second Max said, 'This the right place?'

Stepping back, I checked the number. 33.

'Ahha.' I hit the buzzer again.

It was one of those old Victorian places with bay windows. There were dark curtains downstairs and up so we couldn't see in. There was a narrow gap between the pavement and the house; you could see a basement down there, but it was curtained up too.

'Yes?' Bill on the intercom.

When I told him the codeword, the lock clicked and I pushed the door open.

'Allen sent Max Ward with me,' I said.

I was already inside, Max right behind me, when I heard Bill say, 'Fucking hell.'

There was a short hallway leading straight to the stairs and an open door off to the right. I went in, calling Bill's name.

'Christ, minimalist or what,' Max said, following me into the front room. 'Who is this guy?'

The walls and ceiling were a dirty cream colour, and the floor had a grey carpet that looked brand-new. There wasn't one piece of furniture in the room. The overhead light was bright, a single bulb, its glass cover was sitting on the floor in the corner.

'He lives here?' Max said.

Footsteps came down the stairs, Bill appeared in the doorway. He looked at me hard. I did the introductions but he didn't bother to shake Max's hand.

'Where's the note?' he said.

I gave it to him. While he was reading the note, Max said to him, 'Shouldn't you be out there?' Max gestured vaguely. London. The world. He wasn't angry, more like confused about exactly what was being done to save his old man.

Bill looked up. 'Is your father on any medication?'

'What?'

'Does he have to take anything?'

'Some pills,' Max said. 'For his heart.'

Bill asked what type, and how often, and Max explained that they weren't that important.

'He just pops one when he's a bit stressed.'

Bill stared at him. Max told him the name of the drug.

Then Bill handed the note back to me. I read it again while he fired more questions at Max. The note said, 'Sebastian Ward will be released upon the delivery of 5 US Treasury bonds, each to the face value of one million pounds. Place and time of the exchange to be notified.'

That was it. The typeface was dark and bold, and the note unsigned.

'They haven't phoned?' Bill asked Max.

'Not yet.' Max touched his jacket pocket. 'I've got home and office redirected to the mobile. Not a squeak.'

'The note was addressed to you?'

Max fished in his pocket and pulled out an envelope. M. Ward Esquire, it said. The three of us were looking at it as the door buzzer went. I took a step that way but Bill grabbed my arm.

'It's not for you.' He gave me a look as he went into the next room. We heard a button click. 'Yes?' he said.

A man's voice came back over the intercom, just the code, 'Full Cover'. Then we heard the front door open.

Bill came back through, pointing at us on his way by. 'No questions.'

He met the man in the hall, they talked quietly, I guess Bill was telling him about me and Max.

Max whispered to me, 'No questions? Who the fuck's he think's paying for all this?'

When Bill came back in with the other bloke, they walked past us as if we weren't there. The man was wearing a duffel coat and carrying a sports bag, he had a crew cut that made the top of his head look blue. He looked big and tough. Max didn't say a word.

'The others are down there,' Bill told the stranger.

I put my head round the door just in time to see the blue head disappearing down to the basement. Bill turned and waved me over, so I left Max behind.

'When I sign a confidentiality agreement,' Bill said quietly, 'I'm not playing games.'

'Max was in Allen's office. Allen told me to bring him.'

'Then Allen made a mistake.' Bill glanced over my shoulder, tense.

I got the message. This wasn't just the usual check-up on a fraudulent claim, some people telling lies and others losing money. This was Sebastian's life on the line, Bill wasn't fooling around.

Voices came up from the basement, a clatter of metal. When I looked at Bill he avoided my eyes. I offered to take Max away.

'Too late now.' He headed for the hall. 'When I call, bring him up.'

I rejoined Max; we heard Bill charging up the stairs.

'What goes on here?' Max said. 'What is this friggin' place?'

I leant back against the wall and slid down. Reaching across, I picked up the lampshade and spun it like a top.

'Hey!' Max said.

I almost gave him a blast, but the look in his eyes stopped me. He was angry, sure, but more than that he was scared.

'Give it a break, Max. He'll call us upstairs in a minute.'

Max did a lap round the room. Over the years my opinions about Max had changed. He came across as arrogant, but his main problem was he was weak, and kind of under his old man's thumb. Not hard when your old man's a guy like Sebastian Ward. And after I had my bust-up with my own old man, I got to feeling a bit sorry for Max. There was just him and Sebastian, no other family. it made them unusually close. Close, but Sebastian still called all the shots.

And now Sebastian wasn't here to tell him what to do.

'Okay Ian?' Bill called down the stairs.

I led Max up there. The same grey carpet ran up to the landing. Bill was standing by an open door. He showed us in. More grey carpet and cream-coloured walls. There was a bench piled high with electronic gear, a bloke sitting there twiddling knobs. He turned to us and nodded.

'Where's your mobile?' Bill asked Max.

Max took it out. Bill gave it to the man.

'Number?' the man said.

Max recited the number then he asked what was going on. Ignoring him, the bloke slotted the phone into some kind of modem and started working the keypad.

Bill said, 'Maybe you've saved us a trip to your office.'

Max nodded at the electronic gear. 'What's this?'

'Surveillance equipment.'

'What, phone tapping? Stuff like that?'

Bill told Max they didn't expect the kidnappers to be using the Royal Mail.

Then he asked Max, 'Has your father ever been threatened?'

'With what?'

'Competitors trying to even the score? Personal grudges?'

Max looked blank.

'When you got the note,' Bill said, 'did anything occur to you immediately?'

Max shook his head. Bill gave him a sideways glance.

'Your father only took out the K and R policy three months ago. I don't suppose he had any particular reason?'

I butted in, reminding Bill of what I was sure he knew already. Sebastian had agreed to take out the policy as a sales gimmick to help us get into the market. 'Him actually getting kidnapped,' I said, 'wasn't meant to be part of the deal.'

Bill nodded, his eyes still on Max. Then the surveillance man started grilling Max about the phone system back in the WardSure offices, and Bill's attention moved on. He questioned Max too. I propped myself against a table, watching and listening.

Bill wasn't as big a man as Allen Mortlake, probably just as tall, but leaner. He was in his mid-forties, ex-SAS, he'd fought in the Falklands, won some medal, but a few years later he'd chucked it in to go and work for a private security company set up by ex-officers from his regiment. Now he'd split from them and set up his own operation. We'd used him as an expert witness on security in a few disputed insurance claims like Ottoman. But K and R was a different kettle of fish.

Questioning Max now, Bill looked seriously wired. Wired, but still in control. After a couple of minutes he went out the door, beckoning me after him. He crossed the landing into the back room, and once I was inside, he closed the door.

'Who's the beneficiary of the K and R policy?'

'WardSure.'

'Currently being run by your friend out there?'

I nodded.

Bill walked a few steps away from me, then back.

'Listen, as far as I'm concerned my client is you guys, the Mortlake Group. I don't need this prat hanging over my shoulder.' He meant Max.

'He's harmless. Come on, Bill. It's his old man.'

Hands on hips, Bill bent towards me. 'Max goes,' he said. 'He goes and he stays gone. I don't want to see him again for the rest of this operation. Any contribution he wants to make comes through you, unless I ask for it.'

'Okay, okay.' My gaze drifted to the three bunk beds, the three piles of sheets and blankets. 'What's all this?' I stepped over to the window and pushed back the curtain. The street was empty.

'What are you doing?'

'Just looking.'

'Well don't,' Bill said.

I let the curtain fall back. I thought he was taking the Secret Seven stuff a bit far, but I didn't say anything, he really wasn't in the mood. While he went for a leak, I strolled out to the landing again then in through the door at the back. There were three more bunk beds in there, and more blankets and sheets. I took a quick peek out the window. A van was parked in the narrow yard. The yard backed onto a lane, a big tin gate marked the boundary, it was secured with a shiny new chain and padlock. Across the lane, a warehouse was covered in purple graffiti.

Leaving the room, I met Bill at the head of the stairs. I asked him how many blokes he had coming, and if the police were involved.

'Need to know,' he muttered. 'And you need to know bugger all.' Then he stuck his head into the surveillance room and said to Max, 'Right, son. When you're ready.'

We followed Bill down the stairs and into the front room again. Voices, the sound of horseplay now, came up from the basement.

'What do we know about the fire?' Bill asked me.

I turned and looked at Max.

'When I left, the place was all taped off,' Max said. 'The engines were gone, the cops were waiting for some fire investigation team.'

Bill asked just how bad the fire had been.

Max made a scoffing sound. 'It's a write-off, Jesus. Bad?'

Bill told him to wait out in the hall. Max went reluctantly.

'Get over there,' Bill said to me quietly. 'Find out what they've got on the fire. Arson suspects, anything.' He pulled out a business card, scribbled a number on the back and gave it to me. 'Don't come back here, just call.'

'Why would they tell me what's going on?'

'Take Max. But make sure he understands that blabbing about the kidnap won't help his father.'

Bill put a hand on my shoulder to guide me out, but then there was a rumpus from the basement and we both looked that way. The bloke with the shaven head appeared up the stairs, he laughed down to the others below. But when he turned and saw us, he stopped dead. In his hands was a whacking great rifle, with a telescopic sight.

4

You could smell it from out on the road, charred bricks and mortar; the misty drizzle of rain wasn't doing much to hold it down. The iron gates were open so we just walked right in past the gatehouse and on up the drive. It used to be you walked out from under the trees and there was the house, white and massive, with a few expensive cars out front. It wasn't going to look like that again for a while.

The roof was gone, you could see the sky through the glassless upstairs windows. The right wall of the house had collapsed, and the ground-floor windows looked like a row of burnt-out fireplaces. Max went on ahead, ducking under the police tape, but the smell got too strong for me, I had to stop. He looked over his shoulder, called me on, then disappeared around the back of the house. My breath suddenly shallowed. I could feel myself slipping but I held down the urge to turn and walk away. I covered my mouth with a hankie, forced myself to keep looking. It wasn't as bad as that time in the Room; I didn't choke, but suddenly I was back at my parents' house again, the flames and smoke rising. I jumped out of the car, yelled at Mum to stay put in the passenger seat, then ran to the front door. When I opened it, the heat surged out. The stairs were burning, and the wall. I stepped back a few paces and screamed up to Dad. No-one came.

'Oi!' someone called now.

I spun right and left; I couldn't see anyone. Then there was a noise inside and a policeman stepped out through what used to be the front door. He came across.

'I'm with Max,' I told him.

'You what?'

'Max Ward.'

I repocketed the hankie and he gave me the once-over. He asked who I was.

We'd dreamt up a cover story on the way over, so now I gave it to him. I gestured to the gutted house and said, 'The loss adjustor.' He looked blank, so I added, 'For the insurance.'

I stepped up beside him as if I had a right to be there. We gazed at the house. The ribbon of police tape went right around the place, strung on pickets. The pickets were already leaning.

'What happened?'

'You can't go in,' he said. 'The arson boys haven't finished.'

'Did it go up last night?'

'Early this mornin'.'

I heard noises inside now, men talking and moving around. Over to one side there were half a dozen cars and a van parked under trees off the drive.

God, I thought, turning back to the house. Here again. Another pile of burnt rubble, and me. And then the memories I'd been holding off since hearing about Sebastian's place, they came flooding through.

It was on one of my rare visits home, the place where I grew up, a two-bedroom semi out in Walthamstow. I'd go back there maybe once every couple of months for dinner; I thought I at least owed Mum that. Since my sister Katy had left for college I'd gone round there a bit more often, I knew they missed her pretty bad. That night, as usual, Dad drank and said about two words to me, then after dinner I gave Mum a lift down to her bingo. I was tired, and looking forward to getting back to my own place, so I wasn't too happy when we got to the bingo hall and Mum realized she'd forgotten some ticket she needed.

But I gritted my teeth. No, I said, no problem. I'd take her back home; she could pick up the ticket; we'd be back at the bingo hall in half an hour. She apologized all the way home.

We didn't see the fire till I parked the car out front. At first I thought the smoke was just clouds, but then I saw the flames, and I jumped out of the car, telling Mum to stay put.

But when I couldn't get through the front door, and when Dad didn't answer when I screamed up, I ran. I didn't think, I just ran. I vaulted over the fence into the neighbour's front yard and banged on his door. No lights came on, so I did the same into the next yard, thumped the door, and this time it opened. I nearly knocked the poor old bugger down in my rush for his phone.

By the time I got back outside, neighbours were coming into the street. I went to my car, looking back at the burning house; flames were coming out of the windows now.

I'd opened the passenger door and said, 'Mum,' before I realized the car was empty. And somehow I knew straight away. I ran across the road, but the flames were solid by then, the heat so fierce you couldn't get near the place.

The fire engines arrived. The firemen stood well back and sent great jets of water into the blaze, the water ran in a stream down the street. And it was while I was watching the firemen that a neighbour came over and told me how she'd tried to stop Mum going in. An ambulance arrived; I saw the chief fireman shake his head at the driver, like saying, Too late.

I sat down on the pavement, the water sloshed over my feet, and I cried.

'Ian!'

Max came back out from his father's wrecked house now, signalling for me to join him by the cars. I made an effort to get a grip. When I got over there, Max was already digging around in the van. He tossed me a pair of rubber boots, and some overalls.

'Put these on. The boss man says don't touch anything in there.'

While I pulled them on, I asked him if anyone had seen the housekeeper. As I remembered it, she was always around. But Max said she had her feet up at home, watching telly.

'She didn't know about this?'

'She's been off sick three days. When I rang her this morning and told her, know what she said? She said she had to have at least a month's notice if she wasn't needed.' Pulling on his own boots, Max said, 'Bloody cow.'

'So who was here last night?'

'Just Dad.'

'Didn't he have that bloke doing security?'

'Who, Eddie Pike?'

I nodded. Eddie was someone from the dog world, a track rat who had latched on to Sebastian. Sebastian kept him round as a kind of errand boy.

'Yeah, great security.' Max swore. He said that Pike had gone missing too. 'But when I get hold of him, he's out on his ear along with the old cow.'

We finished pulling on the overalls and went back up to the house, a long walk. The garden was about two acres. A stone's throw from Regent's Park, it must have been one of the most expensive stretches of lawn in London.

The boss of the fire investigation team met us round the back; he warned us not to touch anything, then he led us in. Most of the structure was still intact, only the one side wall had collapsed. When I remarked on that, the bloke pointed to the rubble. That, he told me, was a post-war extension.

Then he slapped his gloved hand against an intact wall. 'This early stuff you couldn't knock down with a dozer.'

'What's it look like?' I said. 'Arson?'

'Looks like,' he said. 'Have to do the lab tests, but probably petrol.' Then he glanced back at Max, adding, 'And this is the fastest insurance claim I ever heard of.'

Max was too busy staring at the wreckage to take that one in.

I glimpsed a German Shepherd working up ahead.

'Sniffer dog,' the bloke said, but I knew that already. It was a sniffer dog that had found Mum and Dad.

We went into what used to be the dining room, he said the dog had finished in there. There'd been a wooden floor, but now it was a thick layer of charcoal and ash, it crunched beneath our feet as we walked. The bloke told us to stay put, then he went deeper into the house; we heard him talking with his team.

'Christ Almighty,' Max said. He turned a slow circle, trying to take it all in. He said it again. Christ Almighty.

The ceiling had collapsed and burnt, and the only signs of what used to be furniture were the thicker patches of charcoal. And the smell. It was so sour it was making my eyes water; I took out my hankie again.

Sebastian Ward's house. The last time I'd been there I'd been served whisky from a crystal decanter. And now? It looked like my parents' house had looked, only bigger. And I was sure there was another difference too, one you couldn't see. I tried not to think about it, but it kept coming back. Unlike Dad, Sebastian Ward would have kept his house insured.

There was a shout from somewhere deeper in the house. When I looked at Max, he shrugged. Then the shout came again, someone calling for the rest of the team.

'Come on,' Max said, and before I could stop him he went blundering through.

I called after him. He didn't come back, so I followed.

We found half a dozen men in blue overalls in the drawing room. They were gathered together in a circle, crouching round a bunch of tangled wires, all that was left of the grand piano. One of them had hold of the dog.

Someone said, 'Get some pictures,' then a camera came out, the flash went off a few times.

One bloke started ordering us out. But the boss, our guide, said, 'Leave them a sec,' then he said to someone else, 'Bag.'

A clear plastic bag got handed to him. He pulled some tongs out of his pocket and poked around in the mess. A few moments later, he lifted something. It was a pistol. He studied it a while, then dropped it into the bag, running his fingers over the seal.

He bent forward again, prodding with his tongs.

'Mr Ward,' he said, still prodding.

Max made a sound.

'Do you recognize the gun?'

'That?' Max said, nodding at the bag.

The boss man looked up. 'Was that a yes or a no?'

When Max didn't answer, the bloke went back to fossicking with the tongs; he was turning over other stuff now.

He said, 'Some private security people think a gun's part of the uniform. Sometimes their employers think that too.' It was like he was talking to himself, but I could see Max was looking very uncomfortable. 'You know how stupid that is, Mr Ward?'

The tongs brought something else from the mess, metallic-looking, just a couple of inches across. The bloke dropped it into a bag, sealed it, then handed it to Max.

'Recognize this?' he said.

Max went pale. I craned over to see. The thing in the bag was a security badge; you could just make out the name. Eddie Pike.

'My father has a right to protection,' Max said.

The boss of the fire investigation team nodded sadly. He turned back to the debris and gave one more pull with his tongs. I felt my gut heave. The thing was finally uncovered, black and shrivelled, and twisted into a grasping claw. But unmistakably human. A hand.

The bloke looked up at Max again, and said, 'You wanna tell that to Eddie here?'

5

The news of Eddie Pike's death shook Allen, no question, and Angela too. If they'd had any doubts about how serious this thing was, or if they were hoping for some painless resolution, the news I gave them about Pike put them right. I told them I'd already phoned the bad news through to Bill Tyler.

Allen Mortlake was a serious-looking bloke at the best of times, but now he had a face on him like the grave. He looked from Angela back to me. 'Angela's had a thought,' he said, passing me a folder from his desk. 'Look at these.'

'They're from the files upstairs,' Angela said. 'Copies.'

'Copies of what?'

She nodded to the folder and I spread it on the desk. There were about twenty pages, typed and handwritten. I only got to the bottom of the first paragraph before I lifted my head.

'Jesus,' I said.

Angela leant across and turned that page over. 'There's worse.'

The next letter didn't have any paragraphs; not much punctuation either, but the rage came off the paper like heat. I looked up again.

'Who are these people?'

'Names,' Angela told me. 'Unhappy investors looking for someone to blame.'

I turned a few more pages. Anger. Hatred. Despair. Names are the people who act as final guarantors for the risks the Lloyd's syndicates sign up to. Becoming a Name used to be like joining an exclusive club, a handy tax dodge for the moderately rich. Not any more. Too many have lost their shirts in the market.

Flicking through the pages, I said, 'WardSure gets a few mentions.'

Angela told me it was those she'd specifically requested from the files. She reached across me again and flipped to the last letter. 'Look at that one.'

It said,

Dear Sir,

Yesterday I buried my wife. We were married for thirty-two years, and until these last three years she was always in good health. I can tell you exactly when this changed. It was the day I received the first demand from Lloyd's. It was for twenty-two thousand pounds. I knew I had to pay, and I did pay. I was a Name for only three years before this, and in that one go you took back as much as you ever gave me.

After that I told my agent to take me off the syndicates. He said he couldn't. He said I was trapped on two syndicates which no-one would reinsure to close because they had exposure to asbestos. Long-tails, as I think you know. Also he said I was on a syndicate in the excess loss spiral. I went up to London to see this agent who didn't even apologize for putting me on these bad syndicates. Shortly after that the next demand from you people arrived. Thirty-one thousand pounds. And so it has gone on.

We had to sell our farm, which was in my wife's family for six generations, and my wife lost her good health with all the worry of it. Last year she told me she would be better off dead, and now she is dead.

On top of this I have seen in the papers where that Sebastian Ward has made a fortune from broking between these stupid excess loss syndicates, including my own. If I had been told Mr Ward had anything to do with Lloyd's I never would have joined, as I know him to be untrustworthy.

I have also seen in the papers where one of your senior people said, 'If God hadn't meant them to be shorn, he wouldn't have made them sheep,' meaning Names like me.

Well please tell him from me, if God hadn't meant the likes of that idiot and Sebastian Ward to be stuck, he wouldn't have made them pigs.

I will be saving all future demands from Lloyd's for a bonfire.

There was no signature, but along the bottom of the page someone had scrawled, 'For the attention of the police?'

'The others are lunatics,' Allen said, taking the letter. 'But this one?'

'How long ago was it sent?'

'Two years,' Angela told me.

I looked at her. 'Two years?'

She dropped into the sofa. She looked dreadful. The older blokes in the market used to tell me that as a young woman Angela was every bit as stunning as her daughter, Justine. Right up to just before her mastectomy, you could believe it too. But that operation had knocked her, and now this business with Sebastian was almost too much for her to bear. She looked how she felt, as worried as hell.

'How long do you think it would take him to forget his wife?' she asked me.

'So he stews for two years, kidnaps Sebastian, kills the security guard and torches the house?' I frowned. 'I don't think so.'

'Well, have you got any better ideas?' Allen asked irritably. He went and sat at his desk and held his head in his hands. He was worried about Sebastian, sure, but he was also worried about how this was going to affect the merger he had going, and his chances of a seat on the Lloyd's Council.

In fact I did have a better idea. I probably wouldn't have mentioned it, but if some fruitcake letter from two years back was the best they'd come up with, why not?

I said, 'That security guard of Sebastian's, the one who

died in the fire? He was Sebastian's runner.'

They looked at me blankly.

'He used to place bets for Sebastian at the dogs. Collected for him when Sebastian couldn't make it. I used to see him sometimes, you know, with my old man.'

Allen said, 'He wasn't a security guard?'

'Maybe he was a security guard too.' I touched my chest. 'I mean he had the badge, but what if this is some kind of revenge thing? Sebastian upset someone down there and this is the payback.'

'Have you told Tyler?' Angela asked me.

'I wasn't sure it was important.'

Angela turned to Allen, but he kept his eyes on me. 'Payback for what?' he said.

'I don't know. He used to bet big. Could be anything.'

'Could you find out?'

I hesitated.

Allen said, 'Tyler's got his hands full, and the fewer people know about this K and R the better.' You could see him warming to the idea. 'You're sure this Eddie Pike was a whatsit?'

I nodded. Allen picked up the unsigned letter from the ruined Name and studied it.

'You could chase this up too,' he said.

I asked him what was meant to be happening down on the box while I was off playing pin the tail on the donkey.

'We'll get by,' Angela said. 'For a few days.'

Allen pointed at her. 'Done.'

I was caught; even if I'd dug my heels in I'm not sure I could have stopped it. Sebastian was their friend; it was only natural they wanted to do everything they could to rescue him safely. Besides that, Allen wanted the merger kept on track and his path to the Council clear. He needed Sebastian found fast; I think he would have tried anything, but Angela saw my doubts.

'Leave it till the morning,' she said. 'If nobody's had any better ideas by then—'

'Okay, tomorrow morning,' Allen butted in. 'Ring me and check first, Ian.'

Then what? I thought. Play Sherlock Holmes down at the dogs? I was starting to regret opening my mouth.

Allen picked up his phone, punching buttons. That seemed to be it.

Turning to Angela, I said, 'Maybe this isn't the time, but I really need to know about that promotion.'

Allen stopped punching buttons. 'What?' he said sharply.

'On the 486 box—'

'Christ,' he said, throwing up a hand. 'Not now.'

Angela gave me a part-annoyed, part-sympathetic look, the kind she used to give me in the old days when I'd just signed up for an absolutely stinking piece of business.

Go home, she told me.

6

'Katy?'

The TV was on, she'd left a wine glass and a half-eaten microwaved dinner on the coffee table. I took the plate and the empty wine glass through to the kitchen. The cutting board was out, pieces of sliced fruit and peelings littered the bench. In the middle of all this, a tub of cream. The tub was leaking, a white trail dribbling down the cupboard door to the floor.

I leaned back. 'Katy?'

She didn't answer so I took a stab at clearing up the mess, then I got a beer from the fridge and went back to the lounge. When I turned down the TV I could hear the hairdryer going in her room. My kid sister, preparing for a night on the town.

Katy was born thirteen years after me, enough time between us so that I never found her a pain in the arse when we were growing up. When I was in my teens, she was barely in kindergarten, and by the time I hit twenty I was old enough to find her occasional sulks pretty funny. She was cute right from the start; that stayed with her, and as she got older she developed this weird sense of humour; even now she could really make me laugh. Mum and Dad spoilt her rotten, but somehow she never turned into a brat.

Two weeks after Mum and Dad's funeral, she'd shown up on my doorstep with a rucksack and a suitcase, bawling her eyes out. She told me she'd dropped out of her biology course at college; she was looking for somewhere to stay. Short-term, she said.

Just until she'd got herself sorted out.

Six months later, Katy still had the spare room.

'Good day?'

I looked up from the TV. She came out of her room wearing a pink towelling robe, her hair frizzed up from the blowdry.

'Not great.' I sipped my beer.

'Hey, where's my glass?'

'Try the sink.'

She pulled a face and went out to the kitchen. When she came back there was a full glass of white wine in her hand. She rested a knee on the sofa. 'Your friend was hunky.'

I gave her a blank look.

'Yesterday?' she said. 'The guy with that report thing?'

The Ottoman report. Bill Tyler had come round to discuss it. It seemed like a week ago. I turned back to the TV, wondering if I should give Bill a call.

'Is he coming back?'

'He's twenty years older than you, Katy.'

She laughed so hard she spilt her drink. 'You are so unplugged,' she said, 'it just isn't true.'

I didn't take the bait. After I moved out of home into my first flat, Katy used to come and see me sometimes with Mum. Then I was the big brother, out in the big wide world. And later I was a stopping-off point for her; she'd arrive with a couple of friends, they'd get tarted up, then disappear to the West End for the night. The old man would have blown a fuse if he'd known. Back in those days Katy looked up to me. Back then she thought I was cool. But now after six months sharing my flat, seeing me go off to work each morning in a suit and tie, she had a different view of things. Now I was – what? Unplugged?

'Did you ask them at work?'

The promotion. I'd made the mistake of telling Katy how far my neck was sticking out over the penthouse.

I shook my head. 'Something came up.'

'Oh, Ian,' she said.

'I'll ask tomorrow.'

'You said that yesterday.'

'Katy.' I looked at her. Without make-up she could have passed for sixteen instead of going on twenty-one. And she hadn't meant to nag; she was concerned, that was all. She wanted to help but she didn't know how. I said, 'Can we drop it?'

She pressed her lips together, not quite a smile, then went back to her bedroom.

'Where are you off to?'

'Romford,' she called back through the door.

Romford racetrack, the dogs. Again. Apart from the two nights a week she'd picked up pulling beer in a bar, it seemed to be what she did these days.

'Ian.' She peeped around the edge of her door. 'Could you get my face cream? It's in the brown jar.'

I wandered over to the bathroom. Even before Katy moved in I never used it, I had my own ensuite, but these days I couldn't have used it if I'd wanted to. Katy had filled it with stuff. Not just any old stuff. Ecologically friendly stuff. Tubes and jars and bottles, with pictures of green things on the labels. She started on her vegetarian kick back in sixth form; we all thought it was a phase she was going through, but now it seemed to have settled into a way of life. I ran my hand over the ginseng and the herbal extracts, picked up one brown bottle, sleeping pills, then finally located the jar of cream. Black, white, yellow and brown faces, all smiled at me from the label.

As Katy poked her hand round her bedroom door to take the jar, the buzzer went.

'That'll be Tubs,' she said. 'Tell him, two minutes.'

Tubs Laszlo was my father's penciller and best friend for over thirty years. More like one of the family than a friend really. I went and let him in.

'She ready or what?' he said, coming through the door.

He followed me into the kitchen and I gave him a can of beer. As he popped it open, I asked him if Jigsaw was running that night.

'Ran last night at the Stow,' he said. 'Katy didn't tell ya?'

Shaking my head, I went through to the lounge. Tubs fished in his pocket and pulled out last night's programme. Jigsaw was the four dog in the second-last race. Beside his name was the trainer's name, and beside that the owner's name, K. Collier. A few weeks after Mum and Dad died, Tubs bought Jigsaw for Katy as a gift. It couldn't lift a leg, but it had done what I think Tubs had meant it to do, help Katy get over things. Tubs was fat – more than twenty stone I guess – and that made some people not take him too seriously. But how many people would have thought of this Jigsaw business. Not me, for one. Back when Katy was bawling her eyes out each day, I was hopeless.

Now Tubs gave me a yard-by-yard account of Jigsaw's race. Bumped out of the traps, cornered wide, and bumped again in the straight. It finished in the usual way, with Jigsaw coming in last.

Tubs went and slapped his hand on Katy's door. 'Katy?'

'Hang on,' she called.

'Hang on, my arse. One minute, I'm gone.'

He came back and sat down, and drank his beer. I flicked off the TV.

'Tubs, have you seen much of Eddie Pike lately?'

He squinted. 'Pike?'

'Ward's runner. Red hair. Few inches shorter than me.'

Tubs said that he couldn't remember seeing him lately. 'But that means sod all.' He swigged his beer. 'Not the kinda bloke I look out for. Why?'

I said, 'Ward's house burnt down.'

Tubs's head went back.

'It might be an insurance job,' I told him, wondering how far I should take this before I got the all-clear from Allen.

After turning it over, Tubs asked me, 'Ward sued anyone yet?'

I forced a smile. Sebastian had once threatened to sue the track steward at the Stow after a dog fell during a race, a dog Sebastian had money on. It never got to court, but everyone down there still remembered it. Tubs, like a lot of dog people, was no great fan of Sebastian's.

I said, 'I went out to see it. His place is a write-off. Burnt to the ground.'

'Whose place burnt to the ground?' Katy said.

I turned. She'd come into the lounge without us noticing; she had her hands up to one ear, fixing an earring.

'No-one,' I told her.

She bent and kissed Tubs on the cheek. Then she went to the mirror, still working the earring. 'I'm not going to go to pieces, you know. What was it, a house?'

Her eyes met mine in the mirror. This one she really wasn't going to drop.

'Sebastian Ward's place,' I said.

Her eyes widened in surprise. She faced me.

'The insurance guy?'

I nodded. I could almost see the thoughts zinging round in her head.

After Mum and Dad died, we found Dad hadn't kept up the insurance on the house. It was no big surprise to me, but Katy took it hard, like Dad had let her down somehow, and she didn't want to believe it. So when Tubs mentioned to her that Sebastian sometimes wrote business with the bookies, she took hold of that with both hands. She was almost obsessed with the idea those first few weeks before Jigsaw came along. I guess it helped her keep her mind off the real tragedy. She even made me go and speak with Sebastian about it. It was embarrassing and pointless, but I did it, just to keep the peace. He told me what I knew anyway, Dad hadn't gone to him for insurance. He offered me a couple of grand out of his own wallet. Just to tide us over, he said. I turned it down. I never told Katy that.

Now when her thoughts stopped zinging, she nodded to herself.

'Ha bloody ha,' she said.

I held up a hand. 'Katy, I might be involved in this at work. I'd appreciate it if you didn't ha-bloody-ha any mates of Ward's you happen to see at Romford tonight.'

Tubs crushed his beer can and heaved himself out of the sofa. 'You ready?'

I could see Katy wanted to pump me for more details, but Tubs was already halfway out the door. She started to ask me a question, then Tubs called, 'Katy!' and she grabbed her handbag, muttering as she went after him.

I called Bill Tyler. No news.

I called him again, the first thing after waking up in the morning, and he told me to get off his back.

In the lounge I found a half-empty wine glass on the coffee table. Katy's door was ajar, and a radio was playing quietly in her room. When she first moved in it used to annoy me the way she always fell asleep with it on. But now I didn't mind, the procedure was automatic, I reached around her door, hit the switch, and the radio died.

'Thanks,' Katy murmured, her voice drowsy with sleep.

'Good night?'

'I dropped ten quid. Wicked.'

Smiling, I closed the door gently, then I went to prime myself with coffee for the day.

7

Since starting in a seventeenth-century coffee shop, Lloyd's has had quite a few homes in the City. The last three are named after the year the Room moved in, the 28 Building, the 58 Building, and the 86 Building, the shiny new tower where I worked. I arrived early, Allen wasn't in, so I headed across the road to the 58 Building where the Lloyd's Claims Office, the LCO, has its home. Angela had asked me to go over there days before, about the disputed Ottoman Air claim, but I'd put it off. Now if I got the go-ahead to chase up my idea about Sebastian and the dogs I wouldn't have the chance to get over there until we were back in court, so it was now or never.

The LCO is a kind of general back-office to the market, a clearing house for the river of paperwork that flows from the Lloyd's syndicates each day. Only a few of the claims officers were at their desks. I couldn't see Lee Chan, and when I asked for her they directed me to the gym, so I went back out to the marbled hallway and made my way downstairs.

Generally underwriters don't visit the LCO. They think of it as a pit where all the boring paperwork gets emptied, and most Names probably don't even know it exists. But when I joined the Mortlake Group Angela used to send me over there a lot. Trips to the engine room, she called them – any problem with a claim, she'd send me. It was a habit I'd kept up; I guess that's how I met Lee Chan.

Now I paused outside the gym door to gather myself. The music was pounding away in there, Motown, it was

Lee all right. I took a deep breath, lifted my head, then went in.

She was alone. Flat on her back on the Nautilus machine, bench-pressing furiously.

'Lee,' I said. She stared at the ceiling, completely focused. I walked across. 'Lee?'

This time her eyes flickered, took me in, then refocused on the ceiling. Sweat poured out of her. 'Ten.' She pressed, then blew. 'More,' she said.

I sat down and watched her. She was only pressing forty pounds, but you could see it was hurting. And you could also see that she wasn't going to give in. When she groaned it sounded too much like something else. I turned aside and studied the tape-deck.

Just months earlier Lee Chan and me were an item. A lot more than that actually, we were going out for over a year. At first it was just fun, a movie, dinner, a quick romp then home, the usual, and I guess I expected it to end in the usual way, with me getting bored and moving on. But somewhere near the end of the fourth month it occurred to me that I'd broken my record. After five months I found myself thinking about her at work, looking forward to whatever we had planned that night and buying her stupid presents; I suppose that's when I realized I was in trouble. The strange thing was I didn't care, it was like being dragged out to sea by a racing tide and just letting go, set free. It was new to me that, that feeling. New, but I would have to have been an idiot not to understand what was happening to me. I never really thought much about how it might end.

Now she let go the grips, and moaned. Eyes closed, she lay there on her back, fingers to her wrist, and checked her pulse. I bent down and switched off the tape.

She sat up. 'Hi.'

'You'll do yourself an injury.'

'It's called taking care of yourself, actually.' She rolled her head left to right, then back and fore. 'Maybe you should try it.'

But I already had. One morning Lee dragged me out of

bed at six to go jogging. Never again.

'So what's news with you?' she said. 'I guess you heard about Sebastian Ward's house?'

I ummed and ahhed a bit, saying pretty much nothing. The K and R was under wraps, and I didn't feel like discussing Eddie Pike's fried body. Lee knew a little of the history between me and Sebastian, but I didn't want to start down that road.

But just to be polite before we got down to Ottoman, I said, 'What about you?'

'Me?' She got up and went over to the exercise bike. 'Not much. I'm going home.' She bent and fiddled with a bolt; the bike seat dropped a few notches.

Going home. The way she said it, she wasn't talking about her flat over in Pimlico.

'The States?'

'San Fran,' she said. She climbed onto the bike and started pedalling. Slowly at first, but gradually picking up speed.

I stood there like a dummy for a while. It felt like I'd just taken a nasty rabbit punch.

Finally I said, 'New job?'

She looked over at me, then back to the wall, still pedalling. 'Among other things,' she said.

Among other things. One other thing mainly. I bit my tongue and watched her pedal.

After six or seven months of our affair we were seeing each other pretty much every day, me spending the night over at her place, or Lee coming back to mine. And most weekends, when I wasn't out schmoozing with brokers or clients, we generally did something together. She'd drag me off to some gallery and I'd retaliate by taking her to a Chelsea home game, and some nights we'd go out and catch a band, other times we'd get a pizza and a video and stay in, and Sunday mornings we'd lie around in bed, swapping bits of the newspaper, drinking coffee, and spilling toast crumbs on the sheets. I thought everything was just fine. Then one Sunday morning Lee casually dropped it into the conversation that we were coming up to our first anniversary.

Anniversary of what? I said.

She rolled her eyes and told me to forget it. I went back to the newspaper.

In two weeks, she said, it'll be one year since we had our first date.

Yeah? I said. I was studying the property section.

Yeah, she said. And don't you just sound thrilled to bits.

When I looked up she was frowning. I let it lie. But over the next few days the word 'commitment' seemed to come up in her conversation a lot, or maybe it had been there for quite a while but I just hadn't noticed. Anyway, I got the general idea. At least I thought I did. I told Lee to keep the night of our 'anniversary' free, I was taking her out for a special dinner. Special, that's what I said. And I can still remember how she looked at me when I said it. She bought a new dress for the night, white, she wore pearls, and when the waiter showed us to our table she was glowing. She stayed like that right up until I pushed my glass of port aside and took her hand.

It's been a great year, I said.

For me too.

I mean it, I said. One of the best.

She squeezed my hand. I took a breath.

I've been thinking about what you said. You know. Commitment?

She nodded.

I've been thinking about that, I said. And I think, well, we get on pretty well, don't we?

She smiled.

I said, Maybe it's time we took the plunge, Lee.

She nodded, leaning forward.

Lee, I said. How do you feel about moving in with me?

Her eyes, Jesus, the shock and then the hurt; I don't think I'll ever forget it. Her hand slipped out of mine.

That's it?

Lee—

46

But she was already on her feet, heading for the door, she didn't even stop for her coat. And I couldn't kid myself that I didn't know what I'd done. The proposal I'd put to her wasn't the one she'd been expecting; without meaning to I'd cut Lee Chan to the heart.

And now Lee was going home. She sat up straight on the exercise bike, rested her hands on her hips and slowed in her pedalling.

She said, 'You didn't come over here just for a social call, did you, Ian?'

'Ottoman,' I said and she nodded. 'Angela told me you had some queries.'

'Just one,' she said. She concentrated on the wall, thinking, her mind switched on to her work now, she took her job pretty seriously. Her job on Ottoman was to look after the 'following' syndicates, those who'd signed on the Ottoman slip after us. The way the thing works is one syndicate signs for a piece of the business first – this is called the lead line – then other syndicates, or underwriters outside Lloyd's, follow, taking the rest of the risk. Because we'd written the lead on Ottoman, it was now our responsibility to lead the court case against them. They were claiming for a plane of theirs that had been stolen. We were claiming that their security procedures were so lax that they'd breached the terms of their policy. And Lee was the LCO Claims Officer on the case. Now she explained to me that she'd just been through the previous week's trial transcripts. 'WardSure's broker dodged every significant question.'

'Chambers?'

'That's the one.'

'Get real, Lee, he's a broker. He has to keep sweet with us and not upset his client.' Dodging difficult questions, I told her, was part of his job.

She shook her head. She said it wasn't just that.

'Ian, I got the impression from a lot of his answers that he wasn't exactly *au fait* with what was going on. He's not stupid, is he?'

No, I said. Definitely not stupid. In fact he had the

reputation of being a very bright guy. Ambitious too.

She looked down at the pedals going round. 'Then I think he told a few lies. In court.'

'About what?'

She glanced up. That, she said, was what she'd been hoping I might figure out. I was only half-listening. My eyes kept drifting back to the dark ring of sweat on the neckline of her pink leotard. Lee Chan was going home.

'Ian?'

I started back. She rolled her eyes.

'Can you at least have a word with him?' she said.

'Lee, I was there in court. That's just the way he is.'

She turned away from me, gripped the handlebars, and pedalled. Sweat beaded across her forehead and dripped on the floor. All that wasted energy. But she finally started running out of steam, the pedalling slowed, and she gulped in air.

Standing, I said, 'Okay, Lee. If I see him I'll have a word. Is that it?'

She nodded, breathless, and I went to the door. But it didn't seem right, after all we'd shared, for her to announce she was leaving and me to just get up and amble out. How many times since our break-up had I reached for the phone and not called her? But then I had so much else to deal with, Mum and Dad dying, my sister falling to bits, all that. And I was hurt too, and bloody angry, after what I'd found out about Lee. The night after our 'anniversary' I went round to her place with her coat, the one she'd left behind in the restaurant. And what did I find? I found Lee on her second bottle of wine, sitting on the floor of her lounge, staring at a semi-circle of photos she'd arranged in front of herself. They were Chinese men in suits, aged maybe from thirty up to fifty. Lee had scrawled NO across most of them, but on a couple I could clearly read the word POSSIBLE.

What's this? I said, dropping the coat on a chair.

In answer Lee picked up a letter from another pile I hadn't seen. It was a letter from her mother. Lee read it aloud. Deadpan. Basically it was a resumé of both the working and social life of a wealthy Chinese-American accountant, one who Lee's mother seemed to think would make Lee a good husband. When Lee finished reading the letter she put it down by one of the photos, a guy in his mid-forties with specs. One of the possibles. Lee picked up another of her mother's letters and started reading, but this time I cut her off.

When did you get these?

She waved her hand vaguely. I looked at the pile of letters; there must have been a dozen at least.

Lee, I said, feeling my temperature rising. While we've been going out, sleeping together, everything, you've had your mother chasing a husband for you?

Good ol' Mom, she said.

She was drunk, and maybe I'd hurt her worse than I realized the night before, but that was it, I completely did my stack. And Lee didn't just sit there and take it, she was up on her feet and giving as good as she got. It wasn't long – ten minutes max – but in that ten minutes of hurled abuse we really did each other damage. Cheated and betrayed, they were about the two mildest accusations we smacked back and forth. Finally I turned and walked out her door saying, 'That's it, Lee. It's over,' and she shouted, 'Good.' But Christ, it didn't feel that good to me. Then within a week my parents were dead, and large parts of my life went on hold. Parts like Lee.

But now suddenly Lee was leaving. She was leaving, and if I didn't speak up now our six-month stand-off would go permanent; it was just too sudden, I was already spinning with the K and R, Eddie Pike's body, I couldn't hold it all separate enough to be sure how I felt. So when I got to the gym door I turned round and faced her.

'When are you leaving?'

She told me. A matter of days. She had a conference to go to in Dublin, she said she was flying straight on from there to San Fran. She said she'd still be working for Lloyd's.

Trying to make it sound like a joke, I said, 'You can work for Lloyd's here.'

49

She got off the bike and reached for her towel. 'I'm engaged, Ian.' Then she turned and looked straight at me. 'My parents found a nice Chinese-American man for me. His name's Wing Tan. He's an engineer. I flew over there last month and saw him. Now I'm going back to marry him.'

My mouth opened. And then closed.

She said, 'Aren't you going to say anything?'

But what was there left to say? All the anger, those feelings of betrayal, what I'd felt that night of our break-up, it all flared up again and burned. Lee Chan had gone and gotten herself engaged. I looked at her hard.

'Congratulations,' I said.

She made a sound in her throat, spun round, and disappeared into the change room, slamming the door.

8

Tubs lived in Hackney with his mother. She must have been at least eighty, I hadn't seen her for years, but when Allen gave me the all-clear to chase up any possible connection between Sebastian's K & R and the dogs, that's where I went, to Hackney. When I knocked on the terrace door there was movement inside and then silence. I knocked again, harder this time.

'Mrs Laszlo?' Nothing. 'Mrs Laszlo, it's Ian Collier, I'm looking for Tubs.'

There was a sound of creeping boards, then more silence. I raised my hand to knock again but before I could a frail voice said, 'Who is it?'

I told her again. She made me shout my mother's name twice and even then the door only opened a crack. Slight, and wrinkled like a prune, she examined me carefully over the chain.

'Mrs Laszlo, I'm looking for Tubs.'

She pursed her lips.

'It's quite important.'

She seemed to think about it. At last she nodded. 'You're the Collier boy, Ian.'

When I smiled she didn't respond.

'Mrs Laszlo—'

'You went away,' she said.

'Look, is Tubs around? Is there any way I can get hold of him?' Her face was expressionless; I wasn't sure how much of this was getting through to her. 'I phoned, no-one answered.'

'Phoned who?'

'Tubs.'

'My Toby's not here.'

She began to close the door but I set my knee against it and she stopped pushing. She didn't seem frightened or even surprised. I gave it one last shot.

'Here's my card,' I said, taking it from my wallet. 'Could you give it to him as soon as he gets in?'

She studied the card closely but didn't take it. Finally she looked up at me.

'You did go away, Sally told me.'

Sally was my mother. Mrs Laszlo was raving, but it gave me a cold jolt. I took my knee off the door, giving up, and as soon as I'd done that, her expression changed.

'He's at the Gallon,' she said, and immediately the door banged shut.

Like Tubs's house, the Gallon Club was a place I hadn't been to in years. A lot of the shops had changed at street level, the old tailor had gone and there was a kebab house where the butcher's used to be, but just along from there the green doorway to the Gallon hadn't changed a bit. The brass plaque was still fixed to the left of the door too, and when I stepped in and started down the stairs the same smells wafted up from below. Cigars and beer and polish; I could have been ten years old again, following my old man down into the club for the first time.

At the foot of the stairs the room opened out to the right; there was a bar along the far wall. The barman was talking to a customer; he glanced over, took me in and kept talking. Around the tables there were a few more men, no women, and on a ledge up behind the barman a TV. The TV was about the only change in the whole place, it used to be a radio up there. On the TV a pundit was giving his opinion on the lead-up races to the Cheltenham Gold Cup but no-one was watching.

Tubs was at one of the tables by the wall, his back turned to me, gassing to a fellow I didn't recognize. I went over.

'Jesus Christ,' he said, craning round. 'You know you

52

look just like a bloke used to be a member here. Name of Ian Collier.' He was surprised to see me, but pleased too, I think. He introduced me to his friend and pulled out a chair.

'Tubs,' I said, 'can we have a word?'

He looked curious now. 'Sure.' He pulled a roll of tenners from his pocket, counted off seven and dropped them on the table. His friend scooped them up and left.

I sat down, keeping my voice low. 'The other night, you remember, that guy, Sebastian's runner?'

Tubs nodded. 'Pike.'

'Eddie Pike. He's dead.'

I waited for some reaction but Tubs just sat there.

'He was in Sebastian's house when it burned down,' I told him. 'He burnt to death.'

Tubs's gaze wandered to the bar. 'You feel like a drink?'

'That's all you can say? The guy's dead.'

He faced me again. 'The cops've been out rattlin' cages. It's not news, Ian.'

I sat up. 'When?'

He shrugged. 'Just now.'

I chewed that one over. I said, 'Didn't you think it was a bit strange?'

'What, you askin' about Pike, next thing he's dead? Yeah, I thought it was strange.' He fixed me with a look, letting me know strange wasn't quite the word. 'You know what's weirder?' he said, tapping a fat finger on the table. 'You bein' here at the Gallon again.'

I said that his mother told me where to find him but we both knew that wasn't what he'd meant.

He stared at me, sad now and kind of accusing. 'How many years?'

'Tubs, I don't need a trip down memory lane. I need some help.'

He leaned back regarding me, then he pushed away from the table. 'Orange juice, Coke or beer?'

While he was up at the bar I took a look around. The dark crimson wallpaper was peeling up near the ceiling, it had always been like that, and the new wall-lamps were just like the old ones, only without the fringe. At the other tables I vaguely recognized some of the faces; a couple of them even smiled and nodded in my direction. It gave me an odd feeling. Maybe it was just for my old man's sake, but it seemed as if I was remembered. And how long was it since I'd last stepped in there? Ten years?

When I was a kid I couldn't get enough of it. Back then the Gallon Club seemed like the centre of the world, the height of glamour. My old man counted for something down there, I guess that was part of it. Him, Freddie Day, Nev Logan and the rest, all the bookies, they'd gather down the club on Monday nights, the week's big event, the settle-up for the previous seven days. When a bookie doesn't want to hold some bet he's taken, he lays it off with another bookie, and later in the day that other bookie might lay some off back the other way. It's just like the syndicates in the Room really, and it can mean that everybody ends up owing everybody. Some bookies keep accounts with other bookies they trust, it avoids tying up too much cash. That's what my old man did, him and half a dozen others, and on Monday nights they'd go to the Gallon and settle up. The door upstairs was bolted and down by the bar they'd drag two tables together and sit around having a drink and a laugh, passing on track gossip, then the week's books would come out, and the money. I'd sit over in the corner, sipping my Coke. Back then I thought the whole business was great.

I was so busy remembering the old days that I didn't notice Fielding now till he was standing right over me.

'Well, well,' he said. 'Not gonna offer me a seat?'

He'd put on weight, and the grog had left little purple veins on his cheeks, but it was him all right. Fielding.

'No,' I said, 'I'm not.'

It was odd seeing him suddenly ten years older, and out of uniform. Maybe he'd been kicked out of the force, I thought – that figured. I glanced over to the bar, but Tubs appeared to be staying put.

'What's with the suit?' Fielding said.

I told him to get lost.

'Worse manners than your old man,' he commented, and then he just looked at me.

For a moment I thought he was going to offer his condolences; I'm not sure I could have taken that. Fielding was not a nice cop. From the time he first set foot in Walthamstow he was trouble. He didn't seem to like many people, but he really hated my old man. It was Dad who heard from someone over at White City that Fielding's old man was once banged up in Brixton for theft. Dad didn't waste the good news. He lined up everyone he knew at the track one night, got them all standing there on the terraces. When Fielding did his usual walk past the terraces at the end of the night, Dad conducted everyone like an orchestra. A couple of hundred voices chanting, 'Brix-ton! Brix-ton!' The look on Fielding's face as he cottoned on was something they still talked about, it must have been the longest walk of his life.

Now he said, 'What brings you back here?'

'Until you arrived, the company.'

'Sir,' a young bloke called, and Fielding turned.

Sir?

Fielding went over, they had a brief conversation, then they disappeared up the stairs.

Tubs came back from the bar. 'Catchin' up on old times?'

'What's his game?'

'Same as yours,' Tubs said. 'Eddie Pike.' He explained that Fielding had arrived half an hour before; it was the first time anyone had seen him in four or five years. Only now he wasn't in uniform. Now he was a detective. I gazed up the stairs where Fielding had gone.

'Anyway,' Tubs said, sliding my Coke across the table. 'What kinda help you after? You in some kinda trouble?'

'It's for work. We need to know if Sebastian had acquaintances who might go in for arson. If he was in trouble himself somehow.'

Tubs chewed that one over. 'You think he dug himself into a hole, got someone to burn him out of it?' He saw me hesitate. 'Well, am I right, or am I right?' he said.

'It's one possibility.'

He made a scoffing sound.

I'd been wondering just how much I'd have to tell him about the K and R, but now that he'd latched onto this other idea I saw that I wouldn't have to mention kidnap at all. He could nose around just as easily thinking he was trying to pin an arson on Sebastian.

'It has to be discreet, Tubs.'

'How much was the place insured for?'

I plucked a figure out of the air. 'Eight million.'

He smiled, his eyes disappearing. 'Some fuckin' house. Sebastian Ward, ay.' He studied his beer. 'Figure that one. Bloke has his arse hangin' out; twenty years later he's got a house worth eight million quid.'

'Not any more.'

'Yeah, not any more.' Tubs took a swig from his beer. 'Anyway I can tell you for nothin', he hasn't dropped that kinda money. Not at the dogs.'

'He doesn't have to have dropped it. He could've had other problems.'

'Like what?'

'That's what I'm trying to find out.'

Tubs moistened his lips, considering. 'His insurance thing, that's the real money. What are the dogs to him these days? Chicken shit. Maybe he lost big on his insurance racket.'

'Broking,' I said.

Tubs cocked an eyebrow.

'It's not a racket, Tubs. It's an insurance broking company.' When he smiled like he thought I was splitting hairs, that got my goat, so I added, 'And businessmen aren't in the habit of burning each other's houses down.'

He stopped smiling. 'Oh yeah? And us lot down here, we are, are we?' He thumbed his chest. 'Things go wrong, we up and torch an eight million-quid house?'

'I didn't say that.'

'Sure.'

He sculled the rest of his beer and put down his glass,

staring past me. I glanced around but no-one was looking our way.

'Tubs,' I said, 'will you help?'

'The man's a tosser.'

'You'd be helping me, not him.'

He thought about that. He'd never liked Sebastian, even in the old days, and what he'd said about Sebastian having his arse hanging out back then, it wasn't strictly true. I was about fifteen when Sebastian started appearing for the occasional Monday night session at the Gallon. He wasn't a bookie, he was a punter – I think it was Nev Logan who first brought him along. Sebastian had sold Nev some insurance on the cheap, Nev thought the other bookies might be interested. It turned out they were; Sebastian did business with just about all of them. And not just insurance, he started betting with them too, on account, and then he'd come in to settle up at the Monday night session. Tubs never liked that. And he never liked the way Sebastian would pull out this little blue book he had, and write insurance for everyone like he was taking bets, just one of the lads. Sebastian came pretty regular at first, but as his business got bigger we saw less of him; he was down to about one visit every three months when I saw his name in the paper. He'd bought an insurance broker; he'd told the journalist he was going to change its name to WardSure. I remember that I showed the article to my old man. He just leant across the kitchen table, flipped me a copy of *Greyhound Life*, the racing form, and told me to keep my mind on the job. Later on I tore out the article about Sebastian and kept it. I'm not sure why I did that, maybe because Sebastian had this air about him, sophisticated, he wasn't like anyone else I knew. Down at the Gallon he seemed like a visitor from another world.

'If we find he's involved somehow,' I told Tubs now, 'we don't pay out.'

'You don't pay out nothin'?'

'Not a penny.'

'He's down the gurgler for eight million?'

'Maybe. But I need to get to the bottom of this fast.'

'How fast?'

'Hours.'

Tubs snorted.

'Okay, days, but it can't drag on.'

Tubs stuck out his bottom lip. I could see it appealed to him, the idea of upsetting Sebastian's apple cart.

'I'll be wastin' my time,' he said, 'but if that's what you want.'

Before I could thank him, someone came over from another table. He was completely bald, his face was like a skull, and it wasn't till he spoke that I recognized him.

'Ian,' he said, offering me his hand. 'Been a while.'

It was Nev Logan; I tried to hide the shock. His grip when we shook was almost nothing, like a ghost.

'Nev,' I said, trying to look him in the eye.

'Just wanted to say sorry I couldn't make the funeral. Terrible bloody thing,' he said. 'Terrible. How's the sister?'

'She's staying with me.'

'Good. Stick together. Good people, your Mum and Dad. Good people.' He rested a hand on my shoulder and I felt the most desperate urge to get out of there. At last he smiled; it made him look even worse, and his hand fell away. 'Come and see us sometimes, ay?' Turning gingerly he shuffled back to the bar.

'Jesus Christ.'

'Yeah. Looks shockin',' Tubs remarked. From his tone he could have been sizing up a dog at the track. 'He's not normally that bad. Must be the treatment or somethin'.'

When he saw the question in my eyes, Tubs nodded. 'Cancer. They told him six months ago.'

'You never told me.'

He looked up. 'Would you've been interested?'

This again. Tubs always thought I'd betrayed Dad somehow when I went and joined Lloyd's. And not just Dad, but all of them, like I thought I'd become too good for dog people once I started to wear a suit. There was no point arguing the point now, I had real problems to deal with, so I stood and put my card on the table.

'I really need this, Tubs.'

'Okay,' he said raising his hands. 'Okay.'

As I went up the stairs I looked over to the bar. Nev was leaning against it, the barman pouring his drink, they were laughing. Nev Logan the joker, the man who used to fill my head with tall stories, he was old suddenly, and dying, and no-one had thought to tell me.

The Gallon Club. Nev. But I had other worries. I hurried up the last stairs and out the green door, into the bright glare of the street.

9

'So you're it,' Bill said, leading me into the surveil-lance room upstairs. 'The fall guy.'

I'd just finished explaining what Allen had asked me to do.

'He thinks it might help.'

'Oh, it'll help,' Bill said smiling. 'You find whoever's got Ward, you'll get your fuckin' head blown off.' He propped himself against the table. 'Big help.'

Green lights bobbed up and down on the surveillance gear, the needles on the dials bouncing to and fro. The soundman had his headphones on lopsided, just one ear covered. He turned to me and nodded.

'We've got monitors on the direct lines into the senior WardSure people,' Bill said indicating the sound gear. 'Another one on their switchboard, Max Ward's home line, and his mobile.'

'Anything?'

'Dick shit. Tell me again who that security guy was?'

I took him through it a second time, explaining what Eddie Pike used to do for Sebastian. When I added that I already had someone digging round, Bill frowned. You could see he didn't think much of our chances in that direction.

'What about the Name?' he asked.

I gave him the note from the pigsticker and he read it.

'How old?'

'Two years.'

Bill pulled a face. 'Fucking hell,' he said.

He handed it back to me, saying maybe I didn't have to

61

worry about getting my head blown off after all. Then he stared at the sound gear a while, watching the green lights flicker up and down the scale.

When I was helping Bill on the Ottoman report it crossed my mind at least once that maybe he wasn't up to the job. He went at things like a bull at a gate, crash through or crash, he had a way of really upsetting people who might have been helpful. There was an Ottoman Air stewardess he spoke to, a bright girl; he grilled her like she was responsible for stealing the plane herself. When he left the room she asked me what Bill's problem was. She said he was worse than the crooks she worked for, but when I asked her what she meant by that she immediately clammed up. I told Bill later but he dismissed it out of hand. Fucking airhead, he said.

But the K and R business was different, you could see he was loving every minute of it. Men with guns, phone taps, the urgency and secrecy. I think if Sebastian had suddenly turned up safe somewhere, Bill would have been disappointed as hell.

He reached across to the sound gear now and hit a switch. A woman's voice came over the speakers; she was talking about commissions on some WardSure policy. Bill pressed a button. Now it was a man's voice, another WardSure employee, he seemed to be bitching to his wife about their nanny.

'Dickhead,' Bill said, pressing the button again.

The next channel was a blank. Bill was about to hit the button a third time when a high-pitched beeping started up.

'Max Ward,' the surveillance man said. 'On the speaker?'

Bill nodded. 'Put him through.'

The man flicked two switches, Max's voice came over the speaker, excited as a kid.

'Hello. Hello, Bill Tyler?'

Bill shook his head, theatrically. 'Is that the code?'

'What?'

'The code. I gave you a fucking code.'

'Full cover. Full cover.'

'Great,' Bill muttered. The surveillance man grinned, enjoying the show.

'It's an e-mail,' Max said, completely wired. 'It just came in, you want to hear it?'

'Max.'

'I'm here.'

'Calm down.'

'Did you hear me? It's an e-mail—'

'For fuck's sake,' Bill exploded. 'Get a grip, Max. Calm down and read us the sodding message.'

We could hear Max breathing. Bill glanced at the surveillance man who nodded; he was getting it all on tape. He picked up a pen as well.

'Now, Max,' Bill said, 'Whenever you're ready.'

'You ready? Okay. Here it is. It's like a list. The first line says, "Re Sebastian Ward, further instructions". Then the next line's the date, today, and then it says 5 p.m. The next line there's an address, you want me to read it?'

'Yes,' Bill said, rolling his eyes.

The surveillance man watched the speaker.

'Lower Park Barn,' Max said; 'Park, P.A.R.K. Brentwell near Lepping, Kent. No postcode.'

'What about the money?'

'Doesn't mention money. Just Brentwell near Lepping, Kent, that's it.'

When Bill looked at his watch I glanced at mine. Three thirty.

'What happens now?' Max said. 'You going down there?'

Bill tapped his hand on his thigh. The surveillance man was already digging through the pile of ordinance survey maps in the corner. He found what he was looking for and opened it out on the spare table. Bill went over and joined him, both of them studying the map.

'Bill?' said Max over the speaker.

'Hang on, Max,' I said.

'Ignore the bastard,' Bill muttered to me. He studied the map some more then he looked over his shoulder. 'Max?' he called.

'Yeah?'

'Stay put. If anything else comes through, call us. And fax over a copy of that e-mail.' He told Max the number. A second later Max was quizzing him again, asking if he was going down to Brentwell.

Bill turned, muttering, and stalked back to the sound gear. He asked if Max had the fax number. When Max said 'yes,' Bill said 'goodbye' and flicked the switch. All we heard on the speaker now was the dial tone. Bill returned to the map. The pair of them traced their fingers left and right, searching; they seemed to be having some trouble finding it.

I said, 'I know where it is.'

They both turned.

'Brentwell?' Bill said, looking at me curiously.

I had a sinking feeling. 'Yeah, Brentwell,' I said, glancing down at my shoes then back up. 'Brentwell, and Lower Park Barn.'

Ten minutes later we were in the van motoring through the City, heading for the Old Kent Road. There was a driver and Bill and me in the front, and four men with guns in the back. I caught a glimpse of the Lloyd's Building; it made me wonder what the hell I was doing.

Bill had the folded map on his knees, now he pointed to Brentwell. 'Which way from the village?'

I told him I wasn't sure, there were a couple of lanes, but I'd know when we got there. He glanced at me like he was having second thoughts about taking me along.

'There's no racetrack marked on the map,' he said.

'It's an old flapping track,' I told him. 'It's probably just fields now.'

He grunted, folded the map up and tossed it onto the dash. 'You're sure this barn's derelict?'

I reminded him that I hadn't been near the place in fifteen years, and his glance lingered on me just long enough this time to make me feel uncomfortable. I suppose I couldn't blame him for having doubts; it must have seemed pretty strange to him, me knowing about the barn. Right then it seemed pretty strange to me too.

Lower Park Barn. I hadn't given the place ten minutes' thought in the past ten years; it was just one more place on the circuit where the old man used to put up his stand. Flapping tracks are the bottom rung of the dog-racing ladder. Not properly regulated, the dogs racing there are generally third raters, trained by their owners, and the tracks aren't much more than sandy circuits on a conveniently flat stretch of ground. Thirty or forty years back there were dozens of them all over the country, but now most of them have gone the way of Brentwell, abandoned and ploughed up or turned into industrial estates. As a kid, going out for a day at some flapping track was like going on a picnic. Good times.

'What's on your mind?' Bill said.

I looked at him, he was watching the road. 'The place,' I said. 'The old track.'

'Exposed?'

'What?'

'The barn,' he said. 'Is it out by itself, in a hollow, up a hill, what?'

I tried to remember. 'In a hollow.'

'How many access roads?'

'Come on, how many roads? This is fifteen years ago.'

'There's four guys in the back,' Bill jerked his thumb that way, 'who'd be grateful if you tried to remember.'

I tried. 'I'm not sure. I think just farm tracks, I couldn't swear to it.'

'Any woods nearby?'

He just didn't seem to get it. There were heaps of these flapping tracks we used to go to, and the years had blended them all in my mind. I was confident that once we got to Brentwell I'd remember the way there; I used to be the old man's navigator on those trips out of London. To Dad and Tubs, out of London was off the edge of the world. But exactly what we'd find at Lower Park Barn now I couldn't say. I was even having second thoughts about it being in a hollow. I reached for the map. There were a few patches of dark green around Brentwell. Woods?

'Maybe,' I said.

'Maybe?' Bill rolled his eyes. 'Jesus.'

A voice came over the CB. Bill picked up the handset.

'Go ahead.'

'We got the fax.' It was the surveillance man we'd left back at the house, you could hear him quite clearly, it wasn't your average CB. 'Reads just like Max Ward said. Name, time and address.'

'Any chance of tracing the e-mail?'

'No.' There was a pause. 'Your friend Max, he scrubbed it.'

Bill stared straight ahead.

'Bill?'

'Okay, keep us in touch.'

Bill double-clicked the button on the handset then hung it back on the hook. He stared ahead a few seconds, quiet, thinking. Then he lifted one leg and drove his foot straight through the glove-box; the sound of breaking plastic was like a gunshot, but the driver didn't bat an eye. We drove on in silence.

After nearly an hour we got to the King's Head in Brentwell; I felt like I was on home ground.

'Straight on,' I said. 'On past the Post Office.'

I handed Bill the map. He'd calmed down a bit; he even tried to fix the glove-box, but when he couldn't he tossed the lot out the window.

'Don't bring us out right on top of the barn,' he warned me.

Leaning forward, I gave the driver directions. They were quiet in the back; we'd slowed to about thirty, Bill started to take an interest in where we were. We headed out of the village past the council houses; there were a lot more than I remembered.

'How far?' Bill said.

'Couple of miles.'

'When we're down to half a mile, tell us.'

I nodded. Back when we'd passed through the City I'd

had doubts about what I was doing, but those doubts were a lot stronger now. The others were tense, I knew that, but somehow it didn't make me feel any better. They were professionals and I was what? A mug?

'Left,' I said, 'up this lane.'

We turned off the main road; we hadn't seen any houses for a while. It was still a way yet but the next building I expected to see was Lower Park Barn. There was a ridge along the left shoulder of the lane, wooded, with a thick undergrowth. I saw Bill inspecting it. After a while I pointed to the right. Where the ground dipped, there was another stretch of woods.

'Just past there.'

'Near the wood?'

'Other side,' I said. 'About half a mile.'

The van slowed, then stopped. Bill asked me where the lane went and I told him. Straight on. I couldn't remember if the barn was visible from the lane.

I said, 'There's a track comes off it down to the barn.'

Bill had a few words with the driver, then he turned and flicked up the canvas flap.

'The barn's at two o'clock, far side of the woods, half a mile. You two, get out of here, make your way down under cover. Get yourselves close enough without being seen, then call in. Clear?'

There was a general agreement from the back. The van door opened and closed, someone in the back said 'right', and we were away again. I glanced in the side mirror. Two men in jeans and heavy coats scrambled up into the woods on the left bank, you couldn't see their guns, but each of them hugged an arm to his chest.

The whole operation seemed so matter of fact it made me feel naive, like I'd just got a glimpse of reality for the first time. Facing the front again, I said, 'How many K and Rs have you guys done?'

Nobody answered. Bill kept his eyes fixed on the woods to the right.

The farm track appeared on our right, and about a quarter of a mile down it you could see the half-collapsed roof of the barn. It was derelict.

The driver's head swivelled as we passed the muddy track, then he turned to Bill. 'Tyre tracks. Someone's been down there.'

We went on up the lane; when the barn roof dropped out of sight we stopped. Bill gave more instructions and the other pair in the back got out and disappeared over the ridge on our right. Bill told the driver to find somewhere to turn.

I said, 'Do you think Sebastian's down there?'

Bill reached behind the seat and pulled out some electronic gear, and a pistol. 'If he is, these are the dumbest kidnappers so far. Not impossible.'

We found a small lay-by further along. As we turned, Bill passed me a handset with a stubbed aerial; he explained how to use it. By the time he'd finished we were parked, facing back down the lane, engine idling.

'We'll drop you at the turnoff to the barn,' he said.

Maybe I should have expected that, but I hadn't. A slow rising wave of fear rippled up from my gut. Four of the hardest men I'd ever seen were on the job, and Bill was tipping me out there to join them? And with what? A glorified walkie-talkie?

'Why?' I said.

'Why?' Bill grinned. 'Because if you don't get out there, you'll have to stay with us. And we're driving down to the barn. Fair enough?'

'You're just going to drive down there?'

He nodded. Yes, he said, that was the general idea. Once he'd heard from the lads.

What could I say? I shut my mouth, holding tight to the handset now, like it was some kind of security blanket. Bill put his pistol on the dash, and we waited. After five minutes the first pair called in. They were in position, fifty yards west of the barn, and there was no sign of anyone. Another minute and the other pair called in, a hundred yards northeast of the barn. Again nothing.

Bill nodded to the driver; we moved off. As we trundled down the lane Bill told the others what he planned to do;

he didn't refer to me by name now, he called me the lookout. It felt like one of those bad dreams when you've been picked for England, you're all set to take the field, and you suddenly realize you don't know what the game is. At the turnoff, we stopped.

'You'll be alright,' the driver told me. He seemed to have a better idea than Bill what I was thinking. 'Nothin's gonna happen till the money comes out.'

Bill reached across me and opened the door.

'Keep out of sight. Any cars come along, get their plate numbers. If they turn down to the barn—' he pointed to my handset – 'let us know.'

It seemed like there had to be more to it, something else I should know, but when I hesitated Bill lifted his chin, indicating the open door. I got out and he closed the door quietly behind me. The van turned onto the muddy track; I stood there watching it head down to the barn, then Bill's arm suddenly shot out the window, waving me back to the woods. He swore at me over the walkie-talkie.

Turning, I hurried off the lane. I leapt the ditch, dropped ankle-deep in mud, then trudged on up the ridge. Fifteen yards up there was an old hedge, some low bushes with a flat rock just behind. I sat down on the rock. You were pretty well hidden there, but you had a decent view up and down the lane. You were high enough to get a proper look at the barn too, but I couldn't see the van at first, it was hidden by the dip. I wiggled my toes. My shoes were covered in mud, and soaking. A hundred and seventy-five quid up the spout. I took off my tie and shoved it in my coat pocket, then I checked my watch. Five to five.

The van appeared again, crawling along, almost at the barn now. It looked so exposed down there, exposed and vulnerable, I was suddenly grateful to Bill for turfing me out when he did. Just short of the barn, the van stopped. There was some talk on the two-way, then I saw one man to the west and one man to the northeast of the barn, on their feet, moving in. I couldn't see the other two. Bill got out of the van. I couldn't hear anything, they were too far away, just moving figures in the distance, slightly unreal, but Bill seemed to be speaking, maybe calling into the barn. When nothing happened he went forward slowly. He sure had guts.

By the time he disappeared inside the barn, the other two were at the side-walls, aiming their guns through the windows. A few seconds later Bill's voice came over the handset. 'Relax. No-one here.'

He wasn't talking to me but I breathed out, relieved. I hadn't realized how tense I was. I stood and stretched my legs, bending to flick the mud off my pants, and that's when I heard the car.

It came down the lane from the west, the way we'd come in, and immediately I crouched and picked up the handset. I shuffled closer to the hedge.

Keep calm, I thought. Check the plates. My heart was somewhere up near my throat.

The car appeared then, a green Porsche idling along at about twenty. It started slowing the moment I saw it.

'Go on,' I whispered. 'Keep going.'

But somehow I just knew it wouldn't. It was kind of inevitable the way it slowed and finally stopped at the muddy track.

I lifted the handset. 'There's a car.'

A moment later Bill snapped, 'Where?'

Where? Here, I felt like shouting. Here, you crazy bastard, right where you left me. Instead I said, 'It's stopped at the turnoff.'

Down at the barn I saw the van suddenly lurch forward, it veered right and disappeared behind the barn. Whoever was in the Porsche was too low to have seen anything; from there all they could see was the barn's roof.

'How many?' Bill's voice on the handset.

'One.' My throat was dry, I swallowed. 'A green Porsche.'

'Not the car, tosspot. How many in it?'

'I can't see.'

The Porsche reversed a few feet, stopped, then swung hesitantly onto the track.

'It's coming your way.'

Its back tyres had just left the tarmac, then it stopped again. The seconds ticked by. It just sat there.

'Hang on,' I said. 'It's stopped.'

The engine burbled, the only sound apart from my strangled breathing. And then the engine died.

'Well, is it coming or not?' Bill barked.

I snatched at the volume, now he raved at me in a whisper.

'No,' I said. 'He's turned off the engine; he's just sitting there. I think there's just one, the driver.'

The car door opened, I felt my heart thud against my ribs. A man got out, back turned to me; he looked down the track. He was holding something. I thought it was a newspaper at first, then he tried to unfold it and I realized it was a map.

'He's got a map,' I whispered to the handset. 'I think he's lost.'

I'm not sure if I really thought he was lost; maybe I was just hoping. It didn't matter anyway, because right then he turned and rested his map on the car roof and I saw his face.

'Jesus,' I said.

He studied the map, then lifted his head, looking up the lane and down the track. I huddled over the handset.

'Bill,' I said, 'it's Max.'

'A map? I heard you the first time. Listen—'

'Not a map. Max. The guy in the Porsche, it's Max.'

There was a pause. 'Max Ward?'

'Affirmative,' I said. I haven't got a clue where that came from. 'Max Ward.'

Then I released the speak-button and the handset squealed like a pig. Max spun round and looked straight up the ridge. I held myself stock-still, eyes fixed on a leaf on the ground, and tried not to breathe.

'Tyler?' Max said.

I glanced up, Max was edging along the car, looking straight up to where I was hidden.

'He's seen me,' I said to the handset. 'I'm going down.' I got to my feet and looked over the hedge just as I heard Bill cry, 'Don't!'

I froze. Max stared up at me. For a second I thought I'd made the most God-awful blunder, then Max dropped his head to one side. 'Collier?' His brow creased in bewilderment; he smiled uncertainly. 'What the fuck,' he said, 'are you doing here?'

The van trundled up a minute later. Bill didn't wait for it to stop; he jumped out and made a bee-line for Max.

'Stay put,' he shouted. 'You call this staying put?' He gave Max a sharp poke in the chest. 'This isn't frigging play school, is it? You think this is frigging play school?'

Max swiped the hand away. The pair of them stood glaring at one another, two schoolyard bullies facing off.

But Max wasn't in Bill's league, and he cracked. He started explaining why he'd come down, the same Just Helping Out story he'd practised on me while we were waiting for the van. But Bill wasn't interested, he lifted his hand again and pointed.

'Go read your K and R policy. Your company's ceded control of this, now it's Mortlake's responsibility. The Mortlake Group appointed me. You interfere and you void the whole thing. Mortlake won't have to pay a penny and your old man's out on his own. Am I getting through to you, Max?'

Max gave him a sideways look. The possibility that what he'd done might void the K and R policy had taken the wind out of his sails.

Bill swayed forward. 'Is that clear?'

'It's clear, okay?' Max gave me a lopsided grin, like saying, Can you believe this guy? Then he turned back to Bill. 'What was in the barn?'

'None of your business.'

Another stony face-off, then Bill turned on his heel and stalked across to the van while Max stood there fuming.

'Collier,' Bill called back, 'you coming?'

I went over and climbed in, the van eased around the Porsche and Max, and started down the lane.

'Bloody dipstick,' Bill muttered.

The driver was smiling, there was laughter in the back

too; I guess everyone was pretty relieved that the worst they'd had to deal with was Max.

Bill said to me, 'When you used to come here with your old man, did Sebastian Ward ever come down too?'

Not with us, I said. But sure, he might have come down here.

'And Max?'

I took a moment with that. 'Same,' I said. Bill didn't say anything, so I steeled myself and asked, 'What was down in the barn?'

Bill lifted his leg. I braced myself for another explosive disintegration of the dash, but it didn't happen. All he did was rest his boot up there. He picked at the clods of mud with a pocketknife.

'Nothin'.' Max's Porsche sent up a spray of mud as it roared past us, slewing down the lane. Bill concentrated on the mud on his boots. 'Absafuckinglutely nothin',' he said.

10

O n the way back to London I tried calling Tubs at
home but the phone just kept ringing; Mrs Laszlo
was turning a deaf ear. Then I tried the Gallon; the
barman put Nev Logan on and Nev said Tubs had left
straight after me that morning and hadn't been back. 'Any
message?' he asked me. But I'd just wanted to warn Tubs
that it seemed a whole lot more likely now that the arson
at Sebastian's place was tied up with the dogs; who else
would have known about Brentwell? I suppose I wanted to
tell him to be careful, I was feeling a bit uneasy now about
having gotten him involved at all. But I said to Nev, 'No.
No message.'

In the back of the van they were quiet, the rush of relief
wearing off. The driver smoked. Bill and me sat silently,
watching the road and thinking our thoughts.

'Just say,' Bill said, 'Sebastian Ward kidnapped himself.'

I looked at him.

'Just say,' he said.

'Is this before or after he killed Pike and burnt down his
own house?'

'The place was insured.'

'Get serious. Pike's dead.'

'Hang on.' Bill lifted a hand. 'Go with me. The K and
R policy's good for five million. Think about it. What's he
really got to do to get the money? Disappear for a few
days, send a few e-mails, race us round the country. When
we're good and worried, Mortlake coughs up, Sebastian
comes stumbling out of a cellar somewhere.'

'What's put this in your head? Max?'

Bill didn't answer, but he didn't have to, I had to be right. Max showing up at Lower Park Barn like that had really set Bill thinking.

'Max Ward,' I said, 'is a dope.'

The driver piped up, 'That how come he's in the Porsche and we're in the van?'

I said to Bill, 'Sebastian and Allen are friends. And Sebastian doesn't need stunts like this to make money.'

Bill stared straight ahead. We were on the Old Kent Road again, not far from the City but passing through a different world. Grog shops with metal grilles across their windows and most of the shopfronts boarded up. When we stopped at some lights an old woman came out of a newsagent next to us. She put down her shopping and scratched at her instant lottery card. A loser. She dropped the scratchie, picked up her shopping and trudged off.

As ~~we~~ pulled away from the lights Bill said, 'Is he really a dope or j~~ust a~~ good actor?'

I opened my mo~~uth~~ then hesitated. Bill saw that. He nodded to himself.

'We'll drop you after the bridge,' he said. 'You'll be wanting to have a word with Allen.'

I took the lift, avoiding the Room, and went straight up to the Mortlake Group offices. Since Bill had dropped me off, I'd had fifteen minutes to think about his theory and I'd decided it was bollocks. If Max and Sebastian were working together to get the ransom money, why burn the house down and kill Eddie Pike? And why would a man as rich as Sebastian get involved in something like that anyway? It was crazy.

I found Allen at his desk. He looked up at me hopefully.

'Nothing,' I said.

His face fell.

I gave him the run-down on the trip down to Brentwell, and halfway through my story he went over to the cabinet and poured us both a drink. When I finished, he went and poured us both another.

76

'Max?' Allen recapped the bottle. 'I don't believe it. He just turned up?'

I nodded. When he brought my drink over I slugged it back. I said, 'Bill's got an idea maybe Sebastian and Max are working together.'

Allen's hand paused; he looked at me over his glass.

'Ian, that's got to be one of the stupidest bloody ideas I've ever heard.'

I raised my hands. I said it was just a feeling Bill had.

'Bugger's not paid to have feelings.' He sat down, one hand on the desk, fingers tapping.

'If there was nothing at the barn, why'd they send the message?'

'Bill thinks maybe they were watching.'

'Watching what?'

'The van. Bill's team.'

I explained what Bill had told me. He'd said it was the kidnappers' way of drawing the team out, getting a look at what they were dealing with. He said it happened like that sometimes, generally when the kidnappers were smart.

Allen gave a wry smile. 'Did he mention where Max fits into that?' Rocking forward in his chair, he turned over some papers. His thoughts moved on. 'By the by, we're due at the WardSure offices in forty minutes.'

'What for?'

He lifted his gaze. 'They've lined up a meeting with Mehmet. No lawyers.'

We look at each other. Barin Mehmet was the owner of Ottoman Air; Sebastian had been trying to line him up for a face-to-face meeting with us for months. Until now he'd refused all our calls and fended off Sebastian's efforts with a wall of silence. He seemed to be quite happy for Ottoman to take its chance in court.

'They?' I said.

Allen told me he'd just taken the call. 'Some young twit. Chambers?'

Nigel Chambers. Mentally I shifted gear. Sebastian's rescue wasn't my responsibility, not directly, it was Bill Tyler's, and after my surprise trip to Lower Park Barn I had a keen sense of my limitations in that direction.

Sorting out Ottoman's claim was a different kind of headache, more familiar, one I thought I could handle.

'What's he talking?' I said. 'Settlement?'

'Chambers wouldn't say. Just said Mehmet would be there and it might be helpful if we went along.'

There was a knock at the door and I turned to see Angela coming in. She looked terrible, really drawn. Before she could ask, I shook my head. No news. Then I excused myself and went to dig up the paperwork on Ottoman. As the door closed behind me I heard Allen launch into the Brentwell story, and I was glad to be out of there.

As I walked across the reception, Pam, our receptionist, looked up from her magazine.

'Did they find Mr Ward?' she said.

I shook my head, then paused. 'What was that?'

'Mr Ward,' she said. 'I thought maybe they found him.'

I walked on to the underwriters' office. 'Who said he was missing?'

'He's been kidnapped, that's what everyone's saying, and his house burnt down too.'

Opening the door, I turned. I saw it cross her eyes as she spoke: she'd suddenly remembered my parents; she didn't know which way to look. But that wasn't what worried me right then. What worried me was that if Pam had heard about the K and R, someone who should have known better had talked.

'It's just a rumour,' I said. 'Do us a favour, Pam. Don't pass it on.'

I gave her a stern look, the kind Angela would have laughed at, but Pam was only twenty-three and she nodded apologetically. I turned and went into the office.

Inside there were three desks, all facing the centre of the room. Beside each desk was a filing cabinet. I unlocked the one for the 86 box, flicking through folders till I found the Ottoman files, four of them, bulging with copies of Bill Tyler's investigation notes. He'd taken a good few statements from the Ottoman employees out in

Turkey but their London office hadn't been nearly so cooperative; certainly he'd got nowhere near to speaking with Barin Mehmet since their first meeting in Izmir. Thumbing through the statements, I wondered why Mehmet had suddenly popped out of his hole.

'What's the buzz?'

Glancing up, my heart sank. Frazer. He flicked the door closed behind him and ambled across to a desk. 'Sebastian still on the critical list?'

I nodded to the door. 'Pam's heard.'

'Ahha.' He slumped into a chair and leant back. 'Pam and everyone else with ears.'

'It's out?'

'All over the market.'

When I groaned, Frazer leant forward.

'If Allen thought he could keep it quiet he's losing his grip.' Then he noticed the files. I'd had them out quite a bit lately; he knew exactly what they were. He folded his arms. 'How's the case going?'

'Ottoman?'

He didn't answer. He looked straight at me.

'Not bad,' I said.

'Justine said the barrister's called you all over for a chat.'

'Tomorrow,' I told him.

He indicated the files. 'What's this, homework?'

'Mehmet's asked Allen for a meeting.'

He gave me a doubtful look. 'Last I heard, Mehmet didn't want to dirty his hands.'

'Change of heart.'

'Just like that?'

'Apparently.' I did a quick trawl through the files, making sure it was all there. Frazer's eyes stayed on me; God knows what he was thinking, but I sensed the tension climb.

Finally he said, 'What do you want, Ian?'

I glanced up.

'Do you think Allen's going to thank you? Something extra in the bonus?'

There was one file we wouldn't need; I put it back in the cabinet, locked it away safely, then turned.

'Good lad, well done, suck my dick while you're down there?' Frazer stood, smiling now, but only with his teeth. 'You think it'll get you Angela's job? Give me the elbow?' He elbowed the air.

'I'm doing my job, Frazer.'

'Great job,' he said sarcastically. He nodded to the folders in my hand. 'Ottoman Air, ay? Tell me about it. Get in some practice before you have to explain it to Piers.' Piers Crossland, he meant. The man on the other side of Allen's merger plans. Frazer never passed up the opportunity to remind me that he and Piers Crossland had once worked on the same box together. The implication was that if Piers ended up in the driver's seat instead of Allen, I was out.

Counting silently to ten, I headed for the door.

He called after me, 'The big move into K and R not looking so good now, is it.'

I swung round. 'What's that?'

He drew back a moment, not sure he hadn't gone too far. But when he saw he'd rattled me, he smiled again.

'If we have to pay out on Sebastian's K and R policy, Allen will drop you like a turd.' He held out his hand, opening his fingers as though dropping something that stank. 'The only way your career's going from here, my friend, is down.'

I suppose I could have said something. What I did was turn on my heel and walk out.

11

The WardSure offices were over on the other side of Leadenhall Market, so we walked.

Allen said, 'Angela was asking if you'd chased up that Name.' When he saw my blank look he explained, 'That kook. You know, the pig-sticker.'

I told him I hadn't had a chance yet, that there'd been no time.

'Well bloody well make time,' he said. His eyes were on the pavement; I don't think he saw me wince. It felt like being eighteen again, getting a blast from my old man after a bad night at the dogs. I wasn't used to that from Allen. Sebastian's kidnap, I thought, was eating him.

Sebastian and Allen went way back, nearly twenty years; they'd met through some racing syndicate they'd both bought into. It was Allen who'd smoothed the path for Sebastian at Lloyd's, and Sebastian had returned the favour later by sending plenty of WardSure's business the Mortlake Group's way. They played golf together sometimes, and Sebastian would often drop into the Mortlake Group offices. I suppose they were about as friendly as two blokes who do a lot of business with one another can ever be. Allen seemed to know his way to the WardSure offices pretty well too; I was going hard to keep up.

In the lift, when we were alone, he seemed to make an effort to shake off his troubles. He inspected himself in the mirror and pulled at the cuffs of his shirt.

'Let Mehmet do the talking,' he said. 'Wait and see if he mentions a figure.' A settlement figure, he meant. The amount we'd agree to pay if Mehmet dropped the court case.

'Have we got a number in mind?'

Allen didn't answer. He straightened his shoulders and faced the doors.

'Are we planning to settle?' I asked.

The lift slowed; Allen ran a hand over his face.

'Maybe.' He turned to me as the lift stopped. The doors opened. 'But if anyone asks, the only number I have in mind is zero.'

Nigel Chambers was waiting for us in the WardSure reception.

'Allen, Ian.' He shook our hands, trying hard to look the serious professional; it made him seem even younger than he was. 'Mr Mehmet's waiting, we'll go straight through.'

The main part of their office was a big open-plan space, islands of desks in lines and PCs everywhere. Down one end of the room was an area rigged out like a library, scores of shelves and thousands of files, racked and labelled, the full policy details for all the business they brokered. Most of the desks were empty; the WardSure brokers were out doing their rounds, touting business to various underwriters across the Square Mile.

At the far side of the room was a row of doors with nameplates, the managers' offices, each one glass-walled. The shutters in Sebastian's office, I noticed, were down.

'Where's Max?' I said.

Nigel frowned. 'You need him?'

I glanced at Allen, who thought a moment then shook his head. Nigel opened the door to the conference room and ushered us in.

There was a packet of Gitanes on the table, and a silver lighter, and behind these Barin Mehmet. He stubbed out his cigarette and stood. He was dark like his picture in the Ottoman Air annual report, and he had a thick black moustache that made his teeth seem snow-white now when he smiled. Nigel did the introductions and we all sat down.

Our dispute with Ottoman had been running for

months, the past few weeks of it in court. It was one of the policies the 86 box wrote the lead on while Angela Mortlake was in hospital. Even though it was Justine who signed us up for it, theft and accident on the whole Ottoman fixed-wing fleet of twelve planes, it was me that was meant to be supervising her at the time. But at the time I was still trying to deal with the loss of my parents, my break-up with Lee Chan, and with Katy crying herself to sleep each night in my spare room. That's why when Justine brought me the Ottoman slip, telling me she wanted to sign, I maybe didn't give it quite the attention I should have. So now here we were, Ottoman suing us for a payout on their plane that had been stolen from a hangar out in Izmir, and us fighting them on their security procedures. And WardSure, the broker on the policy, trying to broker a settlement.

'I think I've got everything we need,' Nigel said, shuffling his papers.

Mehmet told him, 'You don't have an agreement.'

Nigel looked up.

'The only thing you need,' Mehmet said, 'is an agreement. And you don't have that there.' He pointed to the papers.

You could see Nigel didn't know quite how to take that. I had the impression he'd thought he had Mehmet's number, but that Mehmet had suddenly blown that idea clean out of the water.

'Well,' Nigel said, 'that's what we're here for.'

Mehmet grunted.

Lowering his eyes to the papers, Nigel started recapping the situation, but Mehmet immediately interrupted.

'Should we wait for Sebastian?'

Nigel kept his eyes down. 'He's been delayed.'

'I've got time.' Mehmet looked at Allen. 'How about you?'

When Allen said that he'd rather get started, Nigel began again. But Mehmet cut him off.

'Is this how you normally reach an agreement, Mr Chambers?' He took a cigarette slowly from the packet while Nigel squirmed. 'Some people might think you were playing favourites. I'm just one small client. On the other hand, Mr Mortlake here, you're doing business with him every day. It wouldn't pay you to upset him now, would it?'

Nigel said, 'It was you asked for this meeting.'

'I didn't ask to be trampled on,' Mehmet told him. He pointed the cigarette at Nigel. 'And unless I see Sebastian, this meeting is now concluded.'

Beside me Allen made a sound; this wasn't going the way he'd expected. Nigel sat there like a dummy for a moment then he got up, saying he wasn't hopeful but he'd just go and check Sebastian's office.

He got as far as the door before Allen said, 'Nigel? I think you should sit down.'

'I'll just be a second.'

Allen pointed to a chair. 'I said, sit down.'

Nigel came back to the table and sat down.

Allen rested his forearms on the table. He studied his hands then looked up at Barin Mehmet.

'Sebastian won't be coming.'

'Is that so?'

'He's been kidnapped.'

Mehmet stared at Allen. Finally he said, 'The joke's in bad taste.'

Allen turned his head from side to side.

Their eyes stayed locked a moment before Mehmet picked up his lighter and lit the cigarette. He blew a stream of smoke towards Nigel.

'How interesting,' he said.

Nigel started explaining why he hadn't been able to say anything, but Mehmet stopped him with a glance.

'Mr Chambers?'

'Yes?'

'I think,' Mehmet remarked thoughtfully, 'that it's time for you to piss off.'

Nigel stiffened in his chair.

'In fact,' Mehmet went on, turning to me, 'it might be helpful if Mr Mortlake and I had a few minutes to ourselves.'

Allen nodded to me so I got up and headed for the

door. I didn't need a second invitation, the atmosphere in there had turned to pure poison. Nigel snatched up his papers and followed me out.

'Wanker,' he said to the door when it closed behind us.

Alone with him for a moment, I asked Nigel if he happened to know anything about Ottoman that hadn't been properly gone over in court. He shook his head, his mind still back there with Mehmet. Figuring I'd done my duty to Lee Chan, I asked him if there was any chance of a coffee. He pointed to a machine down by the filing cases then he stalked off, furious, and I wandered down to the machine, not sure if I should be strolling unaccompanied around a broker's office like that. It didn't matter anyway because I didn't get very far. Passing Max's office, I put my head in at the open door.

'Watcha.'

Max looked up from his desk. 'What are you after?' He looked past me, eyes narrowing. 'Who you with?'

Gesturing vaguely behind me, I said I was in for a meeting with Nigel. 'Can I come in?'

He beckoned me in then came over and closed the door.

'You didn't bring Tyler?' He looked through the big window into the main office.

No, I told him.

'Guy's an animal.' Relaxing a little, he returned to his desk. 'My father's being held by a bunch of nuts, and you've got an animal on the case.'

'He knows his job.'

'Yeah? Then how come he had you doing the GI Joe bit down at Brentwell?' He searched through some papers. 'I tell you, it looked pretty Mickey Mouse to me. I mean, that van, for fuck's sake. Can't he afford a new one?'

'We didn't expect to see you there.'

'I bet you didn't.'

'Max. Bill thought you'd want to stay here. He told you to stay here.' I nodded to the PC. 'They could have tried to contact you again.'

Max shrugged that off, saying he'd left his secretary to keep watch. 'Look, what's the odds? I'm here or I'm there, and that's where I thought Dad was.' He stopped searching his papers and looked up at me. 'For Christ's sake, Ian, it's my old man they've got. My old man. What am I meant to do, sit on my arse?'

There wasn't anything I could say to that. When it came right down to it, Max had more at stake here than anyone. He was an only child; his mother had shot through to the States and remarried donkey's years ago, so Sebastian was all Max really had by way of a family. It was like me and Katy, just the two of them, and when I thought about it like that I could really understand what Max was feeling. Assuming, of course that Bill Tyler's theory was wrong.

'Tell me,' Max said. 'Honestly. Do you think Tyler's up to it?'

'He'll get Sebastian back.'

Max studied me like he was willing himself to believe it. I said, 'Have you had any other ideas?'

'Not one.' He threw up a hand. 'You insure him against kidnap, he gets kidnapped. What's that say?'

He shook his head and suddenly there was a commotion in the main office. We both turned to the inner window. Nigel Chambers was standing toe-to-toe with another broker, and shouting, his face twisted with rage. The other bloke was bigger; he wasn't moving an inch; I had a feeling he was getting set to pummel Nigel through the floor. Max must have thought the same thing; he stuck his hand out the door.

'Hey! Nigel!'

Nigel raved on till Max shouted a second time. The office went quiet, everyone looking over.

'I don't care what the problem is,' Max said, 'but shut it.'

Nigel made a crack that I missed. Max pointed this time.

'Shut it, Nigel. Or you're out on your friggin' ear.'

Now those few brokers I could see through the window were either looking at Nigel or keeping their heads down. Finally Nigel dropped his head and turned on his heel. Max came back in, closing the door.

'What was that all about?'

'At a guess?' Max slumped into his chair, 'Our staff equity scheme.'

I raised a brow and he explained. Nigel, among others, had loaded up with WardSure shares that were meant to be held in escrow. The shareprice had been soft lately, but since the fire, and the rumours about Sebastian, it had moved sharply south. And now it turned out there'd been a grey market in the office too; the WardSure brokers had been trading their escrow allocations. In this grey market, Nigel had been caught long. Long and wrong. But given my own problems, my heart didn't exactly bleed for him.

'But listen,' Max said. 'This Tyler, if he's not up to it I can get someone else. We can ship some real people in.'

'Real people?'

'Whatever it takes.'

I held up my hands. 'Max. What Bill told you down at Brentwell, he wasn't kidding. You try to involve anyone else, Sebastian's K and R policy's void. You don't just get rid of Bill, you get rid of us too.'

He peered at me. 'Right,' he said tapping his forehead. Never the sharpest knife in the box, Max wasn't improving under pressure. 'Right.'

'Can I make a suggestion?'

He nodded.

'Let Bill Tyler get on with his job. Do what he tells you, and no more peeking over his shoulder.'

Max screwed up his face. I could see he was about to object, but then the phone rang and he grabbed it.

'Hello,' he said, voice strained. 'Max Ward.'

After a second his face relaxed, he leant back in his chair. Whoever it was, it wasn't the kidnappers so I opened the door and backed out. He gave me a wave and a look of despair. Prat though he might be, right then I felt more than a little bit sorry for Max.

On the way down in the lift I asked Allen how things had gone with Mehmet. 'We still in court?' I said.

He had his arms folded and his mouth shut and he stayed like that all the way down. As we went across the foyer I asked him again.

He kept walking. 'Do you see me smiling, Ian?'

I turned my head warily. He most definitely wasn't smiling. Their quiet chat together hadn't gone too well at all.

We were halfway back to the Lloyd's Building before Allen lifted his gaze from the pavement. 'Mehmet says he asked Sebastian for a meeting with us three weeks ago.'

I did a double-take. 'Crap.'

'I don't think so.'

We crossed the road, dodging traffic.

'Sebastian never mentioned it,' I said as we went up into Leadenhall. 'Not to me.'

But Allen was staring a yard in front of his feet again, lost in thought. If Mehmet was telling the truth, instead of bringing us together to get a resolution, as a broker was meant to, Sebastian had been holding us and Ottoman apart.

I did some thinking of my own. 'Why would he lie?'

'Mehmet?'

'Sebastian. It was no skin off his nose if we reached a settlement with Ottoman. Why not just tell us Mehmet wanted a meeting?' I hadn't much cared for Mehmet, and now I cared for him even less. Once or twice I'd heard envious blokes getting sarcastic about Sebastian's success, and I felt then like I felt now, a bit hot under the collar. After all Sebastian had done for me I couldn't believe how casually these guys could throw the mud, but then they didn't know him like I did. Like for instance, not long after I turned seventeen, when I wanted to buy my first car, an old banger, and I was a hundred quid short. I didn't even tell Sebastian, he just overheard me asking some of the blokes down the Gallon for work. I think it was Tubs who told him what I really wanted, and next thing I know Sebastian's slipped me a ton. Call it a loan, he told me when I tried to give it back. I paid it off ten quid a time over six months; he wouldn't take any interest. It turned out the car was a lemon, but when you're seventeen and broke that kind of open-handed help means a lot. After that I used to give Sebastian odd bits of goss I'd picked up from the kennels about which dogs were trying, and when. Dad would have flipped if he'd known, so I didn't tell him. But that loan, I thought that was Sebastian through and through. Open-handed and generous. And now this prick Mehmet was trying to smear him. 'Mehmet's taking the piss,' I said as we veered around some tourists pointing their cameras at the arches overhead. 'Has to be.'

Allen considered that as we passed out from the cover of Leadenhall. The giant silver tubing of the Lloyd's Tower came into view.

I said, 'Did Mehmet mention a number?'

'Yes, he did.'

'Not acceptable?'

'Seven million.'

Quietly I whistled through my teeth. Seven million. Mehmet was still holding out for the full claim. Unless someone had a very sudden change of heart, we were heading straight back to court. I mentioned that Clive Wainwright, our solicitor, was taking me and Justine over to see our barrister the next day.

Allen said distractedly, 'Can't Frazer handle that?'

I stopped dead in my tracks. Allen went on a few steps then he stopped and looked round.

'Frazer?' I said.

Glancing left and right, Allen came back and took me by the elbow. He led me down the stairs to the coffee shop under the Lloyd's Building; the place was closed for renovation. Standing outside the sealed door, we were alone.

'Ian, your priority is Sebastian bloody Ward. If Ottoman's going to distract you—'

'It won't.'

'I think it is.'

'What does Frazer know about Ottoman?' I said, warning bells ringing in my head. I had to think on my feet. 'And I've got to do the witness bit in court anyway, Frazer can't do that. Allen, it'd be crazy to let Frazer take over now.'

'Oh?' He gave me a look. He knew damn well about Frazer and me.

'And if the court case runs on?' I opened my hands. 'Look, you've already pulled me off the box. Tyler doesn't want me hanging around him twenty-four hours a day. So I'll chase up this Name, the pig-sticker, then what? Allen, I've got the time. I can do it.'

I heard a faint note of desperation creeping into my voice. This idea of taking the Ottoman case away from me, I knew it must have been Frazer who put it into Allen's head. Office politics, the new Cold War. Frazer sensed that he was back in the running for Angela's job and he was turning on the screws.

'And the LCO,' I said, 'they already said they want me there tomorrow. Drop Frazer on them, they won't be pleased.'

I doubt that it's carved in stone, Ian.' Allen shoved his hands in his pockets and walked away from me a few paces. He wasn't a fool, he knew Frazer and I were both trying to stamp on each other's fingers, but he also must have known that what I said made sense. The Room was busy, he couldn't afford two senior underwriters off the job. He turned. 'Okay,' he decided. 'Stay with Ottoman, but Sebastian's still the priority.'

His pager bleeped, he took it out and pulled a face. Reading the message, he backed away to the stairs.

When I said his name he paused, one foot on the first step, and half-faced me.

'Thanks,' I said.

'For what?'

'Trusting me.'

He took a moment with that while he buttoned his jacket. Then he said, 'I haven't forgotten who wanted us involved in the K and R market.' He gave me a look that sent my heart into my boots, then turned and started up the stairs.

'Don't thank me yet, Ian,' he said.

12

There was a halo of light over the track, and lots of people walking that way. The car was warm and dry; I wasn't looking forward to getting out.

'Down here,' Katy said. 'At the end.'

I slowed, edging the car down into the lane. The Stow car park was full, and when we'd tried to park in the old place, the spot where the old man and me always used to leave the car, they'd built a supermarket on it. Now Katy was giving me directions to some other spot she knew.

'Are you sure?' I asked her, peering into the dark beyond the headlights.

She nodded. She said she was pretty sure, at least it was still a good spot a year ago.

I looked at her. 'A year ago you were down at college.'

'Yeah.' She pointed up ahead. There was a badly battered sheet of corrugated iron that said 'Keep Out', and just to one side of it enough space for a car. There was a great lump of wood like a railway sleeper right across that space. Katy smiled at me as if to say 'See?'

I stopped the car and we got out to move the sleeper. It felt strange to have Katy helping me.

I said, 'What was on six months ago, some big race?'

She grunted, heaving her end of the sleeper; it hit the ground with a thud. She swiped her hands together then rubbed them over her jeans.

'I used to come back up all the time,' she said.

'What, to the Stow?'

'Everywhere. Wherever Dad went.'

'The tracks?'

She nodded and gave me a sideways look. I guess she must have thought I knew that, but now she saw that I didn't. She frowned.

'You know,' she said. 'Like you used to.'

Like I used to. Doing the rounds of the tracks with Dad, and after figuring out that it was taking my life nowhere, getting more and more pissed off. Not quite like I used to, I thought, tossing her the keys. Katy and the old man. While she parked the car I tried to picture the pair of them heading off to the dogs, but all I kept getting was a picture of the old man and me. Once the car was parked we went back up the lane and made our way down to the track.

I wasn't there for the outing or for old times' sake. It was Tubs I was after; I hadn't been able to get hold of him all day. I'd spent the afternoon trying to pin a name to the Name who sent the pig-sticker note, but the Lloyd's bureaucracy wasn't too cooperative and I'd got pretty much nowhere. When I got home I rang Bill; there was no news there either. He said not to come over, he had my mobile number, if anything happened on the K and R he'd call. That's when Katy breezed out of her room saying she was on her way to join Tubs at the dogs. I'd grabbed my coat and now there we were, at the Stow.

The Stow. Walthamstow Stadium. For the first twenty years of my life, the centre of the world.

When the old man and me used to come here we hardly ever went through the public entrance; it was nearly always the side gate, and always before the crowd moved in. While he set up his stand I'd go round to the kiosk and get us some soup or something, whatever they had. Everyone knew Bob Collier, and I was his son so they knew me too. Dad and me. The olden days.

Now we shuffled forward in the queue, the turnstile ticked over and I handed the bloke a tenner. He gave me two programmes plus change.

Inside, the stand was filling up fast. Katy saw some friends and went off to join them and I wandered down to the rails, trackside, where the bookies had their stands.

After my bust-up with Dad I didn't go back to the Stow for almost a year. And when I did go back it wasn't a regular thing, maybe once every couple of months – it just wasn't the same any more. Dad was down on the rails, I couldn't hang round down there, so I ended up sitting way back in the stand. Each year my connection with the dogs got weaker. Even when I went home occasionally to see Mum it was the one subject that never came up. Dog talk, as long as things were like they were between Dad and me, was taboo.

But even though my connection with the dogs got weaker, somehow it never quite broke. There were more Monday nights at the Gallon, but of a Friday night, every few months, I'd find myself back at the Stow. I'd get my programme, do a half-arsed study of the form, then have a few beers and a bet. Strange, really, how I seemed to need that. Something in the blood I guess.

Now I stood there with the other mugs, glancing from my programme up to the changing odds.

Fair Island, the four dog, was in the red everywhere; it was pretty much two-to-one the rest. But Swordplay was being offered at fours by Abes Watson, the bookie Tubs was pencilling for. I took out a twenty and stepped up.

'Twenty on Swordplay.'

When he heard my voice Tubs looked up sharply. Abes took my money and scratched me a ticket.

'What the fuck you doing here,' Tubs said quietly, pencilling my bet in the ledger.

I told him I was backing a winner.

He gave me a look. I turned the ticket through my fingers.

'Have you had any luck, Tubs?'

He didn't answer; he looked over my shoulder at the punters just behind.

'How about I come back after the race?'

'This is work-time, Ian.'

I told him I'd have to see him later anyway. 'Collect my winnings,' I said, but Tubs didn't smile.

A punter reached past me, pushed fifty quid up at Abes

and I drifted back into the crowd. I eased out of the crush and up onto the terraces.

The dogs were being led out. The steward was in his hunting kit up front, the kennel lads with the dogs just behind. Swordplay was a fawn bitch, shallow in the chest, she had loser written all over her.

In my pocket I fingered the betting slip. So familiar. Dad used a pile of betting slips just like this one to teach me how to count. I wasn't even at school then; I couldn't have been five years old. He'd spread them out on the floor in the kitchen while he sat up at the table studying the form. I had to make them into stacks, one beside each table leg, then he'd call out instructions getting me to move the tickets from one stack to another and adding them up. Later on, when I got the hang of it, I wasn't allowed to count them; I had to keep track of it all in my head. If he'd been a carpenter it would have been a toy hammer, but he wasn't, he was a bookie, so I got the betting slips instead. He didn't force me to do it, he made it a game. I spent hours under that bloody kitchen table. Hell, thirty years back. A long time.

'What 'ave you got in this one?'

I turned, it was Nev Logan who'd come up beside me. He wasn't looking nearly so bad as he had at the Gallon. Swordplay, I told him.

He checked the form then pulled a long face.

'Just twenty,' I said.

He smiled. 'Just as well.'

There was an announcement – the race was delayed for five minutes – and Nev led me away to the bar.

I had a beer and Nev had a lemonade; we sat watching the dogs up on the big screen. I wondered where Katy was, if she was okay, but when I mentioned it to Nev he waved it off.

'She's got plenty of mates here. Let her be.' He sipped his lemonade and studied the screen over the brim of his glass. 'What's the problem with Ward?'

I looked at him. He kept his eyes on the screen.

'Tubs,' he said. 'He's been asking around.'

'Has he?'

He smiled at that. 'Ian, you show up at the Gallon the first time in Christ knows how many years, next thing Tubs is askin' about Sebastian Ward?' He put down his glass. 'I've got cancer, Ian, but it hasn't made me brain dead.'

His look went right through me; I wasn't sure what to say.

'You don't wanna tell me,' he said turning back to the screen, 'no big deal.'

The dogs were being taken up to the traps, the announcer's voice came over the speakers in the bar. Nev meant it; it hadn't put his nose out of joint not being in on things, he'd just been curious, that was all.

Changing the subject, I asked him how his betting shops were doing.

He said, 'Tubs never told you?' When I shook my head, he shrugged. 'They're on the block.'

'For sale?'

'No pockets in a shroud.' He explained that he wanted to cash in while he still had some chance of spending it. So far the only one to show any interest in the three leases was an American hamburger chain.

I mumbled something stupid about him still having plenty of time.

'Right,' he said. 'The other one plays "Jingle Bells".'

He reached over and clinked his glass against mine. What the hell, I thought.

I said, 'Sebastian's house burnt down.'

'I heard.'

'Eddie Pike died in the fire.'

'I heard that too.' He coughed, it racked his whole body. 'Can't say as I cried me eyes out, the man was a bloody weasel. Always was.'

Surprised, I asked how well he'd known Eddie.

'Well enough,' he said in a wry kind of way. I raised a brow and he leant forward. 'Just about the biggest hit I ever took,' he said, 'was down to Eddie bloody Pike.' It was in the Cesarewich, one of the classics; there'd been big money on the favourite but Nev hadn't taken much on it, he thought the favourite was a certainty. Then ten minutes before start time another big wave of money came into the ring, this lot on the second favourite. Nev took a set against her, and by the time he realized he'd overdone it, the odds had plunged everywhere; he couldn't lay off without taking a bath. 'So I held on.'

'A mistake?'

He laughed. It turned into a cough, he covered his mouth. 'Lost me soddin' shirt,' he said. Above his hand his eyes glistened; you could see Nev Logan wasn't long for this world.

He said, 'A week later, I drop in at the favourite's kennels. Took a bottle with me, you know. Me and the trainer, drown our sorrows.' He turned up a hand. 'Guess who's just resigned from the place?'

'Eddie Pike?'

'Our friend Eddie.' Nev paused, his look becoming less cheerful. 'Eddie, the nobbler.'

'They tested the bitch?'

'Clear on the night, but she died two weeks later.' Nev watched me as I took that in. He had another shot from his lemonade. 'Like I said. A weasel.'

Up on the big screen the kennel lads were stuffing the dogs into the traps. Around the bar, heads were turning. Swordplay, I noticed, was making trouble.

I said, 'How long was Pike working for Sebastian?'

'Eddie Pike never worked a day in his life for anyone 'cept Eddie Pike.'

The bar went quiet; the announcer's voice rose then paused. Like everyone else, we looked up at the screen.

The hare shot out from the chute and swept down by the traps. The traps flicked open and a roar erupted from the bar.

'Swordplay,' I said. 'Get up there.'

'Three dog!' Nev shouted at the screen. 'Three dog!'

They were leaning into the first turn, Swordplay drifting wide, going out of the picture. I found myself tensing, urging her on. When they straightened she was second last.

I made a fist. 'Get up there!'

She made an effort, got past one dog, but then they hit the next turn and she drifted again. Now the whole bar was shouting at the screen. The favourite bounded through the finishing line two lengths clear – Fair Island – there was a big cheer. Swordplay came in stone last. The tension left me, I turned to Nev again.

'Unlucky run,' he murmured.

'Jingle Bells,' I said, and he laughed. Then I said, 'Eddie was working as a security guard for Sebastian.'

'Bullshit.'

'Straight up.'

'Eddie Pike?' He shook his head. 'I wouldn't a trusted the bugger to guard a tuck-shop.'

I asked if he'd seen much of Eddie lately, if Eddie was up to something that might have landed Sebastian in trouble.

'Haven't seen him for six months. Not since the summer.'

'Together with Ward?'

'Nah. Seen Pike here at the Stow.' He jerked his thumb over his shoulder. 'Sebastian came down the Gallon a while back, not long before . . .' His words trailed off, then his eyes dropped, and I filled in the blank. Not long before Mum and Dad died. 'Done okay for himself, ay,' Nev finished.

I nodded. Doing okay for himself was probably what had got Sebastian kidnapped, I thought, and his house burnt down. Maybe even got Eddie Pike killed. I was a bit surprised to hear about Sebastian being down at the Gallon back then too. It must have been around that time that Sebastian took me out to lunch, a weird occasion, a one-off that I couldn't help remembering. He'd grilled me in a roundabout way on ethics in the market, a lot of hypothetical stuff. Assume this, assume that, it took me till halfway through the main course before I figured out he was testing me, feeling me out. I was sure Allen was behind it. Checking up on me like, before I got the big promotion. But Sebastian never mentioned he'd recently been down the Gallon.

'I always said you done the right thing, Ian.' Nev looked up from his glass now, I wasn't sure I wanted to hear this. 'Gettin' out,' he said. 'Takin' that job Sebastian got ya. You done okay too, ay?'

I nodded, embarrassed.

'Yeah,' he said. 'I told your old man that. You think the bugger'd listen?'

I put up a hand. 'Nev—'

'Your old man could be the stubbornest bastard in the world.'

'Nev—' I stood – 'I have to find Katy. I'll see you around.'

He looked at me from somewhere way back in those glistening eyes.

'He was prouda you, Ian.'

I walked away quickly as Nev Logan said goodbye.

There wasn't much of a queue behind Abes Watson's stand, he'd had Fair Island in the red early. Tubs left the book with Abes and we strolled along the rails. Then we turned, rested back on the rail, and looked up at the stand.

Tubs said, 'If I'd found something I woulda called.'

'I couldn't get hold of you.'

He folded his arms, settling back, legs splayed. His gut hung over his belt. 'Night like this,' he said, 'your old man woulda cleaned up.'

But I'd already had more of that than I could take from Nev. I said, 'Tubs, I wasn't exactly honest with you about Sebastian.'

He glanced across. 'Not exactly?'

'It wasn't his house we insured.'

He turned, eyes fixed on me now. 'Well, do I get to hear the rest or you gonna run me all over the place with some other bollocks?'

I hung my head, scuffing my shoe on the tarmac.

Trying to excuse myself could only make it worse.

'Jesus, Ian, you take the fuckin' cake. You know that? The fuckin' cake.'

'Sorry.'

'Well, don't be sorry. Just cut out the bullshit.'

'Sebastian's been kidnapped.'

Tubs peered at me, the annoyed look fading. When I glanced around, there were a couple of kids picking up torn betting slips but nobody else close by.

'That's what we insured him for,' I said. 'Kidnap and ransom.'

'Straight up?'

'Straight up, Tubs. He's in real trouble.'

Tubs's mouth hung open a little, slack in his podgy face. I told him what Max had told us too, about Sebastian's dicky heart.

He squinted, then said, 'How much is the ransom?'

'Five million.'

His eyes widened. 'And you gotta pay?'

I said that was right, unless we found Sebastian first, we'd be paying. Tubs shook his head, smiling. He said something about Bonnie and Clyde.

'Say you find him, Ian. Then what?'

'There's a team. Listen, Tubs—'

'A team. What kinda team?'

'Listen.' I faced him. 'There's a team of people trying to rescue him. I was with them today. We went down to Brentwell Lower Park Barn.'

Tubs pulled a face. 'The old flappin' track?'

'The kidnappers sent us there. They didn't show up, and no sign of Sebastian.'

'Why there? Jesus, no-one's used that place for years.'

I nodded. That, I said, was the five million-pound question. Tubs turned a puzzled look up to the stand. After a few moments he seemed to figure it out.

'It has to be dog people. Shit, that place, who else is gonna know it?' His brow creased. 'Bugger me.'

The punters were gathering around the bookies again, the action on the next race getting started. The tic-tac man signalled over the heads of the punters with his white-gloved hands, and Tubs watched him, reading the odds.

I said, 'I think you should drop it.'

'What's that?'

'The questions. Asking around about Sebastian.'

He tugged gently at a jowl. 'I thought you said this was important to you.'

'It is.'

'Well.' He shrugged. He was going to go on with it.

'That rescue team, Tubs, they're armed.'

He made a sound, dismissive. Then he signalled up to Abes. The five dog was opening at evens.

'Pike's dead,' I said. 'Sebastian's been kidnapped, and after this morning's trip down to Brentwell I'm pretty sure it's tied up with the track. Tubs, what I'm saying is this is serious shit.'

'What you're saying is you don't think I'm up to it.'

'No I'm not.'

He stepped away from the rail, reached out and thumped my shoulder. 'I can take care of myself, Ian.' Then he headed back to Abes's stand; it was more of a waddle than a walk. Hitching his belt, he looked back over his shoulder. 'No problem,' he said.

13

There's no fixed procedure for the meetings a Lloyd's underwriter has with his lawyers when a claim goes into dispute. Sometimes the lawyers descend on the offices of the managing agent, and sometimes there's a gathering over at the 58 Building, the LCO. But now, midway through the Ottoman Air dispute, we all trooped along to Lincoln's Inn where our barrister had his chambers.

I met Lee Chan outside in the street; she was wandering up and down peering at lists of names beside each door.

'Lost?'

She turned, I was ready for the real cold shoulder, but what I got was a half-arsed smile. 'Bewildered,' she said.

She fell into step beside me and we continued on down the street. We hadn't gone ten yards before she asked, 'Any news on Sebastian Ward?'

I didn't say anything.

'No comment?'

'None you'd like to hear, Lee.'

'Do they know who's holding him?'

I stayed silent.

She sniffed; she wasn't too pleased with me. I guess she'd been looking forward to giving her friends back at the LCO the inside gen, but all I could think of was how quickly the story had spread. How long would it be now before the media got hold of it, and what would Bill Tyler do if they did? And Frazer. He must have been back in the Room there, rubbing his hands together, just waiting for it all to go pear-shaped. K and R. He was going to drive it like a stake through my heart.

Inside the chambers it was another world. We stepped off the street and back fifty years; the place was shabby like you wouldn't believe. The carpet in the hallway was worn threadbare in patches and when I grabbed the banister flakes of old paint came off in my hand. They made big money – millions each year in fees must have gone into those chambers – but they didn't waste much of it on decorations. Lee Chan's nose wrinkled up. We went along the corridor, glancing through the occasional open door.

Lee Chan said, 'Is this guy Batri any good?' Rajan Batri was our barrister. Lee hadn't been to any sessions in court.

I explained that Batri had done five cases for us, won three in court outright, and settled two others on better terms than we'd hoped for. 'If you can afford him,' I said, 'one of the best.'

Right then he stepped into the corridor up ahead. He stopped and pivoted, didn't even seem to break his stride as he came back and offered me his hand. I introduced him to Lee Chan, and he ushered us into his office where his phone was ringing.

'Bear with me a minute,' he said.

While he talked on the phone we unzipped our bulging leather hold-alls. It was really Justine and me he wanted to see; Lee Chan was just along as an observer, making sure the interests of the other syndicates on the policy weren't being walked over.

Then Justine arrived with our solicitor, Clive Wainwright. Batri beckoned them both in.

'Ready for your big part?' Clive whispered, pulling up a chair beside me. 'I swear by Almighty God, the truth, the whole truth—'

'Can't wait,' I told him quietly. 'Where've you been?'

A break in Paris for a few days, he told me smugly. He'd gone straight from the airport to his office, where he'd picked up Justine. Now he reached across me and shook hands with Lee.

I really wanted to speak with him. Privately. Clive did

criminal law for a few years, but when he realized it wasn't going to make him rich, he switched to commercial. At least that's what he told everyone. But in a funny sort of way he'd never really left the Old Bailey behind. Down at Lloyd's, Clive's office had become the first port of call for more than one market person with serious problems completely unrelated to the market. He had a reputation for good and discreet advice, and if things were really bad he could point you at the most appropriate criminal barrister. He seemed to enjoy this sideline more than his real job, cases like Ottoman, and I thought Allen was wrong not to tell him straight off about the K and R. But now that the news had spread, I knew he'd hear it as soon as he got back to the office. I wanted to tell him before he picked it up secondhand.

Batri hung up the phone. He asked Clive if we'd been briefed. Wainwright glanced at Justine and me.

'I think they know why they're here.'

I nodded, and Justine said, 'Some rehearsal?'

Batri smiled. 'Not quite, Miss Mortlake. Rehearsal implies a script. There won't be one of those in the court.' He picked up a pen, holding it in both hands, and rocked back in his chair. He must have been in his mid-forties. His black hair was flecked with grey and there were bags under his eyes, but that air of sleepiness he had, it was pure bullshit. I'd seen him looking like that when he went into court one morning to cross-examine some claimant who was trying to rip us off. Two hours' verbal assault later and the claimant crumbled, the case was over by lunchtime. 'No, not a rehearsal, Miss Mortlake. Shall we call it rather—' he paused – 'an exploration of possibilities?'

Beside me Wainwright was nodding. Justine had her head cocked, like she was still trying to figure Batri out.

Batri said to her, 'I understand Mr Wainwright furnished you with the transcripts of some of the evidence already given in court.'

Justine agreed, she laid a hand on her hold-all.

'Have you read them?' he asked.

'I've looked at them.'

'Yes, but have you read them?'

'Mr Wainwright's told me what's—'

'Excuse me.' Batri raised a finger from the pen. 'Let us take it, shall we, that you have not found time in your busy schedule to read them. Can I ask that you find the time tonight, perhaps?'

Justine tensed. But Batri smiled then, a sudden flash of warmth, and the pissed-off look on Justine's face slowly faded.

'You'll find it helpful, I think. And if there's anything in the evidence with which you disagree, anything you believe needs further elucidation, please tell Mr Wainwright as soon as possible.'

Wainwright broke in, 'I've mentioned to Miss Mortlake the queries raised about the case vis-à-vis her family.'

'Yes,' Batri remarked. He looked at Justine. 'Would you mind if we explored that a little?'

'How do you mean?'

'Well.' Batri made a face. 'What if I were to put it to you that this case isn't about syndicate 486 rejecting a valid claim? What if I put it to you, Miss Mortlake, that this is about a father using the full weight of his position, imperilling other people's money—' Batri gestured to Lee Chan – 'and all this just to protect the underwriting reputation of his daughter?'

Justine turned her head from side to side, smiling crookedly. She'd heard the line before.

'Could you answer that?'

She shrugged. 'What's to answer?' she said.

'It's not true?'

'Of course not.'

'And how would you prove that?'

'Mr Batri, at work I'm treated the same as everyone else.'

Batri considered that a moment, then he turned to me. 'Would you agree?'

Caught by surprise, I said I supposed so. More or less.

'Treated the same as everyone else,' he said, 'or "more or less" the same?'

I hesitated. Justine made a sound of disbelief.

Batri leant forward, uncapped his pen and jotted a note to himself. 'Well, Miss Mortlake, I take it you see our problem.'

She glared at me. 'I don't believe you,' she said. 'What do you mean, "more or less"? You're ticking me off the whole time.'

'Let's not debate it,' Batri cut in. He recapped the pen and placed it on the desk. 'Enough to say, this is a point our opponents will press. And if I may make a few general remarks about your presentation in court – both of you – please resist being drawn into argument.' He looked at Justine. 'Have you been into court before?'

'No.'

Batri turned from Justine to me and back. 'When you're cross-examined, the opposing barrister will attempt to lead you to the destination of his choice. He might try to draw you into argument. He might try to have you agree with certain statements he makes; he will certainly try to put words in your mouth. But whatever he does, do not attempt to second-guess him. Keep the broad thrust of our case in your mind, and, in the light of that, and after considering the particular question he puts to you, give your answer truthfully. Do you both follow me?'

I nodded.

Justine said, 'What if I make a mistake?'

Batri, ever so slightly, lifted a brow.

'If he gets me to say something I didn't mean,' she said. 'How do I get out of it?'

'The best advice I can give you is that you don't get yourself in that situation. Think before you answer.'

'But say if.'

'Then correct yourself immediately. Don't wait for him to use your mistake as a premise for a line of argument that will take you somewhere we none of us wish you to be.'

Wainwright murmured his agreement and Batri flashed

that smile again. But this time Justine didn't respond, she looked worried. I think it was dawning on her that once she got into the court she'd be pretty much on her own, but it wasn't just that. Somehow she didn't seem her usual cocky self; something was eating her. I think Batri sensed it too.

'One other matter they've raised in passing,' Batri told her, 'is your relative lack of underwriting experience. It's something they'll press you on.'

I said, 'What's that got to do with the claim?'

Batri opened his hands. 'Absolutely nothing.' He turned to Justine again. 'So don't be defensive. Your *curriculum vitae* will be before the judge. I take it the picture it gives is full and fair?'

She nodded.

'Then don't rise if they bait you. Our expert witness is quite satisfied you were more than experienced enough to write the Ottoman business, and he will make that plain to the judge when he's called.' Batri reached forward and flipped his notepad open. 'Clive, I understood Mr Tyler was to be here too.'

Wainwright said, 'I couldn't get hold of him.'

Not surprised, I thought.

Then Wainwright looked up from his notes, grinning. 'Justine tells me he's busy sorting out a kidnap.'

He meant the news to be amusing, but I could hardly believe my ears. When I looked at Justine she stared at the floor.

'The Ward kidnap?' Lee Chan said.

That did it. It felt like I'd taken a punch in the gut. Batri straightened. 'Ward?'

Lee Chan turned to me, suddenly uncertain. Justine did too, and out of the corner of my eye I saw Batri swivel.

'Mr Collier?'

I breathed out a long breath. It was too late to lie. 'Sebastian Ward took out a K and R policy with us. He's been kidnapped. Bill Tyler's working on it.'

'Sebastian Ward,' Batri said, 'of WardSure? The Ottoman brokers?'

'Yes.'

There was a second's silence, then Wainwright said, 'Shit.'

I glanced over to Justine. 'The whole thing's meant to be extremely confidential.'

'I'm sure,' Batri said, and the sound of the words went right through me. He was unhappy, and it wasn't just courtroom make-believe. 'Would it be too much to ask why I wasn't told?'

I mumbled some half-arsed apology, then I said, 'We didn't think it affected the Ottoman case.'

'Who is "we"?'

'The Mortlake Group.'

'Specifically?'

His dark brown eyes bored right into me. I felt pinned to my chair.

'Allen,' I said. 'And me and Angela.'

'I see,' he said softly, looking straight at me. 'How widely is this known?' he asked. 'The kidnap.'

'Too widely,' I told him, shooting a look at Lee Chan and Justine, 'for Sebastian Ward's good.'

Then I added, 'But I don't see as it affects the Ottoman case. I really don't.'

He took a moment with that then he leant forward and flicked through his notebook again. 'Neither do I yet, Mr Collier, but should anything come to mind, you'll be the first to know.' He glanced up. 'And I trust that's a courtesy that will be reciprocated.'

When I nodded his gaze lingered on me a few seconds, coldly. I got the message. He was thoroughly and completely pissed off. 'Let's move on,' he said, pursing his lips like an old woman.

He gave us some general advice then – it was news to Justine but I'd heard it all before. I'd been to court maybe half a dozen times in my career, giving evidence over contested and fraudulent claims, and each time the barrister had given me a few pointers, either like this at his chambers, or informally outside the courtroom door. It always came down to the same thing. Keep your side of

this case in mind, and don't put your foot in your mouth.
Justine sat forward now, drinking it all in.

Next Batri ran through the main points concerning me,
a checklist. I'd already been through it in detail with
Wainwright, my duties as an underwriter on the syndicate, my experience, and my supervision of Justine. That
part bothered me a little, and when Batri asked, 'Nothing
out of the ordinary in supervising the Ottoman business?'
I said, 'No,' but what I should have said was 'maybe'. But
the last thing I felt like was raking through the ashes of the
fire again, explaining how having Mum and Dad die like
that had completely fucked me up for a while. Supervision? It was all I could do just to get into work each
morning in the weeks straight after the fire.

Batri opened another file.

'Miss Mortlake, the same with you now, I won't keep
you long.'

When Batri looked up, I raised a finger. 'I've got an
appointment.'

He nodded to the door, dismissing me.

'I just need a quick word with Lee,' I said.

Pissed off again, he waved a hand in the air and Lee
Chan followed me into the corridor. As we walked away
from Batri's office she started apologizing for dropping
me in it, tying Ward's name up with the kidnap.

'I thought everyone knew,' she said.

'Matter of time,' I muttered.

'Well, I'm sorry.'

'Forget it. Listen,' I said, 'can I ask you a favour?'

She nodded warily. After dropping me in it with Batri I
guess she thought she owed me one.

'I met the bloke who runs Ottoman. Barin Mehmet.
He's a villain.'

Lee frowned and closed her eyes. 'Oh, give me a break.'

'I'm not kidding, Lee. We've had Tyler checking Ottoman's security systems, turning the hangars inside out.
What's he found?'

'According to his report? Their security wasn't up to
standard.' She stopped and looked up at me. 'You don't

need a villain, Ian, this is a slam-dunk. Ottoman didn't measure up to the security specs, that's it, game over. We don't pay.'

'That's if the judge accepts Tyler's report.'

She smiled. She said, 'What's the favour?'

At the far end of the corridor a barrister stepped from his office, a black gown under his arm. He strode away from us, head down.

I said, 'Find out what other companies Mehmet's been involved with, say, the past ten years.'

Lee snorted.

'It's one trip to Companies House, Lee. When you've got that, do a search back at the LCO. See what kind of claims they've made.'

She shook her head. 'Ian, Ottoman's plane got stolen. Everyone agreed from the start we'd hammer their security. That's their weak point. That's where they breached the policy. Now what? You want to turn this into some fancy fraud thing?'

'It's a feeling. I don't know.'

'Well, I do. You start down that path now, Ian, the judge is gonna have a bird.'

A door opened just behind us, two lawyers sharing a joke inside. We turned and ambled back towards Batri's office.

She thought for a bit. 'Do you know something else about Mehmet you're not telling me?'

'No.'

She asked me how often I'd seen him. I told her.

'Once?' She looked at me like I was simple. 'You met the guy once and already he's a villain?'

I touched her arm and we stopped again. I faced her.

'Lee, if you don't want to do it, just say.'

We looked at each other. Her eyes were dark, and deep, and for a moment I felt myself slipping. She bit her lip. Maybe she'd just thought of the same thing as me, her fiancé over there in San Fran.

She said, 'All right, but it's not my number one priority, okay?'

111

I smiled and squeezed her arm. Then Wainwright stepped into the corridor and called, 'Ian?' I was wanted on the phone.

It was Allen, he just had a brief message; he gave it to me and rang off. I stood there for a few seconds, phone to my ear, listening to the dial tone. Then I reached over and hung up the handpiece.

Wainwright and Batri pretended to study their files, but Justine and Lee Chan both watched me.

I said, 'I have to go.'

Batri glanced up. 'No trouble? Allen sounded rather concerned.'

'No.' I reckon he saw straight through me but I forced a smile onto my face. 'Just the usual cock-up.'

Wainwright reminded me of when I was expected in court. Nodding to Batri, I said my goodbyes and retreated out the door. My heart was thumping like I'd just dropped a bundle on Derby night.

Outside I hailed a taxi, gave the driver an address just along from Tyler's safe-house in Islington. I sat there, a hand resting on the seat to either side of me, and tried to stay calm. It was a mistake, I told myself, some misunderstanding. Max had spoken to Tyler, Tyler to Allen and Allen to me, and somewhere along the way the lines had been crossed. I could accept that the kidnappers had finally demanded the money – sure, I'd been prepared for that. I'd hoped Bill might find them first, do the right thing by my career and rescue Sebastian unharmed, but I could accept that that hadn't happened.

But what I couldn't accept, the thing I refused to swallow, was that the cretins who'd kidnapped Sebastian and murdered Eddie Pike had decided they needed someone to act as a courier. They wanted someone to take them the T-bonds. Sitting silent in the back of the taxi, my hands going cold on the seat, I refused to believe it. How had it happened? Stay calm, I told myself. Probably a mistake, I told myself.

And all the while I kept thinking, Why me?

14

Bill took me across to the basement stairs.

'Another e-mail,' he said. 'Untraceable, but we got a printout this time.'

He pulled the faxed copy from his pocket. I read it as I followed him down the stairs.

The kidnappers were demanding five million pounds' worth of US Treasury bonds, five slips of paper, each with a face value of one million pounds. They wanted Ian Collier to act as courier. The details for delivery, the fax said, would follow.

Bill put his hand over his shoulder and I gave him back the fax, all my pathetically hopeful thoughts about a mistake completely blown out of the water.

I said, 'I don't get it, why pick me?'

He stopped at the bottom of the stairs, and I stepped down beside him. The van driver was standing by the table, and the other four blokes were sitting there, playing cards. They stopped their game and looked up.

'Couldn't keep you away, ay?' the driver said.

The others smiled but I didn't say anything. I glanced around the bare walls, at the five bunk beds, and up to the single fluorescent tube overhead. There was a door too, leading out to the back. Comfortable it wasn't.

Bill led me across to the table, pointing the men out one by one. Instead of their names he told me their codes, all animals. The driver was Horse. 'If you happen to hear a name,' Bill told me, 'we'd like you to forget it. Fair enough?' Bill pointed at my chest. 'And for the purposes of saving Mr Ward's fat arse, you're Dog.'

I dropped my head to one side. 'Can we talk?' I said.

When I went back to the bottom of the stairs, he joined me. Behind us the men picked up their card game.

'You've forgotten something,' I said quietly.

Bill frowned, brow creased. After a bit he said, 'I don't see it.'

'Bill, you're looking straight at it.'

I glanced past him at the men. They were playing loud, politely ignoring us.

'See this?' I touched my tie and tugged at the lapels of my jacket. 'This is me, Bill, a suit. I write insurance for a living; I'm an underwriter for Christ's sake!'

He made a gesture with his hands, Keep it down.

'What the hell am I meant to do, throw a bagful of money over some fence, then run?'

'We'll give you a few tips,' he said.

'Oh, great.' Hands on hips, I considered him. 'A few tips.' I looked at the lads at the table. Six professional hard men, plus me. 'That'll help a lot,' I said.

Bill leant towards me, finger raised. 'Listen, I didn't pick you. Nobody here picked you. If it was our choice we'd have kept you right out of it, but that's not the way this thing's gone, all right? Now, if you've got a problem with that, Ian, go find some other post to piss on, because us meatheads down here, we're busy.'

He turned away from me angrily and without thinking I reached out and grabbed his arm. He looked from my hand up to my face.

What did I mean to say to him then? Sorry? Goodbye? And if I had, would he have just let me disappear up the stairs and out the door? I don't know, even now I'm not sure.

But what I said was, 'Bill, I don't want to do this.'

He didn't say anything, just waited.

'I can't understand where they got my name.'

'Brentwell,' he said.

I squinted like, I don't get it. Please explain.

'When we dropped you out of the van,' he told me,

114

'remember I said maybe they were checking us out? I reckon they seen you.'

'I wasn't wearing a name tag.'

Bill nodded and waited for me to figure it out for myself. When I did, something tingled up my spine.

'The kidnappers know me?'

'Bingo,' he said.

The noise from the card game seemed distant all of a sudden, the light hurt my eyes. I thought about back when I was hiding behind the bushes, watching Max's Porsche come up the lane. While I'd been watching him, Sebastian's kidnappers had been watching me, maybe deciding right then that they'd rather deal with me than with the professionals in the van. And they knew me. Dropping my eyes, I touched my fingers to my forehead.

'Which means,' Bill said, 'that maybe you know them.'

I froze, staring down at my shoes. It wasn't so much the words, more the tone. After a moment I said, 'Is that some kind of a suggestion, Bill?'

'Just a remark.'

I lifted my eyes. 'If you want me to play courier for you, keep the remarks to yourself.'

He stepped back and raised both hands, making a joke of it, but it was still there in his eyes, what he'd been thinking. He wasn't sure any more if I was just the innocent bystander in all this that I seemed.

When I told him I wanted to speak to Allen, he led me back upstairs. He left me with the surveillance man and I called Allen at the office.

'Where are you?'

'With Bill,' I said. 'At the safe-house.'

He asked if Bill had given me the T-bonds.

'Just a sec, Allen.' I wasn't quite sure how to say this, he sounded so bloody gung-ho. 'We can't afford to have this go wrong, can we. It's Sebastian's life, I mean look what they did to Pike.'

'What?'

'Allen.' I faced the wall. 'I'm not sure I can do this.'

There was a long silence.

'Allen?'

'I heard you.'

'I really don't—'

'Now you hear me,' he said evenly. 'You either do what Tyler tells you to do, or you can forget about stepping into Angela's shoes down on the box. Is that clear?'

I was too stunned to answer.

'You got us into the K and R business. And if you've got any sense of loyalty to the Group, you'll do whatever you can to get us out of it. Right now that means helping Tyler.' After a pause, he added, 'Now I think we both know what's at stake here, don't we?'

I knew bloody well what was at stake. My hundred grand deposit on the penthouse, and the past thirteen years of my life. Everything I'd worked for since my bust-up with my old man.

'Allen, these guys here, they've got guns. I'm just an underwriter.'

'Your call,' he said. 'If you don't want to do it, Ian, that's your call.'

Before I could reply he hung up. Swearing quietly I put down the phone.

'Bad news?'

I turned to find Bill watching me. I looked at the surveillance man and the surveillance gear and Bill. I was so far out of my depth it just didn't matter.

I said, 'I think this is a mistake.'

Nodding, Bill said, 'Maybe.' As he walked out the door he said that whatever it was, it was time we went down and got things sorted with lads.

Horse had a tattoo around his wrist, I saw it when he handed me his spare jumper. The tat was red and blue, a snake swallowing its own tail, when he saw that I'd seen it he smiled.

'Big night in Hong Kong,' he told me.

I took off my jacket and tie. He said to take off my shoes as well, and when I'd done that gave me a pair of black gym shoes. I sat on a bunk, pulling the shoes on, lacing them up, while Bill and the others discussed me like I was their number one problem. Each of them seemed to have a different idea about what I needed to know: it wasn't exactly reassuring. The word 'hardware' came up a lot, and they weren't talking about computers.

When I started pulling on the jumper, Horse said, 'Hang on.' He went to the bag by the guns, dug around there a while, then brought back a navy-blue vest. At least that's what I thought it was. He handed it to me and it was thick and stiff and heavy.

'Slip this on first,' he said. He lifted his own jumper to show me he was wearing one just like it, then he helped me on with mine. 'It'll stop a knife. Bill reckons a bullet too, long range.'

A knife, I thought, appalled. A bullet.

He finished tying me into the thing then he went to join in the discussion with his mates. I sat alone on the bunk wiggling my toes in the gym shoes, trying not to listen.

Take a punt, that's what the old man used to tell me. I'd be up there on our stand calculating odds, whispering to Tubs, getting the book in order, and then I'd feel the old man at my elbow. Take a set against the four dog, he'd say. Bag the four dog. And I mightn't want to, but it was his book, so I'd do that. And if the four dog got bumped and finished out of the money, he'd clap me on the shoulder and tell me that that's how bookmaking was done. But if the four dog won there'd be a payout queue behind our stand that was something to see and my old man would just shrug it off. Take a punt. Big bold Bob Collier.

All things considered, it wasn't the best time to start proving that I was Bob Collier's son.

'Can you use a pistol?'

I looked over, they were all facing me, waiting.

A pistol, I thought. A bullet.

'No,' I told Bill, my voice strangely husky.

When I coughed into my hand they huddled again, I

guess figuring out if there was anything at all they could do to help me. They must have thought I was a useless bugger but they hid it pretty well. I stared at the floor. I thought of Sebastian and my old man.

By the time I was twenty-one I knew that Dad was going nowhere. After a winning night he'd take whatever the book had won, bung a few score to Tubs, give some to Mum and me, and blow the rest. After a losing night he'd close his bag, go home and wait for the next meeting then repeat the whole thing over again. Financially he was just treading water, but that really didn't matter to Dad; at the track he was someone, he loved the life. But it sure as hell mattered to me. I wanted so much more, and finally it was Sebastian, not Dad, who offered me my one big chance.

It was a Monday night at the Gallon, I'd just watched Sebastian pull out his little blue book and write some house insurance for Freddie Day. When Freddie left the table, I went over. I guess Sebastian knew me pretty well by then, or at least he knew I was ambitious and thwarted, kind of straining at the leash. After a few beers and some talk he made me an offer clean out of the blue. If I came up with ten grand he'd take me on in his office, show me the insurance-broking ropes, and after a few months he'd set me up in my own one-man agency. We'd split the profits fifty-fifty. It was a good deal all round, and for me probably the only chance I'd ever get to break away from the dogs. I could hardly believe it. The problem was I didn't have ten grand. And the only way I could get that kind of money was through the old man, but when I told him about Sebastian's offer he just didn't want to know. Sebastian's charm cut no ice with Dad.

'It's unanimous, Ian.'

I looked up, then across the basement. Bill gestured to the others.

'You don't get a gun,' he told me. 'If things get that serious, we'll move in.'

I nodded, not really with it, just letting things happen

now. They went back to their discussion and I went back to my thoughts. Sebastian and Dad.

Dad and me argued, we argued a lot. I was burning inside, desperate to get on with this other life I'd been offered, and finally the old man cracked. He didn't just give me the ten grand, and I hadn't really expected him to. What he did was agree not to blow his winnings: he'd try to build the float in his bag, if we got it up to fifteen grand I could have ten and do what I liked with it.

Night after night, meeting after meeting, I watched that float like a hawk. It grew by hundreds, then thousands, stalling occasionally, even falling back sometimes, but overall I think it even surprised Dad how fast it grew when he just left it alone. After five months it went through fourteen grand and I knew it was going to happen. That night we went to the Stow with a float of fourteen thousand seven hundred quid. The first two races, I set the book, we made six hundred quid and I was there. I'd get my ten grand, Sebastian would set me up in my own business, I couldn't stop smiling. When I handed the bag over to Dad I was walking on air.

And then for the next three hours I watched as big Bob Collier had the worst losing run of his life. First a few hundred, then a grand. Trying to recoup he took a set against the next favourite and suddenly he was three grand in the hole. He upped the ante. Lost again. And again. I went to the bar so's I didn't have to watch but I couldn't stay away. He started chasing his losses, trying to punt his way into the black, but it just cost him more and more money. It even crossed my mind that the losses were something more than accidental, but I didn't really believe it – I almost wished I could have. What it was was an exhibition of everything I wanted to escape. The roller-coaster ride that flung you around for a bit then dumped you right back where you'd started, the ride my old man had been on all his life. The future that was no future at all. By the end of the night the float was down to less than three grand,

and the dream Sebastian had held out to me was gone. Dad didn't even apologize. He believed a man should take his losses on the chin.

'Here, try this,' Bill said.

This time when I looked up he was bringing me some radio gear from upstairs. He showed me how to use it. The little thing that looked like a Walkman I slung from my belt.

'Say something,' he said.

When I did the radio man with the receiver shook his head, he couldn't hear it on his set. I huddled over, mouth nearer to the inbuilt mike, and tried again. This time he gave me the thumbs-up.

Bill pointed to the coil of thin wire. 'Try the earpiece.'

I put it in. Immediately a voice boomed through it, I tore it out and adjusted the volume. On the second try the radio man's voice came over smooth and clear. I nodded to him, one hand to my ear.

He switched off his set. I took out the earpiece.

'This is for what?' I said. 'In case we get separated?'

Bill didn't answer at first, and when I turned to Horse he looked away. The others glanced at each other; there were a few seconds of awkward silence.

'You're the courier,' Bill said finally. 'Chances are, Ian, some of the way at least, you'll be on your own.'

Nobody looked at me. The radio man took his set out to the van, and the card game started up again at the table. I didn't move from the bunk; I sat there very quietly and stared straight ahead. This was all about Sebastian Ward. Sebastian. I had to keep reminding myself of that. Sebastian, the one man who'd really seemed to understand what I wanted from life way back when, and who hadn't just dumped me when I couldn't produce the ten grand. When I'd explained to Sebastian what had happened at the Stow, and told him that with or without money I intended to make the break from the dogs and my old man, he'd understood that too. A few days later he'd called me to say a friend of his had a job going at Lloyd's, just something junior, but an in.

He said he could arrange an interview if I liked. If? Half an hour later I was down Jimmy the Greek's trying on a shiny new suit. Allen Mortlake interviewed me the next day, and the next week I was chief coffee boy on the 486 box.

When I came back home from my first day's work at the office, and Dad realized this wasn't just some half-cocked thing, that I'd really made the break, he went spare. Lots of swearing and slamming doors and shouting from both of us. Twenty-one years of frustrated hopes erupting. He had plans, he said. If I'd only been patient, in a few years I could have taken over his stand. He just wouldn't face it; by then his stand at the Stow was part of everything I wanted to escape. By then I'd glimpsed a bigger world, Sebastian's, and I'd made the leap. When the rage of our argument died away I heard Mum crying in the kitchen. Dad heard her too. We stood there staring at each other, listening to Mum, knowing that something between us had died.

Finally Dad said, You'll be moving out then.

In the morning.

He nodded to himself, gave me one last look, then as he walked out the door he said, Be sure and say goodbye to your mother.

The next morning I did just that, and that's how my new life began. Since then I'd worked my balls off, sweated blood to get myself taken seriously as an underwriter, got myself within a whisker of the top job on the box, but without that start Sebastian gave me, none of it would have happened. My career, the chance at the penthouse, my whole damn life after the dogs, none of it would have happened. Sitting there in the basement of the safe-house, it came to me absolutely clearly that everything I had I owed to Sebastian.

And now he needed me. Stretching out on the bunk, I dropped my jacket over my face and closed my eyes, hoping to God that I wouldn't let Sebastian Ward down.

15

I t was pitch dark when I woke up; there was a sound of
footsteps running overhead; I didn't know where I was.
The footsteps got louder, I sat bolt upright, and someone
hit the lights.

I looked around. The basement. The K and R team.

Bill came charging down the stairs, shouting, 'We're on,
boys. Grab your gear.'

Wiping a hand over my face, still dozy with sleep, I
swung my legs out of the bunk. The others were up and
moving; Bill put his hand on my shoulder.

'Got the two-way? Got the bonds?'

I reached down to my belt and touched the set and the
earphones, then the bonds in my pocket. When I nodded
he hauled me to my feet.

'Right,' he said, 'get in the van.'

I stumbled across to the basement door; Bill unbolted it
and shoved me up the steps into the backyard. It was
night and the air was cold and damp. I was wide awake by
the time I got to the top of the stairs. Horse was right
behind me; he pushed past, opened the rear van door and
almost lifted me in. Seconds later the others came piling
in after me, and the van started up.

I said, 'What's happening? Is this it?'

Someone said, 'Nippin' out for a pizza,' and the others
laughed.

Bill climbed in telling us to shut up. He slammed the
door behind him then reached up and banged his fist
twice against the roof. The van moved off. I needed to
take a leak.

There was a dull yellow light glowing over my head, and small green and red lights pulsing on the radio gear up front. Apart from the radio man, we all sat along the two bench seats down either side. I was opposite Bill.

He looked dead serious. 'It's a paperchase, Ian. They've given us a phone box to get to down in Greenwich.'

'Why?'

He shook his head. 'They want us there, we're there. You feeling okay?'

I nodded.

'There'll be a note in the box,' he said. 'They want you to pick it up.'

'Then what?'

'Read the note to us on the two-way. I'll tell you what to do.'

'Who'll be with me?'

He looked straight at me. 'They don't want to see anyone else around the box. Just you.'

Just me. My mouth went dry.

'This could be like down in Brentwell,' I said.

'I don't think so.' Bill was speaking to everyone now. 'We're down to business here. This is it.'

Up front the radio man was talking into his mike, one of those no-hands jobs attached to his head. It sounded like he was speaking to the police, but when I asked Bill about that he just shrugged and said, 'The less you know the better.'

We bumped along for a while, no-one speaking, just the blurred chatter from the radio echoing round the van. I still felt cold. Then I thought of something else.

'What did they say about Sebastian?'

Bill lifted his head, face blank.

'I mean, if I can't do what they ask in the note,' I said, 'what happens?'

'Why shouldn't you be able to?'

'I don't know. Just say.'

'Ian—' Bill rubbed his forehead – 'it's too late to back out of this.'

I felt the others watching me now. I stayed how I was,

hunched forward, and looking at Bill.

I said, 'What happens to Sebastian then?'

'If you don't go through with this?'

'If anything goes wrong.'

He dropped his head. He fiddled with a lace on his shoe.

'Bill?'

He muttered something, but I missed it.

I said, 'Come again?' and this time his head rose slowly.

He gestured round. 'We fuck up—' then he pointed at me – 'or you fuck up, they'll kill him. This isn't the time for doubts, Ian. Anything goes wrong now, Sebastian Ward ends up dead. Are you with us?'

I stared straight ahead. I smelt smoke.

'Ian,' he said. 'Are you with us?'

Like a man in a dream I felt myself nodding. 'Sure,' I mumbled. They were all watching me. 'I can do it,' I said.

They dropped me fifty yards from the phone box. It was a quiet street, the deli on the corner was closed and the only light was coming from the phone box and the streetlamp just past it. Horse gave me a smile of encouragement as I went around the van and up onto the pavement. Almost immediately I heard Bill's voice in my ear.

'How'm I coming over, loud and clear?'

'Fine.' I bent my head, speaking into the mike. I'd hooked the Walkman thing inside my jumper. 'You're coming over fine. Can you see anything?'

'Just keep walking. Take it steady.'

I did like he'd told me in the van, no faster or slower than normal. I wasn't in danger, that's what he'd said. But the closer I got to the phone box the harder it was to believe that. I glanced over my shoulder. At the far end of the street a car turned in.

'Do you see that?'

'We've got it covered,' Bill said. 'Don't go into the box till it's past.'

I slowed, I wasn't twenty yards from the phone box. The car came on down the street; its headlights washed over me. As it went by I saw children in the back seat, I told Bill that. Then I stopped and turned to watch as the car passed the van.

'Don't stop,' Bill barked at me. 'Get on to the box.'

I started walking again.

It was one of those new boxes, blue; I stopped outside it with my hand on the door. No turning back now, I stepped in.

Bill said, 'Right, what can you see?'

I glanced left and right through the glass, I'd never felt that exposed before.

'Speak to me, Dog.'

'Is that car gone?'

'Forget the bloody car. Find the message. Look around you, what's there?'

I turned to the phone.

'Flyers,' I said.

'What?'

'There's a whole pack of flyers stuck up. You know, call girls. Advertising.' I looked around but that seemed to be it, just the flyers. I ran my eyes over them. 'No, nothing. Do I come back to the van?' Then my eyes stopped, my stomach turned over. 'Hang on.'

I looked at it a while, not a flyer but a white envelope slotted into the rest so that it looked like a flyer. There was no picture of a naked lady in fishnet stockings, or even a phone number. Just two words. Ian Collier.

'What?' Bill said. 'Have you got it?'

I reached out and plucked the envelope free. A flyer fluttered down.

'I've got it.'

'What's it say?'

I turned the envelope over. Blank. Then I tore the thing open. There was a single page inside, a hand-drawn map photocopied onto the top half, and a route mapped out in red ink. Underneath there were instructions, I started to read them to myself.

Bill yelled, 'Speak to me!' His voice rasped in my ear.

'It's a map,' I said. 'Instructions too. Listen. Follow the

route on the map. You are at the point marked R. Ward is at the point marked W. Proceed alone to the point marked W where the handover will be made. You have twelve minutes to reach W. If you fail to reach W within twelve minutes, or if anyone follows you from the phone box, Ward will be shot.'

My spine tingled. I read the last bit again. Shot.

'That's it?'

'Yeah,' I said, then the phone rang. I looked up at it.

'Answer it,' Bill said; he must have heard it through my mike.

I reached out and picked up the receiver. Nothing. Then a man's voice. 'The twelve minutes start now. And don't bring the geezers in the van.' Then a click.

I hung up and told Bill word-for-word what the voice on the phone said. There was a silence; it seemed to go on forever.

Finally Bill said, 'Get out of the box, Dog. Follow the map. You aren't on your own. Joey and Tim are out there with you. Get out of the box.'

Joey and Tim, real names, that reassured me somehow; maybe Bill meant it to. Glancing at my watch I pushed the glass door open. Nine forty.

'Now move!' Bill said.

Walking quickly from the box and the van, I held the map up, taking my bearings. The van didn't start up like I expected it to.

'They're bluffing,' I said.

'Concentrate on where you're going, Ian. Read the map out to us. Where are you headed?'

'I go left here,' I said crossing the road. Now the van started up behind me, when I looked back I saw it swing around and drive away. I slowed.

'Keep bloody moving,' Bill barked at me. 'Just tell us where you're headed, where's W?'

The van disappeared, I strained to hear its engine but the sound was lost in the traffic noise from up the main road. I was alone. I checked the map again, walking faster now, almost jogging.

'There's no street names,' I told Bill, reading the map. 'I keep heading this way then I do a sharp right and left and then I cross over.'

'Cross over what?'

I studied the map. The red line stopped at the edge of what looked like a main road. It became a broken line, crossed over, then joined up again for a short way on the other side. The W was right where it ended.

'I don't know, some kind of highway?' I said. 'They won't really shoot him, will they?'

There was a pause, then Bill said, 'That isn't a highway, Ian. It's the Thames.'

I lifted my head and peered into the darkness. Ahead there were lights, a boat passing on the river. The trip in the van had really thrown me.

I bent over the mike. 'W's on the other side, just over the bridge.'

'Yeah?' Bill said, 'And what bridge would that be?'

Confused, I looked down at my watch. Nine forty-four. I hurried on, then it dawned on me as I neared the river. We were in Greenwich. There is no bridge over the Thames at Greenwich. I looked up from the map to the river and back to the map again.

My heart was in my throat; I thought I'd blown it. I said, 'The map's wrong.'

Bill said, 'It's the tunnel. They want you to go through the tunnel.' His voice was even, as if he was working hard not to explode.

And then I saw it just ahead of me, the sign and the entranceway to the Greenwich pedestrian tunnel. I kept moving, on automatic pilot now. Once I went down into the tunnel no-one could follow me without being seen, and when I came up on the north side I'd be completely on my own, a sitting duck.

I reached the entrance, stopped and turned. No Joey, no Tim, and no bloody van.

Trying to sound calm, I said, 'Do I go in?'

No answer.

'Bill, are you there? For fuck's sake.'

I heard the van then, revving hard as it swung round a bend up the road. As it raced towards me I looked at my watch. Nine forty-five. Seven minutes to go.

The van pulled up, Bill shot out the door. He ran up to me with his hand out. 'Show me the map.'

I gave it to him.

'Shit,' he said, studying it. 'Shit.'

'Do I go down there?'

He didn't seem to hear me. He pushed the map back into my hands. 'Once you're in the tunnel, we'll lose radio contact. We can't follow you down there or they'll kill Ward.'

'They can see you with me now.'

He shook me. 'The tunnel's the filter. We'll get a chopper up quick as we can. Remember—' his grip tightened – 'don't hand over the bonds till you've got Ward close as this. But don't piss about. Once they've got the bonds they'll scarper. You sit tight with Ward.' He glanced at his watch. 'Soon as you get out of the tunnel the other side, talk to us. Okay?'

'Talk to you,' I said, nodding.

I saw two men jogging towards us along the embankment. Joey and Tim, the cavalry, but they couldn't help me now. Bill released my arm, giving me a shove towards the tunnel entrance.

'Run,' he said.

The stairs spiralled; I went down them starting to sweat now. Immediately the quiet hiss from the earpiece cut out. My gym shoes slapped quietly on each step; that was the only sound apart from my breathing. There was a smell of dampness and a touch of cold air on my face.

Down the last steps and the tunnel opened out in front of me. A dimly lit tube it looked like, with no side passages and no places to hide. The floor was damp, and the stretches of wall. I set off, jogging now, checking my watch. Five minutes left. The bullet-proof vest was getting heavier, and I found it harder to breathe. All that water pressing down, I imagined the walls cracking and water flooding in.

But Sebastian was out there somewhere, waiting for me. Waiting and praying.

I kept jogging till I ran out of puff, then I slowed and looked back. More than halfway along. I walked again, tried to jog. Security cameras pointing down at me, but was anyone watching? The walls seemed to hum, maybe a barge up on the river. I ran again. At nine forty-nine, I reached the far end of the tunnel and took one look behind me. It was empty.

'Jesus,' I said, sucking in air. 'Oh, Jesus.'

Then I turned and grabbed the handrail and started up the stairs.

I came out into the night looking skyward; there was no sign of a chopper. Then I looked all around me, and down at the map.

'I'm out,' I said.

No reply. Maybe Bill was busy calling in the chopper, or reinforcements, some police. I stood still a moment, sucking in more air. There was a wall to my left alongside the path out to the road. I checked the map. W was just further on, a bit to the left, out along the road.

'Bill,' I hissed, tapping the earpiece. 'Bill, I'm out.'

Nothing. I checked my watch. So close to twelve minutes it didn't matter. I found myself walking down the path towards the road. At the end of the wall I stopped and leant against it and spat up phlegm.

'Bill?'

Again, nothing.

It was just me. The only thing that stood between Sebastian and a bullet.

I thought, 'Don't think, just do it,' then I pushed off the wall and stepped out into the road and walked, turning, looking round.

I'd got about ten yards when a voice shouted, 'Collier!'

I spun and looked up the road. Forty yards away there was a parked car, and two men nearby. One of them had his hands behind his back, like handcuffed, and a bag tied over his head. The other wore a balaclava. When I stopped, the second one lifted his arm, pointing a shotgun at the bag.

'Nearly time up,' he called to me. 'Mr Ward was gettin' worried.'

Fixed to the spot, I stared at them. Less than an hour earlier I'd been fast asleep. A few days earlier I'd been writing business in the Room, dreaming about my penthouse, waiting for my promotion, and now I was meant to deal with all this?

'Eleven minutes, ten seconds,' he called. 'Come on!'

Sweat dribbled down my neck. I took two steps, then stopped.

'Sebastian!' I called.

'What's your bloody game?' The guy pushed the gun right up against the bag, still looking my way. 'Bring it here!'

I wanted to. I wanted to walk right up there, hand him the bonds and get Sebastian away from that gun. But something in his voice stopped me. He was scared. Maybe scared enough to shoot both of us once he had the bonds. My muscles went rigid, like I was straining against some invisible leash.

'Eleven minutes thirty!'

I swayed forward, almost started walking, but then the kidnapper pointed the gun at me. I turned right and ran to the protective cover of a wall. The sweat wasn't just dribbling now, it was pouring off me: I felt it running down the backs of my thighs.

'You little shitbag! Bring it here or I'll blow his fuckin' brains out!'

'Settle down!' I shouted back. 'I've got the bonds, for Christ's sake. I'm alone. How about you stop waving that fucking gun all over the place.' I wiped the sweat out of my eyes. The tunnel entrance wasn't far but I couldn't get over there; he'd have a clear shot at me the whole way. My head lolled back against the wall. I closed my eyes.

'Five seconds, arsehole!'

'Okay!' I shouted. 'Okay! I'm coming out.' I put my hands out past the wall first, waving the bonds, to show him I was unarmed, then I stepped slowly into the road. 'Sebastian? It's Ian Collier—'

'Shut the fuck up!' The gun pointed at me again, then up at the sky, then back at the bag. 'Bring it here!'

But by now I was sure he was scared witless, he could have done anything.

'I'll put the bonds down here,' I said, keeping my eyes on him as I crouched and placed the bonds on the ground. 'I'll back off, you come and get them.'

The gunman yelled, 'Get here now, or he's dead!'

I looked up at the night sky, still no sign of the chopper. Then I whispered urgently into the mike, but no voice came back. I couldn't piss around any more, it would have to happen his way whether I liked it or not.

'Collier?'

'Okay,' I said, picking up the bonds and standing slowly. 'All right.' I took a step, then stopped. 'But you point that gun at the ground.'

'You're tellin' me?'

'If you want me to bring these bonds anywhere near you,' I said, 'point that fucking gun at the ground.'

'Listen shithead—' he shouted, but then he stopped suddenly. I didn't hear anything, but I had the definite impression that Sebastian spoke to him. The gun swung left and right, then pointed at the ground. 'Come on then!'

I cocked my head. I was sure I hadn't imagined their brief exchange.

'Sebastian,' I called, 'are you okay?'

'Jesus fucking Christ,' the gunman shrieked. 'Get here, arsehole. Now!' This time it wasn't just fear in his voice, there was a real note of panic, and I knew then that there was something about this whole business. Way wrong.

I squinted at the pair of them in the darkness. 'Sebastian?'

'Ian!'

I spun round, confused. It was Bill's voice, but not through the earpiece. The shout came a second time and I turned to face the tunnel. Sounds came up, voices, and men running. Then Bill appeared in the mouth of the tunnel. Right behind him the rest of the K and R team came bursting out, weapons at the ready.

'Go back!' I shouted. 'Stay back. He hasn't been shot.'

I waved Bill and the others back, but they kept on coming.

'No!' I shouted.

I spun round and looked up the road. I was helpless, the situation out of my hands now. But the gunman didn't shoot Sebastian. He didn't shoot me either; he leapt around to the passenger's side of the car and scrambled in while Sebastian, hands miraculously freed, head-bag still on, jumped into the driver's seat. The engine kicked into life, the tyres screeched, he pulled the head-bag off, and they were gone.

I stared after them in disbelief. A second later Bill was beside me.

'Have you got the T-bonds?'

'Sebastian got in the car,' I said, stunned. 'Did you see that? He was driving.'

Bill grabbed me by the shoulders. 'Did you give them the bloody bonds?'

Still staring down the empty road, I lifted my hand and showed them to him. Bill laughed as he took them.

'Good man,' he said.

'Bill.' I faced him. 'What the fuck is going on?'

The team joined us. Joey and Tim and the others gathered round and Bill showed them the bonds. Someone clapped me on the back.

'Sebastian drove off with the fucking kidnapper,' I said.

Bill said, 'I don't think so, Ian.'

He folded the bonds and pocketed them. Then he jerked his head towards the tunnel and the team wandered back that way. They were talking together now, even laughing, the atmosphere of tension completely gone. Bill spoke into his two-way, calling off the chopper. That done, he turned to the tunnel. I grabbed his arm and he looked at me.

'You don't think so?' I said.

'Game over, Ian. We just got the call.' He pulled his arm free. He was sweating, not breathing normally yet, still charged with adrenalin. The pupils of his eyes were enormous. 'That wasn't Eddie Pike that got fried in Ward's place,' he told me. 'That was his boss.' Bill's mouth twitched. 'Our friend, Sebastian, he's dead.'

2

1

Underwriters get plenty of surprises – usually expensive ones, it's the nature of the business. But Bill's story as we'd walked back through the Greenwich tunnel, it really took the biscuit. When he'd called in the police chopper, some bright spark in the control room had remembered that other bit of information that had come through an hour earlier, a dental report on the body in the Ward house fire. Not Eddie Pike, they told Bill, it had been checked and double checked; the body was definitely Sebastian Ward's, the homicide people would be informed in the morning. When Bill couldn't raise me on the two-way, he'd led the charge through the tunnel.

So what was that back there? I'd asked him.

Not our problem, he'd said.

And sitting on the 486 box the next morning, I could almost believe that. The news was out, Sebastian Ward was dead, and the WardSure shareprice had tanked. You could just about spot the WardSure brokers by the worried faces as they circulated around the Room doing business, their job prospects suddenly looking grim. One unhappy man used our photocopier to run off a dozen CVs.

'Relieved?' Frazer said to me when he arrived. He dropped his folder on the desk as he sat down opposite me at the box, then he leant forward, grinning past the PC. 'By the skin of your teeth, boy. Admit it, you were shitting bricks.'

'Frazer.'

I looked him in the eye. He lifted his chin.

'Stick it,' I said.

He smiled so hard his eyes turned to slits, then a broker approached him and I was spared any more for the moment.

Sebastian Ward was dead. He was dead and business was still being written in the market, life was going on pretty much like normal, and somehow it didn't seem right. The tradition at Lloyd's when a ship goes down is to ring the Lutine Bell. When it rings, the Room goes silent, and everyone feels it. Something has happened. I couldn't help feeling that there should have been something like that for Sebastian, but there wasn't. The only way you could tell he was gone was by looking at the worried faces of the WardSure brokers, and after the life Sebastian had led it didn't seem like very much of a goodbye.

We wouldn't be paying out on the K and R policy either. Being completely mercenary about it, Sebastian's premium would pretty much cover the cost of Bill Tyler's team and – who knows? – the syndicate might even come out a few quid in front. The K and R market I'd got us into, Sebastian's death had got us out of. Careerwise, Sebastian's death was a real break for me, but I really could have done without any more cracks from Frazer.

Sebastian Ward was dead. A bloke who had more life in his little finger than the average Lloyd's man has in his entire body, and he'd been snuffed out just like that. Sitting at my desk, watching business being written at the boxes around me, I felt strangely distanced, like I was watching fish feeding in some kind of aquarium. I guess even then I still hadn't got my head round the fact that he was gone. You don't expect these things, then they happen, the same with Mum and Dad, and you're left floundering around wondering what the hell the whole business means, or if it means anything at all.

Sebastian Ward was dead. In my mind's eye I kept seeing that flame-shrivelled human claw.

'Ian, they want you upstairs.'

I turned to Angela; she was hanging up the phone.

'Who wants me?'

'Allen,' she said. She pushed her glasses up into her hair and rubbed her eyes. They were red, a bit puffy, it looked like she hadn't had much sleep since I'd called to give them the news last night. She pulled the glasses back down. 'He's got Tyler with him. The police want to know what you know.'

'About what?'

'You'll have to ask them.' She turned wearily to the line of brokers and beckoned the first one forward. Ever since the mastectomy she hadn't been the same old Angela, and Sebastian's death had knocked her hard. 'They're up there too,' she said.

As I left the box, Frazer smiled at me and waved.

Bill Tyler was wearing a suit. As I went in, he said, 'Man of the moment,' but he didn't get up. The policeman did though, he was a short man in plain clothes, Allen introduced him as Inspector Dillon. We shook.

He said, 'Mr Tyler tells us you saved the day.'

I looked across at Bill. He spread his hands and I felt my face go red. I went over and sat on the sofa.

Allen said, 'Inspector Dillon's been brought in to investigate Sebastian's death.'

'Murder,' the Inspector said.

Allen paused behind his desk and focused on Dillon.

'When a man's hands and feet are tied, and someone burns a house down on top of him, homicide seems a fair guess.' Dillon raised a brow.

Allen drew up a chair. He told Dillon the whole market was in shock, that the Mortlake Group would do whatever it could to help him.

Dillon turned to me. 'You're an underwriter, Mr Collier?'

'Yes?'

'How did you get caught on the front line last night?'

I gave a crooked grin. 'Long story,' I said.

139

He didn't say anything to that, just sat there and waited. I explained about the trip down to Brentwell, glancing at Bill for a clue about what had already been said. No reason really, just the way I was brought up. Never give a cop a break. But Bill's face was expressionless.

When I finished, Dillon said, 'Mr Tyler says that the next time they contacted him, they asked for you by name.'

I glanced at Bill, he was nodding.

'Yes,' I said.

'Were you surprised?'

I made a sound. More than surprised, I said. Gobsmacked.

'Any clue who they might be?'

A bit wary now, I said, 'I don't know. I thought after Brentwell, maybe someone from the dogs.'

'Sending messages by e-mail doesn't strike me as the average dog person's usual method of communication.'

No, I agreed. It didn't.

'And US Treasury bonds,' Dillon said. 'I don't imagine they're common currency at the tracks.'

I shrugged. I told him I couldn't make much sense of it either.

'Maybe Brentwell being an old flapping track was just a coincidence.'

'Yes,' he said, unconvinced. 'Maybe.' Then he smiled. 'But it seems you acquitted yourself rather well last night. Perhaps they got more than they bargained for.'

I shot another look at Bill, wondering what the hell he'd told them but his face was blank. When I turned back to Dillon he was still smiling and it occurred to me that his last remark might have more than one meaning. A meaning I didn't much like. His attention returned to Allen.

'His son Max tells me you and Sebastian were more than business acquaintances.'

Allen explained that he was on a few of the same horse racing syndicates as Sebastian. 'We used to see each other at the track quite a lot. Not so much lately.'

'Is that why he took out the kidnap policy with you?'

'He took it out with us because the Mortlake Group has a good relationship with his company.'

I was worried my role in getting Sebastian signed up for the K and R policy was about to come up, so when the Inspector glanced at me, I said, 'We were cheaper.'

Dillon smiled into his hand, but the joke didn't go down at all well with Allen. He gave me a frosty look.

'Inspector,' he said, 'the kidnap was a hoax. Some opportunists after the payout.'

'I agree,' Dillon said. On the coffee table someone had spread out a few back copies of the insurance trade press. Headlines about the Mortlake Group's move into the K and R market, one with a picture of Sebastian smiling. Dillon considered all these for a moment. Looking up, he said, 'Incidentally, whose brilliant idea was it to announce to the world that Ward would be worth five million pounds to anyone who kidnapped him?'

Bill Tyler looked smug. It was exactly the question he'd raised when he'd found out Sebastian was going for the full publicity splash.

Allen said, 'No-one took it that seriously. Sebastian wanted WardSure to broke more K and R business. We wanted to write more.' Allen gestured to the coffee table. 'It was just advertising. Promotional.'

Dillon looked up. 'It sure was,' he said.

You could see Allen didn't like that, but he bit his tongue.

Dillon went on, 'The big question is whether or not these opportunists knew Sebastian was already dead. If they did—'

'They killed him?' Bill said.

Dillon turned his hand over, then back. Maybe. Maybe not. I thought of the man with the gun, and the other one with the bag on his head. Sebastian's murderers?

Without thinking, I said, 'They could have known Sebastian was meant to be off stag hunting.' There was a pause, the sticky kind, while the three of them turned to me. I had to say something. 'Max told me.'

'When?'

Instead of answering Dillon's question I shrugged. When? When had Max told me? And then I remembered, it was a few days before Sebastian's house burnt down, before the whole kidnap thing started.

But I said, 'I think it was when we came over to you,' and I pointed at Bill.

He frowned. 'What, with the kidnap note?'

'Yeah,' I said.

Dillon wasn't a hundred per cent satisfied, but he let it pass for the time being. I'm still not sure why I told that lie. I guess it was just the way Dillon's questions were shaping up, I didn't like the way things kept drifting back to me. Paranoia City, Katy would have said. But it was more than that. Dillon knew something, but he was holding back and waiting. For what? One of us to put our foot in it?

Next Dillon asked Allen how Sebastian was regarded in the market.

'He was very successful,' Allen told him.

'Not the question, Mr Mortlake.'

Allen lifted his head, he wasn't used to such blunt treatment and it looked like he didn't much like it.

'He had a lot of friends, Inspector. And if you don't mind me saying so, here at Lloyd's we're in the business of insuring against disasters like fires. Not causing them.' Almost word-for-word the line I gave Tubs. It made me squirm to hear it now from Allen.

Dillon's gaze shifted to the paintings on the walls, big red and blue slashes of paint that looked like real money, then on to the atrium window. 'Success would pay well here?'

'Well enough,' Allen said.

'A million a year?'

'For some. Very few.' Allen gestured vaguely. 'A handful.'

'Was Ward one of the handful?'

'I'd be guessing.'

Dillon faced Allen again. 'Then guess,' he said mildly.

There was a pause while Allen seemed to trawl the question. Maybe he sensed the same as me, that Dillon was holding something back. Finally Allen said, 'At a guess? Yes, I expect he was.'

'House by Regent's Park. Million a year. Mr Ward seems to have lived the life. All a bit flashy, wasn't it?' Dillon looked over to me now. 'Must have put quite a few noses out of joint here. No?'

I kept my mouth shut. I didn't like this at all.

'For every one loser that envied Sebastian,' Allen said, 'there were ten good men who admired him. If you're saying there were people here who wanted him to take a fall, well then, I don't doubt it. But in the eyes of the reasonable, he was highly respected.'

'Because he was successful,' Dillon said.

Allen opened a hand as if to say, Believe what you like. He had that bored look now, he put it on when he thought someone was wasting his time. Dillon must have noticed it, but he didn't seem to give a toss.

'Over at WardSure,' Dillon said, 'they told me Mr Ward had a life insurance policy here at Lloyd's too. And another one. Key Person?'

I said, 'Not with us.' He raised a brow, and I explained that we'd taken on too much Key Person business, so when Sebastian's came to us we'd turned it down.

Dillon asked who took on Sebastian's life policy. I said I didn't know, but he could try a few of the specialist syndicates. I gave him the numbers and he jotted them down.

'And who would be the beneficiaries?'

I explained that on Key Person policies it was always the same, the company. In Sebastian's case, WardSure.

'And the life policy?'

'Just Max, I guess.'

'The son?'

'There aren't any brothers or sisters.' I don't know how I'd got dragged into telling him this. Something about the way he just kept his eyes straight on me. 'Sebastian's been divorced twenty years. So probably just Max.'

Dillon gave me another long look. He must have been wondering how come I knew anything about Sebastian's

143

family, but explaining it would only have dug me in deeper, so this time I stayed stum.

Then Bill piped up, 'Max Ward was down there at Brentwell.'

The comment hung in the air.

At last Dillon said, 'Let's hear it,' and Bill told him that part of the K and R story, I guess he hadn't thought it worth mentioning before. With Sebastian dead, Bill had given up his Max and Sebastian conspiracy theory on the kidnap. But now when Bill was done, Dillon's hands came together; he seemed to mull the whole thing over. I heard a knuckle crack.

Then there was a knock at the door and Inspector Dillon's colleague came in.

Jesus, I thought. Please, no.

He made a phone with his hand, held it to his ear. 'We've had a call,' he told Dillon.

Dillon got to his feet, we all got up, then he thanked us for our time. On his way to the door he looked back.

'Mr Collier, I understand you've met my colleague, Detective Sergeant Fielding.'

He didn't wait for a response, just turned and went out. Fielding gave me a lopsided grin. He ran his eyes over me in a mocking kind of way, as if my suit was some kind of pathetic disguise.

'Watcha,' he said, then he followed Dillon out.

'Who's that?' Bill asked me.

'No-one,' I said.

But it was someone all right, Bill saw that, and he asked me again a few minutes later as we walked out to the lifts. There were a hundred Fielding stories I could have told him, but in the end I settled on the big one. The one I still saw festering behind Fielding's eyes.

A few pubs in Walthamstow, I told Bill, just a few, still have a resident SP bookie. Usually an old bloke in the corner who studies his *Greyhound Life*, spends an hour over his flat pint of bitter, and keeps one eye fixed on the telly. In the olden days there used to be a Starting Price bookie in every pub, but when the gaming laws were relaxed and legal betting shops sprung up all over, most SP bookies either gave up the game or started shops of their own. But some stayed just as they were. Generally old blokes who'd been around the dogs all their lives, retired, some of them, they kept the bookmaking up as a hobby. These aren't the kind of blokes who celebrate a good night with a magnum of champagne. A good night for them would be to cover their beers, maybe a meal, and fifty quid ahead; these aren't rich men, not in anyone's book. And that's what got Dad and everyone else at the Gallon so pissed off when Fielding started shaking the old SP bookies down.

As Bill pressed the lift button, I said, 'Fielding's bent.'

'Cops have to do things.' Bill shrugged. The natural sympathy, I guess, of one man who's worn a uniform for another.

I said, 'Ugly, bent,' and when Bill cocked a brow I told him about Peg Leg Keene.

Old Peg Leg worked in a freight yard as a lad, that's where he had his leg crushed by a rolling lorry. After the leg was amputated the freight company gave him a clerical job. The pay was peanuts but he worked there for almost fifty years; it was the only compensation he got for his leg. Apart from his job the only interest he had in life was the dogs. When he wasn't down the Stow he was at the Bull and Bear, taking small bets; he was their resident SP bookie. One day Fielding showed up, took Peg Leg aside and reminded him that SP bookmaking on unlicenced premises was illegal. He threatened to throw Peg Leg in the slammer. Either that, Peg Leg told us at the Gallon later, or cough up fifty quid. Peg Leg coughed up.

'Community policing,' Bill remarked wryly. He pressed the lift button again and looked up. 'Nothing quite like the bobby on the beat for knowing the lie of the land.'

'It wasn't just Peg Leg. Once Fielding got a taste for it he was into all of them, he was making a packet out of the old buggers. Four months he was at it.'

'They all paid up?'

'What else could they do?'

'So what stopped him?'

'Me,' I said, and this time Bill looked at me in surprise. 'You?'

Everyone was pissed off with Fielding's little venture, but nobody, not even the old man, knew quite how to stop him. Telling the cops was useless even if we'd wanted to: SP bookmaking was illegal, and the cops weren't going to take Peg Leg's word over Fielding's. But then I remembered Sebastian. During the Monday night settle-ups down the Gallon I often got chatting with Sebastian at the bar. We didn't talk dogs. What I wanted to hear about – I guess I made it pretty obvious – was his other life. Sebastian Ward wasn't like anyone I knew, and when he talked about the insurance business and the City, he made that world seem real to me, not just some fantasy place where rich men swanned around in suits getting richer. And one of the things he told me about was insurance fraud. Insurance fraud and surveillance.

I never told Sebastian why I needed the gear and he never asked. It was in the days before everyone had videocams. I had to practise a bit before I got it working, and hiding it properly was a real pain. Even then the results weren't great, but they did the job. All up I put together twenty minutes of footage, Fielding shaking down Peg Leg at the Bull and Bear, and four other old codgers all in different pubs. The next week when Fielding came back for another fifty quid from Peg Leg, Tubs and Dad and me asked him into the back room where we had a projector set up. He watched about five minutes of it before he hit the lights. He knew he was stuffed.

So? he said.

Tubs and Dad both looked at me.

I said to Fielding, Give them back their money.

He shook his head, saying, So this was your idea, you little shit.

Dad told him to lay off Peg Leg and the others, and in the New Year he could have the film footage. Dad knew we had to offer Fielding something.

Fielding went to the door, telling us that he didn't

negotiate with scum, but at the door he turned and looked me straight in the eye. He said, If that film doesn't make it to me on the first of January, I'll be looking for it. And don't get clever and make copies or I'll be looking for you. Son, he said to me, you've just made a very big mistake. One day I'm going to take your fucking head off.

Then he turned on his heel and walked out.

Now as we got into the lift, Bill said, 'What happened to the film?'

'My old man mailed it to him on the first of January.'

'No copies?'

'Nope.' It seemed pointless to explain that my old man regarded that as part of the deal. And my old man never reneged on a deal in his life.

The lift doors closed; we started down.

'And did Fielding ever do like he threatened? Take your head off?'

'I started here at Lloyd's a few months later. He never got the chance.'

After a moment's thought, Bill shook his head. 'Some cop.'

Yeah, I thought, some cop. Folding my arms, I leant back against the lift wall, closed my eyes and considered the awful fact. Under my feet the floor trembled gently. Fielding was back in my life.

2

'You first,' Lee Chan said, taking a bite from her apple.

She'd rung me at home to let me know she might have something for me. I'd walked up to the corner and met her taxi, I don't know why. Maybe thoughts of her leaving soon had been bubbling away at the back of my mind. Maybe I just needed the air.

'You wouldn't believe what I've been hearing at work,' she said now. 'People running around with guns and stuff, the full bit.'

'What have you got on Mehmet?'

She shook her head, still chewing, and pointed a finger at me from her apple.

'You first,' she repeated.

So as we walked the few hundred yards to my apartment block I gave her the edited highlights. Every now and again she interrupted to get more details, and sometimes she laughed; she was pretty surprised at how I'd been sucked into the whole thing. But mostly what she did was listen. When I finished she was quiet for a second or two.

Finally she said, 'So all that kidnap stuff?'

'Complete bollocks. Ward died in the fire.'

'I still don't get why they wanted you to be courier.'

I smiled at that. I said maybe she'd get it if she saw Bill Tyler and his team in action. 'Who would you rather deal with Lee? Me, or half a dozen guys trained to kill you with their bare hands.'

She nodded, holding her apple core out, looking for a

bin. The paved wasteland stretched away on all sides, a few leafless saplings planted here and there. There were no other signs of life, and no bins. She handed me her briefcase, dug around in her coat pockets and found a clear plastic bag. She put the apple core in there, then dropped the bag in her pocket.

'You still trying for the underwriter's job?' she asked, taking back her briefcase. 'Top man on the box?'

'Who said I was?'

'You did,' she told me. We kept walking, almost at the door to my apartment block now, her eyes fixed straight ahead. 'Remember?' she said.

And then I did remember. It was in one of those weak moments, pillow-talk after a heady romp from the lounge room, through the shower and on into bed. Probably the last time I slept with Lee Chan. Which would make it the last time I slept with anybody.

'Yeah,' I said. 'I do. And yes, I still am, but that's not for general broadcast, Lee.'

She ran a finger over her lips, sealing them.

When we reached the big glass door, I held it open for her. Stepping by she gave a wry smile. 'At least you remembered, Ian. I guess that's something.'

Upstairs Katy was watching TV. She said hello to Lee when we went in, but it was a little awkward all round. They'd only met the one time before, not long before Mum and Dad died, when Katy was up paying me a visit from college. Back when Lee and me were still going strong.

Now Katy said, 'I've put another lasagne in the oven.'

Lee glanced at me. I thought she was about to turn down the offer, so I quickly nodded to her briefcase, saying we could look at what she'd brought over, then if she was hungry, we could eat. Giving me a look, she went into my study. As I followed her in, I turned and saw Katy grinning at me like an idiot, arms wrapped around herself, smooching the air. I raised a warning finger and closed the door.

My study wasn't that big, just enough for a couple of chairs, a desk, a filing cabinet and a bookcase. The window looked out over the paved wasteland we'd crossed from the station, the lights glowing in the early evening.

Lee opened her briefcase and dumped a pile of papers on the desk.

'Mr Mehmet,' she said, 'has a surprising history.'

'History of what?'

'Look at this.' She handed me the top pages from the pile.

I pulled up a chair and studied the pages. The first few were printouts from the CHORUS files at Companies House, the general details of Ottoman Air. Board members, no names I knew apart from Mehmet's, profits for the past few years, balance sheets, all the usual blah.

'We know this.'

'Keep going,' Lee told me.

I dropped my eyes again and ploughed on.

The next pages were more CHORUS file printouts, but these were for two other companies, Vector Computing and Black Sea Traders. Barin Mehmet had been on the board of both companies. With Vector Computing until three years earlier, and Black Sea Traders until just twelve months before. I flicked through the pages, then I looked up at Lee and shrugged. So Mehmet was once a director of two obscure private companies turning over less than ten million a year. So what?

Lee pushed that first lot of papers aside, clearing a space. Then she dropped a pair of stapled sheets in front of me, saying, 'Read.'

This time it wasn't information from Companies House; the top of the first sheet had the ILU letter-head. The ILU, the Institute of London Underwriters, a competitor insurance market to Lloyd's. The two papers were a general internal memorandum relating to Vector Computing, and it sure as hell wasn't a letter of recommendation. It was what Angela would call a

DNT, a Do Not Touch. The Institute was indicating to its members that Vector might have scammed one of the general insurers. The general insurer couldn't prove it, so the wording was diplomatic, non-libellous, but the general intention of the memo was clear. It was a flashing red light. Don't touch these guys if you value your profits, it said. Not with a bargepole.

I kept my eyes down. 'Where'd this come from, Lee?'

'A friend.'

When I looked up at her she stared straight back. I wasn't going to get a name. She reached across me and replaced that pair of stapled sheets with a wedge of papers.

'This one's the humdinger,' she said. 'Black Sea.'

'You've really worked on this, haven't you.'

'No, Ian. I just sat on my butt and it all fell out of the sky.'

Before she could get really wound up, I thanked her. She pulled a face. She told me to read what she'd found.

'ILU?' I flipped the first page. 'There's no letterhead.'

'That one's us,' she said. 'Lloyd's. The LCO.'

I started reading. This lot wasn't any kind of memorandum, it was a series of letters and faxes, correspondence between the LCO, the insuring Lloyd's syndicate, the policy broker and Black Sea Trading. They were photocopies. The syndicate number, and the Managing Agent's name, wherever it occurred, had been whited out.

I mentioned that to Lee.

She said, 'Basically it's none of your business.'

I raised a brow. 'You?'

'Me,' she said. 'And don't ask, Ian, because you don't need to know.'

She was drawing the line. She'd do what she could to help me but she wasn't going to let me have anything she thought was commercially sensitive. And she was right too: reading through the correspondence now I saw that the syndicate number was irrelevant; what really mattered was what had happened. Black Sea had been leasing ships, running freight round the Mediterranean and insuring the freight with a syndicate at Lloyd's. Black Sea said that on one of these trips a leased ship had sailed into a bad storm; the freight, several hundred new mopeds, had shifted and been badly damaged. Black Sea had tried to claim two hundred thousand pounds on its freight insurance policy, the difference between the new price of the mopeds and the knock-down price at which they said the damaged goods had had to be sold.

The loss adjustor's recommendation was that the claim shouldn't be paid. He'd flown out to Athens where the mopeds had been offloaded, and after digging around for a week he'd discovered that the initial damage assessment on the freight had been made by the brother of the biggest motorcycle distributor in Greece. And – surprise, surprise – the brother's motorcycle shops all appeared to be well stocked with undamaged new mopeds, none of them carrying a manufacturer's guarantee.

Lee Chan said, 'What do you think?'

I held up a hand, still reading.

After the loss adjustor's report the correspondence became heated. Black Sea threatened legal action, the syndicate threatening a counter-suit for fraud, and the broker tried hard to be helpful without actually committing itself to either side. Then came another letter from the loss adjustor. This time he'd found conclusive proof that the mopeds hadn't been damaged, a statement from a disgruntled officer aboard who'd overseen the unloading of the mopeds at Piraeus. After this the syndicate simply drew up the shutters, inviting Black Sea to sue and see what happened. Black Sea blustered, the broker recommended they withdraw their claim, and finally the correspondence petered out. The broker was WardSure.

Leaning back, I said, 'It never got to court?'

'Not even a writ.'

I folded my arms, considering the pile of paperwork. It sure raised a few questions, Mehmet being on those boards. I wondered what Allen would make of it when I told him. And the fact that WardSure had been the broker on the Black Sea business, that bothered me too. They'd clearly known about Mehmet's background: it was exactly the kind of thing they should have told us about when they brought us the Ottoman slip.

'I'd like to revise my opinion,' Lee said. She tapped the paperwork with a finger. 'I'm not so sure that security's the real issue with Ottoman Air. Not with this Mehmet running the show.'

'Giving him the benefit of the doubt, Lee, none of this amounts to a row of beans.'

She laughed. 'He's been involved with two companies trying on insurance scams. Three, if you count Ottoman. And you want to give him the benefit of the doubt?'

'Okay, so he looks like a wrong'n.'

'Villain, you said.'

Getting up from my chair, I did a turn round the study, stretching my back. I had said villain, and after the correspondence I'd just read it wasn't likely I'd be revising my opinion. But it was all surface, a side-issue to Ottoman, nothing that couldn't be shrugged off in court. I told Lee that.

'So what do you do?' She waved a hand over the pages. 'Forget about this?'

I paused by my bookcase. Ran a hand across the videos along the top shelf, the collection of fire stories I'd built up over the past several months. Clips from the news, the Waco fire in Texas, real-life and documentaries. When I'd come back from the Greenwich Tunnel I'd pulled them out and watched a few minutes of each one. It wasn't normal, I knew that, but it didn't seem to be something I could stop. Not yet anyway.

'Ian, I busted my butt to put this stuff together.'

I turned from the bookcase. 'Thanks.'

'Thanks? I don't want your thanks, I want you to use it.'

I asked her if she'd be showing the papers to the other syndicates on the Ottoman Air slip. Probably, she said.

Leaning against the wall, I looked at the paperwork on my desk. I remembered Barin Mehmet, how he smiled. White teeth.

'Are you thinking you can win the Ottoman case just on the security issue?' she asked me.

'I'm thinking,' I said, 'that you were right when you told me the judge'd have a bird if we dragged this fraud angle in now. If we can win without it, why bring it in?'

She put a hand on her hip. 'If you don't bring it in, you'll lose. And so will the following syndicates on the slip. That shouldn't happen.'

'That's just your judgement, Lee. I think we'll win. So do the lawyers.'

She nodded to herself, studying me. Then she reached into her briefcase.

'They haven't seen this,' she said, handing me another sheet. This time she sat down in a chair and swivelled while I read.

It was a handwritten note from the underwriter of one of the following syndicates on the Ottoman Air slip. This time the syndicate number wasn't whited out: I knew the man, a doddery old bugger who was losing his grip. He said he thought he should bring it to the attention of the LCO that the security man who'd been employed by the Mortlake Group as an expert witness in the Ottoman case might have his credibility undermined in court. He said he had it from first rate sources that Bill Tyler's departure from the army wasn't quite as voluntary as Bill's CV made out.

Finishing the note, I screwed up my face. 'Come on, Lee, you're not serious.'

'If Bill Tyler gets smacked out of the ball park, what have you got left, Ian?' She stopped swivelling. 'You've got a stolen plane, and insurers that look like they're holding out against a legitimate claim. You'll lose.'

'When did the old bugger come up with this?' I flicked the note.

'Yesterday,' she told me. 'But he said he gave you a verbal warning already.'

Handing back the note, I breathed out a long breath. I had a vague recollection of the old sod coming over to our box. He'd asked me if I thought concentrating our whole case on the security angle was wise. I hadn't paid much attention then, but now I could guess what must have been going through his head. If he didn't tell anyone what he'd heard about Bill Tyler, then maybe Bill would sail through court untouched and win the case for us, and then the old bugger's own syndicate wouldn't take a hit. Then again, risking everything on Bill's credibility . . . The silly old tosspot just hadn't been able to make up his mind.

'It's too late now anyway.' I spread my hands. 'Bill's report's in, he's set to be cross-examined in two days.'

'I thought this was important to you.'

It was, a lot more than she knew. I might have got through the K and R disaster, but if we took a hit on Ottoman, Allen wasn't likely to sack his own daughter. The hunt would be on for a scapegoat, and I was shaping up as candidate number one.

I went over to my desk and flicked through the papers. Barin Mehmet had been involved in both companies. Lee was right: too much of a coincidence, not something we should ignore.

I said, 'What do you suggest then? Cry fraud?'

'When does the court reconvene on Ottoman? Tomorrow isn't it?'

Tomorrow, I told her. 10 a.m. sharp.

Her forehead creased, all eight stone of her concentrated on the problem. Finally she said, 'If I keep digging in the LCO records I might get more on Mehmet. That'll help but it won't be enough. What this really needs is a loss adjustor or someone turning Ottoman inside-out.'

'The judge won't wait.'

'I know.' Her forehead cleared, she looked straight at me and smiled. 'And as I'm busy, Ian . . .'

156

I laughed, I guess it seemed funny at the time. Then we heard a voice through the door, Katy calling us out there to dinner.

When Lee was gone I helped Katy clear up the plates. As she was loading the dishwasher she said, 'I could've gone out, you know.'

'What for?'

Still bending, she looked up, rolling her eyes.

'She's a colleague,' I said. 'From work.'

'So?'

'She has a fiancé in San Francisco.'

Katy closed the dishwasher and hit the button. She stood up and faced me.

'So?'

'So isn't it past your bedtime?'

'She still really likes you. I can tell. She really does.'

I didn't say anything.

Pushing by me, she picked up the half-empty bottle of wine. 'Get a life, Ian,' she said.

I heard her cross the lounge to her room, then the door closed behind her with a bang.

Once I'd wiped down the kitchen bench I dropped the cloth in the sink and went out to the lounge. There was a smell of Lee's perfume in there, some flower. I went and opened the balcony door and let in a blast of air.

Sinking into a chair, I picked up the remote and turned it over in my hand. Then I looked over my shoulder. Music came through Katy's door, I knew I wouldn't see her again till the morning. I reached across, turned out the light, then I pointed the remote at the video recorder, finger poised.

Why? I thought. Give it up and go to bed. Sleep.

And then I hit Play.

The TV hissed for a second, the screen snowed, then the picture came. The news team had got the helicopter up just in time; beneath the smoke you could still see the outline of the mansion, the collapsed roof and the walls lit by the uneven light of the flames.

I turned down the volume. I drew my legs up beneath me in the chair. Hunched up in the quiet and dark safety of my own home, I watched Sebastian Ward's house burn.

3

'All rise,' said the court usher.

We got to our feet as the judge came in through his private door. He was all wigged up, robes flowing, and he went up behind his bench and sat down. Then we sat down. He seemed to be getting things in order in front of him, but you couldn't see exactly what, his bench was up on a podium.

At the back of the court, Clive Wainwright leant across to me and whispered, 'Five quid he says, "Let's not waste any time then." '

The judge glanced around the court. There were all the usual faces, the barristers and solicitors from both sides, the court stenographers, and the usher or associate, or whatever he was, and Ottoman's finance director and me. There were two new faces as well. Up front, in the witness chair, was Dean Potter, Ottoman's expert witness on aviation underwriting. I had a vague memory of his jutting jaw from his time in the Room. I never knew him, but Angela reckoned he was okay. The judge gave Potter a nod but pretended not to notice the other new face sitting two seats along from me, the other side of Clive. He pretended not to, but he noticed her all right. You couldn't help noticing Justine Mortlake.

Turning to the court usher, the judge said, 'Shall we begin?'

Clive groaned and slid me a fiver across the desk.

The usher swore Potter in, then Ottoman's lead barrister got up.

'Mr Potter, is the report you have submitted to the

159

court your full and fair opinion?'

'Yes,' Potter said.

The barrister mumbled something I missed and gestured to Batri as he sat down. Now Batri rose. He half-turned to Potter; from behind him we could only see one side of Batri's face.

'Mr Potter, I see from your resumé that you're not actively underwriting at the moment.'

'I'm managing the run-off of a syndicate.'

'You're not actively underwriting at the moment?'

'That's correct.'

Batri looked down, consulting his notes. 'If you don't mind, I'd like to spend a few minutes reviewing your experience.'

'Yes.'

Batri lifted his head and smiled. 'That wasn't a question, Mr Potter.'

Potter smiled back coldly, he'd obviously been in the chair before. Batri put him through the hoops then; who he'd worked for, in what capacity, and how long. Potter answered each question briefly. After five minutes of this, Batri seemed to wind up.

'And you left active underwriting a couple of years ago?'

'Yes,' Potter agreed.

'Only a couple?'

'A few.'

'A few isn't a couple, Mr Potter.'

'I stopped active underwriting six years ago.'

'Six?' Batri seemed surprised. 'But you still believe you're sufficiently well informed about current market practice – notwithstanding the plethora of recent reforms at Lloyd's – to offer a valid opinion on a policy signed not twelve months ago?'

'I'm administering the run-off of a Lloyd's syndicate. It's not as though I've retired to a convent.'

'Well, you wouldn't have, would you?' Batri grinned at him. 'As you're a man, I'd expect a monastery might be more the thing.'

'I meant I'm still in touch with the market.'

'I dare say you truly believe that, Mr Potter.' Batri turned and handed a sheaf of pages back to his assisting barrister and Potter was left with his mouth half-open. He'd been made to sound like he wasn't just out of touch but maybe a little self-deluded. 'Perhaps we should move on to the substance of Mr Potter's report, my lord,' Batri said.

The judge nodded. 'Thank you, Mr Batri.' Then he laid a finger along his cheek and rested his chin on his thumb. He looked bored. There was no jury. The whole case was being laid out for the benefit of the judge; in the end it would be for him to decide whether or not we paid up. His were the only pair of ears in the courtroom that really mattered, and so far the morning's performance didn't seem to impress him. So far not much in the whole case seemed to have made any impact on him at all.

Batri started in on Potter's report then, pulling it to pieces bit by bit. Did Potter really believe that Justine Mortlake would have been given the authority to sign up the Ottoman business unless her syndicate thought she was able? Did Potter expect the judge to accept that supervision of Justine Mortlake was so superficial? Hadn't Potter overstated the case when he said that no-one of Justine's relative inexperience should ever be permitted to write that business? And behind all this, Batri kept tapping away at the idea that Potter was so out of touch anyway that his opinion in this case was worthless.

Unfortunately for us, Potter was a model witness. He conceded points that weren't worth arguing about but held firm to the rest. After more than an hour of push and shove Batri had got nowhere.

Then he said, 'Mr Potter, your position seems to be that Justine Mortlake was in no way competent to write this business. Is that correct?'

Hands clasped on the table in front of him, Potter considered a moment. 'Yes,' he said finally.

'And yet she was allowed, by her syndicate, to write it.'

'Evidently.'

'Yes, evidently.' Batri clutched the lapel of his own robe, standing upright now, and peering over Potter's head. 'Why would the syndicate do that?'

'You'd have to ask them.'

'You're here as an expert witness, Mr Potter. You've been very free in your opinions as to Miss Mortlake's competence. Now I'm asking you, in your position as an expert, to give us your opinion on this matter.' Batri dropped his gaze to meet Potter's. 'Why, in your opinion, was Justine Mortlake permitted to write this business?'

Potter glanced towards the Ottoman barristers. All I could see of them was the back of their wigged heads. When one of them shrugged, Potter turned to Batri again and said, 'Her name. She's a Mortlake.'

Two seats along from me, Justine swore quietly. Clive whispered behind his hand, telling her to keep it down. She glared across the room at Potter.

'She's a Mortlake,' Batri said, 'which implies—' He paused, as if puzzled. 'Tell us, Mr Potter, exactly what does that imply?'

Potter looked up at the judge. 'It's possible her family gave her too much leeway too early.'

'Possible?' Batri said. 'Meaning maybe they did and maybe they didn't?'

'I think they did.'

'You're saying, are you, that Justine Mortlake was promoted by her family above her level of competence?'

Potter nodded. Batri pointed up to the microphones suspended from the ceiling.

'Yes,' Potter said aloud.

I leant across to Clive. I whispered, 'What's Batri doing?' but Clive just shook his head, concentrating on the exchange up front.

'So,' Batri said. 'Allen Mortlake, the chairman and managing director of the Mortlake Group, promoted his daughter Justine too quickly.'

'I believe so.'

'And the consequence of that is that we are all here in court today.'

'Yes.'

Batri turned to his assisting barrister and was given a sheet of paper. He glanced over it then propped it on his lectern. He addressed Potter again.

'Correct me if I'm wrong. You have just said that the managing director of a Managing Agency, a man with all the fiduciary duties which that position implies, has materially disadvantaged the shareholders of that Agency by vesting an unwarranted authority in one of the company's employees.'

Potter hesitated, caught by the question. For the first time since he'd started he seemed confused, unsure of his ground. He asked for it to be repeated.

'Certainly,' Batri said, and stooping to read from the portable PC, he repeated the question word-for-word. Then he stood up and scratched his throat theatrically. Everyone in the courtroom waited.

At last Potter said, 'All I'm saying is, she's his daughter.'

'With respect, Mr Potter, you were saying rather more than that, were you not?'

Potter moved from side to side in his chair, suddenly uncomfortable. Up behind on the bench, the judge had his eyes fixed on Potter. It was obvious that Potter was having second thoughts about his whole line of answers. Batri had led him out further than he'd meant to go.

'I wasn't suggesting anything illegal happened,' Potter said.

'Good. Now that your mind is quite clear on the matter, perhaps I might revert to the initial question.' Batri rocked forward, hands resting on the table, and levelled his gaze right on Potter. 'Justine Mortlake is a member of the Mortlake family. Exactly what, in your opinion, does that imply?'

Potter was quiet a long time. Everyone in the court, apart from the stenographer, was watching him.

At last Potter said, 'Nothing,' very quietly.

'I beg your pardon, Mr Potter?'

Potter lifted his head, all the confidence knocked out of him now.

'It implies nothing,' he said.

Batri thanked him, made a few brief remarks to the judge, then sat down.

'One-nil to the good guys.'

The court had recessed for lunch; Clive and me were standing on the pavement outside St Dunstan's. He seemed pretty pleased.

'At least smile,' he said. 'That was a good session for us.'

We watched Batri lead Justine away. He wanted to run her through the morning's Q and A over a sandwich. I noticed Clive's gaze linger on her arse.

I said, 'They'll go for her, won't they? This afternoon?'

'Batri'll prep her for it. She'll be right.'

I nodded, unconvinced. Potter was ten times steadier than Justine, but Batri had still managed to rattle him. When Batri's opposite number was let loose on Justine, I didn't want to think about it, what might happen.

Clive said he knew a pub nearby that did decent food; if we hurried we could beat the rush. We started off that way but we hadn't got twenty yards before someone back near the court called out, 'Wainwright!' We both stopped and turned.

'Bugger,' Clive said when he saw who it was. 'All I need.'

Nigel Chambers came up to us jogging, a folder gripped tight in one hand. I nodded to him but Nigel wasn't interested in me.

'I want a word,' he said, eyes locked on Clive.

Clive said he'd be back at his office by five thirty. 'I'll see you then.'

Then he turned, but Nigel grabbed his shoulder.

'You'll see me now,' Nigel said, and it was only then that I realized how angry he was.

Wainwright shrugged the hand off. 'If you want to make an ass of yourself in public, Nigel, go ahead.'

I offered to leave, I told Clive I'd meet him after lunch, but he said, 'Stay.' He looked at Nigel again. 'If Nigel wants to have his say in public, that's his choice.'

'You knew!' Nigel pointed at Wainwright. He really was too angry to worry about the scene he was making. 'I came to get some advice—'

'And I gave it to you.'

'You gave me the shaft is what you gave me.'

Clive's jaw clenched but Nigel didn't seem to notice.

'When I asked what I should do,' Nigel said, 'you said "Be open. Spell it out for them." Well how open were you? Was that professional?'

'When you came to me, Nigel, I hadn't been taken on by WardSure. They hadn't even discussed it with me.'

'Bollocks.'

'No, Nigel. It's the truth.' Clive looked him straight in the eye; you could see Nigel waver. 'And really, I don't want to discuss this in the street.'

A few pedestrians went by, Nigel stayed silent until they'd passed; he seemed to be having second thoughts. He shifted his weight from one foot to the other.

Finally he said, 'What the fuck do I do, Clive?'

'Get a lawyer.'

Nigel gave him a desperate kind of look.

'I'm sorry, Nigel, I can't help you. I've taken WardSure on as my client.'

'What about me?'

'You were never my client.'

Nigel nearly burst. 'This isn't over. I'm gonna sue you for professional negligence. And I hope you're not insured because if you're not you're gonna go down.'

'Is that right?'

Nigel tapped Clive's chest with his folder. 'See how you like it when the lawyers take the shirt off your back.'

Clive brushed the folder aside. He seemed about to give Nigel a piece of his mind, then he thought better of it. Turning, Clive said to me, 'We can still beat the rush,' and he walked off towards the pub.

I nodded to Nigel in an embarrassed kind of way and hurried after Clive. When I caught him up I couldn't resist asking, 'Not the WardSure staff equity scheme, by any chance?'

He gave me a sideways glance. I told him to forget I'd asked.

He screwed up his face. 'Hardly matters, I guess. Must be all over the market by now the way Nigel's carrying on.'

I didn't say anything, just walked along, waiting.

Finally Clive said, 'Nigel got out of his depth on the WardSure incentive scheme. Borrowed up to his eyeballs. He came and asked for my advice a while back when the WardSure shareprice was looking shaky. I told him he either had to stump up the cash or lay his cards on the table.'

'And did he?'

'Did he hell. He borrowed more from WardSure against his future salary and bonus. Dug himself in deeper.'

I put two and two together. 'Now they've pulled the plug on him?'

'He took a punt and lost.' Wainwright jerked a thumb over his shoulder. 'He's not taking it too well.'

'How much did he do?'

We stopped before crossing the street. I looked back towards St Dunstan's and saw Nigel disappearing into a crowd of pedestrians, head hanging down.

'The lot,' Clive said. We crossed over, Clive pushed the pub door open. 'I filed the papers yesterday. WardSure got a lien granted against Nigel's house and the rest of his assets this morning.' A couple came out, Clive let them pass. All the steam had gone out of him now. He was a decent bloke, you could see he didn't like the idea that he'd just helped send someone down the pan, even a prat like Nigel. 'You know,' he said going in, 'I really could do with a beer or two. Maybe the full liquid lunch.'

We got back to court late. We bobbed our heads at the judge and made for our seats, Justine was already in the chair, answering questions. I was halfway into my seat next to Clive when I froze. At the back of the courtroom, on the Ottoman side, Detective Sergeant Fielding was watching me. Head cocked, he seemed genuinely surprised to see me there.

'Sit,' Clive whispered, tugging my sleeve.

I sat down. After a moment I leant back and looked again and Fielding's eyes were still on me. I rocked forward and rested that side of my face in my hand. I tried to focus on the Ottoman barrister up front. What the hell was Fielding up to?

Clive nudged me, as if to say, Listen up. With an effort, I concentrated on the action again.

'Miss Mortlake, could you tell us how much aviation business you wrote the lead on prior to the Ottoman Air policy?'

The barrister clasped his hands behind his back and swayed forward. He was tall and skinny, and on the same side of the room as the witness chair. When he swayed forward like that he could almost have reached out and touched Justine. She said, 'I've been involved with aviation policies for six years.'

'Writing the lead line?'

'I've been writing aviation business myself for three years.' She looked up at the judge. 'The Ottoman policy was the first time I'd written an aviation lead line.'

'And have you written any similar leads since?' the barrister asked.

'I'm sorry?'

'Since the Ottoman policy.'

Justine thought for a moment. 'No,' she said.

'And why is that, Miss Mortlake?'

'The market's been soft. We don't think it's a good time to be writing that kind of business.'

The barrister raised an eyebrow. 'Oh really?'

Justine's look turned icy but she didn't fly off the handle like she normally would have. She glanced over to Batri, he was nodding. Too much of that and the judge would pull him up, but for now the judge let it pass. I guess Batri was pleased with her so far; she'd been fielding questions for a good half hour.

'Yes,' she said to the Ottoman barrister. 'Really.'

'Come now, Miss Mortlake, isn't the truth rather that you've been warned off writing leads by your senior underwriter?'

'That's not true.'

'But it is true, is it not, that having Ottoman Air claim against the first aviation policy you've ever led has had a somewhat deleterious effect on your professional reputation?'

'If no-one ever lodged a claim, there'd be no such thing as an insurance business.'

'I concede your point.' The barrister swayed forward again. 'Do you concede mine?'

Looking down, Justine mumbled something to herself. The barrister gestured to the overhead microphones and asked her to speak up.

She lifted her head. 'It hasn't helped.'

'No, it hasn't, has it? But it would be fair to say that it would help, and help greatly, if Ottoman's claim was successfully contested here. Your reputation could then recover from the knock it's taken, and your parents could be reassured that you would have the credibility within Lloyd's to successfully take over the family firm. Isn't that what this whole dispute is about?'

'No.'

'You haven't discussed this with your father?'

'No. I mean—'

'Yes, what do you mean, Miss Mortlake?'

'My lord,' Batri broke in, rising to his feet. 'Perhaps if my learned friend would not interrupt, he might discover what Miss Mortlake meant.'

Batri sat down as the judge gave the Ottoman barrister a mild ticking off. Fielding chose this moment to make his exit. He did a quick bob towards the judge on his way to the door, and when he got there he held the door open. Out of sight of the judge, he turned back and crooked a finger at me, beckoning me over like I was some snotty-nosed kid. I would have ignored him, but Clive saw it too.

Leaning across to me, he whispered, 'I think you're wanted.'

Out in the hall, Fielding rested his back on the wall and put his hands in his pockets. He asked, 'Is it always that boring?'

'You don't have to stay.'

He said, 'I don't intend to, smartarse,' and when I turned to go back in, he raised his voice. 'How's it gonna look if I have to come in there and ask the judge for five minutes of your time?'

I stopped. Then I faced him again.

'What do you want?'

'I never been in that Lloyd's place before. Old man Mortlake's office is somethin'.' He rubbed his chin. 'How much you takin' outa them then?'

'What I earn is none of your business.'

'Depends, I'd say.'

The bastard could really get under my skin. It wasn't just the aggressive bad manners, it was his whole attitude, the way he looked at things. To him I was still that brat from the dogs, Bob Collier's kid who'd somehow managed to pull the wool over the eyes of the suits at Lloyd's. The bastard thought he saw straight through me. To him I wasn't a professional in the insurance market, I was just an East End punk on the hustle. The way he looked at me now, I really could have smacked him.

'What are you doing here, Fielding?'

He nodded towards the courtroom. 'Nice lungs on the daughter. You wanna tell me in English what's goin' on in there?'

Through gritted teeth, I gave him a two-minute summary of our dispute with Ottoman. I told him that they were an air charter company, not a regular client, a piece of business that had gone wrong from the start. One of their planes had been stolen within weeks of us issuing the cover note for their fleet. And I explained that a string of other cases ahead of ours in the High Court's schedule had been settled; that's how come the Ottoman Air case had landed in court so fast.

'So where's Ward fit in?'

'WardSure was the broker on the policy.'

'He stood to gain from all this?'

'No.'

'Lose?'

'It didn't matter materially to him either way. As it happens, he was probably recommending that Mehmet hold out for a bigger settlement than we were offering.'

Fielding asked who Mehmet was, and I told him.

'Anyway,' I said, 'Sebastian didn't broker the deal personally, he just got involved at the end.'

'Says you.'

I took a deep breath. Turning aside a little so's I didn't have to see his scowling face, I told him, if that was all, I had to get back.

'Not yet. I got a couple more.' Stepping away from the wall he opened a notebook and licked the end of his pencil. Looking up, he said, 'Where's Eddie Pike?'

'I don't know?'

'Who wanted Sebastian Ward dead?'

'I don't know.'

'What was your relationship with Sebastian Ward?'

'This is bullshit.'

He flipped the pad closed, looking straight at me. He poked his pencil at the air in front of my eye.

'When we thought it was Pike in the fire, the first place I went was the Gallon. Who was there? You. Askin' about Eddie I found out later. Max Ward tells us his old man was havin' trouble with some court case, so I came down here. You again. And between times that kidnap and ransom bollocks. Who was in the middle a that?'

'Get serious.'

'Oh I'm serious. I'm serious about turnin' you over, Collier, and givin' everyone a good look at what's underneath.'

In the old days I would have laughed in his face. But in the old days he wasn't working homicides, I didn't have that much to lose, and nobody I mixed with believed in the bill. But now here I was dressed in a suit, standing in the High Court, waiting for a result on a multi million-pound insurance dispute. This wasn't Walthamstow. My life had moved on, and it had cost me a lot to move it on. Not just all the twelve-hour days I'd put in over the years with the Mortlake Group, but my bust-up with Dad – that was part of the price too, and I'd paid. I'd paid big to get this life I had, and now this bastard was threatening to bring me down?

I looked up and down the hallway, there was no-one about. Then I bent toward him a little and said, 'You aren't dealing with a fucking geriatric SP bookie here, Fielding. Back off.'

He held my look. Very evenly he said, 'I told you I'd be here when you fucked up. And now, guess what?'

Maybe he would have said more if Clive hadn't come out of the courtroom right then. All Clive saw was the two of us facing each other at the far end of the hall, and he said, 'Private party?'

Fielding kept his eyes on me a moment longer, then he nodded and repocketed his notebook.

'Thanks for your time, Mr Collier,' he said. He smiled at Clive before he turned and walked away. Then Clive came over to fill me in on the progress in court, and Fielding stopped down the hall and looked back. 'Mr Collier?' Clive and me both lifted our heads. Fielding pistolled his fingers at me. 'I'll be in touch.'

He seemed to be waiting for some response, so I nodded. When I did that he smiled again and pulled the make-believe trigger.

4

Whacking little white balls around a golf course is something I only learned to do after I joined Lloyd's. Angela used to give me the occasional quiet afternoon off to practice. An investment in the future, she said, and I was so naive at the time I thought she was kidding. Golf. It wasn't a pastime that featured much out our way when I was growing up. We went to the football sometimes, but mostly it was just the dogs. Dad lived and breathed it, the kennels and the tracks – if you'd offered him a day at the golf course he'd have thought you were nuts. Me too, probably, until our big bust-up.

But once I'd taken a few lessons, and I could hit the ball in the general direction of the flag, I slowly came round to it. It could never in a million years fill the gap that was left after I'd turned my back on the dogs – doing the form, the crowd at the trackside and the thrill of seeing the outsider at full stretch pipping the favourite – but it was better than sitting in the Room on a quiet day and twiddling my thumbs. Besides, it brought in business.

I got to be okay at it too – not great, but good enough to hold my own against most of the guys in the market. But Piers Crossland wasn't most of the guys in the market.

'You need to take it left,' Allen told him as Piers stepped up to tee off. 'It gets you round the trees; you get a good second shot up the green.'

Piers nodded politely, eyeing up the fairway, you could see the flag flapping through the trees. He set himself and took a few practice swings.

'Allen,' I said, but Allen gestured with his hand, silencing me. He watched Piers's form closely.

'You think left?' Piers said without looking round.

'The best shot,' Allen said. 'Gives you a clear second.'

Piers gazed down the fairway then stepped up to the ball, rolling his shoulders. I leant against my two wood, still not quite sure why I was there, but hoping. Allen had phoned me at seven thirty telling me to bring my clubs and meet him for tee-off at ten o'clock. I'd arrived to find him and Piers Crossland waiting for me at the first. There hadn't been time for small talk; we were getting straight into it.

Privileged, that's how I felt. Curious too, but mainly privileged. Allen and Piers were serious people: they didn't play golf with just any old one who happened along, and yet here they were with me. Not with Frazer, with me. Standing at the first tee with them, Angela's job seemed to be right at my fingertips, there for the taking. Threats from Detective Sergeant Fielding seemed like bad but distant memories.

Piers drew back, paused, then swung. It was smooth and strong, there was a thwack, and the ball went sailing out, not left but straight as a die. On, on and right up over the trees, I lost sight of it then, but the last I saw it was headed straight for the flag. It was a shot I wouldn't have tried in my dreams. Piers bent and picked up his tee then he strolled back over.

Allen smiled, but you could see it was a struggle. He went and teed up and smacked his ball down the left of the fairway. I did the same, about twenty yards past Allen's, then the three of us set off with our buggies.

By the third hole the pattern was set. Allen and me were fighting it out for second place.

'You've got a nice swing,' Piers told me as we stood together on the fourth fairway. He'd been giving me his views on the London property market, how he thought it was set for a big rise. But when he sensed that London property wasn't my best subject right then, he dropped it. He watched Allen at the edge of the bushes, searching for his ball. 'You've been with Allen quite a while.'

'Twelve years.'

'That long?' He took out a club and swung it gently a few times, clipping the grass. 'Seen a few ups and downs then.'

'Mainly ups.'

'Mainly?' He smiled confidentially.

It was an awkward moment, I wasn't even sure if he was asking for what I thought he was asking for, a quick run-down on the Mortlake Group's blunders over the past twelve years. A kind of informal due diligence on the company. My gaze drifted across to Allen. 'Yeah,' I said. 'Mainly.'

Piers dropped his head, swinging gently again. 'What's the feeling on your boxes about the merger?'

'Positive.'

'And what's your personal feeling?' He glanced up. 'And don't say positive.'

I mumbled a few words about inevitable changes in the market, corporate capital, get big or get out. He stood up straight, squinting towards the green.

'In a word,' he said, 'positive.'

I looked at him. 'In a word,' I agreed.

He smiled then, a genuine smile, and for the first time I got a glimpse of the real Piers Crossland. Behind all that good breeding I sensed there was someone I might even get to like.

Allen found the missing ball; we watched him shape up to it and belt it back out onto the fairway. Then I took my shot, then Piers, and we trundled off with our buggies again.

The merger was going to happen. I'd never quite believed it until then, but something in Piers Crossland's manner finally convinced me. A merged company made sense, sure – half the market was doing it – but things that made sense didn't always happen. Now that so many Names had pulled out, the financing for the Lloyd's syndicates had to come from somewhere. Bright guys like Piers had seen the change coming; they'd set up limited liability companies to invest in the syndicates, and now these companies were pairing off with managing agents like the Mortlake Group. But Piers must have known Allen had his sights set on the Lloyd's Council. And to get there, his best chance was if he was running the merged company, so where did that leave Piers? Getting fat on a yacht in the Bahamas? He didn't strike me as that kind of bloke.

Eyes to the front, Piers said, 'How do you see things after Angela's retirement?'

'Professionally?'

He nodded.

'She'll be a big loss,' I said.

'Irreplaceable?'

'She's one of a kind.'

A bit further on, he said, 'I understand she wasn't there on the box when her daughter wrote the Ottoman lead.'

I told him that was right.

'But you were,' he said.

I kept my eyes on the grass. I suppose I could have mentioned my parents, but I didn't.

I said, 'I made a mistake.'

He studied me a moment. He said, 'You know I've worked with Frazer before.'

I nodded. How could I ever forget it? It was Frazer's favourite subject. And I didn't care for where this was going now. It occurred to me that I might have read this all wrong, that I might not have been invited to the golf course to be promoted; I might have been brought here to be dumped. If Piers Crossland had any say in it, who was he likely to want as the new underwriter, someone with Frazer Burnett-Adams's background, or me?

He glanced across at Allen who was thirty yards away and closing. 'I tend to think there shouldn't be any extended period before her successor is appointed. Bad for morale on the box,' he said. 'Don't you agree?'

I nodded again; what did he expect me to say?

Allen joined us then and the talk immediately switched to golf. I didn't realize how rattled I was until I topped my next shot, it went skidding into the bunker below the green. Allen and Piers went off to wait up near the hole where their shots had landed while I trudged over to the bunker. What if Piers and Allen had decided to let me down easy out here on the golf course, while Frazer was back in the room right now doing a victory lap, handshakes and back-slaps all round? I felt sick.

I stepped into the bunker; the sand was white, still damp from the dew. My confidence back at the first tee suddenly seemed like lunacy, the dreams of a guy who had lost it.

A picture went through my mind. Me sitting at my desk, Justine at hers, and up there in Angela's chair, Frazer grinning at me like the cat that got the cream. A scene from hell. The bastard would make my life impossible. And then I thought of Kerry Anne Lammar, and the penthouse and the five-thousand-quid-a-week penalty.

I planted my feet firm in the sand, looked up to the flag and back to the ball. There was a sharp twinge in my gut. The first sign of an ulcer? I swung, my wrists jarred as the clubhead stopped dead in the sand, and the ball stayed right where it was. A spray of sand arced onto the edge of the green.

Up there, out of sight, Allen called, 'Now the ball.'

The next shot I got it up there, then I grabbed the rake and smoothed my footprints out of the bunker. First Fielding, now Frazer and Kerry Anne.

I triple-bogeyed the next three holes.

The clubhouse change rooms were like an echo chamber; inside the shower cubicles you couldn't hear a thing. I stood there for a good five minutes letting the jets of hot water needle into me, hands braced against the wall. Since those few brief words with Piers the subject of Angela's replacement hadn't come up and I was starting to hope that maybe I'd got myself into a state for no reason. Turning off the tap, I reached for a towel. Then I stepped out and I found Allen sitting on the bench by the wall. He was alone. Towelling off, I crossed to my locker.

'Piers left already?'

'Gone to the bar.' Allen studied our scorecards. 'That was the worst round of golf I've ever seen you play, Ian.'

'Can't win 'em all.'

'You didn't win any.'

I shrugged. The only hole Allen had won was the sixteenth, a par three where he'd fluked a tee shot that ended up six inches from the cup, but it didn't seem like the moment to mention that.

'Something on your mind?' he asked.

I told him no, nothing in particular. 'Maybe a delayed reaction,' I said. He gave me a blank look, so I added, 'All that Cowboys and Indians with Bill Tyler. Not too good for the nerves.'

'You want some time off?'

'No.'

But I said it a touch too quickly, defensive, and I saw that surprised Allen. He asked me if I was sure.

'The past week, I haven't put in two full days on the box.' I slung my towel over the locker door. 'The sooner I get back there the better.'

As I pulled on my jocks he binned the scorecards, staring after them a moment. He looked like a man with worries; I hadn't seen him like that too often before, but I guess he had his reasons. His friend Sebastian dead; Angela not recovering too well from the mastectomy; the merger talks with Crossland coming to a head. Plenty of reasons. But when he spoke it was about a different worry. Turning to me, he said, 'How was Justine in court?'

'Okay.' I reached for my shirt and tugged it on. 'They pushed her pretty hard. She stood up to them.'

He wanted details, so as I pulled on my pants I gave him what I could remember. I was a bit surprised really that Justine didn't seem to have spoken to him herself. Or maybe she had, I thought, and he was just after a second opinion. When I'd finished, I said, 'Didn't Clive call you?'

'Wainwright's a lawyer.'

I waited for the rest of the explanation but apparently

that was it. Sitting down, I hauled my shoes and socks from the locker.

Allen said, 'Who is this fellow, Fielding?'

I kept my head down, concentrating hard on my socks. First the left, then the right.

'He's a cop.'

'I know he's a cop, Ian. Who is he?'

Now the shoes. Left, then right.

'Someone I used to know in a previous life.' I stamped my feet firmly into the shoes. 'Basically,' I said, 'he's a prick.'

There was a pause. Then Allen said, 'Wainwright told me this Fielding came to see you in court yesterday.'

Funny how these things catch you. I sat straight up; I had to work to stop myself from smashing my foot through the locker door. The past – I'd thought it was done with, gone forever, but now Fielding was reaching out, clutching at my ankles, dragging me back there. Another time and place. Another fucking planet.

I said, 'He was chasing leads on Sebastian's murder.'

'So he went to you?'

'He went to the court.' I got up and crossed to the basins. Glancing at Allen in the mirror, I ran a comb through my hair. 'He'd heard Sebastian was involved in the Ottoman dispute. He wanted to know what it was all about, who was involved, what the stakes were.'

'What did you tell him?'

I turned, bum resting against the basin. I dropped my head to one side.

'What did I tell him?'

'The truth, I assume?'

'Right,' I said, but I was thinking, What am I missing here?

Allen got up from the bench. Slipping into his jacket, he said, 'Confidentiality, Ian. You know how much that means to us.'

'He's a cop.'

'Is he our client?'

I didn't answer.

'Well then.' Allen plucked at his shirt cuffs under the jacket sleeves. Looking up, he saw that he'd unsettled me. 'If the brokers convince themselves we're passing on confidential information about their clients, Ian, where does that leave us?'

'You want me to lie to him?'

Allen winced.

'If he thinks I'm lying,' I said, 'he'll come after me.'

Allen raised his hand. 'Cooperate, by all means. I'm not suggesting otherwise. Just keep it in mind that there are degrees of cooperation.' He looked grim. 'This Fielding's going to be stamping on toes around the market. I don't want you to be seen helping him when he does that.'

Me helping Fielding. The thought of it made me smile and shake my head, but I saw now what had Allen so worried. He didn't want the Mortlake Group sucked into Fielding's investigation, made a clearing house for any market talk on Sebastian. In the eyes of the brokers and the other underwriters we'd be tainted, and if we were tainted business would start to dry up. As usual, there was a lot of smart business sense in what Allen said.

The far door opened and three men came in talking and laughing, their spiked shoes clicking on the tiles. Golf talk. I zipped up my bag and Allen followed me out onto the terrace. He must have thought our conversation was over because he seemed surprised when I asked, 'So what degree of cooperation do I give him?'

Allen shrugged. He said that was for me to judge. 'You're not an idiot.'

Not much, but about as big a vote of confidence as I'd had from him in quite a while. And as Piers Crossland was nowhere in sight, now seemed as good a time as any to mention that other stuff.

'Allen, something's turned up on Mehmet.'

There was a long pause as he took that in. Two golfers came up from the practice putting green and stepped past us. Finally Allen nodded to the car park saying he'd come over with me while I dumped my bag.

Clear of the terrace, out of anyone's earshot, I told

Allen what Lee Chan had found. He didn't say a word all the way to my car. 'One probable scam, and one certain,' I finished, tossing my bag into the boot. 'Now Ottoman. I don't think Mehmet just happens to be accident prone, Allen. The way I read it, the man's a crook.'

I slammed the boot shut. We looked at one another.

He said, 'That's not how you were reading it two weeks ago. Two weeks ago it was a security balls-up at Ottoman's hangar and Bill Tyler's expert evidence was going to blow them out of the water. Blow them out of the water. Your words. Or did I misunderstand you?'

'I didn't know Mehmet's history two weeks ago.'

'And now that you do it's "all change"?' His hand went up to his face and back down. He turned, looking up to the clubhouse. He was, as maybe I should have guessed he was going to be, completely pissed off with me. Quietly, he said. 'They'll crucify her.'

Justine, his daughter, his little girl. If the case turned into a messy fraud dispute, the Ottoman barristers would have Justine back in the witness chair so fast it'd make her head spin. The duffing up she'd got first time round would look like kid's stuff then; they'd tear her to pieces.

Allen went slightly pale. He faced me.

'We can win it on the security angle. Stick to that.'

'I can't.'

His voice rose. 'I'm not asking you, Ian—'

'I mean,' I said, 'it might be out of my hands.'

He paused. 'You haven't told Wainwright. Christ, you told Wainwright before you told me?'

'I haven't told anyone. The stuff on Mehmet, it came to me through the LCO, and they might have no choice. They could pass it on to the other syndicates on the Ottoman slip.'

'Oh, great.' He covered his eyes with one hand, shaking his head slowly. Once the other syndicates heard about Mehmet's dubious past they might come pounding on Allen's door, demanding he up the ante in the court case. The whole thing could turn nasty, and Justine would be caught right in the middle. Right where her father didn't want her.

I said, 'If we can pin the missing plane on Mehmet, Ottoman'll back down. They won't pursue the court case, and Justine won't go through the mincer.'

Poor choice of words. Allen gave me a smouldering look; it was pretty clear now who he blamed for dragging his daughter into the firing line in the first place.

'Who was it in the LCO that dug up the information on Mehmet?' he asked. 'One of the Senior Claims people?'

I nodded.

He took a moment with that. 'Not your bit of Filipino fluff, was it?'

Looking down at my shoes, I explained that Lee Chan was American Chinese.

'I don't give a flying fuck,' he said quietly, 'if she's an eskimo. She wouldn't have gone looking for problems with Mehmet unless someone sent her. And that someone – that was you, wasn't it?'

'Mehmet's trying to rip us off.'

'Oh grow up, man. Grow up.' He took a few steps towards the clubhouse then came back, steaming mad. 'I don't give a stuff if Mehmet's a bloody criminal mastermind, that's the police's lookout. I'm running an insurance business, not sodding Interpol. What I'm interested in is minimizing Ottoman's claim.' He pointed at me. 'That should be yours too.'

'It is.'

'Is it?' He stepped up close to me, dropping his voice, 'Then maybe you can explain why you've just turned a probable maximum payout of a million quid on the security angle, into a possible payout of seven million. Because that's what it'll be, Ian. If this fraud accusation gets floated, and we can't prove it, the judge'll give them the full payout. And if Mehmet's feeling lucky he'll come after us in the civil court for slander.'

Allen was furious, his fists clenched at his sides, his face getting redder all the time. It set me back on my heels, not just how angry he was, but hearing him put it like that, what I'd done. There didn't seem much point explaining that I'd got Lee Chan to dig round on Mehmet when we'd been in the middle of the K and R; what kind of an excuse was that? What Allen was saying was that I hadn't thought it through, at least not like an underwriter, and that me not thinking it through might end up costing us big. Standing flatfooted in the golf course car park, it occurred to me that he was probably right.

'If we can prove Mehmet was involved in the plane theft—'

'If?' Allen pulled a face. 'If? Can you hear yourself?' He made a half-choked sound.

Up at the clubhouse someone called Allen's name, we both looked over. It was Piers Crossland; he cupped his hands to his mouth and called 'Kitchen's closing.'

Head hanging now, I started up the path.

But Allen said, 'Where are you off to?'

I stopped and looked back. Allen was still by my car.

'Lunch,' I said.

He kept his eyes on me. A second before it happened, I knew what he was going to do. My heart sank as he moved his head evenly from side to side.

5

I went out to the airport, Gatwick, where the Ottoman flights left from; they had their office out that way too. When I'd rung their office, they'd told me Mehmet wasn't there; he'd gone to their booth at the airport and they expected him to be out all afternoon. And when I'd rung the Ottoman number at the airport it was permanently engaged, so I just got in my car and went.

Stupid, I can see that now, but after my session at the golf course with Allen and Piers Crossland I felt like I had to do something. The morning had been a write-off. Just remembering that moment on the first tee – me leaning on my club thinking how great I was, patting myself on the back for getting to the upper branches of the tree – just remembering it made my face flush with embarrassment. And then the car park, and the snub from Allen. I told myself it didn't matter. I told myself that at least twenty times. Ian, I said, forget it; it doesn't matter. But if it didn't matter, how come I felt my grip tighten on the steering wheel whenever I thought about it, and how come after half an hour's driving I still couldn't stop thinking about it?

I'd made a mistake, fair enough. I'd got Lee Chan involved when maybe I shouldn't have. Was that the end of the world?

Grow up, Allen had said.

But just how grown up was it to invite me along to lunch then get in a huff and pull the rug out from under my feet?

I reached over and turned on the radio, cranked it up

loud, and told myself one last time to forget it. By the time I got to the airport, I just about had.

The concourse was swarming with people, everyone queuing up to escape the winter, clutching tickets to somewhere warm. The Ottoman Air logo was splashed in big purple letters above three of the booths. I went over there, bypassed the queues and asked the check-in girl if I could see Mr Mehmet.

'Just a minute,' she said. She finished dealing with the old man in front of her, then beckoned the next passenger forward.

'Is he here?' I asked.

'If you have any complaints, you'll have to telephone.'

'I'll keep it in mind. In the meantime, I'd like to speak with Mr Mehmet.'

She took the next passenger's ticket, a middle-aged woman this time, and put the luggage through, tagging both cases. When she was done, she handed back the ticket. She beckoned the next man from the queue.

I stepped up to the counter, blocking the way. 'Tell Mr Mehmet that Mr Collier's here to see him. Mr Collier who insures the Ottoman Air aeroplanes.'

She wasn't impressed. She gave me a cross look.

'I don't think he's here.'

Nodding to the door behind her, I raised my voice. Do you want to check, I asked her, or shall I?

She turned it over for a second then decided I wasn't kidding. Scowling, she went back through the door. Forearms resting on the counter, I dropped my head. That girl was getting paid peanuts; she had to deal with the great holiday-going public all day long, and here I was behaving like a jumped-up prat, bullying her. And I was angry with Allen?

I told myself, very firmly, to get a grip.

It was a couple of minutes before she came back out.

'He isn't here.'

Her tone had changed; she wouldn't look me in the eye. Mehmet was there all right, but apparently he wasn't too keen to see me.

I said, 'Thanks for checking.'

She looked over my shoulder to the queue. 'Next,' she said.

Upstairs in the coffee shop, I got a table with a view over the concourse. I sat there for a while dipping biscuits in my coffee, watching the Ottoman booths, and considering my future.

Option one was to let things slide, do nothing, but after Allen's little lecture I knew that doing nothing was sure to cost me the chance of stepping into Angela's shoes. If I did nothing I saw now that the whole business was likely to pan out just like Allen had said – bad for Justine and expensive for the Mortlake Group, in particular the 486 box. He could put the K and R down to bad luck, but I knew how it was with Allen; he didn't give second chances. If I sat on my hands now, Frazer was going to get the nod for Angela's job.

The second possibility was contacting Lee Chan, persuading her not to spill the beans on Mehmet, getting the situation back to where it was before I'd dragged her into it. But after a minute's thought, I realized that was fantasyland. She'd probably done it already, and even if she hadn't, there was no way she'd withhold information from the other syndicates that the rules obliged her to give them. Not Lee.

That left me staring into my coffee cup, considering option three. I had to nail down the Ottoman claim as a fraud. I had to get enough evidence to make Mehmet call off his barristers, get him to see it was all over, turn tail from the courtroom and run away. Which I suppose is why I'd driven out to Gatwick in the first place.

Brilliant. I'd thought my way right round the problem. Where I wanted to go was right where I was.

Down at the Ottoman booths, the check-in people were still hard at it, processing passengers. I picked up my cup, watching that girl I'd bullied – now she was dealing with some other troublesome bastard. What a life.

Mum used to try and line me up with girls just like that all the time. Someone's daughter she'd met, someone's

187

niece, and I'd crack about once every year and take the girl out. A mistake, it just encouraged Mum to keep trying. She never really gave up until I turned thirty; by then I'd learned to turn down all her offers point blank. I never introduced her to Lee Chan.

Girls just like that, I thought, sipping my coffee, looking down there, thinking of Mum. Of Mum and Lee Chan. Then slowly the rest of the picture came into focus. That bloke at the Ottoman counter, the troublesome bastard, he looked familiar. I put down my cup, peered over the railing now. I wasn't sure, not at first, he had his back to me. Then as I watched he stepped up through the luggage scales, the girl tried to hold him off but he brushed past her; people started turning to see what was wrong.

He tried to open the door, then he put his shoulder to it and I had him in profile. Nigel Chambers. I stood up.

At that moment the door opened. Nigel spoke to someone inside and the door opened some more and he went in. A security man arrived at the counter; it looked like he was asking what was up. That same girl gestured behind to the open door as if telling him, 'ask them, not me.' He did just that, leaning over the counter and calling through to the back office. A few seconds later, out came Barin Mehmet. He smiled and patted the air, a 'keep calm' kind of gesture, as he had a word with the security man. Satisfied, the security man nodded and wandered off. Mehmet spoke to the girl then turned and went back through the door.

The whole thing was over in thirty seconds; already the passengers were stepping forward again with their tickets, the incident not even a ripple in the crowd.

Beside me, someone said, 'Finished?' and I looked around to see the waiter scooping my cup onto his tray. I headed for the stairs.

Halfway down I started having second thoughts about barging right in on them. There was no guarantee I'd get that far anyway, what with the girl and the security guards. Pausing, I looked over the heads to the door, shut now, and wondered what was going on inside. Nigel

Chambers, like me, was a long way from home-ground, and I couldn't for the life of me figure out one good reason why he should have dropped in on Barin Mehmet unannounced. Curious, I went and took up a position to one side of the queues, from where I had a good view of the Ottoman door.

Less than five minutes later Nigel came back out. He brushed past that girl and stepped through the luggage scales again. For some reason he seemed to be reaching for his wallet. I followed him, at a distance, through the concourse. I can't say why – I guess he just seemed more accessible than Mehmet, and the fact of his being there anyway, I don't know, it just seemed so cock-eyed.

He went out under the 'Taxi' sign, his hand still tucked inside his jacket. Outside, at the taxi rank, there was a very long queue and not one taxi in sight. Nigel was loitering at the head of the queue; I sidled up behind him and watched as he tried to slip the first man in line a tenner. The second man in line saw it too, a big man; he reached over and tapped Nigel's shoulder.

'Your spot's back there, sunshine. Fuck off.'

Nigel's shoulders sagged. He went back down the line.

Some people came out through the sliding doors, pushing trolleys, and as they went by I stepped up to Nigel as if I'd come out with them.

'Nigel?' I said.

His head shot round; he nearly jumped out of his skin. I didn't wait, I walked on: it wasn't that unusual to bump into people from the market at the airport. There were always freebies going somewhere, clients being seen off.

Looking back, I said, 'Going into town? I've got my car here if you want a lift.'

Nigel took another look at the queue, then he fell into step beside me. His hand went into his jacket again. When I told him I wasn't charging for the ride, he forced a smile. He let his hand fall free.

'I guess Wainwright told you the story,' Nigel said.

I kept my eyes on the road as we pulled out onto the

M25. So far all we'd done was tell each other a few lies about what we were doing out at the airport, but now it seemed like Nigel wanted to talk.

I said, 'He mentioned you were in some kind of strife.'

'I bet.'

'Serious?'

He leant his head back against the headrest and closed his eyes. 'My job. My house. My friggin' car. How serious does it get?'

I slotted us in behind a truck. I said, 'If it's none of my business, Nigel, tell me. But a year back, weren't you blitzing it?'

'Yep.'

'Big clients, big bonuses?'

'Yep.'

'What went wrong?'

'The guy who should be answering that question,' he said, opening his eyes, 'is dead.'

'Sebastian?'

'The one and only.'

Ahead of us, the truck slowed, I moved out to overtake. The heater hummed quietly. When I pulled back into the lane past the truck, Nigel said, 'What kind of bonus scheme you got at your shop?'

'Pretty good.'

'I mean share options? Money? What?'

'Money.'

Nigel nodded to himself. He said he'd learnt his lesson. Cash, he said, is king.

'You took your bonus in shares?'

'Never again, I'm telling you. Stupidest move I ever made.'

'Just you?'

'All the senior guys. Sebastian made it sound like a win on the lottery. Chance to buy into WardSure. Christ, I must've had my head in my arse.'

After a bit, I said, 'I don't see why you're losing your house over it.'

Nigel smiled a crooked smile. 'Yeah, well.'

That seemed to be as much as he wanted to give me. But Clive had told me the rest anyway. Sebastian Ward had offered Nigel the chance to buy more WardSure shares, over and above his bonus. WardSure lent him the money to do it against the security of Nigel's house. Now the shares had collapsed and WardSure – or a company at arm's length from WardSure to make it all legal – was calling its security in. A lawyer's job. That's where Clive came in.

'You know what I can't believe,' Nigel said suddenly.

I kept my eyes up front.

'I can't believe I actually bought Sebastian's bullshit. I mean, I'm a broker. Wouldn't you think I'd have seen it coming?'

'If Sebastian hadn't been killed—'

'Bollocks.'

I looked across at him.

'WardSure was already on the slide,' he said. 'Sebastian dying like that just tipped it over the edge.'

I told him that from where I sat in the Room, it looked like WardSure was doing fine. He smiled at that. He said you had to hand it to Sebastian, the man knew what good PR was all about.

'Only problem was,' he said, 'he was spending the dosh faster than we were making it. You know, he had twelve horses in training? Twelve, and all of them on the Ward-Sure tab. How much do you reckon that lot cost?'

'You knew that when you took the shares?'

'Of course I knew. Everyone knew. Fuck, we were out at the tracks every Saturday knockin' back Sebastian's champagne, watchin' the bloody things go round.' He gave a strangled kind of laugh. 'Ascot last summer, we had a private box.'

Nigel touched his forehead like he'd just woken up from some bizarre dream. But it hadn't been a dream – at least not the box at Ascot. I'd been out there last summer as one of the freeloading guests. As I remembered it, the champagne was Krug and flowing pretty fast. Expensive days.

But the picture Nigel was painting of WardSure; it was so different from the one in my mind that I just couldn't get my head round it. I'd always believed Sebastian Ward was a successful man. I'd always thought WardSure was a successful company. And now what was Nigel telling me? That the whole thing was a front, the success just a trick done with mirrors?

'But you guys had stacks of clients.'

'Yeah,' Nigel said. 'And the last six months we've been cutting our own throats to keep them. Every time we turned round another broking shop was being taken over. The big ones merging, all the time their costs coming down. They go for market share, drop their commission rates, what does Sebastian do?'

'Drop the rates?'

'The rates, but not the fucking horses.' Nigel folded his arms, closing his eyes again.

The rain came down. It pattered against the windscreen, and I slowed and flicked on the wipers. Ahead, a blurred line of tail-lights winked on. I slowed some more.

Could I really have gotten Sebastian that wrong? I mean, this was a guy who'd come from nowhere, in the space of twenty years he'd built up an insurance broking business with a real reputation in the market, friends with everyone who mattered. He'd employed scores of people, paid them good money, and now what was Nigel saying, that Sebastian was bent? It just didn't square with the bloke I'd known, the one who'd given me a leg-up into the Mortlake Group way back when.

But thinking about it, Nigel had blown a packet this last little while. Thinking about it, Nigel Chambers had a very big axe to grind. But then there was that other little fact nagging at the back of my mind. WardSure had known about Mehmet's history, and failed to tell us.

'Nigel, did you personally broker any slips for Mehmet before the Ottoman thing?'

Eyes still closed, he shook his head. Said nothing.

The rain kept up all the way to Clerkenwell, Nigel dozed most of the way. He seemed shattered, but he woke up at King's Cross and directed me around the streets towards his home. I'd thought of a hundred ways to ask him the question, but in the end I just went with the direct approach.

'Is Mehmet going to settle?'

'Go left here,' he said.

I took the left, then idled along, face turned to him now.

At last he cracked. 'Anyone's guess: I'm not exactly on the bloody man's Christmas-card list.'

'You must have talked about the trial.'

'With who, Mehmet?'

I nodded. Nigel turned his head.

'Haven't seen him,' he told me. 'Not since that day in the office.'

Somehow I must have been ready for that answer, because I didn't even blink. Nor did Nigel; he gave me a bit more bullshit about Mehmet not being the most open client they'd ever had, wasn't that the way with wogs, never trust a man who smoked Frog cigarettes, then suddenly he shut up like he'd just realized he was overdoing it.

I turned where he showed me, into a small square. Nigel pointed out his house, three storeys tall and covered in scaffolding.

'Plenty of work there.'

'Someone else's problem now,' he said tight-lipped. When we pulled up behind the skip he sat staring at his house, his seatbelt still buckled. You could see it hurt him to look at the place, but he didn't seem to be able to take his eyes off it. All the money he must have spent buying the house, then doing it up, and now when it was just about finished – bam. Every last brick of it straight down the gurgler.

He'd gambled and lost, but unlike my old man, Nigel didn't seem to have the stomach to laugh.

He said, 'It wasn't me that brokered the Ottoman deal.'

I didn't say anything. After a while he turned to face me.

'I put all the paperwork through, but it wasn't my baby. Uh-uh.'

'You brought Justine the slip, Nigel. When she signed it, you were sitting right next to her. And you never said any different in court.'

He unbuckled his seatbelt and reached for the doorhandle. He said I could believe what I liked.

'If you weren't the real broker, Nigel, who was?'

He looked at the house again; it seemed to decide him. 'Sebastian,' he said, pushing the door open. 'The one and only.' As he got out he winced, his hand shot to his side. Immediately he tried to cover the action, reaching into his inside jacket pocket. But he saw that I'd seen it. He swung the door shut and stepped back onto the kerb.

I hit the button and the side window went down.

'Sebastian brokered the Ottoman deal?'

His hand still in the jacket, he nodded.

'Nigel,' I said, 'why'd you decide to tell me that now?'

Reaching over, he tapped the roof of my car. 'Thanks for the lift.' Before I could say another word he was picking his way through the scaffolding, zigzagging his way up to the front door. Left, then right, then gone.

6

Underneath my apartment block there was a secure parking area, the bays all neatly numbered. Mine was 23, like my flat. I pulled in there, turned off the ignition and stared at the brick wall. Sebastian brokered the Ottoman deal, did that make sense? As far as I knew Sebastian hadn't come to the Lloyd's Room to broke deals for at least ten years: whenever I'd seen him there lately he was doing the social round, chatting with senior people like Allen and Angela. All the broking for Ward-Sure was done by his employees, Nigel Chambers and the rest: Sebastian had risen way above that donkey work years ago. It didn't make sense at all, but I couldn't shake the feeling that Nigel'd been telling me the truth, that Sebastian had brokered the Ottoman deal with Mehmet, and that Nigel had just fronted it with us. But why? And why had Nigel told me the story now?

I stared at the brick wall till I knew it wasn't doing me any good, then I got out and went round to open the boot.

I was reaching inside when a voice behind me said, 'Welcome home.'

I knew the voice. With a sinking feeling, I turned.

Fielding. Him and some young guy slouching on a Jag across the way.

Fielding made a sideways movement with his hand. 'Step away from the car.'

'What is this?'

They came across. I reached up to close the boot but Fielding's hand shot up beside mine, holding it open. I

195

pulled down, he pushed up – down, up again – then I let go and stepped back, shaking my head. I even laughed.

Fielding stooped, looking inside the boot. 'What's this?'

'That,' I said, 'is the bag where I keep all my guns.'

He signalled to his offsider, the bloke reached in and hauled out my golfbag. Fielding looked from the clubs up to me.

'Satisfied?'

'Golf?' Fielding looked at his offsider. 'This isn't the weekend. Is this the weekend?'

The bloke shook his head.

'This isn't the weekend, Collier. Don't tell me you've been skiving off.'

Eyes on me, Fielding made a tipping gesture with his hand. His offsider upended the golfbag, and the clubs slid out, clattering onto the concrete, the sound echoing. Fielding smiled.

'You're a juvenile bastard,' I said.

He glanced at his offsider. 'Check the car.'

The bloke dropped the bag, and stepped towards the car. I lifted my key ring and hit the button. The locks clunked.

'Open it,' Fielding said.

I folded my arms, not in the mood for cooperation now. Just the opposite. Fielding bent into the boot again, rooted around a bit, and came out with a tyre lever in his hand. He went and stood by the windscreen.

'Open your fucking car,' he said.

I turned to the offsider. 'You see the kind of wally you're working with?'

Fielding lifted the tyre lever. Without unfolding my arms, I pressed the key ring button. The locks clunked again, open this time. Fielding called me a cunt.

While his mate leaned in, searching under the seats, Fielding chucked the tyre lever onto the golf clubs, then he started rooting out bits of old rubbish from the boot.

'If you tell me what you've lost,' I said, 'maybe I can help.'

A tool set hit the floor, then a jack. Inside the boot

196

Fielding grunted, heaving at the spare tyre. It finally dawned on me that they were being serious, not just winding me up, but actually looking for something.

I said, 'You're so far out of line, Fielding, it just doesn't matter.'

'Right, smartarse,' he muttered. 'It doesn't matter.'

The offsider finished with the front seats and moved on to the back.

Then over in the corner of the basement, the lift doors opened and three people stepped out, a man and two women. The man had apartment 25, two doors along from mine, and the women were from the next floor down. All of them were on the apartment block committee. Their conversation carried on for a few seconds, then they saw us and it died. I smiled at them. The man attempted a wave. God knows what they were thinking.

'Everything all right, Mr Collier?' the man called.

I waved back. 'Fine.'

He looked doubtful. One of the women gave him a prod.

'You sure?' he said.

And then Fielding lifted his head from the boot.

'We're from the Metropolitan Police,' he told them bluntly. 'We're investigating a serious crime. Mr Collier here's helping us with our inquiries.'

He looked like butter wouldn't melt in his mouth, the bastard. I could have kicked him in the balls.

My three neighbours went to their cars, looking our way but pretending not to. No prizes for guessing the main topic at next week's committee meeting. I waited till the last car drew out past me, then I said, 'Get your head out of my boot, Fielding. And get your mate out of my car.'

Fossicking deep in the boot, Fielding said, 'People got a right to know what they're livin' with. Didn't think you could fool 'em forever, ay?'

I opened my mouth, then closed it. What was the use? Fielding thought he had his big chance at me; nothing I said now was going to make him give up and walk away. But it wasn't simply revenge. Fielding had made up his mind that I was conning everyone – my job at Lloyd's, my flat, my whole bloody life, all a con. That was something he understood, and if he could manage it he was going to rip and tear until he brought the whole package undone.

'Hello,' he said then, his whole face brightening. He'd found a side panel; I heard it flip open.

'Nothing up front,' the offsider told him, slamming the door. He came round and stuck his head in beside Fielding's.

'Get out of it,' Fielding said sharply.

The young bloke shrunk back like a whipped dog. Learning the ropes from Fielding, he almost had my sympathy.

'Wouldn't remember offhand what you keep in this hidden compartment?' Fielding asked me.

'There's nothing hidden about it. And yes. A red plastic container.'

'So I see. Containing what?'

I spread my hands. 'I don't believe this.'

He picked up the tyre lever and hooked the plastic container out, careful not to touch the thing with his hands. He told his offsider to go fetch him an evidence bag, then he felt the container's weight. 'Not much left. Used any lately?'

'What are you trying to prove, Fielding? I've got a car. It needs petrol. I carry some spare, just like everyone else in the country.'

He brought the dangling container closer to his face, studying it. 'Should be a few good prints.'

I made a sound of surprise. We'd suddenly moved on from the mean-minded to the bloody ridiculous. 'My prints, on my container, in my car.' I shook my head. 'How do you do it, Sherlock? You're a fucking inspiration.'

He gave me a smouldering look.

A car pulled into the basement and idled into its bay. The driver got out and walked straight to the lift without even glancing in our direction. Fielding's offsider returned with the evidence bag. Fielding tipped up the lever, and the plastic petrol container slid down into the bag. The offsider pressed his fingers together along the seal, then took the lot back to their car.

I said quietly, 'Don't come back here, Fielding. Ever.'

Fielding dropped the lever into the boot. 'You might wanna pick up your golf clubs. Someone's liable to drive over them there.' He turned and headed for the lift. 'You're flat 23, right?'

I bent and scooped up the clubs, then tossed the golfbag into the boot after them. Slamming the boot shut, I hit the button on my key ring and jogged over to the lift. Fielding was studying the numbers above the lift doors.

'My flat,' I said, 'is private property.' He didn't say anything, so I stepped closer. 'Did you hear me?'

The lift arrived and the doors opened. Stepping in, he said, 'You've picked up some funny ideas, Collier.'

I stepped in after him and he yelled to his offsider, '23! See you up there.'

The doors closed. Fielding's finger hovered over the buttons.

'Second floor?'

When I didn't answer, he hit it anyway and we started to rise. I stared at him.

'Before you ask,' he said, 'I've got a warrant.'

'Show me.'

His eyes dropped from the numbers to me. He said if I didn't mind my manners, he was going to nail me into the floor like a tack. 'A fucking tack,' he said.

The lift doors opened. When we got out he looked left down the passage, then right. He glanced at me, but when I made no move he went left. A good guess, I had to follow.

We stopped outside my door. I said, 'I'd like to see the warrant.'

'Jesus, aren't you just the one.'

But he pulled the warrant out and handed it to me. While I looked through it, he jingled the change in his pocket, impatient to get the door open, to get inside and turn my life upside-down. The warrant meant nothing to me, lawyer language, but it was signed by a judge, and Fielding looked so damn smug about it the thing just had to be real.

I touched my forehead. What, I thought, goes on here?

'When you're ready.' Fielding nodded at the door.

I handed back the warrant. 'This is crazy.'

'Yeah? Arson and murder. Real crazy.'

He pointed a finger at the door, and the feeling I had then, it was something I hadn't felt in years. Powerless. Powerless and angry – more than angry, bloody enraged at the injustice of what this prick was doing to me. I wasn't a kid any more, this whole scene, it shouldn't've been happening, but there I was, and there he was, both of us knowing I had no choice now but to open my door to him. He looked so bloody pleased with himself too, I could have thumped him.

Taking out my keys, I stepped between him and the door. 'My sister might be in.'

'So?'

I looked at him. 'So mind your manners.' Then I turned and opened the door. 'Katy?'

No reply. I walked in, calling her name again, then crossed to her door, knocked and opened it. A mess, as usual, but no Katy. Relieved, I turned. Fielding was standing in the centre of the lounge, taking stock.

'You own this place, or rent it?'

I didn't answer.

He gave me a weary look, then reached down, grabbed the edge of the coffee table, and heaved. The magazines went flying, the coffee table somersaulted across the room and landed at my feet.

Fielding looked up from his handiwork.

'Own,' I said. 'And if you break anything, I'll be sending Inspector Dillon the bill.'

He strolled around the place, touching things, picking up stuff like the ashtray, tossing it from hand to hand then putting it down somewhere else.

I sat on the sofa, steaming. It took me back, this bullshit. Stuff I didn't want to remember. I must have been eight or nine, Katy wasn't even born, when the cops came calling on Dad. It wasn't their usual thing: if they wanted Dad – I found out later – they generally had a word with him down the Gallon. But this night there'd been some trouble at the Stow: one of the punters had the stuffing knocked out of him after a race the bookies all reckoned was fixed. Whoever beat him up stole everything he'd won on the race; he told the cops it was goons employed by the bookies, and the cops arrived on our doorstep at midnight. I remember staggering downstairs in my pyjamas, rubbing my eyes, hearing the argument raging in the front room. When I put my head round the door I saw some copper pointing a finger at Dad, and Dad pointing back.

They stopped dead when they saw me. Then Dad bellowed for Mum, she came and hooked me away from there, dragged me upstairs and put me back to bed.

That was the first time I remember the cops being in our house; it left a real impression on me because for the next few days the old man went out on a bender. When he came back Mum didn't speak to him for a week.

'What's out here?'

Before I could answer, Fielding was sliding the glass door open, stepping out onto the terrace.

'Knock knock,' someone said behind me.

I looked over to the front door and saw Fielding's offsider coming in. But he hadn't been on the job long enough yet to build up a skin as thick as Fielding's, and finding me alone in the room now he looked a bit unsure of himself. He glanced at the upturned coffee table, and the magazines strewn across the floor.

'Your colleague,' I said, 'is out on the balcony. You'll excuse me if I don't offer you a drink.'

He went out to join Fielding and I picked a copy of *Lloyd's List* off the floor. They couldn't do much harm out there on the terrace, but when they came back in I'd have to keep my eyes peeled. Especially with Fielding. If he couldn't find any evidence of my involvement with Sebastian's death, or the fire, he sure wasn't above planting some of his own. After a minute they hadn't come back in so I dropped the magazine and went to see what they were doing out there.

They were side-by-side, forearms resting on the railing, looking out at the view.

I said, 'Do what you have to, then bugger off.'

Turning, Fielding tut-tutted. He told me to get back in my cage.

'When we're done,' he said, 'we'll let you know.'

Then his offsider touched his arm; they both looked past me. I pivoted.

'You're such a pig,' Katy said, dropping her handbag on a chair and stooping to pick up the magazines. She hadn't seen Fielding or his mate. 'Why'd you leave the front door open?'

God, I thought. God, not now.

I went back in, speaking to her quietly.

'Two cops are here searching the place.' When her eyes widened in surprise, I added, 'Shoot through. I'll tell you about it later.'

She reached for her handbag, leaning across to see around me and out to the balcony.

'Go, Katy.'

'What do they want?'

'Go.'

She pulled a face. Behind me I heard the glass door sliding wide open.

'Afternoon,' Fielding said, coming in.

I made a flicking gesture in front of my chest where Fielding couldn't see. Katy ignored it.

'Hello,' she said.

'The slapper or the sister?' Fielding asked.

Her eyes shot back to mine, seeking guidance now. She knew she'd made a mistake.

Go, I mouthed silently.

But it was too late now, Fielding's offsider came in too.

'Introductions?' Fielding said.

I made them reluctantly, explaining to Katy that Field-ing had a warrant to search the flat.

'What for?'

I looked at Fielding but he didn't respond. He kept his eyes on Katy in a way I didn't much like.

'So you're the sister. Now we know which one of you got the looks.' Fielding glanced at me. 'Be a bloody miracle if you didn't beat him hands down in the brain department too.'

I told him, very firmly, to get on with his search or get out. He sent his mate into the kitchen, and after a moment we heard cupboards opening and pots rattling around.

'Call that a search?' Fielding yelled.

There was a pause, then the pots and pans started clattering onto the tiled floor. Katy took a step that way but I grabbed her arm. She was glaring at Fielding now. My kid sister, my own flesh and blood, I knew exactly what she was feeling, all the fury, the impotence and the rage that were in her. I stepped between her and Fielding.

'You wait here,' Fielding said, pointing at Katy. Then as he went by me he muttered, 'Your room first, boyo. I'm feelin' lucky.'

I whispered to Katy to keep an eye on the other one, make sure he didn't plant anything, then I followed Fielding.

My flat was on one corner of the apartment block, and my bedroom on the outside corner of my flat, the windows facing south and east. I wouldn't say I've got a bachelor's mania for tidiness and order, but generally I like to be able to find things where they're meant to be. Since Katy'd moved in I'd lost control of the public spaces, but my bedroom was still a sanctuary for me, somewhere I could withdraw to when I wanted to be alone.

So when Fielding went in ahead of me now I really had to grit my teeth. I leant against the doorframe, arms folded. 'How long will this take?'

Ignoring me, he pointed to the side door and gave me a questioning look.

'Ensuite,' I told him.

He nodded at the cupboard.

'That's a cupboard,' I said.

He scowled at me.

'It's just clothes and shoes.' He looked doubtful, so I added, 'If you find anything else, it'll be something you dropped.'

He started on the drawers, pulling them out one by one and emptying them onto the bed. For some reason a picture came to me of Fielding stretched out on that psychiatrist's couch, whatsaname, Dr Thomas. It would have taken a doctor to figure out what was going on in Fielding's fat head right then.

I pushed away from the doorframe and went in closer where I could see what he was up to.

He glanced over his shoulder at me and dropped the last drawer on the bed. Then he went and poked around among my suits.

Now that same unpleasant feeling I'd had earlier in the basement came back, that he wasn't just playing a game here, but really searching. My heart flip-flopped, I felt a light sweat break out on my neck. Unfolding my arms I stepped up close to him.

I said, 'A canister of petrol in my car, and clothes in my cupboard.'

He stopped his search and looked up at me.

'What do you deduce from that? That I murdered Sebastian?'

He cocked his head. 'Is that a confession?' I swore. He smiled and turned his back on me, digging through the suits again. 'You might be wonderin',' he said, 'if I intend plantin' somethin' in here. Somethin' that puts you at Ward's house the night he died.'

'It wouldn't stand up.'

'Don't bet on it. But that's not what I'm doin' anyway.' He paused, waiting for me to ask the obvious, but when I didn't, he said, 'Know what I'm doin'?'

'Wrinkling my suits.'

'I'm lookin' for your mistake, Collier. I'm lookin' for that one little error you made that lets me put you where you belong. You and Eddie both.'

It caught me; I swayed back like I'd taken a hard smack in the mouth. Squinting, I said, 'You what?'

'Don't give me that.' He reached into the back of the cupboard behind the shoes. I couldn't see his hands.

'Pike?' I said. 'Me and Eddie Pike? What are you setting up here?'

'Next thing you'll be telling me you haven't seen him for years.'

My hand chopped the air. 'I saw him sometimes at Sebastian's place. He was there. I saw him, that was it. I don't remember even speaking to him.'

'Just clothes and shoes, you reckon.'

'What?'

He looked up over his shoulder. 'In the cupboard. You said just clothes and shoes.'

I stared at him in disbelief. Shaking my head, I said, 'Don't try it.'

He came up, grinning, a football clamped between his big hands. It must have been lying there for years. He bounced it on the floor a couple of times, then rolled it up and down one arm.

'You got a pump?'

It wasn't easy, but I controlled myself. I took a long deep breath before I spoke.

'If you've marked Eddie Pike's card for Sebastian's murder, that's between you and Pike. Leave me out of it.'

Spinning the football in one hand, Fielding said, 'So we won't find Eddie's prints on the canister?'

That one set me back on my heels. But when I thought about it there really was no time when Eddie would have been rooting around in the boot of my car. At least none that he should have been.

'No,' I said firmly. 'You won't.'

Fielding dropped the ball onto his foot, it rolled past me into the lounge. Then he went across to the ensuite, stuck his head through the door and looked around. 'Haven't spoken to him in years, you reckon.'

'That's right.'

He crouched by the bed and flipped up the quilt. The base was solid; he went and checked the other side: there were no drawers there either. Getting up, he wiped his hands.

'But that'd make you innocent, Collier. And that can't be right now,' he said, brushing past me. 'Can it?'

In my study he went through the same routine; he didn't even raise his head when we heard Katy shouting at the offsider in the lounge. He just said, 'Maybe someone should tell her she'll be arrested if she obstructs the search.'

When I didn't move, he glanced up. He told me he wasn't kidding. While I was weighing that one up, Katy shouted again, and I backed out of the study trying to keep him in view. Katy was standing in front of her bedroom door, a Mexican stand-off with Fielding's mate.

She said to me, 'He can't go in my room.'

'He can, Katy. Let them get on with it. The sooner they're done, the sooner they'll be gone.'

I coaxed her away from the door. The offsider went in and began his search.

'What's happening?' Katy whispered, gripping my arm. I realized then that this whole business was frightening her. From where she was seeing it, Fielding and his mate had arrived out of the blue, intent on stamping their grubby boots right through my life. Seeing it, in fact, pretty much how it was. 'What do they want, Ian?'

When I told her I'd explain the whole thing later, she gave me a doubtful look. Then we heard the cupboards opening in her room, she darted past me and gave that bloke a bollocking, so I left her to it.

Back in my study Fielding was by the bookcase, one hand resting on the videotapes, looking around. The tapes of the fires, real-life and documentaries. I went rigid. All those fires: what would he make of them if he knew?

I looked him in the eye. 'Finished?'

His hand dropped; half a dozen videos hit the floor. 'Sorry,' he said, shoving past me.

Out in the lounge again, he pointed along the rear corridor. 'What's down there?'

'The bathroom.'

He noticed the football sitting by the TV. He took three steps and kicked hard; the ball smacked into the wall, ricocheted off the ceiling, and careered down the rear corridor, stuttering from wall to wall. Miraculously, nothing broke. Then Fielding dropped into the sofa, picking up the remote.

'The way I remember it, you and Eddie Pike used to be bum chums.'

'You've got a bad memory.'

'Yeah?' Fielding said. 'Then how about you and that little Paki settin' fire to the school. Bad memory there too?' He was talking about Sanjay Patel. One school holiday me and Sanjay, both about thirteen at the time, put on an unofficial barbecue with our mates in the school grounds. Fielding was one of the cops who sprung us. Now he turned the remote over in his hand and I felt the hairs prickle up my neck. My tape of Sebastian's house going up in flames: it was in the machine, rewound and ready to play.

Don't, I thought. Please don't press the button.

He said, 'Funny how things work out, ay? Like you. Start out as a toe rag and wind up in a place like this. Mr Respectable, the full bit, but you just can't help yourself. It's like a Jekyll and Hyde thing. Someone pisses you off, you go back to type.'

'Unlike you.'

He glanced up. 'I put you away, they'll promote me.'

Keep him talking, I thought. While he's talking he won't press the button.

I said, 'You're going to stitch me up for what, enhanced pension rights?'

He smiled. 'Kinda rags to riches. Same as you, only when your story's over it's gonna read like a kinda rags to riches to rags kinda thing.' He looked at me, and then I got it, what he was trying to do. He wanted me to take a swing at him. He tapped the remote on the cushion beside him. 'Remember Jebby Maguire.'

Jebby, I hadn't seen him since he'd been carted off to Borstal at the age of fifteen.

'What about him?'

'Got done for assault and battery last month. Be a bit a company for you down in Dartmoor.' The remote turned over in his hand. 'All together, just like old times.'

He ran through some more names then – most of them guys I hadn't thought about in years, not since school. Breaking and entering seemed to be the common thread. I tried to keep my eyes off the remote.

'Yeah, petty crime except for Maguire and you.' Fielding dropped the remote onto the cushion. 'And now that Maguire's been sorted—'

'Give it a rest.'

Fielding's offsider came into the lounge, Katy following. When Fielding asked if he'd found anything the bloke shook his head. Katy yanked the bedroom door behind her, slamming it shut. And the way she looked at them, Christ, she was angry.

'Me and your brother here,' Fielding said to her, 'we were just talkin' about the old times.' When Katy frowned, he said, 'Oh yeah. Ian and me, we go way back. Back to when he was rippin' off punters at the Stow. Bob Collier.' He cocked a finger at Katy. 'Your old man too? Or just the same old lady?'

For a second I thought Katy was going to flip her lid. I caught her eye just in time, gave her a warning look, and she checked herself. Very matter of factly she went to the sofa and sat down on the far end to Fielding, like she was reoccupying her own territory.

'If you're staying for tea,' she said, 'we can send out for bananas.'

Fielding peered at her. 'Don't piss me off, girl. Ask your brother here where that gets you.'

Katy tucked her legs up under her, making herself comfortable as if Fielding and his mate weren't there.

And then she leant across and picked up the remote.

'Katy,' I said, my heart in my mouth, 'weren't you going out?'

She pointed the remote at the TV. 'No,' she said, then she hit the button. The TV came on, a wildlife programme.

'Do you mind,' I asked Fielding sarcastically, 'if I start tidying up?'

He smiled at me, sitting there on my sofa like King bloody Farouk. 'Your house,' he said.

Bending down, I put the coffee table upright. Then I slid it back into place between the sofa and the TV, but after that I was stuck. I couldn't tell Katy to turn the damn TV off and I couldn't snatch the remote out of her hand, it'd be too obvious. I knelt and picked up the scattered magazines.

'You don't have a cleaner?' Fielding said. 'Man in your position?'

I told him any more visits from him and I'd get one in full time.

He started to laugh, but Katy then said, 'Just for the smell,' and his laughter stopped dead.

Facing her, he pointed at the TV. 'Turn it off.'

Off. Turn it off, I thought. Kneeling by the coffee table it was as if I was praying, willing her to do it. Turn the bloody thing off.

But she didn't. She tossed the remote down on the sofa cushions, petulant, letting him know she wasn't taking his orders. He reached over and picked the thing up.

Then without turning round to face his offsider, Fielding spoke to him.

'You see these people, Mac? They don't think they're like you and me; the rules aren't for them, not the Colliers. They get their hands on some money, sit back and think they can give us the finger.' He went on talking, facing me now, not even thinking about it as he pointed the remote at the TV and hit Play. My gut heaved. 'Did I tell you how they got their start? Their old man was a bookie down the dogs, drove a Jag while the hard-workin' punters used to walk to the track. Yeah. Big Bob. Wasn't he just the biggest bullshittin' prick, I tell you—'

But he didn't get a chance to tell us anything, because that's when Katy went for him. She launched herself from one side of the sofa and landed on him, clawing his face. He put up his arms, shielding himself instinctively. I jumped up and grabbed Katy around the waist, hauling her off, my other hand snatching at the remote. I missed it. She elbowed me in the gut, wiggling like mad, desperate to get at him again.

'Bitch,' he was saying now. 'Bitch, the fuckin' bitch.'

Katy gave him an earful, still struggling against me.

Then the offsider broke in, saying, 'Sir?'

Fielding spun angrily. The offsider pointed and Fielding focused on the TV. For a moment I really couldn't breathe. Fielding's face slowly changed. He'd dropped the remote when Katy flew at him, but now he picked it up again and turned up the volume.

When she heard the news announcer's voice, Katy stopped fighting me. She craned around to see the screen.

'Oh,' Fielding said after a few moments. 'Would you look at that.'

But I didn't have to look; I'd already watched the tape a dozen times. I let Katy go, stepped over to the armchair and sat down. Fielding leant forward, elbows on his knees, drinking it all in. The offsider and Katy stood stock still, like they were transfixed by the flames. Finally the news announcer mentioned that the owner of the house, Sebastian Ward, was a senior figure in the London insurance market, and with that the screen turned to hissing snow.

Fielding hit the Stop button. Then he glanced over to the study, those videotapes he'd knocked to the floor were visible through the open door. Then he looked at me. I don't know if it was inspiration or plodding cop thoroughness, but without a word he went and picked up half a dozen tapes and brought them back. Then one by one, viewing maybe a minute of each, he put them through the machine. Nobody spoke as we watched the fires raging. It was awful.

When the last tape stopped, Fielding looked at me again, shaking his head.

'Oh my,' he said, grinning. The look on my face seemed to give him a real thrill. 'Oh my, oh my, oh my.'

7

When the doorbell rang it woke both of us; we met in our dressing gowns out in the hall. Katy told me not to answer it, but I did. It was Tubs.

'Come down,' he said. 'I think I found somethin' you'll like.'

When Katy heard his voice she groaned and stumbled bleary-eyed back to her bed. I looked at my watch. Twelve midnight.

'I don't think so, Tubs.'

His voice went quiet. 'Is Katy there?'

'She's in bed, Tubs. Why aren't you?'

A pause, then he said, 'I've found Eddie Pike.'

I rested my forehead against the wall. I was in serious trouble, I knew that. When Fielding and his mate took all my tapes with them, Fielding told me I should expect a call soon. He said maybe I should start thinking about a lawyer. The worst part was it wasn't a joke; somehow this business had got bigger than I think even Fielding expected; it had taken on a life of its own. It might have started out as an opportunity to cause me grief, but now it was turning into a real case. I'd seen that in Fielding's eyes when I'd shown him the door.

Lying awake in bed, tossing and turning, I'd told myself that it was ridiculous. All circumstantial, I'd told myself. Circumstantial evidence. Then I'd realized I didn't even know what that meant, and I decided for once in my life to take Fielding's advice. In the morning, before court, I'd go and see Clive.

Lifting my forehead from the wall, it occurred to me

that maybe I should call Clive immediately. But Tubs wouldn't have liked that. He looked at things like my father had: lawyers weren't much better than police.

Hitting the intercom, I said, 'Give me five minutes.'

'She hit him?' Tubs said. He was laughing.

'It wasn't funny. I had to pull her off before she ripped his eyes out.'

'Why?'

'Fielding said Dad was a prick.'

'No, I mean why'd you pull her off him?'

I looked across at him. He had his eyes on the road; we were headed northeast, out Chingford way, to where Tubs reckoned Eddie Pike was holed up.

I said, 'This isn't like the old days, Tubs. Not with Fielding.'

He shrugged. 'Same bastard he always was.'

'Yeah,' I said. 'The same, but with clout.'

Tubs let that pass. He drove with an elbow resting on the armrest between us, the heater humming quietly. The car was an old Mercedes with plenty of legroom, and plenty of gutroom under the steering wheel, Tubs'd had it for about as long as I could remember. When she was a kid, Katy used to bounce around on the back seat like it was a trampoline.

Now we drove out through the old haunts, north of the Gallon and up past the Stow, and suddenly we were passing the Apollo Bingo Hall. The neon lights were off but you could make out the name from the streetlights. My head turned, watching it go by. Mum used to go there every Wednesday night, week in, week out, year after year; when I got my licence I'd drop her off sometimes on my way to the pub. Usually she'd give Dad and me our tea of a Wednesday night, drop Katy off with Tubs's mum, then go. Around ten she'd come home and if you asked how it went, she'd say, We had a bit of a laugh. And then she'd go upstairs, taking Katy to bed.

A bit of a laugh one night a week, and the rest of the time looking after Dad and Katy and me, as if our lives were the only ones that counted. Selfish of us, but if you'd asked her she wouldn't have said so. And then dying how she did, going in after Dad; if it had been Katy or me in there she would have come after us too. Every time I thought about that, it made me feel small. I pushed in a tape. Buddy Holly. When I tried to turn it off Tubs told me to leave it. He tapped the armrest to the beat.

'So where's Pike hiding?' I asked him again.

Tubs told me to keep my shirt on. Somewhere I knew, he said.

After a while the streetlights thinned out and we were in that territory that isn't town any more, but not country either. Tubs turned down a road with a Dead End sign, cruising slowly. We passed a freight depot and further on a row of small sheds and a house; all the lights in the house were off.

Tubs flicked off his headlights then stopped the car. We sat there, eyes adjusting to the dark.

'He's here?'

'Be down the back.'

'Where are we?'

'Fuck me,' Tubs said. When I faced him he was gazing at me, mouth open a little. 'When you dumped your old man you really did put everythin' behind you, ay? You ever think about us lot at all?'

'I didn't dump Dad. And I don't need a lecture.' I opened the door.

'Ian.'

I looked back.

'Quietly,' he said.

I got out and closed the door quietly. Tubs did the same, then came round to my side of the car with a torch. There was a big sign up ahead to the left. Tubs pointed the torch, flicked it on. Aston Kennels, the sign said. The torch went out; we were in darkness again.

'Know it now?' Tubs asked softly.

'Doug Aston's place?'

'The very same.'

Doug Aston was one of the big Stow trainers. Successful, but his dogs had a reputation for not always trying. Dad used to take me out to different kennels most Sundays, the day the owners generally came round to check on their dogs. He'd chat to the trainers and the owners, keeping up with the goss; we'd spend more time at the bigger kennels, and that meant we spent a lot of Sunday mornings out at Doug Aston's. Him and Dad got along well. But until Tubs had shone his torch at the sign, I hadn't even recognized the place. God, the amount of my life I'd put behind me.

Now Tubs signalled me on with his torch; we went down the side-lane. He whispered over his shoulder, telling me how Doug Aston was away on holiday. 'But I hear he's got short-term help. Remember the shack behind the kennels?'

I made a sound.

'Ten quid Pike's there,' Tubs said.

I reached forward and put a hand on his shoulder. He turned round.

'Tubs, am I trespassing on someone's property in the middle of the night just on the off-chance?'

After a moment he said, 'Yeah.' His head went up and down. 'Yeah, that's what you're doin'. You know why? Because you asked me to help you find this pillock, that's why. You asked me. If you wanna go home, just say so, because this isn't my idea of a good time. Now, do you wanna go home?'

'It was only a question, Tubs.'

'Do you wanna?'

The abruptness surprised me. 'No,' I said, getting a bit pissed off myself. 'No I don't.'

'Settled then,' he said, turning and heading on down towards the kennels. Half a minute later, when he heard me following, he whispered back. 'Hey, Ian.'

'Yeah?'

'Sometimes you're just a big girl's blouse.'

A peace offering. I pushed him in the back and he snorted, laughing quietly.

The kennels were back maybe a hundred yards from

the house. As we walked, Tubs told me what he'd heard at the track down in Wimbledon earlier that night. He'd been drinking with one of the owners after the last race, the bloke mentioned Doug Aston being on holiday. Tubs'd pricked up his ears when the owner said the man Doug left looking after the place kept ducking out of sight whenever anyone came. The owner told Tubs all he ever saw of the guy was the flash of red hair as he disappeared.

'Then I remembered,' Tubs said now. 'Didn't Pike used to work for Doug Aston way back?'

Nodding, I almost walked straight into Tubs as he stopped.

'Up there,' he said.

The kennels were lined up like army barracks, one long low block after another. There were more than I remembered; Doug Aston must have been doing okay.

'The shack's in the middle,' Tubs said. 'Fuck knows how we get past the dogs.'

'I've got a question.'

Tubs looked at me.

'If Eddie Pike's there, what do we do, arrest him?'

'You said you wanna speak to the guy.'

'I do—'

'Then we'll speak to him, Ian.' Tubs started forward again. 'Jesus.'

I went after him more carefully now; the last thing we wanted was to wake the dogs. The smell, that was another thing I'd nearly forgotten. Fifty or more dogs kennelled up and no matter how often the place was cleaned out, the smell of dog piss, food and detergent hung over everything. Not a bad smell, not if you were used to it. It reminded me of Dad and all those Sundays back when I was a kid. It got stronger as we went up the rise. Soon we were on a cement footpath that criss-crossed between the kennels.

You could hear some of the dogs snuffling now, whimpering a little, winning Derbys in their sleep. You could see the shack too, where Eddie might be, just thirty yards on.

Tubs turned to say something, missed his footing, and

stumbled off the path. A dog barked. Tubs froze. I stood still, holding my breath. One second, two, then another bark. Tubs swore and stumbled into the deep shadow by the kennel. The barking and yapping came from all directions then, the sound of paws scratching at the kennel doors. I dived after Tubs as a light came on in the shack.

'Fucked it,' Tubs said to me, apologizing.

Back pinned to the kennel wall, I watched the lit window of the shack. A head appeared and the window flew open.

'Shudup!' the bloke shouted. You couldn't see if it was Pike or not. 'Bloody mongrels. Shudup!'

The dogs kept right on with it, barking their brainless heads off. After a moment the window slammed shut and Tubs said to me, 'You reckon he'll come out?'

He took a step, then the light in the shack went out.

'Wait,' I said. 'If he sees us, he'll bolt.'

We huddled down, crouched in the shadow, the barking nearly deafening now, the dogs going frantic. A few seconds later another light came on in the shack.

'Is this gonna get any easier,' Tubs said. 'Waitin'? I mean, if there's a door out back, he could be boltin' right now.'

I looked at the light in the window. It made sense what Tubs said, we could be missing our chance staying put. I stood and headed off along the wall, Tubs right behind.

At the end of the kennel block we paused again. There was twenty yards of open ground to the shack door.

'Ready?' I said.

Tubs nodded, puffing like he'd already done five miles.

I pushed off the wall, stepped out from the kennels and only got five yards before I was hit fair in the eyes by the light. Blinded, I put a hand to my eyes, swearing. The dogs went quiet for a second, surprised by the sudden blast of daylight.

'Fuckin' security light,' Tubs said. He grabbed my arm and hauled me on to the shack. Now the dogs went absolutely berserk.

'Hang on.'

'Let's just do it,' he said.

I blinked, my eyes refocusing. Tubs let go my arm and grabbed the doorhandle. The door was locked.

'Pike!' he shouted.

I said, 'He's not going to open it.'

'Right.' Tubs turned sideways on to the door. He gave one of the glass panels a sharp nudge with his torch, the broken glass went tinkling onto the floor inside. He reached through carefully; I heard the lock clunk. The door opened. He looked back at me. 'What if it isn't Pike?' he said.

Oh, excellent, I thought.

But before I could say anything we heard movement inside. Tubs shoved the door wide open and we went in. He flashed his torch up and down, found the light switch and hit it. An unfurnished room. Hanging from pegs on every wall there were muzzles and leashes, and between these a few old photos of dogs, some standing at the victory dais, others crossing the finishing line. On a bench at the back, a row of combs and brushes. Feed barrels along one wall.

'Pike?' I glanced at the open doors to the left and right. 'It's Ian Collier. I need to speak to you.'

No answer. Going through the door on the left, I hit the light, calling his name again. It was almost as bare as the first room, a big work-table in the centre and shelves lined with food supplements, pills and powders for the dogs and a pile of boots in the corner. No stairs, and no door out.

'Ian!'

I went back through the first room. Tubs'd taken the other door, I found him waiting for me in there. This room had furniture, a sofa and a couple of chairs. Standing behind the sofa, Tubs nodded to the rear. I went over. There was a kitchen out back, and when I stuck my head through I saw that the kitchen door was open.

'Shit.'

I crossed the kitchen and stepped outside and I knew straight off it was hopeless. Kennels then open ground, and every inch of it in darkness. If it was Pike we'd seen, he'd done a runner. And we weren't going to find him, not tonight.

Back inside Tubs was climbing the stairs, I went up after him.

'You think it was Pike?'

'It was Pike,' he said. 'We fuckin' blew it.'

The stairs went straight into an upstairs sitting room, a few armchairs and a king-sized TV. Another set of stairs went from there up into the loft. Tubs flicked through the old newspapers in the magazine rack.

'Should we be lookin' for somethin'?'

I told him something that proved I didn't kill Sebastian might be handy. He laughed and kept flipping through the papers. I went into the next room. A bedroom this one; two beds but only one of them had been used, the duvet was a crumpled heap on the floor. I glanced out the window just in time to see the path where we'd walked, and the kennels. Then the security light went out. The dogs paused in their barking.

'Ian, the yard light went off,' Tubs called from next door.

'Timer. It must be three minutes or something since we triggered it.'

The dogs howled again. Tubs opened a window and shouted at them to shut the fuck up.

Off the bedroom there was a small bathroom; it looked like it hadn't been cleaned for a while. There was a razor on the sink, and a can of shaving cream. Opening the mirrored door on the medicine cabinet, I found a squeezed tube of toothpaste, a toothbrush and a packet of dispirin. I went back to the bedroom. This was where we'd seen the first light come on, when Tubs set the dogs barking. Pike, or whoever it was, must have been sleeping. It was this window he'd thrown open to shout at the dogs. Then he'd gone next door. Turned that light on.

'Ian, you know anyone called Nigel Chambers?'

I stopped dead in my tracks. Tubs appeared in the doorway, thumbing a business card, turning it over, inspecting it.

'WardSure. That was Sebastian's company, right?'

Numbly I put out my hand. Tubs gave me the card. The WardSure name, address, phone and fax numbers were there and, in the middle of it all, 'Nigel Chambers, Associate Director', in golden letters. I sat down on the end of the unmade bed, held the card between my fingers and stared at it.

'Where was this?'

'Out there.' Tubs thumbed over his shoulder. 'Sittin' on the TV.'

I looked some more at the card. 'Tubs, when the guy stuck his head out the window, could you see him?'

'Same as you did.'

'His face?'

Tubs thought for a bit then shook his head. He pointed at the card. 'What are you thinkin', maybe it was this geezer?'

I shrugged. He asked me who Nigel Chambers was and I gave him a brief description.

'So he's got a house of his own. Why sleep here?'

'Had,' I corrected Tubs. 'Recently repossessed.'

Tubs pulled a face. He said I was being too fancy; the guy who'd bolted out the back door was Eddie Pike, he was sure of it. He screwed up his nose. 'I can smell the little bastard,' he said.

I flicked the card. 'Explain this.'

'I dunno.' He smiled. 'Maybe Eddie was applyin' for a job?'

A last look at the card then I pocketed it. I was lost. Again. If I poked around a bit more, I told myself, I might find a perfectly logical reason for Nigel Chambers's business card turning up in such an unlikely place, but as I got up off the bed I guess I knew in my heart of hearts that the whole thing was running right away from me. 2 a.m., and I was standing in a house we'd broken into; the guy who'd been there was gone. Nigel's card meant something but I didn't know what, and in the kennels outside the dogs were still going nuts.

'Look around,' I told Tubs, stepping past him.

'For what?'

Playing deaf, I went up the stairs to the loft.

There was a large trapdoor; I unbolted it and heaved it open. When it hit ninety degrees it locked into place, and I walked on up. A big room, windowless, the rafters all exposed. There was a piece of string dangling behind me; I tugged it and a single bulb lit up. Very dim. Cardboard boxes were piled along the edges of the loft where the rafters came down to the floor. Crouching, I went and opened a few, but it was just old clothes, back copies of the *Greyhound Life*, race cards and more dog photos. Other people's dreams. I backed out to where I could stand again, then carried on down the centre of the room. The light from that bulb hardly reached to the far wall, and by the time I got to the bits and pieces of furniture down there I was straining my eyes to see. Half a dozen chairs, some kind of desk, and a few framed pictures stacked together and propped further back against a rafter. Other people's junk. I reached over to the desk and tried to open the drawers but they were locked. When I ran my hand over the locks, I couldn't find a key. Then my foot touched something; there was a metallic clinking sound. I bent and picked up the slim wooden box. The lid opened on a hinge; I turned the box to catch the light behind me. Knives and forks. I took out one knife; the blade and handle were both a dull silver colour, and heavy. The handle thickened at the bottom into some kind of crest, onion-shaped, imitation rich man's cutlery. I dropped it back in the box.

Hopeless. Wiping my hands together I returned to the stairs. I'd had enough. In a few hours I was due in court. I'd speak to Clive Wainwright in the morning, but in the meantime I just had to get some sleep. I pulled the trapdoor closed after me, bolted it, then went to fetch Tubs.

He was sitting on the unused bed, feet up, browsing through a girlie magazine. The cover girl was smiling, hands cupped under an enormous pair of knockers.

'Let's go,' I said.

He swung his legs down to the floor saying, 'I found this under the mattress. You still gonna tell me it wasn't Pike?'

'Right now I don't give a toss.'

'Ian.' When I looked back, he dropped the girlie mag and picked up a big white envelope from the side table. He handed it to me. 'I found this under the mattress too,' he said.

I asked him what it was but he didn't answer, just nodded to the envelope.

I turned the thing up, jiggling it by one corner. The edge of a photo appeared. Colour. I pulled it right out and some negatives came along with it. When the negatives hit the floor, Tubs scooped them up and he leant back studying them, holding them up to the light.

He said, 'Sebastian looks like he's enjoyin' himself.'

Staring at the enlarged photo, it was my turn not to answer. I was stunned, completely gobsmacked, I felt like I'd been knocked out on my feet. This was a different league to Nigel's business card. I just couldn't take my eyes off the picture. A bed and two naked people, one of them Sebastian. They were going at it hard. Sebastian had hold of the woman's ribcage; his eyes were closed, the muscles of his neck standing out; you could see he was pumping for all he was worth. And underneath him the woman, her head tilted back, mouth open, her lips pulled back over her teeth like she might be in pain, but you knew that she wasn't.

Eyes still on the photo, I reached behind me, feeling for the bed. Then I sat down. I slid my fingers up into my hair and squeezed. I wasn't dreaming.

I heard Tubs say, 'Don't s'pose you know the tart.'

If only, I thought. The mane of blonde hair and the bright red lipstick, and the firm tits that I saw now were a little lopsided. Oh yes, I knew the tart all right. The tart was a colleague of mine. Her name was Justine Mortlake.

8

For a long time Clive Wainwright gazed at the photo, not even touching it. He just left it where I'd put it, on his desk. Finally he said, 'What do you want me to do?' Then he looked up. 'Has Allen seen this?'

'No.'

'Planning to show him?'

'Oh, sure. Allen, I've got a great snap of your daughter being shafted by a mate of yours. Wanna see?'

Clive gave me a pained look. He went to his filing cabinet, started digging in there.

After Tubs dropped me back to my flat at 3 a.m., I'd slept for four hours, but badly. And over breakfast Katy was on at me about Fielding, telling me I should file a complaint with the Police Commissioner or the ombudsman or someone. When I told her to put a sock in it she got the hump and wouldn't make the tea. And now Clive's reaction to the photo; it wasn't shaping up to be a great day.

I said, 'I thought you might handle it.'

He took a folder from the cabinet. 'Why?' he asked.

I mumbled something about him being a solicitor.

Coming back to the desk, he said, 'Currently working on behalf of the Mortlake Group. And do you know what'll happen if I take that—' he pointed at the photo – 'to Allen?' He dropped the folder on the desk. 'He'll thank me very much, tell me I did absolutely the right thing, and once the Ottoman case is over he'll never speak to me again. I'll lose a client.'

'I don't think so.'

'No?' He put a finger on the photo and pushed it slowly across the desk back to me. 'Then you show him?'

Stalemate. My stocks with Allen had already taken a battering; I read this the same way as Clive. With a photo like that, Allen wouldn't hesitate to shoot the messenger.

'Look,' Clive said. 'I'm not saying it isn't important. I just think it might be best if we put it to one side for the time being. Finish the Ottoman case first; after that take it up with Justine.'

'I can't wait.'

'You can wait.'

'No,' I said. 'I can't.'

He started speaking again but I cut him off.

'It isn't just the photo.' I rested my forearms on the table, interlaced my fingers and looked up at him. 'Clive, I'm a whisker away from being done for Sebastian's murder. I think I might need a lawyer.'

He stared at me a second then shook his head. He laughed nervously. 'You? What, you just up and killed Sebastian? Run that by me again.'

He wanted it to be a joke, but some lawyer's instinct seemed to tell him straight away that it wasn't. Or maybe it was just the look on my face. At that moment, admitting it out loud like that, after the night I'd had, I honestly felt like death.

His nervous laughter faded. He sat down as I started to speak.

'There's this cop,' I said, 'Fielding,' and then I cranked out the story, the whole stupid thing, starting with the hoax kidnap, then what Lee Chan had dug up on Mehmet. I told him about how I'd seen Nigel Chambers with Mehmet out at the airport, and how we'd found Nigel's business card at the kennels. Clive interrupted a bit, getting the details straight, asking who Tubs was, stuff like that. When I told him about Fielding's visit to my flat the day before, and the tapes, he cocked his head.

'So what was on the tapes?'

'Fires,' I said.

His eyes narrowed. Please don't tell me, he said, that you're a pyromaniac.

'Back when my parents died,' I explained, avoiding his eyes, 'I started making tapes.'

'Why?'

I shrugged. Clive waited.

'Okay, I saw a shrink,' I told him. 'You know, when my parents died I was there, I saw the fire. The shrink said I wasn't facing up to something. Maybe the fire, I don't know. I started taping fires off the TV.'

'That helped?'

'Not really.'

Until then he'd been pretty matter-of-fact, professional, but the news about the tapes, I think it shook him. He shifted in his chair, his look changed too, like he was thinking maybe I wasn't quite the bloke he'd thought I was. I had an awful feeling that he was actually considering the possibility that I'd done it, killed Sebastian Ward.

'Then last night,' I said, laying a hand on the photo, 'this turns up.'

'While you were trying to get your hands on Pike.'

'Fielding was trying to stitch us up together. I had to speak to Pike.'

'Had to?' Clive clamped a hand to his forehead. 'Ian, from what you're saying, you are so far up shit creek it doesn't matter. Have you been hearing yourself?'

He got to his feet, and came round his desk, reciting a list of laws I'd managed to break out at Aston's Kennels. I lost track somewhere around number five.

'And now,' he said, wrapping up, 'now you come to a lawyer? Ian, you're a bright boy. What in God's name has been going through your head?'

'I didn't set out to break the law.'

'No? Then what?'

He was waiting for an answer but I really didn't have one to offer him.

I said, 'It just seemed to happen, all right?'

Clive gave a choked sound. 'If you end up in court, Ian, "just seemed to happen" isn't going to impress anyone.'

He looked at the clock. 'Speaking of which, Ottoman's up in twenty minutes.'

He picked the folder off his desk, asking if I wanted to share a taxi.

I put a finger on the photo. Sebastian and Justine frozen like that forever. 'What about this?'

Clive made a gesture, slipping something imaginary into his breast pocket. 'Somewhere safe,' he said, going to the door. 'It's yours.' Glancing back at me, he added some advice. 'If I was you I'd think twice before showing it around.'

The taxi set us down across from the court with five minutes to spare. Clive had spent the ride over studying his notes, preparing for the session ahead. But he was distracted, that was obvious. What I'd shown and told him had thrown a new light on Ottoman's claim. The only problem was it was a murky light: without digging deeper it was impossible to say which side it was going to help, us or Mehmet.

As we crossed the road, Clive said, 'Any ideas on why you think Sebastian was murdered?'

'Hundreds.'

'Prime suspects?'

'Dozens.'

'You're thinking maybe Mehmet, aren't you?'

I said yes, that possibility had occurred to me. When Clive frowned, I asked what was on his mind.

'Among other things?' He stepped up onto the pavement and paused by the revolving doors. 'You're in the witness seat tomorrow. If the Ottoman people get a whiff of what's been going on with you the last few days, they'll take your head off. What's on my mind?' He pushed the revolving door. 'You, Ian. You're on my mind.'

Inside, the security guard was waiting by the walk-through metal detector so I buttoned my lip. There wasn't much I could have said to defend myself anyway; I guess I just hadn't thought how what I'd done might affect our

228

case. That seemed to have been my problem right from the off.

In the courtroom the usual faces were all there, the Ottoman barristers and solicitors in confab on the far side of the room. Down the front, Batri and his second, both wigged and gowned, were sharing a joke. Behind them one of Clive Wainwright's junior colleagues was busy with a portable PC. It was meant to be for the trial transcript – as the court stenographer typed, the words appeared on the screens – but just now the young solicitor had hijacked it for a game of solitaire. He finished the game the instant he saw Clive. I was relieved to see that Fielding hadn't come.

But Bill Tyler was there, sitting at the back reading a paper. While Clive went for a word with Batri, I pulled up a chair beside Bill. He turned a page and kept reading.

'How's Action Man?' he said.

I remarked that for a bloke just about to go into the witness seat, he seemed pretty relaxed.

'Ahha.' He folded the paper and put it aside. 'Long as they don't shoot me, I figure I'll be all right.'

'Batri take you through it?'

He nodded. 'Yesterday.' Then he faced me, cupping a hand against his cheek and dropping his voice. 'Listen, I went round your place this morning, I had something for you.' When I looked puzzled, he said, 'From the lads. We got a bonus for not sending Mortlake's ransom money up the spout. The lads wanted to cut you in.'

It took a second to understand. When I did I felt ridiculously touched, and embarrassed too, a complete phoney. I dropped my gaze to the desk.

'You got three grand,' he said.

'I don't want it. It's their bonus, I didn't do anything.'

'What's your problem? Three grand. They cut you in. That's it.'

I raised my eyes just in time to see Wainwright beckoning Bill down to the front for a final word before the judge arrived. Bill got to his feet, laying a hand on my shoulder.

'Cash money, I gave the bag to your sister. The lads

wanted you to have it, Ian. Don't be an idiot.'

I told him again I didn't want it, and he shrugged then strolled down to the front, buttoning up his blazer, looking confident. A man's man. Three grand. From blokes that needed it – and certainly deserved it – far more than me.

The judge arrived, settled himself on the bench, and Batri rose to get started with Bill. Clive came back to sit with me and I tried to put the lads and the bonus out of my mind.

There was a quick run through Bill's army career, concluding with his entry into the SAS. Batri pointed out that there was a blank on Bill's CV over this five-year period. 'For the obvious reasons, it would be fair to say,' he added, 'that security was a major preoccupation of Mr Tyler's during this time.' That got an approving nod from the judge and a bored look from Batri's opposite number.

Batri went on to a brief question and answer about Bill Tyler's move into civilian life, the special licences he retained, and the work undertaken by Tyler Associates relating to security. From beginning to end it only took five minutes, but when Batri sat down he'd established Bill as about as good an expert witness on security as you could possibly get. And the judge had already seen Bill's report on the Ottoman hangar in Izmir. The young solicitor, Clive's colleague, smiled at me behind Clive's back.

Then the Ottoman barrister rose, clearing his throat.

'Mr Tyler, would you say your career post-SAS has taught you anything?'

'I'm sorry?'

'Have you learnt anything in the past years?'

'I hope so.'

'Yes, you might hope so, Mr Tyler. But my question was have you?'

Bill grinned crookedly. He'd done the expert witness bit before, he was used to the game.

'Yes,' he said, 'I have.'

'And your work in the private sector, perhaps you could

tell us a little about what it entails.'

'Tyler Associates does mainly corporate work. A company wants its security arrangements looked at, maybe beefed up, they come to us. We do a plan for them, sometimes make some suggestions on the hardware – locks, alarms – and if they want we can offer them a service contract—'

'For the alarm systems?'

'Whatever they want. Sweeping a boardroom for bugs; supplying security people for special occasions.' Bill opened one hand. 'Whatever they want.'

'And if they want you to gather intelligence on another company?'

Bill shook his head. The barrister pointed at the microphones hanging from the ceiling.

'No,' Bill said. 'We do security, period. Purely defensive systems.'

'Mr Tyler, have you heard the expression, "attack is the best form of defence"?'

'My lord,' Batri said, rising. 'My learned friend has been answered on the point.'

'Quite,' the judge said, agreeing. He circled a finger in the air. 'Move on, please.'

Batri sat down. The other barrister leant forward on his lectern.

'Since going into the private sector, Mr Tyler, would I be right in saying that the range of your work has expanded?'

'The company's growing.'

'Has the range of your work expanded?'

'Yes.'

'And the tools of your trade. Electronics. Computers. Would it be correct to say that technological advances have changed your business profoundly?'

'Yes.'

'Over five or six years say, almost changed out of recognition.' The barrister smiled and gestured to the stenographer, tapping away at her PC keyboard. 'Just like here,' he said. 'Would that be right?'

'You could say that.'

'Do you say it, Mr Tyler?'

Bill shrugged like it wasn't important. 'Yes.'

'And prior to joining the SAS – correct me if I'm wrong – you were in a specialist artillery unit?'

'Correct.'

'So the situation is, that your pre-SAS career had nothing to do with security, your SAS career is a blank as far as this court is concerned, and post-SAS you have only six years experience during which the nature of work has changed so much as to render the first few of those years, as regards security expertise, redundant.'

Bill puzzled that one out for a second. 'You're saying I don't know my job?'

'I'm pointing out that quite apart from the glaring five-year lacuna in your CV, your security experience may be thinner than it looks.'

'Excuse me,' the judge said, squinting at the Ottoman barrister. The barrister turned to him, surprised. 'The details of Mr Tyler's career in the SAS are covered by privilege,' the judge went on. 'The court accepts that privilege. It hardly seems fair or appropriate to be referring to Mr Tyler's period of service with them as a lacuna.'

I whispered to Clive, 'What's a lacuna?'

'Gap in the argument,' he whispered back. 'Missing link in the chain.'

Up front the Ottoman barrister tried to protest, but the judge cut him off again.

'Please desist,' the judge told him, 'from trying to score cheap points off an honourable record of service.'

Clive whispered to me, 'Who needs Batri?'

A scribbled message went from the Ottoman solicitors to the assisting barrister, who handed it on to his partner, the one who'd just got the dressing-down. He screwed it up and dropped it on the desk.

'If I can refer my lord to bundle sixteen,' he said, 'perhaps we can move straight on to Mr Tyler's report.'

Clive had a hand over his mouth, trying not to gloat.

Ottoman's team had obviously decided that the judge was so biased in Bill's favour that more questions about experience, expertise and the usual guff just weren't going to help them at all. Clive had a copy of Bill's report in front of him; he opened it. Up on his bench, the judge did the same.

'The aircraft in question,' the Ottoman barrister said, 'was one of a fleet of twelve being run by Ottoman Air at the time. And you went out to Izmir, Mr Tyler, shortly after the plane was stolen?'

'Straight away.'

'Hours later?'

'A few days,' Bill said. 'I flew out with the loss adjustor.'

'Yes, tell us about that. The loss adjustor asked you to accompany him?'

'Mr Mortlake arranged for me to go.'

'With the loss adjustor?'

'Yes.'

'Rather odd, didn't you think?' Before Bill could answer, the barrister went on, 'I mean, Ottoman Air notified WardSure immediately the plane was stolen and WardSure notified the lead underwriter, the Mortlake Group. All well and proper so far. But then, in the normal course of things, wouldn't the procedure have been for the Mortlake Group to send in a loss adjustor to make an initial assessment? Find out what had happened?'

'The plane was stolen. Everyone knew what had happened.'

'No they didn't, Mr Tyler. Not the details. Not how it was stolen, for instance.'

Bill folded his arms, but didn't say anything.

'The Mortlake Group received the Ottoman claim, and they didn't wait for the loss adjustor's report, they sent you straight in. You hadn't done any security work for Ottoman Air had you?'

'No.'

'You weren't familiar with their security arrangements?'

'No.'

'Then why did they send you?'

'To see what went wrong. Give the loss adjustor a hand.'

'They didn't trust him by himself?'

'If they hadn't trusted him,' Bill said, 'they wouldn't have hired him. I went strictly to look at Ottoman's security. To see what went wrong.'

The barrister joined his hands behind his back, swaying forward. 'Precipitate, don't you think?'

Bill hesitated. He knew this was building up to something but he couldn't see what. He answered a little warily.

'I don't think so.'

'Mr Tyler, when you flew to Izmir the circumstances surrounding the theft of Ottoman's plane were as much a mystery to you as they were to the Mortlake Group. We know that, because the only man who could have enlightened you, the loss adjustor, the man whose report would give the detail necessary to decide if your advice was even needed, he was sitting beside you on the plane.'

'I don't see your point.'

'Don't you? Let me put it like this. How soon in the piece did it occur to you that the Mortlake Group was going to challenge Ottoman Air's claim?'

Bill's look hardened. 'I'm not party to Mortlake's decisions.'

'Please answer the question, Mr Tyler.'

'I don't recall exactly.' When the barrister stayed silent, waiting, Bill added, 'I suppose it was when Allen Mortlake told me to do a full report.'

'No earlier?'

Bill looked up to the judge. 'Like I said, I'm not party to their decisions. What the underwriter does, that's their business. I just do what they contract me for.'

'I put it to you,' the barrister interrupted firmly, 'that the only reason you were on that plane to Izmir with the loss adjustor was because the Mortlake Group had already decided, prior to gathering any evidence, that the legitimate claim of Ottoman Air was going to be denied. From that day, before you had even glimpsed the security arrangements in Izmir, you knew that you were preparing to end up here, in this court.'

Half-rising, Batri said, 'My lord, does my learned friend have a question he wishes to ask?'

The Ottoman barrister offered to rephrase, and Batri sat down.

'Didn't you know, from the moment the Mortlake Group hired you to accompany the loss adjustor, that Ottoman's claim was going to be denied?'

'No I didn't.'

'You didn't know that they'd already prejudged the claim?'

Bill unfolded his arms. 'You're saying they prejudged it. I never said that.'

The barrister went at it again, the same issue but from a different angle, banging away at the idea that Ottoman had got the rough end of the pineapple, that the Mortlake Group weren't interested in the rights and wrongs of the claim, that Allen Mortlake had made up his mind to fight them way back at the start. And through his questions, the barrister trailed Allen's motive for the fight, protecting his daughter's professional reputation. Bill turned a lot of the questions aside, saying that what happened within the Mortlake Group wasn't his affair. But whenever the questions returned to that business about him being sent out to Izmir so quickly, Bill's answers got more and more defensive.

Beside me, Clive doodled on his pad, the muscles in his jaw clenched hard. In all the pre-trial sessions we'd had on the Ottoman case, nobody had spotted this. Any one of us could have seen it, but the major responsibility for sending Bill into the firing line underprepared was Clive's. And he knew it. While Bill did his best up front, Clive kept his eyes on the pad.

After half an hour, the barrister had made his point in half a dozen different ways, then he saw the judge glance up at the clock.

'So, to move on.' The barrister twisted his wedding ring as he consulted his notes. 'You arrived in Izmir.' He looked up at Bill and smiled. 'Rather earlier than you might have been expected to, nevertheless you arrived. Did you begin your – what shall we call it? Preliminary investigation?'

'Call it what you like,' Bill said, and Clive looked up frowning.

Bill's irritation with the barrister was starting to surface, not a good sign.

'Did you begin your investigation immediately?'

'The same afternoon.'

The barrister gave a fake look of surprise. 'You had access to the Ottoman hangar?'

'Yes.'

'Immediately?'

'They faxed my passport details to Allen Mortlake. He confirmed who I was.'

'And the staff at Ottoman Air never obstructed you? They let you get straight on with your investigation?'

'Mr Mehmet came out to the airport. When he arrived, he took a look at the faxes, I think he rang Allen, then—'

'Allen Mortlake?'

'Yes. Then he told the Ottoman staff to show me what I wanted to see. Me and the loss adjustor both.'

'So the staff of Ottoman Air never obstructed you?'

'No.'

'Were they helpful?'

Bill thought about it a second. 'They didn't obstruct me. They were helpful enough.'

'Did that surprise you, Mr Tyler?'

Bill picked up a glass of water, eyes on the barrister. 'No,' he said flatly.

'I am going to refer you,' the barrister said, opening the Tyler Associates report, 'to page 72 of your own report. Bundle sixteen.' There was a pause while Bill and the judge both turned pages. 'Do you have it?'

'Yes.'

'Please read the second paragraph for us, Mr Tyler. Aloud, if you will.'

Bill glanced down the page for a second, then read, his

236

voice expressionless. 'In short, the general standard of security at Izmir Airport is low, in addition to which Ottoman Air itself has three major weaknesses. One, poor background checks on flight crews prior to employment, and lax monitoring procedures thereafter. Two, failure to render their aircraft inoperable during extended ground time. Three, failure to institute proper security checks, with clear assignations of duty and lines of responsibility among staff members.'

Bill looked up. The barrister rested an elbow on the lectern.

'On what basis did you reach these conclusions, Mr Tyler?'

'I called it how I saw it.'

'Yes—' the barrister looked pained – 'but that is just my question. How did you see it? How were you able to see it? You were in Izmir, what, four days? Assuming you're not psychic, how were you able, in such a short space of time, to discover, for example, what the monitoring procedures for the flight crews actually were?'

Bill saw where this one was headed. He moved uncomfortably in his chair.

'I was told.'

'By whom?'

'I don't remember the names.'

'Let's not be coy now, Mr Tyler. You were given the information, were you not, by the staff of Ottoman Air?'

'I don't see anything wrong with that.'

'Is the answer yes or no?'

Bill fixed him with a cold look. 'Yes.'

'And Mr Mehmet, the owner of Ottoman Air, even he gave you some of the information contained in your report. Is that right?'

'Yes.'

Clive had stopped doodling in his pad. He was watching Bill hard, like he was willing him through each question.

'Mr Tyler,' the barrister said, 'at any time in your four days in Izmir, the days immediately following the theft of the plane, did Mr Mehmet or his staff say or do anything at all that indicated to you they might have doubts about the legitimacy of their claim?'

Bill took quite a while with that. He glanced across to Batri before answering.

'No,' he said finally.

'In fact they gave you, who they knew to be in the employ of the underwriter, every assistance, didn't they?'

'They were helpful, okay?'

The barrister pressed on. 'So the situation is – is it not? – that the plane was stolen. Ottoman immediately notified WardSure, as per policy. The Ottoman Air staff, and the owner, were materially helpful to you in your investigation, and gave no indication that they expected their legitimate claim to be challenged. And the help they gave you is now central to your report, which is central to the Mortlake Group's case here today. I put it to you that actions here speak louder than words. Ottoman Air hid nothing because it had nothing to hide, but the Mortlake Group—'

'My Lord—' Batri broke in, but the other barrister talked over him.

'—the Mortlake Group, by precipitately employing you, showed a clear intent to deny a legitimate claim before examining one shred of evidence.'

'My Lord, I really must protest.'

There was a pause. Everyone looked up to the judge. He seemed to be weighing things up. Then, unexpectedly, it wasn't the judge but Bill who spoke.

'I'm not party to the Mortlake Group's decisions,' he said lamely.

Batri shot him a warning look, but it was too late. The judge leaned back, fingertips touching together beneath his chin, studying Bill Tyler. You could feel the change in mood through the court, that stock answer of Bill's hadn't gone down at all well this time. In fact it sounded just how the Ottoman barrister might have prayed for it to sound, hollow and self-serving. Beside me Clive had his head in his hands.

At last the judge made a note to himself, then nodded to the Ottoman barrister.

'I presume you have more questions for Mr Tyler.'

'Yes, my lord.'

The judge, for the first time in days, had lost his bored look. He gazed down at Bill. He rested a finger along one cheek.

'Let's not waste time then,' he said.

9

'Butchery,' Clive muttered as we came out at the lunchtime recess. 'They butchered him and Batri just sat there.'

While he was telling me this, he had a smile fixed on his face; you'd never have known how angry he was. When I told him I thought the last hour hadn't gone so badly, he barked a dry laugh.

Out in the men's room, we were alone. He dropped the smile then, and swore as he splashed his face with water.

Taking a leak, I said, 'I've had a rethink on Mehmet. I can't see what he had to gain, killing Sebastian.'

'Oh please,' Clive said.

When I turned, he was drying his hands on a paper towel. He glanced across at me.

'Not now, Ian. I've got a real case on my plate here, and it's turning into a stinker.'

'A real case? Clive, I've got a cop trying to fit me up with a murder.'

'So you said.'

He flicked the paper towel in the bin and faced the mirror. He smoothed down his hair. Zipping up, I went to the basin to wash my hands.

'What's that mean, So I said? You think I'm lying?'

'I don't think you're lying, all right?'

'Then how about some advice.'

'I don't have any.' He paused, reconsidering. 'Keep your head down, Ian. Now that's good lawyerly advice.'

While I soaped up my hands Clive braced himself against the next basin, arms locked. He stared at the mirror, a worried man. Keep my head down? Had he listened to a single word I'd said back there in his office?

Then he added, 'That'll be best all round. Don't stir the pot.'

And that's when I got it. Finally. He turned to go and I grabbed his arm.

'You're worried I'm going to mess up your case.'

He jerked his arm free and straightened his jacket. I'd hit the bull's-eye.

'I'm being stitched up for murder, and you're worried that me trying to protect myself is going to fuck up your case against Ottoman. Clive,' I said laughing, not quite believing it. 'Jesus, what is this?'

He looked past me.

'Talk to me,' I said.

And maybe he would have, but then the door opened. Bill Tyler came in.

As he wandered over to the pisser, Bill said, 'How'd I do?'

'Not too bad,' Clive told him. It must have just about choked him to say it, but there was no point in letting rip now. Bill still had another session to do in the witness seat, he needed his confidence intact.

'If that wanker in the wig comes in here,' Bill said, referring to the Ottoman barrister, 'I'll flush him.'

Frowning, Clive went to the door. He reminded Bill of the judge's instructions not to talk to anyone about the case, or his evidence, during the recess. Then Clive made his exit.

Bill looked at me, rolling his eyes. 'Fucking lawyers,' he said.

Out in the hall I ran into Angela. When she asked me how the morning went, I pulled a long face.

'That bad?'

'Worse, but don't tell Bill.' I glanced over my shoulder. 'Clive wants him in shape for after lunch.'

Angela took my arm and steered me outside onto the pavement. She said, 'I've tracked down your Name.'

For a moment I was lost. She saw that.

'Hello, Ian. The Name that sent that note. Bonfires and pig-sticking?' She pulled the note out of her bag. Clipped to one corner there was a scrap of paper with a name and address scrawled in Angela's handwriting. The name was Mr White. 'Seems like he's a farmer down in Kent,' she said, then added, 'Brentwell's in Kent, no?' We looked at each other. 'I wondered if I should tell Bill,' she said, considering the note, 'or just hand it over to the police.'

I took the note and re-read it. It was pretty much how I remembered it, threatening in an unhinged kind of way. But there was a bit I'd forgotten, it was that part that really leapt out at me now. *Sebastian Ward. I know him to be untrustworthy.*

I read it aloud to Angela. 'What's that mean? "I know him to be untrustworthy"?'

She put out her hand for the note. 'Ian, the man's talking about sticking people like pigs. Who cares who he says is untrustworthy? He's bonkers.'

Maybe, I thought. Probably, even. But what would Angela have said if I'd shown her the photo I had in my pocket? Sebastian, the Mortlake family's old friend, giving Justine the shaft. Sebastian and Justine might both have been grown-ups, but fifteen years earlier Sebastian had been giving Justine dolls to play with at Christmas time. An uncle figure in the Mortlake family. But somewhere along the way Sebastian had moved the relationship on, and I wondered what Angela would think of Sebastian if she knew.

I tore off a corner of the note and propped my foot against some railings. I started copying out Mr White's name and address, using my knee for a desk.

'Ian. What are you doing?'

I told her.

'I mean,' she said, 'what are you thinking of doing? With that address.'

I gave her back the note. 'As far as Bill's concerned, the kidnap's over; he's been paid, and that's the end of it.'

'Well, I'll give it to the police then.'

'You can,' I told her, 'but I can tell you right now, they won't be interested.' Angela looked sceptical, so I explained. 'If a note like that suddenly drops into their hands courtesy of the Mortlake Group, they'll think they're having sand chucked in their eyes.'

'By whom?'

'Me,' I said.

Angela gave me a sideways look like she thought I'd lost it, that maybe I'd cracked under the pressure of the kidnap business and the Ottoman case and everything. I was about to put her right when the Ottoman team came out of St Dunstan's, the solicitors and the two barristers, all smiles. As they walked by, the lead barrister, unwigged but still gowned, nodded to me. You could see in his eyes how he was looking forward to it, tomorrow, when I'd be in the witness seat. I nodded back, my heart sinking into my boots.

Once they were out of earshot, I said to Angela, 'The cops think I was involved with Sebastian's death.'

When I faced her again she was staring at me.

'One cop in particular,' I said.

'Why?' She got a worry-line straight up between her eyebrows. 'Involved with? Are they accusing you?'

'Not officially.' I studied Mr White's address. Care-of Horley Farm. 'Not yet,' I said.

When I looked up, she was still staring.

'In case you're wondering Angela, it's not true.'

She shook her head, saying that's not what she was thinking at all. 'Why've they picked on you?'

I told her it was a long story, not one I had the time for just then. I tried to cut the conversation off, get going, but Angela knew me too well. After twelve years on the 486 box together, she could read me like a book.

She said, 'My car's round the corner.'

'I'll get a taxi.'

'Not all the way to Kent you won't.' She turned on her heel. 'I'll drive, you talk. This one I really have to hear.'

★ ★ ★

Leaving out the photo, I told Angela the same story I'd told Clive Wainwright. She did what he'd done, asked a few questions, but mainly she just listened, weaving her car through the traffic. We were well down the Old Kent Road before I'd finished.

Angela was silent for a moment, then she said, 'So you think if I took Mr White's note and showed the police, they'd just think it was you trying to get them off your back.'

Yes, I told her. That's how I saw it.

She mulled that one over. Then she asked, 'If Mehmet's a crook, and Nigel Chambers is tied up with him and this Pike fellow, why do you want to pay a call on Mr White?'

I couldn't answer that one without either showing her the photo of Sebastian and her daughter, or lying. I chose to lie.

'I'd like to rule out all possibilities,' I said, 'before I point the finger at Mehmet.'

'It still doesn't add up.'

I lifted a hand. 'Angela, I'm in a boatload of trouble. Can't you humour me? Please?'

She wasn't completely satisfied, but she knew that I was serious. At least I'd convinced her that I honestly believed I was in a boatload of trouble. After giving me one last curious look, she drove on in silence and I pretended to sleep.

It turned out White's place was nowhere near Brentwell – in fact it was almost at the opposite end of the county. When we got to the nearby village, I had to go into the shop and get directions to Horley Farm. Giving me directions, the shopkeeper referred to it as White's old place.

About a mile outside the village, we found the turn. It was a gravel track bending back towards the village; you could see the church steeple jutting up from the hollow further on. Before the hollow there was a farmhouse; the sign on the open gate said Horley Farm.

I went to the door and pulled the bell-lever. The

farmhouse was three storeys, old red brick, something out of one of those country magazines. Angela watched me from the car.

A young woman opened the door, a child perched on her hip. I explained that I was after Mr White.

'He moved,' she said, pointing past me. 'Down the hill on your right. It's the only place before the church.'

Before I could ask any questions, she closed the door. I went back to the car.

The track got rougher as we went down the hill; the winter rain seemed to have washed most of it away. It was all open fields, sheep wandering down the track in front of us, but we still almost managed to miss the place. We thought it was a shed or a barn or something, but there was no other building between us and the church.

We pulled up and looked at it.

At last Angela said, 'Where's the door?'

Shaking my head, I got out and went to see. Around the back of the building I surprised some more sheep; they scattered. In the middle of the building, there was a door. I stepped back and whistled to Angela, beckoning her over.

Then someone said, 'Hello?' and I spun round. An old man looked at me through the open window about three feet away. I saw him take in my suit and tie; his look changed.

'If you're from the bailiffs, you can ruddywell—'

'No, we're not. We're looking for a Mr White.'

'Jehovah's Witnesses?'

'No.' It looked like he was going to close the window anyway, so I asked him straight out, 'Are you Mr White?'

He nodded. 'Who's with you?' he said.

'I'm Ian Collier.' I gestured to Angela as she came up. 'This is Angela Mortlake.'

He repeated Angela's surname, looking her over as she said hello. It seemed like he'd heard the name before but couldn't quite remember where. He peered at us through the window.

Angela took the bull by the horns. 'Mr White, you

might not recall this, but some time ago—' she fished in her bag and pulled out the note, holding it up – 'you sent us this.'

When he squinted, she held the note closer. He recognized it and his face changed again. His mouth opened but no sound came out.

'It is yours, isn't it?' Angela said.

As he pulled the window to, he said quietly, 'I'll get the door.'

Angela turned to me, eyebrows raised.

I said, 'You don't suppose he's got a gun in there.'

She told me not to be such a drama queen, but I noticed she stayed safely behind me as we walked across to the door. Standing there on the doorstep, waiting, I got a feeling of what it must be like for the cops when they go doorknocking on drug crazies. Maybe the door opens and everyone inside is completely zonked. Maybe the door opens and you get your head blown off. All the possibilities in between.

The door opened. Mr White had a kettle in his hand.

'You'd better come in then,' he said.

The room we walked into was a combined living area and kitchen, the ceiling was so low I had to duck under the light. There was a gas stove by the sink. When Mr White asked if we wanted tea we turned the offer down, but he lit a gas ring anyway and put the kettle on. His back turned to us now, he shuffled plates in the sink. Angela looked at me.

'Mr White,' I said, 'that note you sent—'

'You're from Lloyd's.'

'Yes.'

'Both of you?'

'We're underwriters with the Mortlake Group,' Angela said. 'That note—'

'Some fellow from the hardship committee came to see me,' he said, facing us. 'I told him to sod off.'

'We're not here about your losses.' I took the note from Angela and went and handed it to him.

Without reading it, he crumpled it into a ball in his fist.

'I wasn't well,' he said. He tried to look me in the eye but couldn't quite manage it. It was obvious that he was ashamed of what he'd written.

I started to say something about not wanting to reopen old wounds, but he cut me off.

'Mortlake.' He nodded to Angela. 'That's you?'

'My husband founded the managing agency.'

'Which syndicates?'

Angela rattled off the numbers. Mr White thought for a while.

'I wasn't in any of those.' He looked from her back to me, wary now. 'What do you want?'

'You mentioned Sebastian Ward in your note. Did you know him?'

'Unfortunately.'

'Did you know he died?'

White nodded. 'Bloody thief. He ended up with an obituary in the *Times*, did you see that? Bloody thief the man was.'

'What did he do?'

Mr White ignored my question; just thinking about Sebastian was turning his face red. He shifted his weight from foot to foot, then he reached across and flicked off the gas.

'We'll walk,' he said.

'It won't take that long,' I told him. 'Just a few questions, then we're gone.'

'We'll walk,' he repeated going across to the door and opening it. 'I've made a mistake. I really don't think I want you people in my house.'

Angela stiffened; she made a sound like she'd been jabbed in the ribs. For a second I thought she was going to let rip at him and tell him what she thought of Names who wouldn't take their losses on the chin. But in the end she kept control of herself.

White brought a walking stick; he leant his weight on it as we walked down the hill.

Trying to get things back to where they were before Sebastian's name came up, I said, 'Nice spot here.'

He grunted. He said Horley Farm was mentioned in the Domesday Book. Walking between us, he bent over, leaning to the left, and I had the impression maybe he'd had a stroke sometime. Behind his back, Angela gestured at me to get on with it.

'You saw the farmhouse?' he asked me. I nodded, wondering how to get back to the note. He said, 'My wife was born there. She'd still be there now if it weren't for you lot.'

'With respect,' Angela cut in, annoyed, 'you weren't on any of our syndicates, Mr White. It's hardly fair to blame us.'

White's jaw set hard at that. I shot Angela a look but the damage was already done. He clamped up; he wouldn't answer my questions. In fact he wouldn't speak to us until we were right down by the churchyard wall. Resting against the wall, he reached into his pocket and pulled out a knife. He handed it to me.

'Would you be so kind,' he said, 'as to cut me some of those?'

He pointed to a cluster of white flowers growing near the wall further along. Christ Almighty, I thought. Help the aged, or what? But I went and cut a bunch of them. When I came back I gave him the flowers and the knife, and he thanked me. Now or never, I thought.

'Mr White, since Sebastian Ward died we've run into a few problems connected with either him or his company. You seem to think he wasn't trustworthy. Can you say why?'

He studied the flowers, then lifted his eyes, looking up the hill. You could see Angela's car parked by his shack, and further up the hill the farmhouse that he'd been forced to sell because of his disastrous investment in Lloyd's. He pointed his stick up that way.

'We had some statuary in the garden,' he said, and I thought I'd lost him. Behind me Angela muttered, 'Let's go.' But then White went on, 'Figures, you know. Diana the Huntress, wood nymphs, that kind of thing. Must be, what, twenty years ago? We'd had a burglary the year before and the insurers made the claim difficult for us. Different story. Anyway we weren't happy with our insurers; we thought we'd get a few other quotes. Picked them out of the phone book, half a dozen of them.'

He went quiet, remembering, and I said, 'WardSure was one of them?'

He gave a lopsided smile. 'My wife liked the name.'

'And they insured you?'

'God no,' he said. 'That Ward came out two or three times, trying to get the business. Wouldn't take no for an answer, bloody man.'

Angela said, 'That makes him persistent, not untrustworthy, Mr White.'

'Mrs Mortlake, what some people call persistence, others think of as bad manners.' He nipped off the flower-stems with his fingers.

Angela looked at me like, Can you believe this guy?

She was no soft touch, I knew that, but I thought she was being a little too hard on the old bugger. Considering what Lloyd's had cost him, he was treating us pretty okay.

'It wasn't just his manners,' he said, pushing off the wall and heading for the churchyard gate. 'He made us an offer.'

'Sebastian was a broker,' Angela said. 'That was his job.'

White went on to the gateway, then he turned and looked Angela straight in the eye. 'Ward offered to insure our statuary for eight thousand pounds. He implied that he could arrange a special service. Do you know what that service was?' He paused, but Angela didn't reply. 'It was this, Mrs Mortlake. He would arrange private purchasers for the statuary. The statuary would be removed, and we would file a claim. Mr Ward would approve the insurance payout. The eight thousand pounds from the insurance was to be added to whatever he got from the sale of the statuary, and everything was to be divided between us. Tell me,' he said, 'was that part of his job?'

Angela looked appalled. I was pretty stunned myself.

I said, 'He offered to go partners in an insurance scam?'

But before White could answer, Angela said, 'I don't believe it.'

Ignoring her, White said to me, 'When those Lloyd's losses started coming in, I took a more active interest in where our money was disappearing to. When I found out that Sebastian Ward was a Lloyd's broker, well – I told my agent to get me out.'

'Sebastian wasn't running a syndicate,' I said.

'He was there. Lloyd's let him in, the barrel was rotten.'

Angela looked sceptical. 'And did you report him when he made you that offer?'

White said he wished he had done now, but at the time it happened he was harvesting, rushed off his feet. 'In the end I just sent him packing with a flea in his ear.'

Angela said, 'You've got no evidence for this accusation then, have you.'

'Angela,' I said. A blind man could have seen White wasn't lying: she was pushing the old bugger way too hard.

'Sebastian might be dead,' she told me, 'but that doesn't give anyone the right to walk all over his reputation.'

'Are you suggesting I made this up?' White asked, annoyed.

'It was twenty years ago,' Angela said to him. 'Memories aren't always perfect.'

'It happened in just the way I said.'

She nodded, making it obvious she was humouring him. She told me, 'I'll see you back at the car.'

'You are an impertinent woman,' White said.

Beneath her breath she muttered, 'Bloody old fool.'

His hand shot up, flinging the bunch of flowers in Angela's face. She stepped back and stumbled, falling heavily against the gatepost. Her head hit the wood with a sickening thud and she cried out. But she grabbed at the gate and stayed on her feet. It was all over in a second.

I stepped between her and White. Me versus an old man with a walking stick.

His eyes clouded. I thought it was anger, but then he said, 'Sorry,' and reached out to help her. 'I'm so sorry.'

Pathetic really, he was close to tears.

'I'm okay,' Angela said, brushing my hand off. She touched the back of her head, wincing, but there was no sign of blood. 'Let's just go.'

She pushed away from the gate and started up the hill. White called out another apology, but Angela was just too pissed off to answer.

'She's fine,' I assured him.

Watching her stomp away, he still seemed to be trying to figure it out, why he'd done it. He said quietly, 'She called me a liar.'

Thinking it might help, I explained that Sebastian Ward was a family friend of the Mortlakes. White nodded, not really with it. Finally he bent, leaning on his stick, but he couldn't quite reach the flowers. It really was pathetic. I gathered them up quickly and handed them to him and he picked bits of dirt off the petals.

I watched Angela marching up the hill. What the hell had gotten into her, provoking the old bugger like that?

'There's nothing wrong with my memory,' he said, turning to the churchyard gate. 'Ward made that offer.'

When I opened the gate for him he went through and immediately stepped off the path by a gravestone. I remembered that note. It gave me a queasy feeling deep in my gut when I realized what he was doing. The poor old bugger had come down to visit his wife.

'You will tell Mrs Mortlake I'm sorry,' he said, looking over to me from the grave.

Closing the gate, I turned and set off up the hill.

Angela was leaning against the bonnet when I got up there, her hands locked behind her head.

'Are you all right?'

'I'll live.'

'Did you have to go at him like that?'

She rolled round, facing me across the bonnet. She looked at me like I was nuts.

'Angela, he didn't mean for you to crack your head.'

'Oh well, that makes me feel a whole lot better.' She

252

unlocked her hands, tipping her head gently from side to side.

'And I think he's telling the truth about Sebastian.'

She scoffed.

'Seriously,' I said.

She rested her hands on the bonnet. She reminded me that White had been wiped out by Lloyd's, and she reminded me of that note. 'He wants revenge, Ian.'

'Against a dead man?'

'You invited him to tramp all over Sebastian's reputation. What was he going to do, pass up the opportunity?' Wincing, she reached up and rubbed her neck.

I asked her again if she was okay.

'Fine,' she said. 'Are you finished here?'

I looked down the hill. Old man White was still in the churchyard. What he'd said about Sebastian – and that photo in my pocket, and Nigel telling me Sebastian was involved with the Ottoman slip – well I was starting to see a few things in a different light. But how to tell Angela?

I said, 'Remember when Sebastian took me to lunch that time? It was just before you went into hospital.'

'Does this have anything to do with anything?'

'Did he mention it to you and Allen later?'

No, she said. She asked me what I was driving at.

'I'm not sure.' What I really wasn't sure about was how to say it. During that lunch Sebastian had asked me some pretty strange questions. Hypotheticals, like, Say if this proposition was put to you, how would you react? At the time I'd thought he was testing me out for Allen, giving my integrity the once-over in the lead-up to my promotion. But now, having heard Mr White – and everything else – well I just wasn't sure any more. Couldn't all those strange questions have been testing me out for something else? Finally I said, 'If Sebastian used to pull this scam with statuaries, what's to say he hadn't graduated to planes?'

'Oh, come on.' Angela nodded wearily down towards the churchyard. 'Some twisted old so-and-so spins you a line, and you're just going to buy it, Ian? It's preposterous. You're acting like you never knew Sebastian.'

'I'm not sure that I did.'

'What?'

'Nigel Chambers reckons WardSure was already in trouble businesswise before Sebastian died.'

Her look changed, like she'd just realized what this was all about. 'Ian, this wouldn't have anything to do with getting the police off your back, would it?'

'No.'

'If they thought Sebastian was in the habit of defrauding people, they'd have a list of murder suspects as long as your arm.' She looked at me. 'Ian, I can't believe you'd do that.'

In frustration, I slammed a fist down on the bonnet. Angela flinched.

'We didn't know Sebastian,' I said, making a real effort to stay calm. 'I thought I did, but I don't think so now.'

'I knew him.'

'I don't think so, Angela.'

I thought I'd shaken her, at least raised a doubt in her mind. But then she looked down to the churchyard saying, 'I'd trust Sebastian a thousand times more than that old sod.'

It was an instinctive thing, just like when old man White chucked the flowers in her face. I took the photo out of my pocket and flicked it across the bonnet, it landed picture-side upward.

She glanced at it, and before she'd properly seen what it was, she picked it up. And then she saw. Her mouth opened like she was struggling for air.

'Angela,' I said, going round the car. I reached for the photo but she put out a hand, holding me off.

She studied the thing a few seconds more, then she stepped away from the car. Sheep scattered up the hill.

'Angela,' I said feebly, 'I'm sorry.'

Bent double, she held the photo to her stomach and chucked her guts up on the grass.

10

Lee's flat was full of boxes. Wooden ones, cardboard ones, big and small – you name it, she had it. It was only a single-bedroom place, but the amount of clothes she kept in there was just unbelievable.

She shoved an armful of dresses into one box. 'Maybe,' she said, 'Angela had concussion from the knock on the head.'

Legs stretched out on the floor in front of me, can of beer at my side, I watched Lee pack.

'It couldn't have helped,' I said. 'But I shouldn't have dropped it on her like that.'

She dug in a drawer. 'How old's Justine? Thirty?'

'Twenty-seven,' I said. 'And Sebastian was pushing sixty. And he was meant to be their friend.'

She got another armful of gear and dropped it in a box. 'And?' she said.

'That isn't enough? Justine's her daughter, Lee. Sebastian was poking her daughter.'

'They were both grown-ups.'

'Sixty,' I said, swigging on my beer, 'is a hell of a lot more grown up than twenty-seven.'

Lee got down on her knees and started shunting the full box across the room. She was wearing a pair of black draw-string pants, Chinese pyjama style, and a white vest on top. The central heating, as always in her place, was turned way up high. When the box hit the pile of other full boxes, she turned and flopped against it, puffing. Wiping the sweat out of her eyes, she said, 'Enjoying the beer?'

I made a token effort to get up but she waved me back

down. She was nearly finished, she said, then she got up and went into the bedroom. She left the door open and after a while there was the sound of another box being packed.

Lee Chan, my sometime girlfriend, was going home. It was real to me then in a way it hadn't been before, all those boxes addressed to San Francisco and the pile of coathangers tossed aside on the floor. In a few days she'd just get on a plane and be gone. No more taking the Tube into the City each morning, no more complaining about the weather, no more dealing with underwriters like me: she was taking the big leap out, just straight up and gone, and I knew there was something I should probably say, but instead of that I just took another swig of my beer.

She'd asked me to come over and collect some clothes I'd left there, and now they were stuffed into a plastic bag by my side. A few T-shirts, that's all. I wondered why she hadn't just thrown them out.

'If Sebastian was bonking Justine,' I said, raising my voice, 'what does that mean for the Ottoman deal?'

'That a question,' she called back, 'or you just thinking out loud?'

'Say that photo was taken before Justine signed the Ottoman lead?'

'Uhha.' She walked across the bedroom with another armful of clothes, passing through my field of view.

I said, 'I mean if what White told Angela and me was right, if Sebastian tried it on back then, what's to say he didn't do the same with Mehmet?' That was the thought that had been worrying me ever since the trip down to Horley Farm, but I hadn't been able to say it to Angela. Our drive back to London was pretty grim. I'd tried to apologize for dropping the photo on her like that, but Angela just didn't want to know. And she'd kept the photo. She'd shoved it in her handbag and pushed the lot down by her feet in the car, and I didn't quite see how I could ask for it back.

Sebastian and Mehmet set up the Ottoman plane theft together, and Sebastian got Justine to sign the Mortlake

Group up for the lead insurance line. When we paid out, they split the profits. It was a lulu, but the more I thought about it the more it seemed to fit. 'Lee?'

She appeared in the bedroom doorway. 'So what happened to Sebastian Ward, hero and all-round good guy?'

'Leave it out.'

'Your words, not mine.'

'I never said he was a hero.'

'Ian.' Her voice dropped. 'When you used to take me out, that's about all I ever got from you. The latest on Sebastian Ward, how shrewd he was, his business going gangbusters.'

'Give over.'

'You thought he was just the bee's knees.' She pointed at me. 'Am I right?'

'No.'

'I am but you don't want to admit it.' She flicked her hair back and swaggered off for more clothes.

It wasn't a great moment for me that, she'd caught me on the raw. The truth was Sebastian was a kind of hero to me – not just because of all he'd done for me: I guess I used to look at him, his success, his house and everything, and I'd see how things might be for me one day. But I hadn't realized that I'd blabbed about him like that, not to Lee. And not to anyone else for that matter. There I was thinking how good I was at playing my cards close to my chest, the professional underwriter bit, and Lee takes a glance and sees right through me. Was I really that obvious?

'Sebastian wasn't my hero,' I called. 'He was good at his job, that's all I said.' Somewhere in there, a door closed. 'Lee?'

'Whatever you say, Ian.'

I crushed my empty beer can between my knees. How can someone five feet two inches tall be so infuriating?

I lobbed the can in the direction of the kitchen bin but it missed, so I went in and binned it. The packing hadn't started in the kitchen, all the cooking gear was hanging on the wall just like I remembered it. Lee took cooking lessons for a while; during the six-week course I was her guinea pig. I'd come over to her place, eat, have a romp, sleep, then leave early to go home and change before work. Good times. Fun. BF, Before the Fire. Before then, I thought, looking round the pots and pans – before Mum and Dad died – I actually had a life. Things I could look forward to.

Returning to the lounge, I did a lap with my hands in my pockets.

'Remember this?' Lee stepped into the doorway, holding up a piece of material. It was a deep turquoise colour, the black flowery pattern snaking all over it.

At first I didn't have a clue what it was. But then the way she was holding it now, pressing it against her body, I tried a little harder and it came to me.

'France?' I said.

'Ahha.'

'A break in Normandy?'

Laughing, she held it out in front of her so she could see it better. It was a sarong, about the only thing she ever wore when we took a long weekend by the beach in Normandy over summer. An American Chinese and me from up Walthamstow way: we had about six words of French between us. We kept to ourselves for three days and lived off baguettes and chocolate and beer. Each morning and evening she'd walk down to the water in that sarong, and I'd watch her from the cottage behind the beach. She'd wade out, swim a few strokes then lie on her back floating, kick her legs through the water and glide. When she came back up to the cottage she'd be shivering, I'd throw her a towel as she ran past on her way to the shower. Sometimes, often, I'd go in and join her. Fun. Way back when. Before the fire.

'Lee, I need you to dig out some paperwork for me.'

Her smile died. She crumpled the sarong around her arm.

'At the LCO,' I said as she disappeared back into the bedroom. When she didn't answer I went over to the door and looked in. She was standing on a chair, unhooking some tapestry thing she had on the wall. 'Lee, there's this guy—'

'No.'

She hadn't even turned; she was still unhooking that thing.

'You haven't heard what I'm going to say.'

To the wall, she said, 'You want paperwork from the Claims Office.'

'There's a good reason.'

'I don't wanna hear it.'

'I need this, Lee. I really do.'

Again she didn't answer. She finished unhooking the tapestry and started folding it as she got down from the chair.

'Listen, Lee, there's this guy—'

'La-la-la-la—'

'There's this guy—'

'La-la-la-la.'

'Lee, for Christ's sake!'

She put her hands over her ears. 'La-la-la.'

I grabbed her arms and yanked them down by her sides, shouting, 'I've been set up for Sebastian's murder, will you listen to me?'

She kicked at me. Then what I'd said seemed to reach her and she stopped struggling. I guess she saw in my eyes I wasn't joking.

'Lee, I need your help.'

She looked down at my hands and I realized then that I was squeezing her bare arms very tight. When I released her she pulled back, rubbing at the deep red fingermarks.

'Set up? You mean like framed?'

'The cop investigating Sebastian's murder happens to hate my guts.'

'Why?'

I waved a hand, brushing the question off. It was pointless going into all that.

'He hates you, so he's framing you?' she asked, and to my own surprise I hesitated.

Yes wasn't exactly the truthful answer. The truthful

answer was that Fielding hated me so he was taking extra special care to hit me with the spotlight. But the spotlight seemed to be lighting up stuff that had nothing to do with Fielding, like the tapes and like me being down the Gallon asking about Eddie Pike. Then the K and R, and now the Ottoman case.

Finally I said, 'It suits him to believe it was me.'

'Can he prove it?'

For a moment I just stood there waiting for the punch-line. But it didn't come, Lee was actually waiting for an answer.

'Get real, Lee.'

I followed her into the kitchen where she pulled down some pots and pans. A minute later I found myself standing over the cutting board, slicing vegetables. Lee had two steaks out, she worked them over with a tender-izing hammer, really going at it, hammer in both hands. I watched her from the corner of my eye. That guy in San Fran, her fiancé, I wondered if he knew what he was getting, and if he had the sense to look after it, appreciate it better than I had. Lee Chan deserved that, at least. But behind this thought was another thought. I hoped that fiancé of hers got hit by a truck.

Back turned to me, she pushed the sizzling onions around. 'The cop that hates you,' she said. 'What's his name?'

'Fielding.'

She picked up the pan, rolling her wrist. Then she put the pan down and sprinkled herbs in there while with her other hand she reached over and turned on the fan. There was something on her mind. I looked at her curiously.

'Open some wine.' She flicked her hand, shooing me off. 'Go lay the table.'

Fifteen minutes later, we were eating. Neither of us had said a word more on the only subject that mattered and I wasn't sure if I could hold out much longer. But then she put down her knife and fork, and studied her glass.

Here we are, I thought.

Offering her the bottle, I said, 'More?'

She slid her half-empty glass toward me. 'Your friend Fielding called in at the LCO today.'

I nodded but didn't say anything. A cold feeling ran up my spine.

'You're not surprised?' she said.

'Encouraged,' I lied. She gave me a Please Explain look, so I told her, 'If Fielding's sniffing around there, maybe it's got through his fat head that Sebastian had more important things to worry about than me.'

'Like Mehmet?'

'Is that who Fielding was asking about?'

Lee put up a hand. 'Me first.' She pushed her glass away, eyes down. 'Ian, I think I need to know why you believe this guy Fielding hates you.'

Meaning what? I wondered. Explain, and I might help you? Explain, or I won't help you? Talk, so I can compare what you tell me with what Fielding told me earlier? I couldn't figure it out, and when she lifted her eyes to meet mine even that didn't give me a clue, so in the end I gave up figuring and just told her. Me and Fielding. Not just recently but right back to the start: our whole stupid history; incidents I remembered even as I spoke, like things stirred up from a stinking swamp. It took me nearly half an hour, finishing with me hauling Katy off him back at the flat, and Fielding walking out with the videotapes.

In the middle of it all, I went and got us another bottle of Lee's wine from the rack.

'And that's the truth, Lee.' I'd ended up in the lounge, on my back, telling the last part to the ceiling. Now I rolled over, head propped on my arm, and looked at Lee. She was still at the table, fingers around the stem of her glass. 'I don't know what Fielding told you,' I said, 'but that's the truth. Start to finish.'

She pressed her glass lightly against her lips. 'But framing you for a murder?'

I sat up, swinging my legs round to the floor. 'The kidnap and all the rest of it. I don't know, he just seemed to fit a few things together. He put two and two together and got five.'

'Did he?' she said.

I looked straight at her. She wanted to hear it again so collecting myself, I mustered every bit of integrity, every bit of sincerity I could, and I gave it to her just like she wanted.

'Yes, he did,' I said. 'Lee, I had nothing to do with Sebastian's death.'

Her eyes stayed on mine a few beats, then she looked away. I knew I'd reached her. She raised her glass to her lips again. Full lips. Red.

I said, 'Do I get to ask one now?'

She nodded, the glass pressed to her lips.

'Was Fielding chasing up links between Sebastian and Mehmet?'

'Yes,' she said. 'Partly.'

'Partly?'

'Ian, after what you've just told me?' She pushed a loose strand of hair from her eyes. 'The other part he wanted to know about was the connection between Sebastian and you. If there was any way he could trace the connection through the paperwork.' She looked at me a moment to make sure I'd got the significance of this. When she'd been taking down the tapestry, when I'd asked her to dig out the LCO paperwork, it was the second time she'd been asked that day. And the bloke that asked her earlier, he was a policeman.

'I wasn't asking you to help me cover my tracks, Lee. There are no tracks. I haven't done anything.'

'But you want the paperwork.'

'Not the originals. Copies. whatever you can get.' I got up and took a turn round the room, expecting more questions. When she didn't ask any, I said, 'You met Fielding. Ask yourself, who would you trust, him or me?'

For a second she actually thought about it. I threw up a hand in disgust, and Lee said, 'Okay, okay, so he's a jerk.' She poured herself another glass of wine. Then she said, 'I put an order through for the paperwork this afternoon.' To the warehouse out in the sticks, she meant, where truckloads of Lloyd's paperwork gets stored. 'I'll get the stuff tomorrow.'

She took a long pull at her wine. She was twirling a strand of hair round her finger, just by her ear. She always did that when she was worried. Worried or tipsy.

I said, 'Am I asking too much?'

'You know damn well you are.' Still twirling her hair, she added, 'Your signature's going to be on quite a few of the leads.'

She was waiting, I knew, for me to tell her to pull them. Mislead Fielding. And I was tempted to, but I had a feeling that if I did she might show me the door.

I said, 'No problem.'

'No?'

'Give him whatever you like,' I said. 'I've got nothing to hide.'

She looked at me. At last she said, 'All right, Ian. I'll get you some copies.'

'I'll need to see all the business Justine signed up for, not just the leads. Everything she did through WardSure that's been claimed on.'

Lee nodded tiredly. After what I'd told her about that photograph I suppose she'd been expecting this, but she looked completely fed up with it all. First Fielding, now me.

She cocked her head. 'Anything else?'

It was pushing my luck, but I tried anyway. I asked if there were copies of any correspondence Justine or Sebastian might have had with the LCO over the Ottoman claim.

Lee got up and went to her bedroom door. She pointed back to where her briefcase was propped by the stereo.

'It might be,' she said, 'that in an unguarded moment, while my briefcase was out of my sight, someone snuck himself a look without taking anything.'

I looked from her to the briefcase and back.

'Two minutes,' she said, disappearing into the bedroom.

It took me a second to realize she was serious. When I did, I went and picked up her briefcase, laid it on the table and flicked the catches. Unlocked, it sprung open. There were a few loose sheets, a diary, and a cheque book, and one thick folder labelled Ottoman. I opened it. The top sheet was the provisional timetable of the trial, a red tick beside the witnesses who'd already appeared. My name hadn't been ticked, but tomorrow's date was pencilled in there, a reminder I really didn't need. I thumbed through a few more pages, it seemed to be laid out in reverse order, the early stuff further back, so I went to the bottom of the pile. There I quickly found what I was after. A couple of faxes, and some e-mail printouts from way back at the start, in the days straight after the Ottoman plane was stolen. The way I figured it, if Justine and Sebastian were in the scam together, they'd have been keen to smooth the path for the claim. I thought I'd find evidence of this in their correspondence with the LCO.

Instead what I found was that most of the correspondence from our syndicate came from me, and on the WardSure side, from Nigel Chambers. All of it standard stuff.

'Two minutes,' Lee called from the bedroom.

Disappointed, I slid everything back into the folder and closed the briefcase. There was nothing in there that was going to help me. Rain was falling now, and the windows rattled noisily, shaken by the wind.

Sebastian and Justine. Had I been a bit quick out of the traps? Wasn't Lee right; they were both grown-ups, couldn't they do what they liked in private together? But all I had to do was think about it for ten seconds and I was back where I started. An idiot could see that something just had to be going on. And that photo showing up at the Aston Kennels like it had, I thought now that maybe Tubs had the right idea when he'd suggested to me that Eddie Pike wasn't above a bit of blackmail. But where did that get me? Nowhere, unless I could speak to Pike.

'I'll phone a taxi,' I called back through Lee's bedroom door. Walking across the room, I said, 'You should keep that case locked. By the way, I didn't take anything.'

No answer from inside. In my ear, the ringing tone from my mobile, but no answer there either. I dropped my hand, thumbing the Off button as I stopped outside her door.

'Lee. I'm getting a taxi home.'

When I started redialling, there was a sound from inside the bedroom and I stopped punching buttons. I put a hand on the doorframe and leant in.

'Lee?'

She couldn't hear me, not over the noise of the shower.

I hesitated. Hesitated and thought, What goes on here? Then after a brief struggle with my conscience, I convinced myself I wasn't taking too much of a liberty, and went in. Without the tapestry on the far wall, the bedroom looked bare. Boxes I hadn't noticed before were lined up at the foot of her bed with dresses draped over them. And there, at the back, the bathroom door was ajar. I said her name again but it hardly came out, my throat was suddenly dry and tight. I slid my mobile into my pocket. The bedroom door open. And the bathroom door ajar. Signs everywhere, if only I could read what they meant. I stood by her bed wondering if that was where she meant me to be, or if she thought I was still in the lounge, calling a taxi.

Lee Chan. The first time I slept with her it was kind of surprising, this small Chinese body wrapping itself around me with a fierce American desire. Lust, even. And that's what I felt then, standing in her bedroom, heart hammering, and listening to the shower. Desire. Lust. A great surge of life, the kind of thing I hadn't felt in months.

And then the shower stopped. No noise now but my breath, short now and shallow, and the windows rattling, and I thought, What the hell am I doing here? Lee was packing to leave the country; she was engaged to another man, and I was tip-toeing around her bedroom like a teenager with an itch.

Pivoting silently on the carpet, I took a step towards the lounge.

'Ian,' Lee Chan said very quietly.

I stopped. Then I hung my head a moment and tried to breathe easily. After a second I faced the bathroom door. There was just silence, then a brief trickle from the shower, then silence once more. After a long time I took a step towards the bathroom door. Then another. I reached out, rested a hand on the door and it swung gently back.

'Lee?'

Steam hung over the shower cubicle, the frosted-glass walls dripping with condensation. And through the glass, a figure standing very still.

As I stepped into the bathroom the heel of my shoe clicked once against the tiles. I paused. Looked down, and then up. She didn't move. I heard her breathing now, behind the glass. The smell of soap was like sweet flowers in the steam.

I took another step, my face very close now, to the glass. My hand went out from my side, I watched it grip the handle of the cubicle door. The heat ran through my fingers, and then I knew there was no way, just no way I could stop this. I leant my weight on the hand and with a slow swishing noise the door slid open.

Her wet hair clung to the sides of her face and her neck, the water trickling down her, and she stood still, not reaching for me or doing anything, just watching me take her in, and what she was wearing. The black and turquoise sarong clung to every curve like a shining wet skin. Then my eyes went back to hers. Staring straight at me, she tugged at the sarong above her breasts. Under its own weight, the sarong began to roll and peel down. She kept her eyes on mine as the sarong passed over her nipples and her ribs and her waist; it caught on her hips and she reached down and touched it again, and it slid over her thighs, down her calves to her ankles. Barely moving, she stepped out of it, standing on it now, a turquoise pool at her feet. And then, so very quietly, she said my name. I felt my throat contract, my heart slam against my ribs, and there we were, where I never dreamed we could ever be again.

I reached for her, my hand rising slowly. Lee. Lee Chan. And when my fingertips touched her wet skin, I was gone.

11

When I got home around six thirty the next morning, I grabbed a carton of orange juice from the fridge and headed for my room. Katy's door was closed and there was no sound from her radio so I didn't have to poke my head in and turn it off. I had a shower, put on my dressing gown, and pulled up a chair by my bedroom window. Sipping from the carton of orange juice, I watched the morning come in, the big NOW SELLING sign on Cooper's Dock gradually lit by the sun. My penthouse. My bloody nightmare the way things were going.

The morning after the night before and I wasn't quite sure I knew what had happened back there with me and Lee Chan. Those T-shirts she'd asked me over to pick up, did I really buy that? And then the meal, the first time I'd eaten at her place since our big fight – hadn't she had most of it ready? But if it was a set-up it was a hell of a lot more pleasant than the one Fielding had going. The only trouble was I just couldn't see where this put us now, and I wasn't sure that Lee Chan knew either. Before I'd left her flat I'd asked, casually, if she was still going back to San Fran. Too late I realized it wasn't a question she expected me to be casual about. Glaring, she told me she had a wedding to get to. When I bridled at that, she pulled the sheets up over her head and rolled over to face the wall. We really had laid the bruises down deep, way too deep to be healed in one single night.

Finally I came to the conclusion that we were pretty much where we'd been yesterday; Lee on her way to

267

California and marriage; me still trying to deal with my problems here in London. After that dismal reckoning, I tried to think about something else.

I finished the orange juice and phoned Wainwright.

'I've been thinking,' I said, 'about that photo.'

'Mm?'

'I showed Angela.'

There was a pause.

'Clive? I showed Angela.'

'I heard you.' The call had caught him asleep, but you could tell he was wide awake now. 'How'd she take it?'

'Thrilled. She kept it for her album.' I went to my cupboard and ran a hand over my suits and ties. 'I'm guessing she's had a word with Allen about it.'

Clive made a sound of agreement. If Angela had done it already, Clive wouldn't have to give the bad news about Justine to his biggest client. 'So all cleared up then,' he said, relieved.

I looked at the phone. Then I said, 'No, Clive. Not all cleared up. I need to see you and Allen before court.'

'What for?'

I took a grey suit and a blue tie and laid them on my bed. 'Remember I told you where we found the photo? Remember I said Nigel Chambers's card was there?'

'Mm.'

'And remember I told you how I saw Chambers out at the airport with Mehmet?'

He took a few seconds with that. Then he made the connection that I'd just made – one I should have made a lot sooner. If there were more copies of that photo of Justine and Sebastian, or others like it, and they'd gone from Chambers to Mehmet, then Mehmet was bound to use them against us. And the best place to use them against us was in court.

'Oh shit,' Clive said.

I told him I'd see him in his office in an hour. 'You call Allen,' I said, then hung up.

While I was getting dressed I heard Katy out in the kitchen. Early for her. For the first month she moved in she was never up before I left for work, and on the weekends she was never out of bed before ten. But gradually, as the weeks went by, she'd got better. Getting over her depression about Mum and Dad I guess, but even now early mornings still weren't her best time. In the early morning, actually, my pretty twenty-one-year-old sister could look like a sixty-one-year-old slob. .

And right then I didn't feel up to the ribbing she was going to give me either, about not coming home the previous night. So I hung around in my bedroom waiting for her to go back to bed. Instead of that, I heard the sound of a pan being shoved around on the stove, and a radio coming on. I groaned. She was going to interrogate me over breakfast. I really couldn't face that, so I picked up my briefcase, opened my door very quietly, and crept silently through the lounge. Something sizzled in the pan.

I was about halfway to the door when Katy shrieked, an ear-splitter that trailed into a laugh. Hesitating, I turned to the kitchen, then deciding it must have been some joke from the breakfast DJ, I carried on towards the front door. I was almost there when she laughed again, but this time it was followed by another laugh, a man's, and it wasn't the DJ either. It stopped me dead. I faced the kitchen again. Just the radio now.

I went over there, she was smiling, and when she saw me standing in the doorway she pointed at me, saying, 'Here he is.'

The bloke in the suit turned: it was Bill Tyler.

'Morning, Ian,' he said.

'You were in the shower,' Katy explained. 'I told Bill he might as well come up and wait.'

'Ready for the big day in court?' he asked me, smiling.

'Ready enough.'

Katy poured some coffees, but when she started on my cup I told her I'd pass. I glanced at my watch: I didn't want to miss Clive.

Bill said, 'How come you didn't make it back for the afternoon session yesterday? At the court.'

'Angela and me had to check something out.'

'Sorted?'

I nodded, thinking sorted wasn't exactly how I would have put it.

'Well, you missed a good one,' Bill told me, and he started to give me a run-down on how he'd handled the Ottoman barrister. Clive, I thought, might have a very different story.

When he was finished, Katy asked me if I wanted some bacon and eggs. I shook my head, but Bill said, 'Don't mind if I do,' and Katy laughed and went and opened the fridge.

While she was poking around in there, I asked Bill what he was chasing. He said to me quietly, 'I came to pick up the three grand. The lads got the hump when I told them you turned it down. You were serious, yeah?'

Nodding, I asked Katy what she'd done with the bag Bill had dropped off the other day. She said she'd dumped it in her room.

'Well, give it back to Bill before he goes,' I said. I looked at Bill: he was really settling in. He was twice divorced: I'd sometimes heard him complaining about how all the alimony payments were keeping him poor. The chance of a cooked breakfast had made his day. I said to him, 'Will I see you in court?'

He frowned and shook his head. Despite the big talk I could see he hadn't enjoyed his day in the witness box one little bit. And I was the next man up.

As I reached down for my briefcase, he said, 'Hey, you don't look the best, Ian. You look a bit tired.'

I glanced over to Katy by the stove, hoping she'd missed it. Some chance. She had a grin on her that almost split her face.

'Yeah,' she said, like she was really concerned. 'Yeah, Ian, you do. Not a great sleep?'

'Just fine,' I told her flatly, and before she could give me any more needle I picked up my case and shot through.

'What if Angela hasn't shown him the photo?' Clive said.

We were in his office. I was sitting on the black leather

couch, flicking through the latest *Lloyd's List*, and not taking a single word in.

'If she hasn't shown him,' I said, 'then we'll have to tell him.'

'We?'

I stopped flicking through the magazine. 'Me then, okay?' Dropping the magazine on the side table I got to my feet and wandered to the window. 'But don't do a runner on me, Clive. If I have to tell Allen, you sit tight.'

Clive nodded, satisfied. He'd get to see what was happening without having to take responsibility for any of it, a real lawyer's approach to the problem. He told me that Bill's afternoon session in court the previous day had been a lot better than the morning session. The way Clive read it, the Ottoman case was nearly over, and we were just ahead on points. In his opinion, the only thing that could cock it up was that photo. The judge would be less than impressed to discover that the broker and the underwriter were, quite literally, in bed together. If that photo was produced in court, Ottoman was bound to look like the injured party. The judge would crucify us.

'Heard any more from that DC?' Clive said. He meant Fielding.

I nodded. 'He's checking up some old policies I've written.'

'Oh? The purpose of that would be?'

'Policies brokered by WardSure.'

'Ah.' Clive gave me a look. This poking around by Fielding was damaging me all over the place. First with Lee Chan, and now Clive. I couldn't blame them for having doubts, but unlike with Lee, I didn't have the time to argue my case now with Clive.

In the end I just said, 'Clive, it's bullshit.'

Before Clive could respond, Allen came through the door without knocking. Clive got to his feet. We did the 'good mornings', and Clive hit the buzzer telling his secretary, 'No calls.'

Allen unbuttoned his jacket and rested an ankle on his knee. I hadn't seen him since the golf club car park. I felt a bit awkward after what had happened there, but he seemed to have forgotten all about it. He cracked some old joke about lawyers and whores; Clive laughed and I tried to smile. Then there was silence.

Allen turned from me to Clive, 'Is this chargeable time?' He wasn't someone who joked about money.

'Ian's got one or two concerns about what happens in court today.' Clive pointed my way. 'Ian?'

Allen looked at me, I cleared my throat.

'Angela and me went to see that bloke yesterday, Mr White. The Name who wrote that note, that business about not trusting Sebastian.'

'The pig-sticker,' Allen interrupted.

'Did she tell you?'

Allen raised a brow, but didn't answer. He wasn't making this easy for me.

'Anyway,' I said, 'this guy White says Sebastian offered to cut him in on an insurance scam.'

Allen's eyes never flickered.

'Not recently,' Clive reminded me.

'Not recently,' I agreed.

'And the supposed scam,' he added, 'was paltry.'

What was he trying to do, soften the blow? I gave him a warning look, then faced Allen again. 'It wasn't a lot of money, and it was a long time ago, but that's not the point.'

Allen said levelly, 'What is the point, Ian?'

'I've heard it from other sources too,' I told him, remembering what Nigel Chambers had said. 'From inside WardSure, his own brokers, there were a lot of people who weren't happy with how Sebastian was running the show.'

Allen readjusted himself on the sofa, legs crossed now, and arms folded. 'I couldn't care less how Sebastian was running the show. What business would that be of ours? Not our worry.'

Turning, I glimpsed an army of suits through the window. Men pouring into the City, ready for battle. In an hour I'd be sitting in the witness seat at St

Dunstan's. Still facing the window I said, 'Did Angela show you the photo?'

No reply. When I finally turned I found Allen gesturing for Clive to leave, and Clive rising to go. So there it was. Allen knew.

'Clive saw it too,' I said quickly. 'I think we need his advice.'

Clive looked at me daggers. Allen considered the pair of us then waved Clive back to his seat.

Allen said, 'Just how long has the picture been in circulation?'

'It turned up a few days ago.'

'And you've been hawking it around?'

'No,' I said.

'Two.' He pointed at me, then Clive. 'Plus Angela. How many more, Ian? Frazer?'

'No. Look—' I pointed to Clive – 'I showed Clive because I thought it might affect the Ottoman case. I thought—'

'Yes?'

'I thought,' I admitted weakly, 'that you and Angela wouldn't have to see it.'

Allen closed his eyes. He wasn't going to break, you could see that, nowhere near it, but Justine was his daughter and that photo had cut him pretty deep.

Opening his eyes, Allen said, 'What changed your mind?' and that threw me.

What changed my mind was Angela behaving like a cow to old man White, but before I could think of how to put that, Clive butted in.

'Ian's concerned a copy of the photo might have found its way into the hands of Ottoman's legal team.'

Allen made a sound deep in his throat.

'But in my opinion,' Clive went on, 'if they had a copy they would have approached you by now. Pressured you to settle so the picture never saw the light of day in court.'

'Blackmailed me,' Allen said.

Clive pulled a face. 'Negotiated a just and equitable settlement agreeable to all parties.' Looking past Allen, he added, 'They haven't done that, by any chance? Run a copy of the photo by you?'

'No.' Allen leant forward, forearms resting on his thighs, and studied the floor between his feet. In his mind he must have been weighing it up, what he'd do if it happened.

Clive said, 'And if they did try it?'

'They haven't,' Allen answered gruffly.

'There's another possibility,' I cut in.

Clive faced me but Allen kept his eyes on the floor. Nobody, I noticed, had said straight out, Maybe Justine's a crook.

I said, 'Say they've got a copy of the photo and they haven't trailed it past you yet. There's still got to be a chance they produce it in court. If they did that today, me in the witness seat, I'd be stuffed.'

Allen lifted his head. You could almost see the wheels turning behind those pale blue eyes. At last he asked me, 'Why?'

We looked at each other. 'Why?' I said. 'Allen, you saw that photo.'

'I saw a picture of two adults doing what adults sometimes do. And if it's produced in court there'll be questions asked about exactly how that photo was obtained.'

I glanced at Clive, hoping for support, but he stared right past me. If someone was going to send Allen off the deep end, it wasn't going to be him.

'This wasn't just any two people,' I said.

'No,' Allen agreed. 'One of them was my daughter.'

'One of them was writing the Ottoman lead, Allen, and one of them was meant to be the independent broker.'

'Meant to be?'

'Christ.' I opened my hands. It was too late to pussyfoot around now. 'You must see how it looks. Justine was having an affair with Sebastian. He put the Ottoman business her way, she signed the lead. Wham. Mehmet files a claim. Next thing we're fighting the claim in court and Sebastian gets incinerated in his own home.'

Allen considered that. He said, 'I hope you're not suggesting that Justine was involved in anything but

274

signing up for what she thought to be a good piece of business.'

'I'm telling you how the Ottoman lawyers might play it. That's all.'

Allen pointed. 'You were meant to be supervising her, Ian. I haven't forgotten that.'

It was a low shot, but a good one: it stopped me dead. If I'd been doing my job properly way back when, maybe there would have been no Ottoman policy on our books, and no court case either. I put one hand on Clive's desk and raised the other to my forehead. Brilliant. I'd put my boss's nose out of joint and got nowhere with the argument. Absolutely brilliant. And then, to my immense relief, Clive took pity on me.

He said to Allen, 'I don't think Ian's suggesting any inappropriate behaviour on Justine's part.' And then to me, 'Are you?'

'No,' I said, taking my cue. I faced Allen again. 'No, I'm just saying that if the photo gets produced in court today, there'll be some pretty awkward questions. And I don't know how to answer them.'

Allen studied me a while. 'Any thoughts, Clive?' he said finally.

Clive doodled on a pad. 'That photo looked to me as if it might be rather old.'

'How could you tell?' I asked.

'Let him finish,' Allen said.

Clive carried on doodling. 'When you think about it, the problem's not so much that there was a relationship between them, is it? As you said, Allen. Two adults. No, I'd think the worst of it would be, say hypothetically, if Justine and Sebastian had deliberately attempted to conceal the true nature of that relationship. If they'd kept it secret, say, from colleagues.'

'But that's what they did,' I said.

Clive winced. 'Please.'

Allen told me to keep my ears open and my mouth closed. 'You wanted advice, Ian, now listen up.' He nodded for Clive to go on.

Clive said, 'What might have happened here is that Justine and Sebastian had an affair that was over long before the Ottoman business was written. An affair that was well-known—' here Clive gave me a meaningful look – 'to at least one of Justine's colleagues.'

There was a pause. Allen took up the thread. 'And if that colleague was confronted by evidence. Say a photo?'

Clive shrugged. 'He already knew all about it. Done and dusted years ago. He might even feel inclined to express distaste that anyone could pry, probably illegally, into such an intimate domain.'

I turned from one of them to the other, feeling like a cornered rat.

Allen stood, flicking at the creases in his trousers. 'I won't make it down to the court today, Clive, but if you could let me have a transcript.'

'Hang on,' I said.

Allen looked at me.

'I'll be under oath,' I told him. 'I can't lie.'

He reached out and squeezed my arm. 'Nobody's suggesting it.'

'There must have been times, Ian,' Clive volunteered, 'when you saw Justine and Sebastian together. The syndicate taking him out to lunch. Drinks. Didn't I see her in his box at Ascot last year?'

'That was all of us,' I said. 'Frazer and Angela and me. That was work.'

Clive pulled a face. 'Work. Play. I'm sure if you thought about it. I mean, memories. Not infallible, are they?'

I stared at him.

Allen gave my arm a pat, then headed for the door. He reminded Clive to bring him a copy of the day's transcript from court. Then, pausing in the doorway, Allen looked back at me. 'The Council wants the final word on who gets Angela's seat on the 486 box.'

Suddenly dry-mouthed, I waited to hear the decision.

'I think I'll wait till I read tomorrow's transcript,' he said. With a smile and a nod, he buttoned his jacket and strolled out and away down the corridor.

12

In the courtroom they were all in the usual seats, but not me. I was in the witness seat, where the clerk had directed me before he disappeared into the private chambers out back to get the judge. The desk in front of me was empty except for a solitary glass of water. Looking across, I saw Batri pinch the bridge of his nose while he read his notes. When Clive and me told him about that photo earlier, and the possibility of it appearing in court, Batri had done his nut. But that was half an hour ago, now it looked like he'd got over the shock. From a seat behind our barristers, Clive smiled at me encouragingly.

It wasn't the first time I'd been in the witness seat. I'd been involved in my fair share of disputed claims, and more than a few of them had landed up in court. But this wasn't like those other times, not by a long chalk. I concentrated on my own breathing, tried to relax. When I leant forward my hands trembled on the desk, so I leant straight back and rested them, bunched into fists, on my knees.

'All rise,' said the clerk. When the judge came in behind him, I felt my stomach turn over.

We did the stand up, sit down bit, then as everyone was settling the judge had a few words with the barristers. While this was going on the public door of the courtroom swung open. Around the room, heads turned. From my seat up front I didn't have to turn, I just looked up and there he was, Fielding, bobbing to the judge as he strolled across to take a seat behind the Ottoman solicitors.

I shot a questioning look at Clive. He shrugged and

shook his head, like I should forget Fielding and concentrate on the job.

'Mr Collier,' the judge said, 'I believe you understand the procedure.'

Shaken by Fielding's arrival I mumbled, 'Yes,' and the judge had the clerk swear me in. Bible in my right hand, I repeated the words mechanically, really working hard to stop myself from glancing Fielding's way. Whatever he was doing here, I knew it couldn't mean anything good for me. After I was sworn in Batri did the usual introductory bit then he handed me over to his learned friend. The Ottoman barrister got to his feet, straightening his wig. I looked past him to Fielding, that bastard actually smiled at me. I snapped my head to the front again.

'Mr Collier,' the barrister said, then immediately paused. Silence fell over the courtroom, all eyes on me.

Here we go, I thought. Just me, alone now, up here on the highwire.

'Let's start with your underwriting experience, shall we?'

When I nodded he trotted me through it quickly, starting with when I joined the Mortlake Group and moving on through the promotions I'd had, right up to date.

'And now you're a senior underwriter on Syndicate 486,' he concluded.

'Yes,' I said.

'But you were the acting underwriter on Syndicate 486 when the Ottoman lead was written by that Syndicate.'

'Correct.'

'Demotion, Mr Collier?'

'The underwriter on the 86 box was off sick when the Ottoman business was written,' I explained. 'Since then she's come back on the box.'

'This is Angela Mortlake?'

'That's right.'

'The mother of Justine Mortlake who wrote the Ottoman lead.'

'Yes.'

'Thank you, Mr Collier.' He put aside his notes on my CV. He opened a folder and set it down on his lectern. 'I'd like to move on now, to the Ottoman Air policy.' He glanced up to the judge and added, 'My lord, I note that we may have cause to take further consideration of Mr Collier's work record at a later time.'

The judge nodded, jotting a note to himself. I glanced across at Clive, but he seemed really relaxed so I tried to put the barrister's last remark out of my mind.

Headgames, I told myself. Just concentrate on the questions.

'Would you say, Mr Collier, that Justine Mortlake was a bad underwriter?'

'No.'

'No? Then is she a good underwriter?'

'If you want my opinion, she does her job well.'

'So she's a good underwriter?'

'Good's not very specific.'

'Oh? The word "bad" didn't seem to cause you the same difficulty, Mr Collier, did it?'

I thought about Allen Mortlake reading the transcript later. I thought about my job.

'Justine's a good underwriter,' I said. 'I just wasn't sure what you were after.'

'Yes, well don't worry about what I'm after, Mr Collier,' the barrister told me, smiling. 'If you could simply answer the questions I put to you, we'll move ahead splendidly.' He consulted his notes on the lectern again. 'What underwriters would you say require supervision?'

The question stumped me. I said, 'You want me to name people?'

'Please don't,' the judge interrupted. I looked up at him. He said, 'I think the intent was a more general question. That is, What type of underwriters require supervision?'

'Yes, my lord,' the barrister said, bobbing his head. He turned back to me, mildly pissed off by the judge's intervention. 'Just so. Within a syndicate, what type of underwriters require supervision?'

I thought about that for a second, then I said, 'Pretty much all of them.'

The barrister made a surprised sound, completely fake.

'There's no hard and fast rule,' I explained to the judge. 'But even the Syndicate underwriter has the Managing Agent looking over his shoulder. It's not so much a question of who gets supervision, but how much they get.'

'And what factors would determine that?' the barrister asked. 'How much each underwriter gets.'

I paused to consider again. 'It comes down mainly to experience.'

'The less experienced get more supervision?'

'Yes.'

'And what form would this supervision generally take?'

'It's not really that formal. You're sitting at the box; brokers are bringing in slips. You talk to your colleagues, get a few opinions. Maybe someone warns you off some business you thought you'd write.'

'That doesn't sound like supervision.'

'I did say it wasn't that formal.'

'And an underwriter with the degree of experience Justine Mortlake had, she'd expect to be offered rather more advice than, say, someone like yourself?'

'That doesn't mean she wasn't up to the job.'

'Please address yourself to the question, Mr Collier.'

The muscles in my neck went tense. 'Yes,' I said. 'She'd expect more advice.'

He asked me another, then another; he must have banged away at it for a good fifteen minutes, establishing again what everyone knew anyway, that Justine wasn't the most experienced person on the box. Finally he produced the original Ottoman policy slip, stepped around from behind his lectern and placed the papers in front of me.

'Do you agree that this is the slip, presented to your syndicate by WardSure, outlining the Ottoman Air policy?'

280

I flipped back and forth through the pages. 'It looks like it.'

'It is it, is it not?'

There didn't seem much point arguing the toss, so I said, 'Yeah, this is it.'

'Do you see Justine Mortlake's signature?'

'Yes.'

'And beside it the figure, seven per cent?'

'Yes.'

'Please look carefully at the paper just above that signature and number. What do you see there?'

'You mean where it's been rubbed out?'

'Yes, do you see that?'

I nodded, then glanced up to see him pointing to the microphones overhead.

'Yes,' I said.

'Can you see that a number has been rubbed out?'

'Seven per cent,' I said, and suddenly Batri got to his feet.

'My lord,' he said, 'is Mr Collier being asked to give evidence on something he can't even see?'

The judge considered a moment. He said, 'He seems to have seen it well enough,' then he nodded for the Ottoman barrister to continue. Batri sunk back into his seat, looking vaguely unhappy.

'Can you explain,' the barrister asked me, 'what the rubbing out indicates?'

'Sure.' I rested my forearms on the desk, touching the slip occasionally as I explained what had happened. 'The broker brought Justine the slip, she discussed it with me, and I agreed she could sign the lead for seven per cent of the risk. Subject to some clarifications from the broker. So we pencilled ourselves in for seven per cent. Once the broker made the clarifications, he brought the slip back to us. Justine rubbed out the pencilled number, inked in a seven, and signed.'

'That's common practice?'

'Absolutely standard.'

'Do you notice,' he said, 'that the figure seven, done in

ink by Justine Mortlake, is a crossed seven?'

I shrugged. 'That's how she writes them?'

'Look, if you will, at the seven above it. The pencilled seven that's been partially rubbed out. It isn't crossed, is it?'

I looked. 'No,' I said.

'Can you explain that?'

'Maybe she didn't pencil it in,' I said. He really seemed to be making a mountain out of a molehill. I shrugged again. 'Maybe I did.'

'Maybe?'

Turning up to the judge, I said, 'It was months ago.'

'You've already told us,' the barrister broke in, 'that Justine discussed it with you. You were the colleague she turned to for advice. Angela Mortlake was off sick as you've mentioned. Who else could have pencilled in that seven?'

'I'm not trying to deny it,' I told him firmly. The guy was really starting to get on my wick now. 'I'm just saying I don't actually remember pencilling it in. If you ask me does that look like my number, that I wrote it? Yeah, it does. Justine probably put it in front of me, told me what she wanted to do, and I pencilled in the seven. Then she got the clarifications, stuck her own number down, and signed.' Looking up to the judge, then back to the barrister, I said, 'I don't see the issue here.'

'I must confess,' the judge remarked dryly, 'that you are not alone, Mr Collier.'

'My lord—' the Ottoman barrister came and took the Ottoman slip from me – 'the line of questioning might seem digressive at present, but in the course of the morning I'm certain its importance will become clear. If my lord will bear with me.'

The judge glanced at the clock on the wall. Sighing, he told the barrister to get on with it.

The barrister shuffled his papers, bending to hear a suggestion from his colleague. I took a swig from the glass of water and a look around. On our side of the room no-one seemed much troubled. Batri and his offsider were whispering together, and when Clive caught my eye he gave me a discreet thumbs-up. That might have meant more to me if I hadn't seen his private and public reactions to Bill Tyler's session in court. But on the Ottoman side – maybe I was imagining it – they seemed more alert somehow, the solicitors looking like they expected something to happen. That photo?

And Fielding. He'd kicked back in his chair; he had his arms folded and his chin resting on his chest. Relaxed. Waiting for me to screw up. Three empty seats along from Fielding, Max Ward was consulting his electronic diary.

'Mr Collier.' The barrister gripped his robe's lapels and rocked forward on the balls of his feet. 'Did you hear the WardSure broker, Nigel Chambers, testify, or have you read the transcript of his testimony?'

'Both.'

'You're aware, then, that although it was Chambers who dealt with Justine Mortlake face-to-face in the Lloyd's Room, Sebastian Ward was in fact instrumental in broking the Ottoman side?'

Sebastian. Now we were getting down to it. He was going to set Justine up on one side, Sebastian on the other, then produce that bloody photo like a rabbit from a hat. And I still didn't have a clue what I could say to that.

I said, 'I don't remember Mr Chambers saying that Sebastian was instrumental in it.'

'That's just splitting hairs now, isn't it, Mr Collier?'

'I don't think so.'

'Sebastian Ward,' he said, swaying back, 'held a controlling shareholding in WardSure. He was the founder of the company. He was joint chairman and managing director, and here he was involved in broking the Ottoman policy, and you're asserting that his role in that, as compared with a junior member of his staff, wasn't important?'

'I didn't say that.'

'So his role was important?'

'Nigel Chambers wasn't junior staff.'

'Not compared with Sebastian Ward?'

'Compared with Sebastian,' I said, 'everyone in Ward-Sure was junior.'

There was a sound at the back of the courtroom, a grunt of agreement. I glanced up and saw the judge frowning directly at Max. Just along from Max, Fielding was sitting up straight, roused now by the mention of Sebastian.

'Let's not get bogged down in this,' the barrister said. 'Perhaps you could describe in your own words what you took to be Sebastian Ward's role in broking the Ottoman slip.'

I shook my head, saying that I couldn't even guess. 'Nigel didn't broke the policy to me. Even if he had, what went on between him and Sebastian wasn't something we'd know about.'

The barrister foxed around some more, playing up the kind of forceful personality Sebastian was, making it seem like Nigel Chambers was more of a messenger boy than a broker in the Ottoman deal. After what Nigel had told me himself, it was pretty hard to raise much objection to that.

Then changing tack suddenly, the barrister asked, 'Do you know Mr Mehmet?'

'I've met him. I wouldn't say I know him.'

'Did you meet him before or during the time the Ottoman policy was under consideration by your syndicate?'

'I didn't meet him till just the other day. The only contact he had with us before that was through Ward-Sure.'

'Through WardSure,' he repeated to himself, glancing at his notes. 'Yes. That's much as you'd expect the arrangement to be, isn't it, considering Mr Mehmet looked upon WardSure as an independent agent?'

If I hadn't known about the photo, the question would have sounded like an offhand remark. Instead of that it set alarm bells ringing. Independent agent?

'All our clients come to us through the brokers,' I said. 'That's how it works.'

The barrister shot me a look from under his brow and

for a second he wasn't play-acting, he really seemed to be figuring it out, just how much I knew. For a moment I wasn't aware of anyone else in the room.

'Mr Collier,' he said, and I thought, Here it comes. I braced myself for the rabbit from the hat. It didn't come. Instead he asked me another general question. Then another. It felt like I'd been let off, we were gradually easing back from the cliff. Then for half an hour he circled around the idea that the Mortlake Group had a good business relationship with WardSure, but it was all very general, nothing that pinpointed the relationship between Justine and Sebastian. I even started to hope my worries about that photo turning up in the Ottoman camp were misplaced.

At the back of the room Max was still paying attention, but Fielding had his hands locked behind his head again. He seemed to be dozing. Clive appeared to be going through his morning mail.

'So would it be fair to say that a disproportionate share of WardSure's clients had their business placed with the Mortlake syndicates?' the barrister asked, summing up.

'I don't know about disproportionate,' I told him. 'But we got our fair share of their business, sure.'

'Not disproportionate?'

'I don't have the figures.'

He held up a sheet of paper. 'The numbers come from Chatset, my lord.' Chatset, the major independent Lloyd's analyst. They usually have a firmer grasp than even the Lloyd's Council on what's happening number-wise in the market. A photocopy went up to the judge, another to Batri, and one was passed to me. 'Do you see, Mr Collier, the average figure, across all syndicates, for the WardSure business?'

'Yes.'

'And the figure for the Mortlake Group?'

'Yes.'

'From these figures, it would appear WardSure is twice as likely to direct its client's policies to Mortlake Group syndicates than to any other. Do you agree?'

I turned to the judge. 'The numbers are a bit misleading. WardSure had a lot of bloodstock and aviation clients. We cover both those areas. A lot of the other syndicates don't touch that business.'

'My lord,' the barrister interrupted. 'The column "Other Syndicates" excludes the non-aviation syndicates. You'll see at the bottom of the page where Chatset's specialist verifies that after taking all such factors into consideration, the Mortlake Group writes a well above average share of WardSure's business.'

The judge glanced at the clock; we were closing in on lunchtime. Then he started to read. Remembering how tetchy I'd seen him get when a witness argued an unarguable point, I said, 'That's probably right. We got more WardSure business than most.'

Relieved, the judge put Chatset's numbers aside.

The barrister asked me, 'Was there any reason for that?'

'Not particularly.'

'Between the Mortlake Group and WardSure there were no—' he paused for effect – 'special relations?'

Now I paused. If I denied it outright he'd flip me over and put the boot in. Forget Justine, the whole market knew Sebastian was a Mortlake family friend. And if I gave him the opening and he started in on Justine, I could be perjuring myself before I knew what was happening.

Finally I said, 'Allen and Angela Mortlake were quite friendly with Sebastian Ward.'

'Quite friendly?'

'I think they owned a racehorse with him.' I gestured vaguely, reaching for the almost empty glass of water. 'That kind of thing.' Sipping from the glass, I looked over to Batri. He was watching the Ottoman barrister carefully. It must have been as obvious to him as it was to me that the 'special relations' had nothing to do with Allen or Angela.

The Ottoman barrister waited for me to put down the glass, then he said, 'Is that all?'

'They socialized together,' I told him. 'They were friends.'

He tilted his head back, looking at me down his nose. 'I meant is that the only particular connection you know of? The only special relationship between Sebastian Ward and anyone in the Mortlake Group?'

The courtroom had gone very quiet. I'd reached the point of no return, I had to make my choice. And the Ottoman team knew their man was about to drop a grenade in my lap. The stenographer's fingers flashed over the keyboard, typing in the questions, then the hands paused, waiting. I saw her glance at me from the corner of her eye. Even the judge leant forward, sensing the change.

In the recess, Clive would report my answer back to Allen. The wrong answer, and I knew what would happen. My promotion to syndicate underwriter – the pay and the bonus and the penthouse, Jesus, my deposit – the whole thing, what I'd worked for since leaving my old man and the tracks, it would all disappear straight up the spout. The only safe answer, I realized, was the one Clive had dreamt up back at the office.

'I was aware,' I said finally, 'that Sebastian was quite friendly with Justine.'

The barrister cocked his head. 'Justine Mortlake?'

'Yes.'

His brow wrinkled like the answer wasn't quite the one he'd expected. His assisting barrister handed him a slip of paper – while he glanced at that my eyes wandered to Clive. He stretched, smiling as if he was pleased I'd stepped down the road he'd mapped out. He thought things were going to be okay.

'Mr Collier,' the Ottoman barrister said, 'I'm now going to ask you three questions, and I would like you to take your time, and think carefully before answering.'

I nodded, on my guard now. When the photo was waved at me I didn't want to over- or under-react.

'This is the first question.' The barrister gripped the lectern and stared at the space midway between me and the judge. 'Did Sebastian Ward make a personal recommendation on your behalf, that secured you your initial employment with the Mortlake Group?'

Taken by surprise, I frowned. He kept his eyes firmly on the back wall.

'My lord,' Batri said, getting up. 'My learned friend has already led us very far from our purpose here, but I really do believe that casting an aspersion on the character of the witness, if that is what is intended, is a step beyond the pale.'

Nodding, the judge said to the Ottoman barrister, 'Just three more questions?'

'If my lord would hear them, and the witness's answers, my lord could then decide if the cross-examination of the witness should continue.'

The judge rested a cheek on his hand, swivelling left and right in his chair, mulling it over. If there had been a jury I don't think he would have let it go through. But there was no jury, only him. And now he was curious. When I pulled my own hands off the desk they were suddenly clammy with sweat.

'Go on then,' the judge said finally. 'Just the three.'

The barrister looked directly at me and repeated his question word-for-word. 'Did Sebastian Ward make a personal recommendation on your behalf, that secured you your initial employment with the Mortlake Group?'

For a few seconds there was silence. I could lie, and line myself up to be skewered. Or I could hum and ha and look like I was hiding something. Or I could tell the truth.

Looking him straight in the eye, I said, 'Yes. He did.'

There was a grunt at the back of the courtroom – Max again. The judge looked that way sternly.

'Question two.' The barrister went up on tip-toe. 'By whose authority on Syndicate 486 was the Ottoman Air policy written?'

I opened my mouth to say 'Justine', but then I thought again and hesitated. By whose authority? Was that Justine, because she'd signed it, or me, because I'd been the acting underwriter? And I had a feeling he was trying to set me up here so that he could blow me out of the water with question number three.

At last I said, 'Justine signed.'

'Yes, but that wasn't my question, Mr Collier.'

'Well, what do you mean by "authority"?'

'Clear enough, isn't it?'

Batri jumped up. 'My lord. Really. My learned friend told us three questions, and now he's badgering the witness.'

'My lord—' the Ottoman barrister spun quickly to face the judge – 'this is a mere clarification of the witness's answer.'

Unfortunately the judge agreed. He said, 'Please sit down, Mr Batri.'

When the barrister asked me if I wanted him to repeat the question, I didn't answer him. Instead I turned to the judge.

'When you talk about authority on the syndicate, I guess that was me. But the way it works is each underwriter's responsible for the slips his signature goes down on.'

'Or hers,' he murmured.

'Or hers,' I agreed. 'The authority's kind of split.'

'Which is how your pencilled seven per cent appeared on the Ottoman slip?' the barrister broke in.

'I explained that.'

The barrister waved it off. 'So your answer to my second question, By whose authority on Syndicate 486 was the Ottoman Air policy written? That would be what? Your authority, supplemented by Justine Mortlake's?'

'It was a joint authority if you like. Me and Justine both.'

'But you were her senior?'

'Yes.'

There was a movement at the back of the room; when I looked that way Max was whispering to Fielding. Clive had his head bowed; I couldn't see his face. I had a feeling he didn't want me to.

'Question three,' said the barrister.

Batri didn't even pretend to be consulting his notes now. He watched the barrister with an expression I didn't understand at first. But then his head dropped to one side, and I got it, what was going through his mind. The bastard was curious. The Ottoman barrister seemed to be setting me up instead of Justine, and Batri was wondering why.

'Once again,' the Ottoman barrister told me, 'think carefully.'

Breathing out a long breath, I braced myself. It occurred to me that I was about to be tied in with that photo somehow; my hands bunched into fists on my thighs. And then it came. The last bolt from the blue.

'Mr Collier, in what manner did you repay your father's gambling debt of one hundred and five thousand pounds to Sebastian Ward?'

My mouth opened. A choked sound came up from my throat.

Batri was up on his feet; his hand slapped the lectern but it was like someone had turned the volume down to zero. His mouth was opening, he was obviously shouting, but I couldn't hear a thing.

I dropped my head into my hands. God, I thought. Oh, God.

My old man and Sebastian. How much? One hundred and five thousand pounds? It didn't even cross my mind that it hadn't happened. Big, bold Bob Russell had punted himself into an enormous hole; the Ottoman team had found it, and they were going to shove me right in there and bury me alive. It felt like there was a giant arm wrapped around my chest, slowly squeezing.

When I came back to myself, the Ottoman barrister was saying to the judge, 'If it were to calm my learned friend, I would be happy to withdraw the question for the time being and recommence after lunch.'

Batri tried to protest again, but the judge cut in, 'Yes, I think that might be appropriate.' Then he looked down at me, unsmiling, and warned me not to speak to anyone about my evidence during the adjournment. He meant it too: in the last fifteen minutes I'd been spun from being a witness into some kind of defendant.

'All rise,' said the clerk.

We rose. The judge got down from the bench and

glanced at me over his shoulder as he disappeared out the back door. The clerk stepped around me like I had the pox.

Alone at the front now, I looked out over the courtroom. Clive was whispering urgently with Batri, the Ottoman barristers were soaking up congratulations from their solicitors, and way down the back Max Ward was heading for the exit. Fielding got to his feet, tucking his shirt in and straightening his tie.

My old man and Fielding, the great inescapables.

When Fielding looked up, he saw me studying him. His eyes swung round to check that nobody else was watching, then he grinned at me and blew me a kiss.

And right then I really could have killed him.

13

'Clive!'

Wainwright looked over his shoulder and saw me chasing after him down the pavement. I thought he was going to blow a fuse. I said his name again as I caught him up.

He kept walking. 'I can't speak to you, Ian.'

'They're stitching me up.'

'Are you deaf?'

I grabbed his shoulder but he shrugged my hand off and walked faster. When we got round the corner he stuck his arm out and called, 'Taxi!'

It drove right on by.

'Clive, I swear to God, I never knew my old man owed Sebastian.'

He didn't say anything; he looked down the street, ignoring me.

'I don't even know it now. The barrister just came out with it – I mean the whole thing, it could be bollocks.'

'Sure,' he said, steaming. 'Bollocks. That number, a hundred and five grand; he just plucked it out of the air.'

'Well, he could have.'

'The Pope could have been a Protestant, Ian. As it happens, he isn't.' He stuck his arm out, signalling another taxi. It shot right past too.

I asked him where he was going. He looked up and down the street, arm at the ready, but there were no taxis in sight now.

His arm dropped. Fixing me with a look he spoke quietly. 'I'm going to see my client, your boss. And I'm going to explain to him that nobody gives a monkey's that Sebastian was screwing his daughter. I'm going to explain to him that Ottoman have found a much better candidate than Justine for a WardSure–Mortlake Group conspiracy theory.'

'But it's bullshit.'

'Ian.' His hand shot out, this time the passing taxi stopped. Then he swung round and tapped me lightly on the chest. 'I have to tell you, it didn't look like bullshit from where the judge was sitting.' Flinging his briefcase into the taxi, he climbed in saying, 'The Lloyd's Building.' He shoved down the window.

Leaning forward, I said 'I honestly had no idea.'

The taxi started to move off and as I walked alongside a few paces Clive looked up at me darkly. He said, 'And I honestly don't know if I believe you, Ian. I honestly don't.'

The taxi accelerated away. I was left standing on the pavement staring after it, my career, my whole bloody life suddenly in freefall. He was going to tell Allen, and Allen was going to think – what? That I'd had some private deal going with Sebastian? That I'd used Justine to get what I wanted, then used her again in court to shield myself? At very least he'd think I'd lied to him. The taxi disappeared into traffic. My old man dropped over a hundred grand to Sebastian, and I – Bob Collier's son – I didn't know about it? Christ, even Clive didn't believe me. And the truth was, if I'd been in his shoes I don't know that I would have believed me either.

Tubs, I thought suddenly. Reaching into my pocket for my mobile, I whispered his name. At his home, no-one answered, and when I tried the Gallon the barman said he thought Tubs'd gone up town to see Nev.

'Where?' I asked. 'At the shop?'

'That's Ian Collier, big Bob's son, yeah?'

'Yeah,' I told him. I'd never felt less like big Bob's son in my life.

'Well, that's where Tubs said he'd be.'

I flagged down the next taxi and gave him directions to Nev's betting shop over on the edge of the City. Just a walk away from the office of Ms Kerry Anne Lammar.

Tubs would know, I was sure of that. Whatever was behind it, my old man couldn't have dug himself into a hole that big without word getting round. And if he'd turned to anyone for help it would have been Tubs, so Tubs just had to know. And I had to find out before the Ottoman barrister got me back in this witness stand after lunch and nailed me into the floor.

By the time I reached the shop, I still hadn't got through on the mobile.

Be here, I thought, going in. It was almost like a prayer. Please Tubs, save my arse, and just be here.

He wasn't, at least not in the front room. There were half a dozen blokes standing round looking from their form guides up to the screens, and a couple more placing bets. A voice droned on in the background, a horse race from up North. It was tatty in there, worn carpet and cheap veneer panelling, like a scene from the fifties. No wonder Nev couldn't sell the place. His punters looked like a mixture of pensioners and the permanently unemployed.

I went to the counter, a woman with a blue rinse was taking bets.

I said, 'I'm looking for Tubs Laszlo.'

She looked me up and down. 'Name?'

When I told her, she flicked a switch in front of her and said, 'Ian Collier looking for Tubs Laszlo.' Another punter came up to place a bet and she asked me to stand aside.

She was too much like Mum for me to argue with her, and it wouldn't have done me much good anyway. She had her instructions, and they didn't include letting impatient young men in sharp suits bully their way past her. I went and sat down. Stood up. Took a turn round the room, then sat down again.

One hundred and five grand. Mum must have known too – why the hell hadn't she let me know? And at the back of my mind another question started to nag – why hadn't Sebastian told me?

'Mr Collier?'

I looked up, the blue rinse lady was pointing to a door at the back. I went over, she hit the buzzer, and I stepped through.

'Twenty-three,' Tubs said, 'twenty-four, twenty-five.'

He picked up the pile of tenners he'd just finished counting, and stuck a rubber band round them. He slid the lot across the table to Nev. Nev made a note in his ledger.

'Ian,' Nev said, giving me a nod.

'Nev.' I closed the door behind me.

Tubs pulled a stack of fivers out of his bag, took the rubber band off and started counting again. 'Got Fielding off your back yet?' he asked me.

'Tubs, can I have a word?'

He nodded to an empty chair by the table.

'Private?' I said.

He made a show of looking over his left shoulder, then his right, then he looked at me. Nev offered to leave.

'Sit down,' Tubs told me, pulling a face. He gestured for Nev to stay put. 'Nev'll pop his clogs by Christmas. How much more private you want?'

Grinning, Nev reached over and pulled up a chair for me. I sat down. Tubs counted out the fivers as Nev watched him.

I said, 'Was Sebastian betting on the dogs again lately?'

Tubs kept his eyes down, still counting. 'Lately?'

'Before Dad died.'

'Could have been.'

'This isn't a joke, Tubs. I need to know.'

He glanced up. 'Now you need to know. Twelve years after you walk out on your old man, you need to know.'

'That's not how it was.'

He returned his attention to the money. 'Eleven. Twelve. Thirteen.'

'I just came from the court.'

Tubs went on counting silently.

'I was meant to be giving evidence on that plane deal,' I said. 'The one I told you Sebastian was involved in.'

'We can do this later, Tubs,' Nev said. It was his shop and his money, but Tubs just shook his head and kept counting.

I said, 'The lawyers on the other side are trying to make it look like I had a scam going with Sebastian.'

'Twenty,' Tubs finished.

He bundled the notes and slid them across the table. Nev made another note in his ledger.

'Are you hearing me, Tubs?'

'Whaddaya want, Ian? Sebastian was a crook, I don't need a buncha beaks to tell me that. And didn't Sebastian set you up with your job? So maybe the beaks got the wrong enda the stick. Am I meant to fall off my chair in shock? Somethin' like that?'

I looked at him. 'Did you tell Fielding?'

'What?'

'That Sebastian opened the door for me at Lloyd's?'

'Listen—'

'I did,' Nev said.

Tubs reared up in surprise. I turned to face Nev: he looked awful. It wasn't just the cancer: you could see in his eyes it was dawning on him that he'd really dropped me in it.

He shook his head. 'Fielding was down the Gallon, bein' a bloody pain, askin' about Sebastian. Shit, Ian, I'm sorry. You know, we just wanted shot of the bastard.'

'So you told him.'

'It didn't seem important. It was from way back, the bloody dark ages.'

'What else did you tell him?'

'Nothin'.' Nev put up his hands. 'I swear.'

I held my head in my hands a moment. Nev had told Fielding, Fielding had told the Ottoman barristers, and they'd used it to skewer me. One small puzzle solved, but I was a long way from jumping for joy.

Tubs asked Nev, 'Why'd you speak to Fielding?' but I cut in then, telling them both it didn't matter.

I glanced up at the clock. I was due back at the court in thirty minutes.

'That's not my big worry, Tubs. My main problem's this other thing, Sebastian punting with the old man.'

Tubs seemed to think about that, then he reached into the bag and pulled out some twenties. He dropped them on the table, and started counting. I reached out and put my hand on the pile.

'The other side's lawyers,' I said, 'are saying Dad was in the hole to Sebastian for a hundred and five grand.'

Tubs didn't say anything to that. He put his hand on mine and tried to pull it off the money. I pressed down hard.

'A hundred and five grand, Tubs.' I looked from him to Nev, who dropped his eyes. 'Now why do I get the feeling I'm the only one surprised by that?'

Tubs said, 'It's over with.'

My hand clenched into a fist around the notes.

Nev said, 'He should know,' meaning me, and when Tubs heard that he just lost it.

'The fuck he should know!'

I faced Nev. 'A hundred and five grand, right?'

'Right,' he said.

Tubs shouted, 'Shut it!' but it was too late, Nev had already confirmed that the Ottoman lawyers knew what they were talking about. In thirty minutes' time they were going to tear me apart.

Tubs glared at Nev like he wanted to do him.

said, 'And nobody thought it was worth telling me? Tubs?'

'Don't ask.'

'I am asking.' I unclenched my hand. Some notes stuck to it, I brushed them off. 'In court they're making out I paid back what Dad owed by doing a favour for Sebastian. Like Dad put me up to it.'

Tubs pointed at me. 'He never woulda done that, not your old man. He never asked you for one single bloody penny.'

'I know that, all right? I never said he did.'

Nev said to Tubs, 'Come on, Tubs. Ian's gotta explain that to the beaks, he needs the full SP.'

Instead of just telling me, Tubs mulled it over. I was bloody angry with him but I couldn't afford to do my block – that could wait – what I needed right then was the real story of how my old man had dropped such a major bundle to Sebastian Ward. If I knew that, at least I might still have a chance of defending myself against the Ottoman barristers. A very slim chance.

Tubs clasped his pudgy hands together on the table. 'In this court business, someone's draggin' your old man's name through the mud?'

I said, 'They're lining up for it. This afternoon they'll cut loose.'

'Cunts,' he said.

My old man's reputation, that really meant something to him. It gave me a twinge when I realized he was more concerned about that than about me. A few seconds' more thinking, then he made up his mind. 'Sebastian showed up at the Gallon, I dunno, maybe eight or nine months ago,' he said. 'We hadn't seen him for donkey's years. Comes in, drinks all round, acts like he's just one of the lads. Only we know he's loaded these days. And he knows we know he's loaded. Between times we've gone nowhere, and he's got rich with his insurance racket thing.' Tubs glanced at me, expecting an interruption, but I let it pass this time. After what I'd found out the past few days, racket didn't seem such a bad description of Sebastian's business. 'Anyway, the usual, we're talkin' dog talk, and Sebastian gets sentimental, tells us the ponies aren't a patch on the dogs for atmosphere – all the bollocks – next thing you know he's showin' up at the Stow.'

'Punting?' I asked.

'Not with me,' Nev said. He glanced at Tubs, then added, 'Not with anyone 'cept Bob.' He got up and went to the safe in the back corner. He twiddled the knobs then pulled the door open. 'We joked about it down the

Gallon. Told Bob if he had a heart he'd share a rich bugger like Ward around, give us all a fair share.'

'Big joke,' Tubs said sadly. 'After a bit Bob starts gettin' in the red with Nev and a couple a others.'

'Nev?' I said.

Nev came back to the table. He picked up the counted bundles and started tossing them across the room into the safe.

'Three grand with me,' he said. 'I think about the same with a couple more blokes down the Gallon.'

Tubs told me, 'That wasn't like your old man,' but I knew that already.

I said, 'But that's just a few grand. How did that get to be over a hundred with Sebastian?'

They looked at one another. They still didn't want to tell me.

Looking up at the clock, I said, 'I've got twenty-five minutes to get back to court.'

Nev went and crouched down by the safe and locked it. Tubs spoke.

'I only found out later, Ian. Sebastian wanted to bet on the tick. Your old man agreed.' On the tick. No money changing hands up front.

'But a hundred and five grand? Christ, how many bets is that?'

Tubs hesitated, then said, 'Basically, two.'

I just stared at him.

He counted off two fingers. 'Twenty-five grand, the first one. Double or nothing makes fifty. Double or nothing again, that makes a hundred. Plus what he was into Sebastian for already.'

'Dad went double or nothing on fifty grand?'

Tubs said defensively. 'I only found out later.'

Nev piped up, 'None of us knew what was goin' on, Ian. It was like this private thing, just Bob and that prick.'

They didn't get it. I wasn't sitting there staring at them like an idiot because I blamed them. I was staring like an idiot because I couldn't get my head round it, what they'd told me. Double or nothing on a fifty-grand bet, that wasn't bookmaking, not at the dogs, and not when you lived in a Walthamstow semi. When you lived like that, fifty grand – double or nothing – was Russian roulette.

I screwed up my face. 'Why?' I said. 'Why would Dad do that?'

Then a voice came over the speaker, that woman with the blue rinse out front.

'Nev, those hamburger people are measuring things. Is that okay?'

Nev swore then went out to see. When Nev was gone, I asked Tubs, 'Did the old man lose his marbles? What?'

'You're reading it all wrong, Ian.'

I got up, shaking my head. Big bold Bob Collier, my old man, in the end he'd finally done it, what I was so afraid of all those years ago. What I'd told him was bound to happen. He'd trusted his luck one time too many, bet the farm and lost everything. Did it even cross his mind what that might mean for Mum?

'Old bastard.'

Tubs's head jerked back. 'You what?'

'I told him,' I said. 'I bloody warned him.' Walking around the table, I put the rest of it together. Fielding must have picked this up down at the Gallon or out at the Stow when he was investigating Eddie Pike's 'death'. And then he'd passed it on to the Ottoman team. My hand went to my head. In the afternoon session they were going to skin me alive. 'I can't believe it,' I said. 'He's been dead six months and here he is again, fucking up my life.'

Tubs came at me like a dog at a hare. He grabbed me by the lapels and shoved me up against the wall. I was so surprised, I froze.

'You wanna know why Bob done it, double or nothin' on fifty grand?'

I tried to shake free, but he held firm.

'You really wanna know?'

'Piss off.'

'Because of you, Ian. You. That's why he done it.'

I pushed him and spun right, breaking his hold. He grabbed my shoulder and pulled me back to face him.

'Sebastian bloody Ward. Every time you went home, it was Ward done this and Ward done that, how much money he made, what a great fucking hero he was.'

'I never said that.'

'You didn't have to say it. Christ, grab a brain, Ian. Howdya think Bob felt? Ward got you that start at Lloyd's, next thing you're in a friggin' suit. You're coinin' it, Ward's coinin' it, and Bob, he's still down the Stow watchin' the bloody dogs go round.'

'I offered Mum money. He wouldn't let her take it. He didn't need to bet with Sebastian.'

'Money?' Tubs looked at me like I was thick. 'He didn't want your money.'

'Well what the fuck did he want?'

Tubs didn't answer, he went back to the table. I followed him.

'No, you tell me, Tubs. When I was working with him, he wouldn't listen to me. When I joined Lloyd's, he just didn't want to know. From the day I left home we never once sat down and talked. Is that normal? That's not normal, Tubs.' I held up a finger. 'Not once.'

Tubs lifted his eyes, he gave me a close look, then his head dropped. 'Forget it,' he said. 'Jesus.' He went to the door and grabbed his coat.

'Tubs?'

He paused, one hand on the door.

'What did he want? Do you know?'

The anger had left Tubs now, he seemed a different man, not menacing, just fat. Fat and old. But how he looked at me, it hurt. He looked like he was disappointed with what he saw.

'He wanted your respect, Ian. Your respect.' He nodded to himself, opening the door. And as he went out I heard him mutter, 'Christ knows why.'

14

The solicitors were late getting back: I sat in the witness seat and stared at my glass of water. Just beside me the Ottoman barristers were discussing some judge, debating whether he was ga-ga or just putting on an act, and in the middle of this one of them leant over and asked if I'd had a good lunch. When I ignored him, he turned back to chat with his colleague again.

My old man dropped a hundred grand, pretty much everything, just to win my respect. Sitting there in the courtroom, Mum and Dad dead, the Ottoman barristers waiting to destroy me, I could have cried. He was my father; I was his son, and yet time after time it had happened, right up to the end. I wasn't like him. He wasn't like me. We knew it, both of us, but somehow our whole lives we just hadn't managed to get past this one painful fact.

When I bought my first flat, two years after I joined Lloyd's, I told Dad how I'd saved the deposit, and how I'd got a special deal on the mortgage. I thought he'd be proud of me, but I was halfway through telling him about the deal I'd got on the insurance when Tubs came by. The old man got up, saying 'Good', like he didn't really give a toss, then the pair of them went down the pub. It hurt like a kick in the balls. Respect. Wasn't that what I wanted from him too? And now, too late, I saw it. How the hell did I expect to win big Bob Collier's respect by showing him how clever I was at playing safe? And how the hell did he expect to win mine by going head-to-head with Sebastian on a hundred grand punt?

All we'd managed to give each other was disappointment, and sometimes a lot worse. But he'd tried. He'd wanted my respect.

Jesus. I bowed my head over the desk.

Then there was a stir of voices at the back of the court, and I looked up. Clive filed in with the Ottoman solicitors, I caught Clive's eye but immediately he turned away. Max Ward followed them in, he went and sat by Fielding and seemed to tell him some news. Fielding nodded.

I sat up straight in my chair. The Ottoman solicitors went into a huddle with their barristers while Clive spoke to Batri in a whisper. Something was definitely up. But before I could go across and speak to Batri and Clive, the clerk came in telling us to rise for the judge.

When the judge sat down, everybody else did too, except the Ottoman barrister and Batri. They glanced at one another, kind of unsure, then the Ottoman barrister gestured for Batri to go ahead.

Batri coughed into his fist. 'My lord, during the luncheon recess my client has managed to find some common ground with the plaintiff. My learned friend and I were informed of this only a short while ago, but it would seem—' Batri turned to the Ottoman barrister and raised a brow – 'that a settlement has been reached?'

The Ottoman barrister nodded. 'That's my understanding also, my lord.'

The judge swayed forward. 'A settlement?'

'Yes, my lord,' Batri said.

A settlement. The thing clicked through my head like dominoes falling. If there'd been a settlement, that was the end of the case. If that was the end of the case, there'd be no more evidence. If there was no more evidence, I wouldn't be sitting in the witness stand all afternoon trying to answer unanswerable questions about my old man and Sebastian. The relief of it almost made me puke.

Looking directly down at me, the judge said, 'A rather sudden change of heart, Mr Batri.'

Batri spouted some bollocks about the Mortlake Group having kept its door open to a settlement all along, but you could see the judge wasn't really listening. His dark eyes bored right into me.

'Would it be premature to enquire as to the nature of the settlement?' he asked.

The Ottoman barrister said, 'My understanding is that the claim will be paid in full.'

My head snapped round. Payment in full? I couldn't believe my ears: that was crazy. We'd had ups and downs through the case, but we hadn't been crushed, not by a long shot. I looked at Clive but he kept his eyes firmly on the judge. When I turned to Max he shrugged like it was nothing to do with him.

There was a bit of talk then between the judge and the barristers, fixing up a time to sort out costs and sort out any other loose ends, but it was like background noise, completely unimportant.

The claim was going to be paid in full. The Ottoman barrister had set me up as the villain, the guy who conspired with Sebastian to take Ottoman's insurance premium while never intending to pay out on a claim, and now the Mortlake Group had just folded. No further contest. What it looked like, I realized, a cold feeling spreading in my gut, what it looked like was that Allen Mortlake had paid out in order to stop the Ottoman legal team from actually proving I'd done what they'd already implied I'd done. It looked like he was protecting me.

'Mr Collier,' the judge said. He leant his weight on his forearms and peered at me down his nose. 'It would appear we have no further need of your assistance. And notwithstanding Mr Batri's protestations, I feel we are all indebted to you for this unexpected but welcome close to the case. This morning's evidence seems to have had a most salutary effect on your employer. Thank you very much.'

The sarcastic bastard; I could have reached up there and wrung the old goat's flabby neck.

'All rise,' said the clerk.

The judge disappeared out back, then the clerk, and around the courtroom everyone started talking. Batri and

305

the Ottoman barrister shook hands, and the solicitors on either side started packing up their bundles of paper. No fireworks and no final bell, just a lot of suits packing up their briefcases. That was it. The case of Ottoman Air versus the Mortlake Group was suddenly over.

Stepping out from behind the desk I went across to Clive Wainwright, he was snapping his briefcase shut. Head down, he said quietly, 'Relieved?'

I waited till he looked up, then I said, 'I'm not sure.'

Over his shoulder I saw Max Ward and Fielding leave the courtroom. I didn't much like the look of that either.

'Clive, we shouldn't have paid out.'

'After this morning? Don't kid yourself.'

'You still don't believe me.'

He glanced left and right. The stenographer finished packing up her portable PC then went and spoke with Batri. Clive took me by the elbow and drew me aside. Keeping his back to the room, he lowered his voice.

'It was Allen's call, not mine. I recommended a fifty per cent payout, but he wanted this case finished. The only way we could guarantee that was handing over the full whack. So that's what we've done.'

'But it looks like he's just settled to save my arse.'

'Ian, he did save your arse.' Clive pulled a face. 'Who cares what it looks like?'

'You're telling me Allen's decision to settle had nothing to do with Justine?'

Clive gestured for me to keep my voice down.

'Seriously,' I said. The whole thing had taken me so much by surprise I was still trying to figure it out. Sure, I'd been spared an afternoon's grilling by the Ottoman barrister, but when I thought about it, what more could he possibly have up his sleeve? He'd already pulled his big surprise. He'd have kept on about my old man owing Sebastian, and he'd have made it seem like I'd paid back the debt by making Justine sign for the Ottoman business, but when I simply told him the truth – that I didn't know about Dad's debt, and that I hadn't pressured Justine to do anything – what else could he have done? Made me look very stupid, I suppose. Maybe even made me look a liar, but what he couldn't have done was brought the case to a close. And as long as the case continued there was a chance Justine's relationship with Sebastian would be exposed. But that wasn't going to happen now that we'd settled. 'Seriously, Clive. I mean this is pretty bloody convenient, don't you think? Justine comes out of it like Snow White, and I'm left holding the baby. You see how that judge looked at me?'

'No-one cares, Ian.'

The assisting solicitor came over to tell Clive that Batri wanted a word. Clive nodded and the bloke wandered off.

'Listen,' Clive said, glancing over his shoulder. There was no-one within earshot. 'This isn't exactly the highlight of my career either. But Allen stopped the case. It's over. Finito. Maybe because he was protecting Justine. Maybe you. It doesn't matter.'

'It matters to me.'

Clive looked at me like I was the naivest thing he ever saw.

I said, 'He's not going to give me the syndicate underwriter's job now, is he?'

He shook his head like he couldn't quite believe I was even hoping. He reached out and patted my shoulder. 'Ian, Justine's his daughter. You don't think he's going to blame her for this, do you?'

'She was fucking Sebastian.'

He sliced his hand through the air. 'The case is over. But if you want some advice you'll steer clear of Allen for a while.'

'None of this is my fault.' I felt my fists bunching, the frustration and anger bubbling up. 'I didn't do anything wrong.'

Clive picked up his briefcase. 'From Allen's point of view, you didn't do much right. And I wouldn't worry about promotion, Ian. The way Allen took it, you're a cat's whisker from being thrown out on your arse.'

He went across to join Batri and I put my hands on the nearest table, bracing myself for a moment. If Allen fired me now, after this, I'd never get another job in the insurance market. Every door in the City would slam shut in my face. It wouldn't just be the penthouse and my deposit then. Without a job, I'd never pay back the mortgage I'd taken out on my flat. I'd lose everything I had, and any chance I had of climbing back up the ladder; the past twelve years of my life would be rubbed clean off the slate. And unbelievably the cause of all this was that same guy who'd first turned my head at the Gallon, the guy who'd given me what I'd always thought of as my one big break. Quietly I swore. Bloody Sebastian.

Wainwright and Batri glanced my way, clearly discussing me. I'd been in freefall, but now it occurred to me that the freefall was almost over. I was about to hit the earth.

'Allen's busy,' his secretary told me.

Reaching for his door, I said, 'I'll just put my head in.'

'He's got Mr Crossland with him.' She raised a brow. 'And the Chairman.'

That stopped me. The Chairman of Lloyd's, the head of the Council, otherwise known as God. If he was in there with Allen and Piers Crossland, they'd be discussing the merger, and they weren't going to welcome an interruption from me. Backing away from the door now, I asked the secretary to give me a buzz when Allen was free. 'I'll be down on the box. Just tell him I need to speak to him.' I held up a hand, fingers spread, and told her pathetically, 'I only need five minutes.'

'Wait on.' She flipped through a pile of memos on her spike. 'You had a message. Here.' She tore it off and handed it to me.

Call Lee, it said. Urgent. And then Lee Chan's number across the road in the 58 Building.

When I got over there Lee wasn't at her desk. One of her colleagues pointed me out to the loading bay where the vanloads of paperwork came and went from the building. Lloyd's produces tons of documents each year; it's too expensive to store it all in the City so it gets piled up in some warehouse out in the sticks. A van makes the trip a couple of times a day, ferrying whatever's needed into town, then back. Lee was out there waiting, glancing at her watch.

'About time,' she said. Then when I was closer, a look of surprise crossed her face. 'You okay?'

'I've just come from court.'

'Ottoman?'

I gestured around. 'What goes on? Your note said urgent.'

She was about to answer but then the van pulled up, we stepped back. The driver opened the van doors, Lee went over and asked him for the box she'd ordered. He dragged out half a dozen, she crouched down beside them and read the labels, shaking her head each time.

And I just looked at her. Lee Chan. She was absorbed in the search; it was like she'd forgotten I was there; her forehead was creased in concentration. With one hand she held her black hair back over her ear and for a moment I saw her. I mean really saw her. Maybe it was the shock at the court, the chance of losing everything I'd worked for, or the news about Dad and Sebastian, I don't know. Maybe it was just the feeling of my whole life caving in. Lee was flying out to Dublin for that conference the next day; from there she'd go straight on to the States. In three weeks she'd be married to some guy she didn't even know, and me, I was just standing there with my hands in my pockets.

'I never said "thanks",' I said now. 'For the other night.'

She looked at me over her shoulder, one eyebrow cocked, and waited.

I glanced at the driver, he was out of earshot. I said, 'You don't have to leave.'

She returned her attention to the boxes.

'Lee?'

She slapped her hand against the last box. 'This one.'

I went and picked it up and before I could speak she turned her back and led me inside. She didn't head for her desk, we took the stairs.

'So how was court? Not good?'

'Fantastic,' I said. She opened a door from the stairs

into a corridor. Stepping past her, I added, 'We settled.'
Pausing in the corridor, I looked both ways.

'Settled, as in, "case over"?'

'Yes.'

'Why?'

'This box's getting heavy, Lee.'

She gave me a look then went left. A short way along
she pulled out a key, glanced up and down the corridor,
then unlocked the room and herded me in. There were no
windows, and when Lee locked the door behind us the
place was pitch dark.

'Don't make too much noise,' she said, hitting the light
switch.

The fluorescents flickered on. We were standing in
some kind of utility room; one wall was covered in
shelves. Plastic bottles of cleaning liquid were lined up
over rolls of hand towels and toilet paper. At the end of
the room a row of vacuum cleaners was buried under a
pile of towels and blue tubing. I dropped the carton onto
the bench by the sink.

I said, 'What's the big secret?'

She squeezed past me. She slid back a low cupboard
door on the other side of the sink then, crouching down,
she reached in there.

'How much does Ottoman get?' she asked. 'For the
settlement.'

'The lot.'

She looked up, surprised. 'Full payout?'

When I nodded she made a hissing sound between her
teeth.

'Let me guess,' she said. 'You showed Allen Mortlake
the photo?'

I nodded again.

'He panicked and pulled the plug?'

'Not quite the full story,' I said. This wasn't the time to
try explaining about Dad.

Lee found what she was reaching for; she pulled it out.
A green folder. When she handed it to me I gave her a
puzzled look.

'You asked me to check out some of those earlier deals,' she said, 'Remember?'

Justine's deals brokered by WardSure, but what good were they going to do me now? And why the cloak and dagger bit? I started turning my head, telling Lee things had moved on, but she tapped the green folder with a finger.

'I think you should read it,' she said.

She went across to the box I'd put on the bench. She started pulling papers out, running an eye over them, then putting them aside. It seemed pretty pointless, I wanted to get back and see Allen, but after setting Lee loose on this stuff I couldn't just toss the lot in the bin and walk out. I pulled over an upturned bucket and sat down. Five minutes, I thought. I owed her that. Just show willing for five minutes, I thought, then I'm gone.

After flicking through the first few pages, I looked up.

'This is the wrong folder.'

'I don't think so, Ian.'

'But these aren't Justine's deals.'

'That's right,' she said. When I opened my mouth again she stabbed a finger in the air, pointing to the folder in my lap. 'Just read it.'

I read. There were only three deals, it took me less than ten minutes. When I looked up again, Lee had the papers from the box sorted. She handed me a wedge of pages, saying, 'Three more.'

'Lee—'

She nodded down to the pages in my hand. Like a zombie I spread them out on the folder; while she stood over me I read through the three older deals, the documentation that had just been brought by the van. Lee didn't say a word. When I was done I stared at the pile of pages. Six policies in total, six different leads, all of them written by Syndicate 486. Every one of them a loser. Lee had pinned her own notes to the first three: she'd discovered that the insured party on each of them was as dodgy as hell. And two of those names appeared on two of the policies that had just come up in the van as well, it wasn't just a whiff of something wrong, the whole thing absolutely stank.

At last Lee said, 'No comment?'

I stared at the signature on the first slip, the same signature that appeared on all six policies. The A and M were big and looping; they hadn't changed at all in the past twelve years. Angela Mortlake. Slowly I closed the folder.

'I don't believe it,' I said.

Lee made a snorting sound. I dropped the folder on the floor beside the bucket, then stood up to get the circulation back in my legs.

I told her, 'I didn't ask you to check Angela out.'

'Well, Justine's hardly written any big leads,' Lee said. 'I zapped through hers, they looked okay, so I spread the net.'

'To Angela?'

'And Burnett-Adams,' she said, then her glance slid past me.

I got a nasty feeling. 'Anyone else?' I asked her.

She pulled a face. 'Angela Mortlake was the only one writing that kind of lead.'

'Lee,' I tapped my chest, 'you checked up on me?'

She didn't answer.

I said, 'I can't believe you'd do that. I ask you to help me and what? You try to put me in the frame?'

'That wasn't it at all.' Lee bent and picked up the folder. 'At all.'

'No?'

'Oh for Christ's sake,' she muttered.

It wasn't anger in her voice, more like she was dealing with some young kid she'd just about given up on. I felt the blood rush into my face.

'Ian,' she said wearily. 'I'm thirty-four years old. You know. An adult. You asked me to help you, fine, but that doesn't make me your puppet. You wanted me to check for bad deals coming into your syndicate through WardSure—' she waved the green folder – 'this is what I found. Angela Mortlake. Take it or leave it.'

We looked at each other. Then voices passed along the corridor outside. Lee glanced back over her shoulder and signalled for me to be quiet. The voices moved on.

She said softly, 'I have to go.'

I put a hand on her shoulder. Then I reached my other hand forward, open, asking for the folder. Silently Lee turned her head.

'I need it, Lee.'

She gave me a sceptical look. There didn't seem any way round it, so I told her, 'In court today no-one mentioned that photo of Sebastian and Justine. They had a better idea.'

Her forehead creased. 'Angela?'

'Me,' I said. I told her about Sebastian and my old man.

'This came out in court?'

'Courtesy of Detective Sergeant Fielding,' I said.

'Then the Mortlake Group settled with Ottoman?'

'Bingo.'

'Jesus.'

'Lee, I'm hanging onto my job by the skin of my teeth. Fielding's still crawling all over me and he's not that interested in finding alternative suspects for Sebastian's murder. As far as he's concerned, I'm it.'

Her eyes dropped to the folder in her hands. 'Maybe if you show this to Fielding—'

'No chance.' I wasn't quite sure if I meant no chance I'd show him, or no chance Angela had anything to do with Sebastian's death. 'Fielding's made up his mind.'

Her brow creased, she touched the folder. 'But you want the paperwork.'

I paused then. I wanted the paperwork because I thought it might give me a chance to figure things out, but Lee's hesitation made me see just how much I was asking of her, how far she'd stuck her head out for me already. For Christ's sake, here we were standing in an LCO utility room whispering together like a couple of thieves frightened of being sprung. It was obvious what was in it for me, but for Lee? And now I was asking her to surrender the paperwork? To be a party to the theft of legal documents entrusted to her care?

I blew out a long stream of air. 'No,' I said. I raised my eyes from the folder to her. 'Not if it's going to screw things up for you. But I really appreciate it, Lee, everything you've done. You know that.'

After a moment she nodded, looking down, and I wanted to reach out and touch her. But I wasn't quite sure how she'd take that.

I said, 'You're still going to leave, aren't you.'

Lifting her head, she gave me a direct look and nodded again. After a moment she said, 'I never asked my mother to send me those letters, Ian. Or the photos.'

More voices passed outside, she glanced nervously around, then facing me again she seemed to make up her mind about something. She pushed the folder into my hands.

'I'm on the four o'clock flight from the City airport tomorrow afternoon. If you get there early, maybe we'll talk.'

As she went to the door I said her name and she turned. But there was too much to say and this wasn't the place or the time, I'd have my chance tomorrow. So all I said right then was, Thanks.

She shook her head. She told me I had a real way with words. Then pointing to the folder, she added, 'And I'll need that back tomorrow too, Ian.'

Lifting my hand, I crossed my heart.

15

Back in the Room, I sat at my desk on the 486 box and tried to concentrate. Business had been building up while I'd been away, brokers who'd been waiting for me to sign their slips suddenly moved in. I spent an hour working my way through the queue and every fifteen minutes I rang Allen's secretary upstairs, but every time she told me he was still in that meeting with Piers Crossland and the Chairman.

Across the box from me, Frazer Burnett-Adams was grinning his fat head off, chatting with the brokers and generally behaving like he owned the place. When I'd arrived from the 58 Building, he'd taken me aside for a quiet word.

Heard about the settlement, he said. Suggest we play a straight bat.

What you talking about, Frazer?

No need to confirm or deny anything, he said. Then he raised an eyebrow. Did your father really owe Sebastian that much?

I thanked him for his support and returned to my desk. Fortunately news of the settlement – and my public skewering in court – hadn't spread yet among the brokers. Most of their gossip was still tied up with Sebastian Ward's death and WardSure, and because of my connection with Sebastian's K and R policy they all seemed to think I wanted to hear their theories. I didn't, but how could I tell them to shut up about it without having them turn the spotlight on me? So I put up with it, signed the slips and let the bullshit wash right past.

Angela wasn't on the box, but Justine was, and I'd dealt with most of my queue of brokers when I saw her go over to the coffee machine. I slid out of my chair and went up behind her.

'White,' I said. 'Two sugars.'

She didn't turn. She said, 'Fuck off, Ian.'

I reached past her for a cup. 'You heard we settled. You think that makes you look bad?'

'It does make me look bad.' She glanced at me, eyes narrowed. 'And actually what I heard was that you dropped us in it.'

'Who told you that? Clive? Your old man?'

She pulled a face, spooning coffee into her mug.

I said, 'Did your old man mention anything else?'

'What my father tells me is none of your business.'

'No? What about your mother?'

She turned, annoyed now. One of our junior people headed over for a coffee, I waved him off.

I said, 'When you signed the Ottoman slip, Angela was off having that mastectomy.'

Justine's brow wrinkled. 'Do you mind?'

'Did Angela discuss the Ottoman slip with you?'

'No.' She reached past me for the milk. 'What's your problem anyway?'

'You're sure you never discussed it with her?'

Swearing, she poured the milk into her coffee. She'd already given me her answer and she wasn't going to argue the toss. Worse, I had a feeling she was telling me the truth. Those six bad deals of Angela's, and Justine's rotten Ottoman deal, they might not be connected at all. So much for that brilliant idea. But I'd taken more than enough of Justine's holier-than-thou attitude, I was fed up with her, she didn't seem to give a bugger what effect the whole business had had on me.

Leaning a little closer, I said, 'You signed the Ottoman slip because Sebastian told you to.'

Her eyes shot up. In that moment before she recovered, I saw that I'd shaken her.

'If I remember rightly,' she said sweetly, 'you approved it.'

'If I remember rightly, Justine, my parents died the week before. I was approving anything anyone waved in front of me.'

'If you were that bad you shouldn't have been working.'

'Probably not.' When she went to step past me, I cut her off. She did that brow-wrinkling thing again, and put her hand up to push by.

I said, 'Then again, if you were signing leads on WardSure business, you probably shouldn't have been screwing Uncle Sebastian.' She froze, like some weird statue, one hand holding the coffee mug, the other up and ready to push me out of the way. 'You were screwing Sebastian, and he asked you to sign the Ottoman lead, and that's what you did, Justine.'

'No.'

'Yes.' I looked over her shoulder. Frazer and some of the brokers out of earshot were glancing across. 'The only thing I'm not sure about is whether or not you knew there'd be a claim.'

Turning away from me, she put down her mug.

'Did you, Justine?'

She swivelled and seemed about to give me an earful. But then she changed her mind. Brushing past me, she grabbed her handbag from the back of her chair and stalked out towards the Ladies. The heads turned to watch her go by, but the appeal of that firm arse of hers was completely lost on me now. She was a brat, she'd cost the Mortlake Group a heap of money, her parents a lot of pain, and me just about any chance I ever had of getting into the syndicate underwriter's chair. It crossed my mind that maybe she'd cost Sebastian more than he'd bargained for too.

Frazer came over to make himself a coffee. Smiling, he reached for the sugar. 'No luck with the boss's daughter then?'

My hands clenched into fists but I kept them down at my sides. I got back over to the box just in time to take the message from upstairs. Allen Mortlake was free.

★ ★ ★

As I stepped out of the lift I saw the lift doors opposite closing. The Lloyd's Chairman, inside, nodded to Piers Crossland, and then the doors closed. Piers pressed the button for a lift going down, glanced back and saw me.

'Bad day at the office?'

'In court,' I corrected him.

'Yes,' he said. 'So I heard.'

I turned that one over. The only person he could have heard it from was Allen, and the only time he could have heard it was just now, in the meeting he'd come from with Allen and the Chairman. Which meant that the Chairman knew as well. And Allen wouldn't have been putting the blame for the Ottoman disaster on Justine, I was sure of that. God. Worse and worse.

Piers said, 'Should I order a transcript?'

I shook my head, telling him not to bother. 'How it looks in the transcript's not how it was.'

'Oh?' The lift came, the doors open but Piers didn't get in. The doors closed and the lift went down without him. He said, 'So how was it?'

'In court?'

'I was thinking more of the Ottoman policy. Obviously a cock-up, but what actually happened?'

I looked away through the glass doors and on down the corridor towards Allen's office. Normally I would have kept my mouth shut, but since Allen seemed to have blabbed already, I said, 'Is the Crossland–Mortlake Group merger going ahead?'

'Does that matter?'

'Yeah,' I said. 'I think it does.'

He considered. 'You don't want to talk out of shop?'

I waited for an answer. He glanced down the empty corridor.

'We've just informed the Chairman that we expect to make the announcement on Monday. An agreed merger.' Facing me again, he said, 'Good enough?'

His openness caught me flat-footed. So the merger was going ahead. Piers Crossland would have a say in the appointment of the new Syndicate 486 underwriter.

While the implications went zinging round my head, he said, 'What happened on that policy?'

'We should never have written it.'

'Because?'

Another pause, then I told him, 'Because Barin Mehmet is a crook. Because it was a bad risk from day one.'

'Justine Mortlake couldn't have thought so.'

I looked at him. In his voice and in his eyes there seemed to be a question. Whatever Allen had told him, Piers clearly had his own doubts about Justine, and the way the case had been settled. With nothing to lose now, I took the plunge.

'Justine was a bit cosier with Sebastian Ward than she should have been. And I think Sebastian was in with Mehmet.' For the time being I left Angela out of it.

Piers absorbed that news without a murmur. I was expecting him to ask me to explain but he didn't, instead he said, 'She told you she was going to sign it, and you waved it through.'

That again. I could have told him about my parents dying, how I wasn't exactly on top of things at the time, but it would just have sounded like I was making excuses, not a good way to start with a man who – if I somehow got through all this – might be my new boss.

Shrugging, I told him what I'd told him before. That it was an honest mistake. He said nothing, but his eyes opened a little wider.

Another lift came, three men got out. Piers reached over and held the lift doors open. When the men had disappeared down the corridor, I said, 'My old man owed Sebastian some money I didn't know about. The Ottoman lawyers made it look like it was me who was a bit too close to Sebastian. That's not true.'

Frowning thoughtfully Piers got into the lift. His head dropped to one side.

'Sebastian Ward and Justine Mortlake?'

The lift doors started closing.

'Ask her,' I said.

319

In his office, Allen was standing at the wall-window looking down at the Room. He had a drink in his hand. He gestured with it towards the bar fridge, telling me to help myself; it wasn't quite the reaction I'd expected. And after the day I'd had, I could have drunk the bloody fridge dry. But I held off. I needed a clear head to face up to what was coming. I had Lee's file on Angela tucked under my arm.

Allen didn't seem quite with it at first. He mentioned some recent US court case that was going to hit the insurance industry hard. He said the Lloyd's Chairman was setting up a working party to look into it.

I said, 'I just saw him.' Allen stopped mid-sentence. I added, 'Out by the lifts, with Piers.'

Allen's eyebrows lifted. He took a pull from his drink.

I asked, 'What were they here for, the merger?'

Allen waved my question aside. 'No,' he said. 'Something else.'

It was the first time since I'd joined the Mortlake Group that I'd actually caught Allen in a lie. There wasn't any satisfaction in it. The lie could only mean one thing, that he didn't trust me any more, that he'd decided to close me out.

We were silent a few moments, both of us wondering who was going to mention it first, the Ottoman settlement. Finally, it was Allen. Peering down into the Room, he said, 'How long was this going on, Ian? Sebastian punting with your father.'

'The first I heard of it was in court today.'

His head turned, he gave me a doubtful look that really ticked me off.

I said tightly, 'I would have explained in court, only Clive came back after lunch with the settlement and I didn't get the chance.'

'You've got your chance now.' He swung round and put down his glass. His face was set like stone. 'We've settled, Ian. You're not in the witness stand. This is a private conversation and it's cost us a very big payout to make it a private conversation. Now what in the name of Christ was going on between you and Sebastian?'

'We didn't have to settle.'

He slammed his fist down on the table, the pens jumped.

'We've settled. Seven million pounds. And now I'd like an answer.'

'I told you.' I held his gaze. 'I didn't know.'

'That's not an answer.'

'It's the truth.'

'Jesus.' He turned in a circle on the spot. 'Do you realize the damage this has done?'

'The money—'

'Not the damn money,' he roared. 'How we look. In particular, how we look to Crossland. One week we're a prime managing agency running good syndicates, the next we've got a rotten apple in the barrel. We look bad. Extremely bad.'

Rocking back on my heels, I said, 'The rotten apple. That's me?'

'If the cap fits,' he muttered.

'But I told you, I didn't know anything about my old man and Sebastian.'

'Ian.' He looked directly at me, leaning forward, hands braced on his desk. 'I'm not convinced.'

It hit me like a punch in the gut. Allen Mortlake, a guy whose judgement I'd always respected, he'd decided my word wasn't to be trusted. He'd decided that I'd conspired with his ex-friend Sebastian Ward to rip the Mortlake Group off.

'Allen, just give me some time. I'll prove this thing between Sebastian and Dad had nothing to do with Ottoman.'

Nodding, Allen straightened some papers on his desk. 'Sure. Take all the time you need.'

I did a quick double-take. He saw he'd taken me by surprise.

'Ian, what you do in your own time's your business. As of now, you are suspended.'

Not a punch in the gut this time, more a kick in the

balls. Suspended. Temporarily removed from the box. Until that moment I must have kept some ridiculous hope alive that I might still get the promotion, but that one word killed the hope stone dead. Frazer Burnett-Adams was going to inherit Angela's seat, and I was going to be sitting at home watching daytime TV. Until Allen decided what to do with me, I was out.

I said, 'You can't do that.'

'It's done.' He went to his desk and sat down. 'Until the merger goes through, I don't want to see you back here.' He nodded to the file under my arm. 'Is that for me?'

'No,' I said. If Angela really was involved in something, handing the file to Allen now wasn't going to help me at all. I clutched it tight to my side, like a drowning man clinging to the wreckage.

There was a sharp knock at the door. Without waiting to be called, Clive came in.

'Excuse me.' His eyes slid from Allen to me. 'You're wanted downstairs, Ian.'

'Not now,' I said.

'Now,' he told me firmly. 'It's Fielding. And he isn't playing games.'

While we went along the corridor and down in the lift, Clive filled me in on what he knew. Fielding had had a busy afternoon. Since I saw him leave the courtroom with Max after the announcement of the settlement, the bastard had got another search warrant for my flat, gone back there and found what he'd told Clive was evidence linking me directly to Sebastian Ward's murder.

'Evidence at my place? You're kidding.'

Standing in the lift, Clive raised his hands. He told me not to shoot the messenger.

'Well what kind of evidence? A box of matches? What?'

'A piece of jewellery apparently. A Ward family heirloom.'

'He must have planted it.'

Clive studied the floor numbers. He wouldn't look me in the eye. 'I took the liberty of calling a lawyer for you.

322

He'll meet us down at the station.'

It took a second for that to sink in. 'I'm going to be questioned officially?'

Clive nodded. 'Don't say anything to Fielding until the lawyer arrives. I'll be with you anyway, but be warned.'

My head was spinning. I'd just been suspended, Frazer was going to get the top job, and now Fielding was about to interrogate me over evidence he'd planted in my flat. I slumped back against the lift wall, tilted my head back and closed my eyes. I was stuffed. I wanted to scream.

Clive said, 'By the by. I went for a drink with one of the Ottoman solicitors. Who do you think fed them that stuff about your old man?'

'Fielding.'

'You knew that?'

'Clive, I told you what he's like. He wants to fry me.'

Clive considered me a moment. 'Why don't you show him that photo?'

I gave him a withering look. 'That photo of two adults doing what adults sometimes do?'

He reached out and held his thumb on the lift button. The doors stayed closed.

'I gave you an option, Ian. What should I have done? Let you go into the courtroom unarmed?'

I pressed my fingers to my temples. Whoever's fault this mess was, it wasn't Clive's. I shook my head.

He said, 'What were you talking with Allen about back there? Justine?'

'Me, actually.'

Clive raised a brow.

'Allen doesn't want the merger with Crossland derailed over this. He needs a scapegoat.' I smiled crookedly. 'As of now, I am suspended.'

Staring at me, Clive took his thumb off the button and the lift doors opened. Stepping past me he muttered, 'Buy a lottery ticket. Your luck has to turn sometime,' but I couldn't even raise a smile.

It was only when I got out of the lift that I realized we weren't on Clive's floor. We were down by the Room, the floor where the Mortlake boxes sat, you could see them through the big glass door. I stopped in my tracks. Fielding was in there, sitting on my desk and talking to Frazer.

I grabbed Clive's arm. 'What's this?' I pointed through the glass door.

'He wanted a word with your colleagues. No big deal.'

Then Fielding looked over and saw us; he must have been waiting for this moment ever since he'd sent Clive upstairs to get me. Fielding lifted his hand and crooked a finger, beckoning me in there. But there was no way I was going into the Room to face him. It was too humiliating.

I said to Clive, 'I'll wait here.'

Clive reminded me to keep my mouth shut till we joined up with the lawyer down at the station, then he went into the Room to fetch Fielding.

I took a turn around the landing, tapping Lee's file on Angela against my leg, wondering what I was going to do with it. I was pretty sure I'd done the right thing not showing Allen. After all, that was what I'd done before, the Justine-and-Sebastian photo thing. Once that got to Allen he'd swept it straight under the carpet, that wasn't going to happen this time. But what was going to happen, I wasn't quite sure. A couple of brokers came out of a lift. I watched them go through the glass door and into the Room.

Kerry Anne, I thought then. Jesus. I was going to have to call her. Now that I'd been suspended, my chance of promotion completely blown, I'd have to tell her that I'd changed my mind about the penthouse. And all the while she'd know that I hadn't changed my mind one bit, that the truth was I just couldn't afford the place. Oh God, she was really going to love that. She'd tell everyone in her office how she'd had me pegged from the start, a wideboy who had his sights set higher than his wallet could ever take him – she'd be gloating about this one for years. And unless another buyer for the penthouse showed up, clause seven on the contract kicked in. As from Saturday my hundred-grand deposit would be disappearing at the rate of five thousand pounds a week.

Stuffed. From every direction possible.

I ran a hand over my face then looked up through the clear glass door. Clive was shaking his head as he spoke to Fielding. Clive looked angry, there was obviously some disagreement. Gesturing back towards me, Clive chopped one hand down on his other palm. At some boxes, the underwriters and brokers had begun to notice, there was a general rubbernecking going on. Fielding was the centre of the show, and he just sat there grinning.

Finally Clive seemed to give up, came back out to rejoin me.

'Plan B,' he said as he came through the door.

I asked him what was happening, what was up.

'He wants you in there,' Clive said, looking everywhere but at my eyes. 'I tried, Ian.'

'Wants me in there for what?'

'You'll just have to go along with it.'

He turned and looked back into the Room.

'Meaning?' I said. When he didn't answer, I reached out and touched his shoulder. 'Clive?'

He breathed out a long breath. 'He's going to arrest you, Ian,' he said. 'In the Room.'

My gut turned over.

'He can't.'

'He can, Ian. And he is.'

Looking through the glass door, I saw Fielding was still sitting on my desk. But he wasn't talking to Frazer now, and he wasn't grinning either. He was looking straight back out at me, seeing how I took the news from Clive.

Fielding was going to arrest me in the Lloyd's Room. The things I thought I'd escaped all those years ago, my old man's reckless punting, cops like Fielding, they'd come smashing back into my life and now they were going to destroy me for good. People do not get arrested in the Lloyd's Room. Not underwriters, not brokers, not even the girls who do the photocopying, nobody. But there was Fielding, waiting for me to go in so he could put a hand on my shoulder and nick me in front of the whole damn market. I'd be finished. Arrested and walked out of the Room by a cop, suspicion of murder and all that bollocks – how was anyone going to be able to trust me after that? And Fielding must have known. This whole business could have been done quietly. Christ, if he'd picked up the phone and told me to get myself down to the station, I wouldn't have liked it, but I'd have gone. But that wasn't how Fielding wanted it. What he wanted was maximum damage. I was big Bob Collier's son, a jumped-up nobody who'd once caused him grief, and now that Fielding had me at his mercy he was going to bring me down.

My glittering career at Lloyd's was over.

Clive said, 'Let's get it done,' and he stepped up to the glass door. He glanced back, but I stayed right where I was. I stared past him at Fielding.

Clive followed my gaze into the Room. Fielding was still sitting on my desk, feet up on my chair, but now he had something in one hand. He held it up a little higher, swinging it gently, so that its metallic sheen caught the light. A shiny silver pair of handcuffs.

I made a sound.

'Oh fuck,' Clive said. 'That man is so far out of order.'

'No way,' I said.

Clive faced me. I shook my head.

'There's no way he does that to me, Clive. No way.'

'Keep your hat on.' He glanced back into the Room. 'I'll talk to him again, we'll sort it out.'

'He won't listen.'

He spun round angrily. 'Well, that makes two of you then.'

Eyes still on Fielding, I edged slowly across to the stairs. When Clive realized what I was about to do, his angry look disappeared. He screwed up his face.

'Don't, Ian. Don't even think about it.'

But I had thought about it, and what I'd thought was that playing things straight had lost me the penthouse, probably my deposit, and got me suspended. Playing things straight had let Fielding walk into the life I'd built since leaving the dogs, and tear it to bits. And finally here

Fielding was, perched on the 486 box, swinging a pair of handcuffs, and waiting to nick me for murder.

'I'll be in touch,' I said.

Clive called me a bloody idiot, and I took one last look into the Room. Fielding had stopped swinging the cuffs, I think it had just gotten through to him that maybe he'd misjudged me. Clive grabbed my arm. 'You can't hide from this.'

'I don't intend to, Clive.'

'Then stay put.' He gestured to the Room. 'I'll talk to him.'

Nodding, I watched as Fielding got to his feet, then I turned to the stairs, clutched the folder under my arm, and ran.

3

1

Men in suits. An anthill has ants, the City has men in suits. By the time I shot out of the Lloyd's Building and through Leadenhall Market I was just one more of them, a guy with worries trying to make his way home. I'd heard Fielding shouting down the stairs after me, but I wasn't even sure if he'd given chase, and once I'd got through Leadenhall I stopped looking back to see.

What now? Where now? The one place I couldn't go was home, Fielding knew I wasn't that stupid, but he'd have to make sure it was covered anyway.

'Taxi!' I shouted, and stuck out my hand.

A miracle, it pulled up right next to me, empty. I scrambled in. The driver asked, 'Where to?' and without thinking I found myself giving him directions to Tubs's place. As we pulled out into the traffic I slumped back in the seat and suddenly felt quite cold. The sweat made my shirt stick to my back like wet plaster.

Swivelling, I looked back through the window. People walked up and down, no-one paying any attention to my taxi going by, and there was still no sign of Fielding. I faced the front again, calming down, my heart gradually eased up thumping against my ribs. And somewhere around then I had an uncomfortable thought. Pulse rate dropping, the zing of adrenalin dying away, I saw the whole performance as Clive must have seen it. Me not a hero standing up for my rights, but me an idiot, crossing a dangerous legal line.

I held tight to the folder on my lap. I prayed to God that Tubs was home.

'Then what, you done a runner?'

'More or less,' I said.

Sprawled across the floor, heads and arms under the sink, Tubs laughed. He'd met me at the door with a monkey wrench in his hand, and now we were back in the kitchen. The relief at finding him home had already passed. I was getting annoyed he wasn't taking my problem more seriously. He rolled and grunted. Under the sink, pipes clanged.

'Shit,' he muttered. 'Jesus fuckin' shit.'

'I can't go home, Tubs.'

A hand came out from under the sink, the fingers opening and closing. 'Pliers.'

I dug through the pile of tools and junk on the table. Handed him the pliers.

'If I go home he'll arrest me.'

'I thought you said you only run because he tried it on at work.'

'I did.'

Tubs grunted some more. His shirt strained open between the buttons, his white belly wobbled. 'Home,' he said. 'That's not work.'

'I don't want to get arrested anywhere, Tubs, okay?' Getting up, I went and stood by the back door. The yard was a mess, overgrown with weeds, and the sheets on the washing line were tangled together; they wouldn't be dry in a week. It never used to be like that, not when Mrs Laszlo still had all her marbles.

'You angling for a bed?' Tubs rolled out from under the sink. He propped himself against the cupboard, breathing hard. His face was almost purple.

'I'll be right.'

'Yeah. The fuck you will.' He lifted his head. 'Take the front room upstairs.'

'That's your Mum's.'

He shook his head. 'Hasn't used it for years.' Reaching back under the sink he gave the monkey wrench a sharp pull. 'She can't do the stairs.'

And the way he said that, and the yard out back, I had a glimpse of how things were for him now, maybe how they'd been for quite a while. On the home front, Tubs was just managing to keep his head above water.

The monkey wrench came out, then the pliers; he tossed them up on the table and hauled himself to his feet.

'How long you reckon before Fielding shows up here?'

I shrugged. 'Couple of days.'

Nodding to himself, Tubs looked at me. Finally he said, 'What's the big plan? You gonna shoot your way out?'

'It'll only take me a couple of days to get this sorted.'

'This?'

I'd put the folder down on the table by the tools. Now I laid a hand on it. I explained that I thought Sebastian Ward had been feeding bad deals into the market through my syndicate.

Tubs reminded me he'd seen the photo. 'Sebastian and the tart.' He meant Justine.

'These aren't Justine Mortlake's deals,' I said. I looked down at the folder. I still didn't quite believe what Lee had found. 'These are Angela's, Justine Mortlake's mother,' I told him.

Tubs whistled. 'No shit. Sebastian was fucking the mother too?'

I kept my head down. I stared at the folder full of slips while I tried to steady myself. Sebastian and Angela? Christ, was that possible?

'Hey,' Tubs said, shaking his head. 'He was a shit but you gotta hand it to the guy. The daughter and the old lady.' He seemed slightly awestruck.

'I don't think that's how it was, Tubs.'

Still shaking his head, he went past me to the door. He told me to come on up and see the room, so I picked up the folder and followed him.

Out in the hallway, he put his head round a door and told his mum he had a friend staying for a couple of days. He got me to stick my head in too so she could see my face; he said that might stop her from having a heart attack if she bumped into me later. She didn't seem to recognize me at all.

The room upstairs was big. A bay window at the front, a single bed over by the wall, and along the opposite wall a wardrobe and a dresser. I dropped the folder on the pillow. Tubs nodded to it.

'How's that meant to get Fielding off your back?'

I sat down on the bed. I thought about Angela, what kind of woman she was, or at least what kind of woman I'd always thought she was. Respectable, that went without saying, but hardworking too, and capable, she would have made it anywhere with or without her family name. A lot more than you could say for Justine. But the Angela outside work, how well did I really know her? I knew she married Allen young, and I knew what a cold fish Allen could be. And if Sebastian had unexpectedly appeared, shining and full of charm, into her life the way he'd come into mine? Then there was the mastectomy. Glancing at the folder I remembered how she'd chucked her guts up when she saw the photo of Sebastian and Justine. And the way Angela behaved with that bloke White, she really hadn't wanted me to believe what he'd told us about Sebastian. In the end I had to face it. Tubs's idea wasn't pretty, but it fit.

Opening the folder, I pulled out the pages. Thinking aloud, I said, 'If Sebastian was running a scam through Lloyd's, maybe that gave someone a reason to kill him.'

Tubs straddled a chair by the dresser. He rested his hands on the chairback, his chin on his hands. 'You find out who murdered Sebastian, you tell Fielding, and Fielding says thank you?'

'Leave it out.'

'Bit hopeful, ay?'

'Tubs—' I lifted my head to give him a blast, then I thought, What's the point? Gesturing round at Angela's slips, I said, 'I really need some time alone to go through this.' Then I went over and picked up the phone and dialled.

Tubs opened his hands like, No problem, but as he got

up from his chair to leave he heard me ask down the phone for Katy.

He whispered, 'Who's that?'

The bar, I told him, where Katy was working. She'd be just starting her shift.

Tubs leant on the chair and waited. After a moment Katy came to the phone.

'Hello, Ian?'

'Yeah. Can you talk?'

'Not really.'

'Okay, then listen. I won't be home tonight. Maybe not for a couple of nights, but don't worry, all right, I'm okay.'

'This is about Fielding, isn't it.'

I told her it was.

'I had to let him in, Ian, he said—'

'Don't worry about that. I don't think Fielding'll come back to the flat now, but if you're scared, anything like that, just move out. Go stay with a friend. All right?'

'Ahha. Where are you?'

'Never mind.' I figured the less Katy knew the easier things would be for her if Fielding came calling again. 'If Fielding does show up, don't get clever. I've got enough problems; I don't need you in the shit as well. Katy?'

'I'm not stupid.'

'Katy—'

'I have to go, Ian.' In the background I heard her boss calling her back to the bar. 'You're seriously okay?'

'I'm fine,' I told her. 'Just stay out of Fielding's way for the next few days if you can. That'll help me more than anything.'

We said our goodbyes and then she rang off. As I hung up, Tubs pushed away from his chair.

'What the fuck are you doin'?' he said.

'What?'

'What the fuck are you doin', Ian?' He took a step towards the bed, suddenly angry. 'You stir up all this shit with Fielding and you leave Katy to take the flak?'

'Come on, Tubs.'

He pointed. 'Come on be fucked. She's your kid sister.

You're her brother, right? You're meant to be looking out for her. You wanna play some bullshit game with Fielding, that's your business. Not Katy's.'

'It's not a game.'

'Don't get smart.'

'Well, what was I meant to do?'

He leant forward. 'You were meant to look after her, Ian. You're her friggin' brother. All the family she's got now.'

It caught me hard, on the raw, and maybe I heard an accusation in his voice that wasn't really there. Bracing my arms on the bed beside my thighs, I said, 'What's that mean?'

'It means pull your head outa your arse.' He stepped back, pushing the chair aside. 'It means think of someone else for a change.'

'You blame me, don't you?'

He stopped, one hand on the chair. He knew what I meant, but I said it anyway.

'For Mum and Dad. You blame me for that.'

He shook his head. 'Nobody blames you.'

'You do, Tubs. Right after the fire, the next morning, when I told you what happened? I saw how you looked at me.'

'You're dreamin'.'

'I went for help and Mum went in after Dad. You didn't say it but you think it should have been the other way round, don't you. You think I should have tried to save Dad.'

'No.'

'You think if I'd gone into the house maybe both of them would still be alive.'

'This is meant to be what I think? You're telling me?'

'I know you do.'

'Then you know wrong, Ian.' He let go the chair, pushed it across to the wall with his foot. 'You are so fucking wrong.'

He made a snorting sound, giving up the argument. I felt kind of stranded then, and stupid too, like I'd just taken a running jump at something that wasn't there. For six months I'd believed it, and now the first time it was out in the open the thing had just collapsed into a big heap. He honestly didn't blame me for not saving Mum and Dad from the fire. Maybe for other stuff, but not for that.

'Right,' I said sarcastically. I shuffled through the papers on the bed, trying to hide my confusion. I felt like a prat.

When I looked up a few seconds later, Tubs was watching me.

Finally turning his back, he walked out, saying, 'Come through here.'

I called after him that I wasn't in the mood for games. He didn't answer. After a while curiosity got the better of me, and I went out to find him. He was in his bedroom at the back of the house. He was standing on a chair digging around the junk piled on top of his wardrobe.

'If this isn't important—'

'Give it a rest,' Tubs said. He gave me a pained look.

Folding my arms, I leant against the door. He wasn't normally such a drama queen; I was really beginning to wonder what this was about. A couple of overnight bags hit the floor, then Tubs made a sound like he'd got his hands on what he was after. He tugged a few times and the thing came out from under the pile of junk. Turning, he dropped it onto his bed.

Bob Collier. The lettering was black on a white background. Bookmaker, it said, and then his licence number. My old man's cash bag. The same one I used to have slung over my shoulder way back when I worked with him. It was badly knocked about, the leather all cracked, but somewhere along the way it had picked up a new shoulder strap. I looked up at Tubs, then back to the bag. Maybe it was just my imagination, but it seemed to give off a smell of the tracks; it was like the old man's ghost had wandered into the room.

Tubs got down off the chair. 'It won't bite,' he said.

I went across and touched the shoulder strap. Rubbed it between my fingers.

Tubs said, 'I think there's somethin' inside.'

Turning away, I said, 'I've got stuff to do.'

'Priorities, Ian.' Tubs pointed at the bag.

Reluctantly I dropped the strap. Then I reached out and touched the silver clasp, it clicked and the bag sagged open. It wasn't what I'd been half-expecting, the usual few grand in grubby notes that my old man kept as a float: there was no money in there at all. I upended the bag on the bed.

Dad's betting ledger fell out, and beside it his medal from the War. I looked at Tubs, but he didn't say a word. I shook the bag, ran a hand round inside, but that was it. I put the bag down.

'Okay,' I said, 'I give up.'

'The stuff's yours.'

I picked up the ledger and thumbed through it. Out of the corner of my eye, I was studying the medal. Dad won it in the War, he never told me how. But it meant something to him. He gave it to me when I turned twenty-one. The day after our big bust-up I put it back in the china cabinet, and neither of us ever mentioned it again.

'Bob wanted you to have it all,' Tubs said.

I turned a page. Numbers and names, lists of bets he'd taken, the only record of Dad's last days. Then the significance of Tubs's remark sunk in. I looked up.

'He what?'

'Sit down, Ian.'

'I don't want to sit down. What do you mean he wanted me to have it?'

Tubs looked past me like he wasn't sure about this any more. I waved a hand at the wardrobe.

'And what's it doing up there?'

'It's where I put it.'

'Don't piss me about, Tubs.' I tossed the ledger down by the medal, and put my hands on my hips. When I saw the pain in Tubs's eyes, I felt the hairs prickle up the back of my neck.

'He gave it to me to keep for you, Ian. He said you should have it.'

Steeling myself, I asked, 'Gave it to you when?'

'Back last summer.'

'Back last summer, when?'

'Look,' he said. 'You've got it, all right?'

Just keeping a grip on myself, I asked very quietly, 'When did he give you the fucking bag?'

Tubs looked straight at me. At last he said, 'That morning.'

It was like some storm I'd been watching, building in the distance, rolling towards me as it grew, and finally breaking right over me.

'That morning,' I said, 'before the fire?'

Tubs nodded. For a long time I just stared at the wall, not aware of Tubs, not aware of the bag or the medal or any damn thing. Last year, on the morning of the day he burned to death, Dad gave the things he most valued in all the world to Tubs. For Tubs to pass on to me.

Eventually I said, 'He knew he was going to die?'

'He didn't tell me that, Ian.'

'But he gave you this stuff.' I waved a hand over the bag and the ledger and the medal.

Again, Tubs nodded. When I screwed up my face, he said, 'He didn't make a big deal of it. He come round when I was on my way out, just give me the bag and said he'd got a new one. Said he reckoned I'd see you before he did, to give you the bag.'

Now I picked up the ledger and dropped it in the bag. Then I picked up the medal and held it in the palm of my hand, thinking, trying to figure it out. Dad knew he was going to die. That meant – what? Finally I dropped the medal in the bag too, and snapped the bag shut.

'You could've given me this the next day, Tubs.'

He didn't answer. When I looked up he turned his head from side to side.

Toying with the shoulder strap, I said, 'I'm not in the mood for Three Guesses.'

'If I'd told you then, I thought it might fuck things up if your old man had life insurance or somethin'. If he did, you'd be the one claimin'.' Tubs saw that I still hadn't got it. Or maybe that I just didn't want to get it. 'I mean,' he said, his gaze sliding past me, 'if they started askin' questions, I thought maybe it was best you didn't know about your old man leavin' you this stuff.'

I felt sick in the stomach. 'You don't believe that fire was an accident?'

Tubs turned his head.

'You think Dad killed himself?'

'I'm no friggin' expert, Ian.'

'But that's what you think happened.'

Tubs bent and picked up some of the gear that had fallen off the wardrobe. He didn't bother with getting on the chair again, he just slung the stuff back up there.

'Fucking Ward,' he said.

Ward? It took a moment, but then it clicked into place. The why of it. Why Dad had done it. Dead Men Don't Pay. Once Dad died in the fire, his debt to Sebastian was cancelled. Dad didn't have the money to pay Sebastian what he owed him, but he wasn't somebody who could have welched on the bet. If he'd done that he never would have been able to hold his head up again, not in the places that mattered to him. Not at the Stow. Not in the Gallon. Dead Men Don't Pay. Tubs kept his back turned to me, letting me figure it out for myself. And I saw it now, why Tubs didn't blame me for not saving them. By my old man's code suicide must really have seemed like an honourable solution to the mess he'd punted himself into.

Only Dad hadn't planned on me and Mum coming back early that night. Jesus, it was too horrible for words. Dad had built himself a funeral pyre, he'd wanted to die, and Mum had walked right into it to save him.

A film of tears came to my eyes. Before Tubs had a chance to face me again, I picked up my old man's bag and walked out.

I didn't look through Angela's deals. I lay on the bed,

hands behind my head on the pillow, and stared at the cracks in the ceiling. Dad hadn't told me. If he'd told me, I thought, I could have helped. I could have paid off at least part of the debt, and I could have spoken to Sebastian too. But I knew Dad wouldn't have wanted that. After the fights we'd had, the bust-ups over how he ran his book, the wild swings up and down, how could he have come to me and admitted that he'd been wrong all along? He couldn't have. Not a proud bastard like him. And I'd bet good money that he hadn't said a word to Mum about it either.

Numb, that's how I felt. After a while I flipped open the bag, took out the ledger and thumbed through the pages. I wanted to be angry with him. And I guess I was angry in a way, but I wanted more than that; I wanted to be furious like I'd been in the old days, but somehow it just didn't come. He'd fucked up, no question, but he couldn't have known Mum would do what she did. And Tubs's guess about life insurance was wrong, my old man never insured any damn thing. The price he'd paid just to make it seem like an accident, the death he'd suffered, that must have been for Mum's sake, I thought, so she'd never know he'd done himself in. Christ. How could I be furious? He was dead.

Then I paused in my thumbing through the ledger. The bet stood out a mile, fifty thousand quid at even money, it dwarfed the other numbers on the page. In the margin Dad had written 'S. Ward', and on the other side was a firm 'L' that marked the bet as a loser for the book. There it was, recorded in my old man's bold hand, the punt that had finally cost him and Mum their lives.

I couldn't bear to look at it, I turned the page. There were a few more bets, then nothing, the carefully marked rows and columns all empty. The end. Race meeting over. Mum and Dad's lives, all done. I was about to snap the ledger closed when I noticed the last entry. It was marked as a lay-off, a bet he'd placed with someone else, but the numbers looked completely cock-eyed. According to the numbers Dad had bet £400 on a 300–1 shot, but no dog in the world had ever run at odds like that, it didn't make the blindest bit of sense. But what really made me sit up straight was that name again, in the margin, S. Ward.

Tubs came in. I pointed out to him the weird last bet in the ledger.

'What do you make of this?'

Tubs's brow creased as he studied it.

'A mistake?' I said.

'Your old man?' Tubs frowned and shook his head.

I turned the ledger towards me and looked at the bet again. There was no L or W next to it, so no way of telling whether Dad lost or won on the bet.

'Payout of a hundred and twenty grand,' Tubs said. 'Some punt.'

We both looked at the numbers in silence. Then Mrs Laszlo's voice came drifting up the stairs; she was calling for Tubs. I snapped the ledger shut and tossed it in the bag.

Priorities, I thought. And right now the priority wasn't figuring out some cock-eyed bet, it was stopping Fielding from banging me up in gaol. As Tubs went to the door, I thanked him for keeping my old man's stuff for me.

He turned to me with a lopsided smile.

'Your fuckin' transparent, Ian.'

'That bad?'

'You want somethin', why not just ask?'

Mrs Laszlo's frail voice drifted up again. 'Toby?'

He rolled his eyes.

'Tubs,' I said, 'I really need to borrow your car.'

2

Driving Tubs's old Mercedes was like driving a tank, but I got to the Mortlakes' country house in just over an hour. It was after eight. I parked in a lay-by fifty yards short of their drive and walked up to the gates. They were open and at the end of the gravel driveway by the house I could see a dark Saab, Angela's car. I'd checked once already on the way over, but now I took out Tubs's mobile again and dialled Allen's number at work. On the first ring he answered, and I immediately hung up. He was probably in another meeting with Crossland, trying desperately to hold the line on the merger. Piers Crossland would be putting the screws on; he might be a gentleman on the golf course but in business he'd take every advantage he could get. And after the Ottoman payout, and me doing a runner, Allen's bargaining position hadn't gotten any stronger. But for the moment I put that aside. I took Lee's folder out from under my arm and walked up the drive, the leafless branches scraping in the trees overhead.

In the car I'd thought of a lot of ways to approach this, but now that I'd arrived the simplest way seemed best. I didn't have the time to frig around, not with Fielding on my case, so I walked straight up to the door and hit the buzzer. Somewhere inside, chimes rang. I glanced around, but there didn't seem to be any security cameras. A dog started barking in the house.

When the door swung open, Angela was standing there in a paint-spattered apron. She was holding the doberman by the collar, talking to it, shutting it up, but when she saw me she stopped. She said my name, surprised. No doubt about it. From Allen or Justine, maybe even Frazer, she'd heard. I was a criminal on the run. I shot a look at the dog. 'Will it eat me?'

'Not unless I tell it to.' Straightening after a moment, she gave a yank on the dog's collar and stepped back. 'Come on in,' she said.

I'd been out to the house more than a few times in the past couple of years, usually dinner parties where all the other guests were people from the market. It became one more of those stupid point-scoring things I had running with Frazer. 'Didn't see you down there yesterday, Frazer. What's that? You weren't invited?' The next week he'd be invited down and I wouldn't be, and then it was my turn to take the needle. Petty. Childish. My only consolation, looking back, was that my old man never saw me in action.

'I suppose Allen's told you,' I said to Angela, following her and the doberman into the kitchen, 'I had a visit at work from Fielding.'

'He mentioned it.'

'And did he mention he'd suspended me?'

She waved a hand towards a cabinet. 'You'll have to mix your own drink.' She knelt on the dust-sheet spread out on the floor. Around it the kitchen chairs had all been pushed back. The doberman went over and slumped down on a giant cushion by the Aga. On the dust-sheet there was another chair. Angela picked up a brush and with neat dabbing strokes, started painting. 'I can't let it dry. It's meant to look like bamboo, sodding thing's taken me two hours.'

I said, 'I'll pass on the drink.'

Angela studied the end of her paintbrush, still dabbing. 'I can't believe I'm doing this. Allen was worried I'd be bored once I retired so he put my name down for some courses.' She glanced my way, raising a brow. You know Allen.

'You don't have to do it.'

'Actually, I'm getting to like it.' She dipped her brush

in the paint, turned the chair, and set to work again. 'Therapeutic. And I don't have to listen to the brokers.'

'Fielding was there to arrest me.'

She pursed her lips, concentrating hard on the chair.

'If I hadn't run,' I said, 'he'd probably have charged me with Sebastian's murder by now.'

Angela wrapped a rag round her finger. She swiped a paint dribble off the chair. 'Aren't you being a bit overdramatic, Ian? You seem to have a real thing about this Fielding. Why don't you just talk to him?' She smiled at me and said, 'I hope I'm not going to get done for aiding and abetting.'

Right then the doberman lifted its head and barked. Angela turned on him and snapped 'Shut up!' and he dropped his head to the cushion again. 'Bloody animal,' she said. She wasn't quite as relaxed about my visit as she'd been making out.

I set my folder down on a side table. 'I've got some slips here I'd like you to look at.'

She returned to her painting. 'No thanks,' she said. 'Show Allen. Take them to Frazer. I've retired.'

Pulling the slips from the folder, I told her, 'These are pieces of business written before you retired.'

No reaction. I'd been watching carefully but there wasn't even a flicker of the eyes. She concentrated hard on the end of her brush, laying the paint on in short even strokes.

'Angela, aren't you the slightest bit curious about why I'm here?'

'I know why you're here.'

I made a sound. She leant back to examine her handiwork on the chair.

'You want me to talk Allen into lifting your suspension.' When she put down her brush, she faced me. 'But I can tell you right now, I'd be wasting my breath. He is livid, Ian. Absolutely livid.'

I put up a hand, I didn't need the reminder. 'That's not why.' I propped myself against the huge kitchen table and flicked through the slips Lee had found. 'Just tell me if these names ring any bells.'

Angela wiped her hands on the apron, curious now.

'Kestrel?' I said.

'No.'

'Connolly and Blythe?'

'No.'

'Astra Freight?'

'No.' She pushed herself up from her knees, turning away from me. 'What are they meant to be?'

'I haven't finished.'

Her head swivelled, she looked like she wasn't too happy.

'Blaxton?' I said.

'No.'

She was lying. And she knew I knew she was lying.

'There's a couple more,' I said, holding out the slips for her to take. When she didn't touch them, I slipped them back in the folder. The atmosphere had changed. The dog had his head up off the cushion now, watching us closely.

'You wrote the lead on all of them, Angela. And they all made claims.'

'Did I ever say I was perfect?'

'They were extremely dodgy pieces of business. Maybe you're not perfect, but you're more than good enough to have seen they were rotten risks.'

She quoted that old market wisdom at me, about there being no bad risks, only bad prices.

'The broker on every one of those slips,' I said, 'was WardSure.'

At that, finally, I got a reaction. She bent over and started hammering lids onto the paint tins with her fist. Her face was tight.

'Where is this going, Ian?'

'It's the same as the Ottoman deal.'

'I didn't write that.'

'No, Justine did. And I think we both know how Sebastian convinced her.'

Angela stood up straight. She gave me a look that burned.

I said, 'Fielding wants me done for murder, Angela. Normally I wouldn't give a toss what goes on in someone else's private life, but I'm not going to let myself get banged up in prison just because I didn't want to hurt anyone's feelings.'

'I'm not answerable for Justine.'

'That's fine. Because I'm not talking about Justine.'

She held my gaze a second longer, then she stooped to pick up her tins of paint. And that, I suppose, was when I knew Tubs's guess was right. When Angela turned away instead of laughing in my face. I stepped back and sat down on a chair. I dropped my head.

'Jesus Christ,' I said.

Ignoring me, she took the paint tins and placed them on a board by the French windows. Then she came back for the brushes.

'Angela. You and Sebastian had an affair? For more than ten years?'

'I've retired.'

'What?'

She pointed a brush at me. 'I'm not responsible for the syndicate any more, Ian. If there's a problem there, it's not for me to sort it out.'

'Problem?' I held up the folder, Angela's six rotten deals. 'Angela, don't you think Fielding might be interested in this?'

She seemed genuinely puzzled. 'Why?' she asked me.

'Because, Angela, you were having an affair with Sebastian for more than ten years, you were assisting him in defrauding the market, and when he switched his attentions to your daughter, his house burnt down. And he went with it.'

She looked at me a moment, and then she did it. She laughed. A forced laugh. She took her brushes across to the bucket of water by the window. 'Oh, come on, Ian. You can do better than that.'

'I wasn't joking.'

'Wronged woman goes mad with jealousy? Jilted lover takes murderous revenge?'

'You wrote these leads.'

'Middle-aged woman has mastectomy and goes stark raving nuts?' She swirled the brushes through the water then stood up, wiping her hands on the apron. 'It's ridiculous.'

I looked at her, a woman who'd just turned fifty and celebrated the occasion with a mastectomy. Jilted, that was her word. Had Sebastian dumped her for Justine?

I said, 'Is it, Angela?'

Her eyes on mine, she undid the apron and slid it off over her head. She tossed the apron on the floor by the paint.

'Up yours,' she said.

She was halfway to the drinks cabinet when I told her, 'Even if Fielding doesn't take these deals seriously, I think Allen will.'

She stopped.

'And the Lloyd's Council,' I said.

She spun round. 'Don't.'

We looked at each other. Two weeks earlier we were friends and colleagues, and now we were – what? Sebastian hovered like a shadow between us. Turning, she continued to the drinks cabinet and poured herself something.

'Has it crossed your mind,' she asked, 'that you might be wrong?'

'These slips—' I touched the folder.

'About Sebastian and me,' she said.

While she came back to the centre of the room, I considered the question. I realized then that she hadn't either confirmed or denied the connection between them, and after a while as she stood there sipping her drink and studying her newly painted chair, I said, 'Well, am I wrong?'

She sat down, crossing one leg over the other. Good legs for a fifty-year-old woman. She rested her glass against her chin. 'No.' She sipped her drink. 'As it happens, you're right on the money.'

She didn't look at me now.

'Angela,' I said. 'Why?'

Smiling sadly, she took a good swig then her head fell back. 'Why? Why marry too young? Why breast cancer?' She took another swig. 'Why any bloody thing?'

She looked tired, completely drained, like she just couldn't be bothered hiding things any more. The mastectomy, then Sebastian's death, and now me dredging up stuff she must have thought was buried forever, it was like she'd come to the end of the road.

I touched the folder. 'Why'd you write these leads?'

'Sebastian asked me to.'

'Just like that?'

She put down her glass and looked me straight in the eye. 'Were you ever in love, Ian?' She waited for me to answer. When I didn't come, she went on, 'At the start – what was that one, Kestrel?'

I flicked open the folder and read her the first of the dodgy slips.

She nodded. 'It didn't seem that important. I did the usual background check, they looked bent so I told Sebastian I was going to turn the business down.'

'You were already having the affair?'

'He said he really needed the business. The brokerage. Things were a bit tight.' Angela shrugged, remembering. 'So I signed the lead.'

'Knowing there'd be a claim.'

'No,' she said quickly.

I thumbed through the folder. 'Connolly and Blythe? Astra Freight?'

Her eyes fell.

'You must have realized sometime, Angela. Sebastian gets you to sign all these leads and they keep turning out stinkers; something must have clicked.'

'He needed the brokerage.'

'Brokerage, my arse.'

She leant forward. 'All right, so after a few times I probably guessed. He was my lover, and I put things through the syndicate I shouldn't have. What am I meant to do now, throw myself off the Lloyd's Building?'

349

She knew she was in the wrong. It couldn't have been too easy for her owning up to all this – the affair, then caving in to Sebastian when he pressured her to sign the lead on those policies. And if I thought back to those lectures she used to give me on ethics and etiquette in the market, I didn't know whether to be embarrassed for her or very bloody angry.

I said, 'Those clients, Kestrel and that, did you meet any of them?'

'No.'

'But you knew they all had bad claims records. You must have guessed they were bent.'

Nodding, she picked up her drink.

'Then you must have had a fair idea Sebastian was bent too,' I said. 'He had to be splitting the claims with these guys.'

I tapped the folder. She didn't say anything.

'Angela, you don't want these deals to go to Allen now, do you?'

Her look hardened. 'I'm not sure that blackmail suits you, Ian.'

'I'm not sure going to prison for murder suits me either. And it's whistle-blowing, not blackmail.'

Angela tapped her knee. I thought it was just nerves, but then the doberman got up and trotted over. She touched its back and it sat at her feet, looking up at her.

Stroking his ears, she said, 'I'm not going to beg, but I don't want those slips being passed on to Allen.'

'Then help me.' I nodded to the folder. 'Did Sebastian ever mention any names, people from those companies?'

'No.'

'No-one he'd had a falling-out with?'

'Ian, don't you get it? When I was with Sebastian, we didn't spend our time talking business.' She held my look for a moment, then her gaze dropped. She stroked the doberman's neck. 'Anyway, I don't see what good it could do anyone, you telling Allen. Not now.'

'Angela—' I spread my hands – 'Sebastian was murdered. His bloody house burnt down on top of him, and then someone tried to pull a K and R stroke on us. And then Ottoman and Mehmet; if all that's connected with these deals you were doing—'

'You don't believe that.'

'I don't want to believe it. But then again, I didn't want to believe you were having an affair with Sebastian behind Allen's back.'

She flinched. I wasn't doing myself any favours. I needed her help, and there wasn't much chance of that if I put her back up.

'Look,' I said, 'I don't want to go to Allen. I just want to figure out what was happening with Sebastian before he was murdered.'

'Then what happens to those?' Angela pointed to the folder.

'They go back into storage,' I told her. 'They'll gather dust for another twenty years, then get ditched.'

She considered my proposition; it didn't take her very long. However else she wanted to spend her retirement, I thought, it wasn't as a divorcee with a reputation for adultery. She shoved the doberman and it loped back to its place by the Aga.

'That Blaxton's policy,' she said, 'was the last I wrote the lead on for Sebastian.'

'That was almost two years ago.'

Angela nodded.

'And that was the last time he asked you for the favour?'

'Yes.'

I waited and she just looked at me.

'What about Ottoman?' I said.

She took her glass back to the cabinet. Pouring another tall one, she said, 'The first I knew about Ottoman was when their claim came in.'

'And you thought?'

'I thought Justine had written a bad piece of business.' She recapped the bottle and faced me. 'And I thought you'd been rather slack in letting it slip through.'

I took that one on the chin. I said, 'So the first you knew about Sebastian and Justine was the photo?'

Closing her eyes, she nodded. And when I remembered how she'd reacted on seeing the photo, it seemed likely. And if she hadn't known about Justine and Sebastian until well after Sebastian's death, then the jilted lover turns murderous idea was junk. Not that I could take it that seriously anyway. I mean, this was Angela.

'I'm not proud of writing those leads for him,' she said, returning to her chair. 'And I don't like the fact that he was sleeping with my daughter – even if, under the circumstances, I'm not in much of a position to complain. But believe me, Ian, when his house burnt down, and later when we found out he'd been murdered, I was more shocked than anyone.' She stared over her drink at nothing. I felt embarrassed then, like some kind of peeping Tom. Just remembering Sebastian Ward was making Angela's eyes cloud over; she wiped them with the back of her hand.

'Angela, could either Allen or Justine have known what was going on between you and Sebastian?'

The meaning of my question seemed to sink in slowly. Did either her husband or her daughter have a motive for murder?

'Now that,' she said, tilting her glass towards me, 'really is crazy.'

I was about to ask a few follow-ups when the doberman suddenly leapt to its feet. He barked at the windows, and a moment later we heard a car speeding down the drive. The dog pricked its ears then turned a circle and slumped by the Aga. A sound he recognized. I got up from my chair.

'Justine,' Angela told me as the car stopped out front. Then she raised an eyebrow in my direction. 'And Allen and I haven't let on that we know about her and Sebastian, either.'

I got the message, she didn't want a big scene. I guess she and Allen had decided the best thing, now that Sebastian was dead, was to forget they'd ever seen that photo. Let Justine get on with her life ignorant of what they knew. That was all well and good for the Mortlakes, but what about me?

I said, 'I already asked Justine about her and Sebastian.'

Angela wrestled with herself briefly, then gave in. 'And?'

'And nothing. She didn't want to hear.'

The front door opened and closed; there were footsteps in the hall. When Justine came into the kitchen and saw me, she stopped cold. Her cheeks glowed.

Looking at me, she said to her mother, 'What's he been saying?' and then, 'Why's he here?'

Angela gestured vaguely to the folder in my hand. She explained there was some syndicate business we were clearing up.

'He's been suspended,' Justine said. The dog went and nuzzled up to her, she shoved it away with her knee. 'The police are looking for him too, they came to the Room to arrest him.'

I told her to keep her shirt on. Justine glared at me.

She said, 'Does Dad know he's here?'

'Oh for goodness' sake.' Angela was ticked off with her daughter now. 'Take your coat off,' she said. 'Have a drink and settle down.'

Justine gave me a withering glance as she pulled her coat off and stepped back out into the hall. Angela took a very long drink from her glass; she seemed absolutely knackered. Living in the same house as her daughter, after all that had happened, must have been hell for her. And those leads she'd written for Sebastian, given the kind of person she was, they'd be on her conscience forever. But I still wasn't sure that I bought everything Angela had told me. Given the kind of person she was, how had she fallen so easily into Sebastian's crooked set-up? Justine – stuck-up and vain – now her I understood. But Angela? Something about it just didn't ring true.

'What's she up to?'

Angela got up from her chair and looked out through the doorway.

'Justine!' she called.

There was no answer. We looked at each other. I think we both realized in the same moment exactly what Justine was up to. The bloody cow was busy on the phone.

I swore.

Angela said, 'I'm sorry, Ian,' but I didn't wait for the rest of the apology. I knocked the painted chair over in my rush for the door, and as I ran down the drive I heard the doberman barking at me from behind the tall French windows.

Two miles clear of the place I passed the first cop car, blue light flashing, siren wailing, headed the other way.

3

When I called Clive he just about chewed my ear off. What did I think I was doing, did I realize the position I'd put him in, wasn't it time I came to my senses, the full bit. After a couple of minutes letting off steam, he calmed down enough to listen.

'There's been a development,' I said, and then I told him straight out that Angela had had a long-term affair with Sebastian. I didn't mention the deals.

After a few seconds' silence, he asked cautiously, 'How long-term?'

'More than ten years.'

He groaned.

I said, 'If either Justine or Allen knew—'

'Stop right there.'

'Maybe they had some kind of motive for murder.'

'I don't want to hear it.'

'Clive, you don't—'

'Shut up, for Christ's sake!'

I looked at the receiver in my hand. Faintly hearing my name, I put it back to my ear.

'There's been what you might call a development this end too,' Clive said. I waited and he added, 'I think you should hear it from the witness's own mouth.'

'What witness?'

'The witness,' Clive said, 'who was in Sebastian's house the night of the murder.'

We met at a lay-by in Epping Forest. I drove past once in Tubs's Mercedes, and saw Clive's car parked there waiting. As my headlights swept over his car I saw two figures in the front but I couldn't make out their faces. Half a mile on, I turned and came back slowly. I pulled off the road and eased up behind Clive's car, the whole business feeling completely unreal.

After switching off the ignition, I flashed my headlights. One from either side, they got out of the car. They looked around into the dark – the forest was thick and low just there – and after a moment they headed my way. Clive opened the door behind me and slid into the back seat without saying a word. Then the passenger door opened and the witness got in beside me. He offered me his hand but I just let it hang there until he got the message. The hand dropped.

'What's up with you?' he said.

I stared over the steering wheel, the muscles of my jaw clenched tight. 'Nigel,' I said, 'you've got the brains of a fucking gnat.'

He made a sound. Clive grabbed the seatback between us and hauled himself forward.

'I didn't come out here to watch a catfight, ladies, so don't bloody start.'

Nigel Chambers turned to Clive saying, 'Why does he have to know anyway? I told you I'd tell the cops.'

'The cops,' Clive said patiently, 'haven't had their lives turned upside-down by your failure to step forward and say what you saw, Nigel. But Ian here, he has. He's owed an explanation. Give it to him, then we're leaving.'

I glanced across at Nigel; he was frowning, clearly unhappy that Clive hadn't taken him straight to the cops. I said to Nigel, 'You were at Sebastian's place that night?'

He nodded reluctantly.

'What for?' I asked him.

'This and that.'

I looked at him. Finally he shrugged.

'The WardSure shareprice was coming off a bit. I was borrowed up to the eyeballs and I'd committed to taking another truckload of shares. I needed some cash. Short-term.'

'You were going to borrow from Sebastian?'

'Ahha.'

'You'd done that before?'

'Yep.' He shook his head. 'Look, this is all beside the point anyway. It never got that far, I didn't even get to ask him.'

Half-turned to Nigel now, I rested an elbow through the steering wheel. Clive was leaning forward, listening.

'I got there late,' Nigel said, remembering. 'I don't know, maybe ten?'

'You phoned first?' Clive asked.

Nigel shook his head. 'No chance. I didn't want him telling me to sod off before I put it to him about the money. Anyway, I get there the front gate's open, so I drive up to the house. Up at the house, there's plenty of lights on, but as I'm walking up the path I hear some noise round the side. When I go round there to look it's that guy Pike, Sebastian's security man. He's got his van backed up to the side door. When he saw me he just about fell over.'

'What was he up to?'

'Wait on.' Nigel collected his thoughts for a moment. 'I asked Pike, "Is Sebastian in?" and at first he looks lost, then he says, "In the library. You know the way, show yourself through." Well I didn't know anything had happened, and I'd come to see Sebastian, so I went in. The library door was closed, I knocked a couple of times but there was no answer, I thought Pike must have got it wrong. But just to be sure, I opened the door and looked in. Sebastian was there all right. Stretched out on the floor.'

'Dead?' I said. Clive poked me in the shoulder.

'Dead,' Nigel agreed. 'But I didn't know that at first. I went over, I couldn't believe it, there was a gun lying under his arm, a pistol. I lifted his head and I pulled the pistol out, I guess I was trying to make him comfortable. Jesus, I don't know.' Nigel ran his fingers up through his hair, and stared out into the forest. I got the feeling he didn't want to look me in the eye. 'I was just like that,'

Nigel said, 'when Pike came running in.'

I tried to picture the scene; Nigel and Sebastian and Pike. It wouldn't come.

'Then what?' Clive said.

'Then like I told you, I'm still shocked out of my head, Pike comes over and takes the pistol off me, holding it in some cloth. Then he starts saying he's going to call the police.' Nigel faced me. 'Well I just freaked.'

'You ran?'

'How could I run? My fingerprints were all over the pistol and Sebastian's body was just lying there. Pike had me by the balls. He knew it too.'

'But you didn't actually see Pike shoot Sebastian.'

Nigel turned to Clive. 'While I was still completely freaked out, Pike got me to help him. You know how?'

I didn't say anything. Neither did Clive.

'The little bastard was robbing the place. That's what his van was doing backed up to the house. He'd taken paintings, anything he could carry, but he couldn't get the big stuff by himself. Some desk he wanted. So he made me help him load it. Little fuck.'

I studied him for a while. 'You're saying Pike murdered Sebastian so he could rob Sebastian's house?'

Nigel's brow creased. 'Well, what else?'

'And he tricked you into leaving your fingerprints on the murder weapon.'

He nodded.

I took a breath. 'Nigel, you knew the cops were trying to nail the murder on me, and you left this till now?'

He mumbled an apology into his chest. When I swore, he lifted his head. 'Hey, I was set up too, remember. And between times I've been busy going bankrupt. It hasn't been a picnic for me either, you know.'

'Perhaps,' Clive said quietly from the back seat, 'Ian should hear the rest of it.'

Nigel turned on him. 'You said we were going to the cops.'

'Let's finish up here first, shall we?'

Nigel looked like he was going into a sulk. And I really

couldn't understand why he'd rather talk to the cops than me.

'So what about the fire?' I asked him.

He shook his head. 'I was already gone. Pike said he'd take the body away in the van, he said if I breathed a word he'd drop me right in it. He still had the gun.'

'With your prints on it.'

'Right.' Nigel turned thoughtful. 'Next morning I'm going nuts figuring out what to do, then I hear the news. Sebastian's house has gone up in flames.' He pulled a face. 'When the rumours got going, I had other worries.'

'The WardSure shareprice.'

'That K and R bullshit knocked it,' Nigel said unhappily. 'And then when it came out he was dead, the bloody thing fell off a cliff.'

I glanced back at Clive; his expression didn't give anything away but his eyes were fixed firmly on Nigel. 'The K and R?' Clive prompted.

'Yeah,' Nigel said. 'Nearly did my head in, that one. I mean, a kidnapped dead man. Then I got to wondering if I'd really seen what I thought I'd seen that night in Sebastian's library. I guess I wanted to believe he was still alive. If he was still alive the shareprice might have turned around; it could have saved me from going down the bloody pan.'

'So you kept your mouth shut.'

Rubbing the back of his neck, Nigel said, 'So I made a mistake.'

It was difficult, but I just managed to stop myself from taking a swing at him. Clive must have sensed that, he put his hand on my shoulder. He told Nigel to go and wait in the other car.

'I want to get this sorted out tonight,' Nigel said to him. 'With the cops.'

Clive nodded. When Nigel opened the door, the cold night air poured in. For a moment I thought the bastard was going to offer me his hand again, but in the end all he did was bob his head and get out.

'Nigel,' I said, 'have you ever heard of a place called Aston Kennels?'

He turned up his collar, frowning as he shook his head. The door closed. We watched him walk back to Clive's car, shoulders hunched, hands pushed deep in his pockets.

While we'd been talking a few cars had gone by, but now the road was empty and as dark as the forest. I stared straight ahead. Behind me Clive sat in silence.

'Clive?'

'Mm?'

I turned and rested my arm along the seatback. 'What the fuck was that all about?'

He didn't answer. He sat slumped back in the seat, his hands on his lap, looking out at the night.

'Nigel just up and changed his mind? And Jesus, that story—'

Clive snorted.

I said, 'How much do you reckon was true?'

After a pause, Clive answered, 'Not much.'

'And why's he suddenly stuck his hand up now? I don't get it.'

'Ian.' Clive touched my arm. 'I don't have a clue what's going on with Nigel. But it's your neck in the noose. I thought you deserved a chance to hear what Fielding's going to hear when I deliver Nigel to the station. Well, now you've heard.'

I faced the front. Clive's car was just a dark shadow. 'Why's he so keen to tell the cops?'

'Pass,' Clive said.

I turned to ask another but Clive raised a hand.

'Look, I've done my bit. And here's another one for you. That piece of jewellery you say Fielding planted at your flat. He's taken it to Max to identify.'

'What is it?'

'A diamond brooch, shaped like a butterfly.' He reached for the doorhandle. 'You've got my number. When you figure out what you're going to do, call me.'

'Nigel could tell the cops you both saw me out here.'

Smiling grimly, Clive said that he'd warned Nigel not

to, but that yes, it was a risk.

'Thanks,' I said.

He faced me. 'Don't thank me, thank Fielding.' When he saw my surprise he explained, 'After you did your escape act today Fielding came up to my office. He pointed out that I was involved in the Ottoman case, that I knew about the K and R, and that I appeared to be someone you trusted.'

'He tried to drag you into this thing?'

Clive opened the door. 'Let's say he convinced me of something that you'd failed to convince me of since the start of this mess.'

He closed the door. I wound down my window.

'Now you know I didn't have anything to do with the K and R?' I said. 'Or the murder?'

Clive walked towards his car, speaking over his shoulder.

'Now I know,' he said, 'that Detective Sergeant Fielding is a prick.'

4

For a few hours, up in Tubs's front room, I slept. I dreamt about Mum and, when I woke up, daylight was peeping round the curtains. It was while I was rubbing my face, still groggy with sleep, that I made the connection I should have made hours earlier. Getting up I wrapped a towel around me then I wandered over and took Tubs's mobile off the dresser. I dialled Clive, praying I'd get something more than the answer machine.

Four rings, then he answered. 'Wainwright.'

'Clive, it's Ian. You said you had dinner at Sebastian's place last week.'

There was a few beats' silence then he said, 'Are you off your rocker?'

'No, listen, was there anything unusual about the silver, or the cutlery? Some mark, anything that sticks in your mind?'

'Cutlery. You're serious?'

'Very.'

A pause, then he answered. 'Nothing occurs to me. By the by, I'm still down at the station. Here's a bit of good news for you. Max Ward can't positively identify the brooch.'

I asked Clive what he thought that meant. He said it meant that whoever tipped Fielding off that the brooch was in my flat, or gave it to Fielding to plant there, had made a mistake. Either the brooch had nothing to do with Sebastian, or Fielding's informant hadn't bargained on Max's bad memory being quite so bad. Clive said his money was on option two.

'Well, does that let me off?'

He told me if anyone ever asked, I hadn't heard this from him. 'But I wouldn't present myself just yet, Ian. Max might still remember.'

'Oh great.'

Clive said he was getting another lawyer to come down to the station and hold Nigel's hand, he really sounded like he'd had enough of the whole business. Then just as I was about to ring off, he said, 'That cutlery?'

'Yeah?'

'I couldn't swear to it, but didn't it all have a bulby bit down the end?' He paused as if he was puzzling it over. 'Yeah,' he said. 'Like an onion?'

Doug Aston was back from his holidays. His wife said he was with the dogs so Tubs and me walked on down the track to the kennels. The place looked different in daylight, more open, but the smell was just the same. We found Doug with one of his kennel lads, both of them kneeling beside a tub of mush, bread and water, Doug had his arms in it up to the elbows. He saw us from a good way off but he waited till we'd stopped right by him before he looked up.

'Watcha,' Tubs said.

Doug nodded, and turned to me. 'Long time, Ian.'

I didn't want to start down that road, so I came right out with it. 'We've come about Eddie Pike.'

Doug gave the mush another stir with his arms, then he scooped a bucket through it. He handed the bucket to his lad, telling him to finish the feeding then hose out the yard. The lad walked over to where the dogs were scrabbling at their kennel doors, yapping.

'Got back last night,' Doug said, wiping his arms with a rag. He nodded towards the lad. 'Just heard this mornin'.'

'What did you hear?' I asked him.

He shot a look at me. He knew now that this wasn't a social call.

'Eddie's in some strife,' he said. He finished wiping,

then flicked the rag over a rail. 'The lad knows more about it than me. Try him.'

'Eddie Pike's wanted on suspicion of murder,' I told him evenly. 'Sebastian Ward – remember him? His house burnt down while he was still in it. Eddie Pike was meant to be the security man there. But since the fire, he's disappeared.'

Doug rolled down his sleeves. 'Yeah?' he said. Then he turned away from us and headed for the converted barn, the place where Pike had been hiding out.

We followed him into the central room downstairs. The pane of glass Tubs had smashed with his torch hadn't been replaced, but the floor was swept clean. Doug threw back the lid on a feed bin and leant over, inspecting how much was left.

I said, 'Doug, you must have known Pike was staying here.'

He screwed up his face. 'You what?'

'He's not here now, is he?'

Doug's mouth opened, he made a sound of disbelief.

Stepping forward, Tubs gestured to the door. 'Sorry about the glass. When Ian and me came over the other night, we had some trouble persuading Pike to let us in.'

At that, Doug's look changed. He tugged at the bin lid, it came down with a bang.

'What do you two want?'

'To look around,' I said.

He waved a hand, telling us to feel free, he was busy. He opened the next feed bin and peered in there.

'Then we'd like a chat,' I told him.

He didn't look up; it seemed like we'd already given him plenty to think about.

Tubs went and looked into the other dog room and came back shaking his head. Then both of us went into the living quarters, where Eddie Pike had bolted from the other night. Downstairs it was all just like it had been, except that the back door leading out of the kitchen was locked shut. Up on the next floor the beds were stripped bare, and the TV had gone; it looked like no-one had used the place for months. Tubs checked under the mattresses. No girlie mags this time, and no photos.

Getting to his feet, Tubs said, 'You reckon Aston cleared the place out, or Pike?'

I pulled a face. Who knows? Then I went to the stairs and climbed up to the loft. Hitting the light switch, I saw straight away that the stuff was gone. Tubs climbed up behind me, we stood side-by-side looking down the dimly lit gallery to the far wall. As my eyes adjusted, I saw a few dust-sheets heaped halfway along.

Tubs said, 'You're sure it was here?'

Nodding, I went forward. I crouched and pulled the dust-sheets back, there was nothing hidden underneath.

'All the silverware was here,' I said, waving my hand over the spot. 'In boxes.' Still crouching, I pivoted. 'The furniture was over there.'

'The desk?'

I stood, walked a few paces, then stopped. 'Right here.'

Tubs stared at my feet as if he was imagining how it had been.

'Fuck,' he said.

And that pretty much summed it up. We'd had our chance and blown it.

Then I noticed something in the shadow, about knee-high, propped against a rafter. You could have mistaken it for a bit of old board, I guess I had till then, but now I saw that it glinted golden along one edge. Crouching down, I went forward, and the last yard I had to get down on my knees. Close up, you couldn't mistake it.

I took out a hankie, placed it over my hand, then reached out and gripped the edge of the thing. Backing awkwardly out of there, I pulled it after me.

'What have you got?' Tubs said.

Standing, I took it over to the light, still careful not to touch it except through the hankie. I spun it round so we could both see.

'A picture?' Tubs reached, but I fended his hand off. He looked surprised, then he got it. 'One of Sebastian's?'

'At a guess.'

It was a landscape; even in the dim light you could make out the trees and the sky. In the field there were dark shapes, maybe cattle.

We studied it for a while, then I picked it up and headed for the stairs.

'Let's see if we can't jog Doug's memory.'

We found him in the room where we'd left him, but now he had a pile of leads and collars out, he was cleaning them. Through the open door to the yard, we heard the lad outside hosing down.

'Satisfied?' Doug said, without looking our way.

I took the picture over and propped it on one of the feed bins. He glanced up. I don't know what bullshit story he'd dreamt up for us, but you could see in his eyes when he saw the picture that he knew a story wasn't going to help him now.

'Not one of yours?' I said.

He had his elbows on the table; he lifted one hand and covered his face.

'It was stolen from Ward's house the night he died,' I told him. 'Along with the other stuff Pike had stashed up there.'

Doug stayed silent.

I said, 'We should probably take this to the police.'

'Leave it out.' He dropped his hands. 'All I did was leave the little bastard a key.'

'Pike?'

'Yeah.'

I gestured round. 'For this place?'

Doug nodded unhappily. Then he got up and slung the leads and collars on their hooks before closing the door.

'Anyway,' he said, turning, 'what's this to you?'

Looking him straight in the eye, I explained that the police had the mistaken idea that I was involved with the murder. 'If I send them round here,' I said, 'maybe you could put their minds at rest.'

He drew back, shocked. 'Here? Fuck me, don't send them here. It's nothin' to do with me.'

'Then why did you give Pike the key?'

'I was goin' on holiday. I had a lad comin' in for the dogs, feedin' and that, but I needed someone a bit responsible if there was problems. Callin' the vet in, say. Buyin' more feed.'

'And someone responsible,' I said, 'that was Pike?'

'He done it for me last year,' Doug opened one hand. 'He won't be doin' it again. I already told him that.'

A blast of water hit the door outside then moved on. Doug didn't seem to realize what he'd said.

'Where is he now, then?' I asked.

He looked down. 'Dunno.'

'You came back last night. Between then and now, you've spoken to him. Where?'

Ignoring me, he turned to Tubs. 'They don't seriously reckon Pike killed him, do they?'

Slowly, Tubs nodded.

'Shit,' Doug said. His hands bunched into fists on the table. He was thinking about his licence. 'I'll wring the bugger's neck.'

'Where is he?'

'I had nothin' to do with it.' He was tense; it was coming home to him just how much trouble Pike might have landed him in. If the police showed up at his kennels, word would get around. He'd find himself hauled up by the stewards at the Stow, maybe even old man Chandler, and asked to explain. If he couldn't satisfy them it might cost Doug his training licence; without that his kennels were worthless. Now he dropped his head. 'He's at the Stow.'

'The track?' Tubs said, amazed. 'He's hiding at the track?'

'Look, I came back last night. Pike just about shat when he seen me. He had the kennel lad giving him a hand loading stuff in his van.'

'From the loft?' I said, jerking my thumb up.

Doug nodded. 'I took one look at it – pictures, classy furniture – Pike said he was helpin' a mate out; I knew it had to be hooky. I got my key back off him, and told him to bugger off. That was the last I seen him.'

'He told you where he was going?'

Doug turned his head. 'He took the kennel lad to help him get the stuff unloaded. He gave the lad twenty quid to keep his mouth shut.'

'Not enough?'

Going to the door, Doug said, 'The kid's not too bright, but he prefers his job here to the dole queue.' He opened the door and called the kennel lad over.

While we were waiting, Tubs poked me in the ribs. I turned to him and he nodded to the far wall. There was a collection of framed photos, the standard winning shots of the dogs as they hit the line at full stretch.

'Bottom right,' Tubs whispered.

I looked down there. At first I didn't see them, but then both names leapt out at me, Lucky Lip and Jeremiah.

'Here,' Doug said, bringing the lad in.

Collecting myself, I listened as Tubs asked the lad a few questions. He wouldn't have been more than seventeen, and it was obvious that helping lug furniture was the sum total of his connection with Pike. I kept glancing back at the dog photos. The lad just about drew us a map of where at the track he'd helped Pike unload the stuff. Doug must have put the fear of God into him earlier. When we had what we needed, I told the lad, Thanks, and he shot out the door like a hare.

Doug said to me, 'Take that with you,' pointing to the painting I'd propped against the feed bin. 'That's the last of it, yeah?'

'I think so.'

Swearing under his breath, he went and pulled another lot of leashes and collars off the pegs, then laid them out ready to clean. You could see something was playing on his mind.

I picked up the painting to go, and he said, 'Listen, there's no need for the cops to know Pike was here, is there?'

His licence. That's what was still eating him.

'I can't vouch for Pike,' I told him, 'but Tubs and me won't say anything.'

Doug looked relieved. It seemed like this might be a good time for a bit of give and take, so pointing to the photos of Lucky Lip and Jeremiah, I said their names. Doug didn't seem troubled.

He cocked his head. 'You wanna see 'em?'

'No,' I said. 'They any good?'

'Hardly lift a leg, either one of 'em.' He touched the photo of Lucky Lip. 'This came in at five-to-one.' Then Jeremiah. 'This one too. Same weekend. Buggers haven't done a bloody thing since.'

Five-to-one. But the bets in Dad's ledger were both at even money, so Sebastian had been very keen to get his money on.

'Were they tested?'

'Yeah,' he said, becoming wary. 'They came back clean. And before you ask, no, I didn't have a penny on either one.'

We seemed to have reached the end of the line. Then Tubs spoke.

'Doug, you weren't on holiday just before they ran that weekend?'

I got it a second or two before Doug; I don't know which of us was more surprised. Doug's mouth dropped open.

Tubs said, 'You didn't happen to leave someone your keys?'

Turning his head, Doug went straight into the next room. He pulled an old calendar off the wall and came back, flipping back through the months. He checked the date on the winning photos then ran his finger over the calendar. His finger stopped. He looked up.

'Ireland,' he said quietly. 'I went to look at some pups.'

'And Pike kept an eye on the kennels for you?' Tubs asked.

Doug nodded, his face going grey. He looked at me like he'd seen a ghost; he turned the calendar around for me to see. He had his finger on something there, and I looked down.

On the Saturday, in red ink, he'd scribbled in: 'Bob Collier, 10 a.m'.

I raised my eyes. 'What's that?'

'An appointment.' Doug's brow furrowed as he remembered. 'Your old man came out for a word.'

Tubs made a sound. I shot him a warning look.

'About Jeremiah?' I said.

Doug nodded, still staring at the calendar. Ten o'clock in the morning of Jeremiah's race. By then it was obvious to all three of us what had happened, but there was no getting round it, I had to ask.

'What did you tell him, Doug?'

Doug looked up slowly, turning from me to Tubs, then back. 'I told him it couldn't lift a leg.' He wasn't a crook, and he wasn't in with Sebastian and Pike, and right now he was absolutely gutted by what he'd accidentally done.

'I swear to God, Ian,' he said. 'I honestly thought that dog couldn't run.'

5

As we drove I felt my gut churning. The two bets that had sent my old man under, they weren't even on the level; he'd been completely stitched up. I was almost sure of it, and when I got my hands on Pike, I'd know. That seemed really important suddenly, to know exactly how it had happened. Since Tubs had given me Dad's bag and the medal and ledger; since he'd told me Dad had probably done himself in, my view of things had changed. Jesus, the old man's reckless punt against Jeremiah wasn't as reckless as I'd thought; every bit deeper I got my opinion of his actions improved. I guess I was a bit ashamed really. Ashamed of what I hadn't done the night of the fire, sure, but more than that I was ashamed of how I'd thought of Dad in the months since he'd died.

'That last bet in your old man's ledger,' Tubs said suddenly.

I looked across at him. He kept both hands on the steering wheel, arms straight, his belly almost touching the seat between his legs.

'Yeah?'

'What was it again, four hundred quid at three hundred to one?'

'So?'

He pulled a face. 'Just thinkin'.' He went quiet for a bit, then he said, 'Four hundred at three hundred to one, that's a hundred and twenty-grand payout.'

'You've lost me.'

'A hundred and twenty grand.' He looked over. 'That's how much Sebastian took Bob for on those two dogs, and then some.' When I didn't say anything Tubs seemed annoyed; he faced the front again. 'If your old man'd won that bet he'd be all square with Ward. Maybe up a bit.'

'Get real, Tubs. Three hundred to one? On the dogs?'

'Who said it was on the dogs?'

That one stopped me. I was about to ask him exactly what he meant, when he pointed up ahead and said, 'Is this us?'

I nodded, and he took the turn to the City airport, and my thoughts slipped into a different groove. Lee Chan was going home. I had the LCO papers in a plastic bag beside me. This wasn't a detour I could avoid even if I'd wanted to; Lee really needed those papers back. *Uberrima Fides*, at the Lloyd's trading standard; there were still plenty of people there who took it seriously. I was in such strife already that the theft of some old documentation couldn't have done me much more harm, but with Lee it was different. If they missed the documents, the LCO people would be brain-dead not to realize I was behind it, and loads of them knew the history between Lee and me. And once they made that connection Lee would be out on her ear.

Besides that, this was it, the last chance I had to say what I wanted to say to her about us. And deep down, I guess I knew that that was the real reason she'd told me to get the papers back to her. She wanted to give me that chance.

When we pulled up in the dropping-off bay, Tubs offered to take the papers in. 'No-one's lookin' for me,' he said.

'No-one,' I told him as I got out, 'including Lee.'

I told Tubs to wait, or to circle round if he got moved on.

Inside the terminal was full of suits. Businessmen on their way to meetings, coming back from meetings, or typing into their laptops, preparing for meetings to come. I bought an *FT* from the kiosk and stuck it under my arm, like camouflage. I couldn't help being nervous, but I didn't really believe there was that much chance of me being spotted. Fielding might have circulated a description of me, or even a photo, but the only faces the cops or Customs people would be watching were those checking in. I stood well back from that area and ran an eye over the suits. Every now and again there was a splash of colour, a woman, and my gaze zeroed in. Two minutes of this, and there was still no sign of Lee Chan.

'You're under arrest.'

When I felt the jab in my back, I flinched. Then I turned.

'Not funny,' I said.

'Oh, lighten up.' Lee smiled, but I could see it didn't come easy.

There was an awkward silence as we carefully avoided looking one another directly in the eye. Finally I held out the bag.

'I brought the papers.'

She took the bag, and slipped her arm through mine and led me back to her luggage.

Glancing left and right, I said, 'Is there somewhere private?'

We got to her luggage and she let go my arm. She crouched down and packed the papers into a padded envelope she'd already addressed. She said she'd have it couriered back to the LCO once she'd checked in.

'And don't ask me why,' she said, standing, 'but I thought you probably had a right to see these too.'

She handed me a few photocopies, about ten pages. I gave her a questioning look.

'Facultative treaties,' she said. Facultative treaties are reinsurance policies on individual items rather than across a whole portfolio of risks. I was still none the wiser.

'Check out the names,' she told me.

Then a security guard went by and I muttered something about dealing with it later. I started folding the photocopies, ready to slip them in my pocket.

'Your funeral,' she said. She picked up her hand luggage then grabbed the handle of her case. The case was on wheels; it glided along behind her as she made for the check-in.

I stood there like a dummy for a second, then I flicked quickly through the photocopies. I checked out the names. The first three were Kestrel, Connolly and Blythe, and Astra Freight, and after that I stopped looking. I strode after Lee Chan and caught up with her just as she was joining the check-in queue.

This time I slipped my arm through hers; she didn't seem surprised. I guided her on past the check-in.

'Where'd you get this?'

She smiled up at me. 'Can we sit down now?'

I veered right to a row of plastic chairs.

Kestrel, Connolly and Blythe, and Astra Freight were all pieces of business Angela had signed because Sebastian had asked her to. At least that's what I'd thought. But then, according to these photocopies, nearly the entire sum of each risk had been reinsured around the market. It was like accepting a bet then laying-off to cover yourself. The dodgy claims these clients had made had hardly cost the Mortlake Group a penny.

Lee sat down. I dropped into the chair beside her. Just along from us a suit glanced up from his *FT*, listening to a flight announcement. It wasn't for him, so he went back to his paper.

With an effort I kept my voice low. 'What goes on here, Lee? All those deals were covered?'

'Apparently.'

I shuffled through the photocopies, not really seeing much. I couldn't understand why Angela hadn't told me the full story of what she'd done.

'I rang Katy,' Lee said. 'She mentioned the police had been round.' When I didn't say anything, she added, 'And I heard what happened at the Room.'

'Public enemy number one,' I muttered.

'You'll get through it, Ian.' Lee reached over and squeezed my wrist. 'I know you will.'

I almost made some smartarse remark, but when I saw in her eyes how serious she was, I bit my tongue.

'Did you see Angela?' she asked me.

I told her I had. Then I swore her to secrecy – some misplaced sense of chivalry – and gave her the rest of it, about Sebastian and Angela's affair. It was probably my imagination, but the suit with the *FT* seemed to prick up his ears.

Lee became thoughtful. She said, 'Did you believe her?'

'Are you kidding?' My voice rose; Lee gestured for me to keep it down. 'Lee, she told me she was having an affair with Sebastian, and signing up business when he asked her to. That's not good stuff. If it wasn't true, why would she tell me?' There was more evidence too, like how Angela had reacted when I dropped that photo of Justine on her, and the look in Angela's eyes when she talked about Sebastian. But the confession, I thought, was the guts of it.

Lee nodded to herself, 'Did you notice who placed the reinsurance for Connolly and Blythe?'

I hadn't, I'd assumed it was Angela who did all of them, but now Lee drew my attention to the signature at the bottom right of the second photocopy. I stared at the scratches. Angela's signature was there, but for some reason, Allen's was too.

'She reinsured the first, he at least knew about the second,' Lee said, flipping on. 'From then on, it was just Angela again.'

'What does that mean?'

Lee gazed at the papers. She said she'd been rather hoping I might know.

I got up, walked along the row of chairs, then back. Allen knew about the reinsurance of the Connolly and Blythe risk. Did that mean he knew about Angela and Sebastian? But Lee was way ahead of me.

She said, 'If someone was sleeping with your wife, and you knew, I guess you'd be pretty mad.'

Stopping, I looked down at her. She tapped the photo-copies into a neat pile on the seat.

'Lee, that Connolly and Blythe stuff went through over ten years ago.'

She said something in Chinese. I asked for the translation.

'Roughly? Revenge is a dish best served cold.'

'I don't buy it.'

'Just an idea,' she said.

But the idea was just too whacky; I shook my head.

'It wasn't just his wife,' Lee reminded me. 'It was his daughter too.'

'He didn't know about Justine and Sebastian.'

'Are you sure?'

Clasping my hands behind my head, I took a long look at the ceiling. Justine was the apple of Allen's eye. It was just like Katy and Dad. And if Allen already knew about Sebastian and Angela, and then suddenly he found out Justine was at it too? But where the hell did Nigel Chambers' cock-and-bull story fit into that?

'Ian, are you okay?'

'Yeah,' I said. 'Sure.'

But I wasn't, not inside. There was a call over the PA, the flight to Dublin, and Lee looked across to the check-in desk. It felt like part of me was dying.

'That's me,' she said, getting up. Her face was set like she'd made up her mind not to cry.

'Lee—'

'Please don't say you'll write, Ian.'

'I was going to ask if you're sure you're doing the right thing.'

She squinted at me.

'This guy,' I said, Won Ton—'

'Wing Tan.'

'You really think he's the guy? I mean, you've only met him once. What happens if you get married and you don't get on? What happens then?'

She considered a moment. Finally she said, 'I don't know, Ian.'

'Then don't do it.'

She reached over and touched a finger to my lips. When she let her finger drop, we looked at one another.

'Lee, you don't even know this guy.'

'I know,' she said, 'that he's willing to take a chance.'

Something inside me crumpled. Lee went up on tip-toe and kissed my cheek and everything I'd meant to say got choked in my throat. Before I knew it she was walking to the check-in, towing her luggage, but I was damned if I was going to let it end like that.

I took a step after her and called out, 'Lee!'

She stopped and turned. And that's when I saw Mehmet. He was further along the line of check-in desks; he must have recognized me just moments before I saw him. He lifted his arm and pointed straight at me, then he spun around shouting for Security.

'Get over here!' he yelled.

I didn't wait to see what happened next, I vaulted over the chairs and ran.

As I shot through the doors I heard Mehmet doing his lolly behind me, but I didn't look back. I hit the dropping-off bay at a run: there was no sign of Tubs. I swung left and bolted down the tarmac. When I glanced back over my shoulder, a couple of security men with walkie-talkies came spilling out the doors with Mehmet at their heels.

'Tubs,' I whispered. 'Tubs, you fat bastard.'

I faced the front again, sprinting now, my legs jarring with each step. And I thought, This is it, I'm done.

And then I heard them coming for me in the car. My lungs were giving out and I slowed, then I realized how ridiculous it was running, they'd get me anyway, so I stopped and bent over. I rested my hands on my hips, trying to breathe. The car screeched to a halt beside me; I put my hands behind my head now and stood up straight, gasping for air. Fielding was going to tear me to bits.

'Oi!' Tubs shouted, 'Comin' or stayin'?'

He pushed open the rear door and I tumbled in, cursing him. The door slammed as the Mercedes lurched forward and I stayed where I'd landed, face down on the floor.

When I could breathe again, I got to wondering how that bastard Mehmet knew I was a wanted man. There was a pain in my chest; I heaved myself onto the seat and looked back through the rear window. To one side of the terminal, a plane lifted off. I realized then, a kind of hollow feeling spreading through me, an aching emptiness, that I hadn't said one bloody word of what I'd meant to say to Lee Chan. And now she was gone. My head fell back; I thumped the seat beside me and swore.

6

'Friday,' Tubs said.

We'd stopped at the lights just before the entrance to the Stow; people were walking across the road in front of us. Young blokes with their girlfriends, the girls done up to the nines, ready for the big night out. Behind them some old codgers, the kind that had been going to the track for the past thirty years. Friday night at the dogs, and half the East End was converging on the place where we'd been hoping to have a quiet word with Eddie Pike.

Tubs turned to me. 'You still wanna do this?'

'Just park,' I told him. 'We'll work something out.'

While Tubs paid the parking attendant I covered my face with the grubby old Panama hat I'd found on the floor, and leant back in the seat like I was sleeping. When I felt the car moving up the ramp, I pushed back the brim.

'Tubs, when Sebastian used to come down the Gallon—'

'Yeah?'

'Didn't he bring that book of his sometimes?' Tubs screwed up his face and I went on, 'You know, he used to write some insurance, didn't he? That blue book he had. Like with Nev. Sebastian did the insurance on Nev's betting shops.'

'Ahha.' Tubs parked. He pulled on the handbrake, then faced me.

I said, 'Mum and Dad's house: how much do you reckon it was worth?'

Tubs's face was blank at first, then you could see him gradually cotton on.

'A hundred and twenty grand?' I asked.

'About,' Tubs said. 'That's gotta be it, Ian. Your old man insured the house with Sebastian. Three hundred to one. Four hundred quid premium and a hundred and twenty-grand payout.' He banged the heel of his hand on the steering wheel. 'Christ, that's it.'

I stared straight ahead. 'Except for the bit,' I said, 'where Dad torched the house he'd just insured.'

Tubs pulled a face. He reminded me about those two dogs, Lucky Lip and Jeremiah. 'Do as you're done by. You can't blame your old man for that.'

Mulling it over, I found Tubs was right. If Sebastian really had got Pike to nobble those two dogs, the hundred grand Dad had dropped to him wasn't a normal loss, it was theft. By insuring his own house then torching it, Dad had simply returned the favour. And now I understood why he'd died in the fire too. It wasn't just for Mum's sake, so she didn't think it was suicide, but so the insurance people didn't think it was suicide either. He'd done it to make the insurance policy stick. Arsonists, as every underwriter knows, do not get drunk and lie down in the flames.

But if that was it, my old man's final plan had gone horribly wrong, not just with Mum, but with the insurance as well. Sitting in the car now, I squeezed my hands over my eyes. Dad. Jesus Christ, it just wouldn't have crossed his mind that Sebastian would do anything else but pay up. It wouldn't have occurred to him that someone like Sebastian, with smart offices in the City, might welch on a bet. I let my hands fall. Mum and Dad died for nothing. And they died for nothing because even when Dad tried to sink to Sebastian's level, he was too damn honest for the game.

When I reached for the doorhandle, Tubs grabbed my arm.

'Hey, the furniture you seen at Aston's place. The gear Pike nicked. There was a desk, yeah?'

'Yeah. There was a desk. I told you, I tried it, it was locked.'

'Locked.'

'What's the big deal?'

'Locked like maybe there was papers in it no-one was meant to see?'

'Tubs, it was from Ward's home. Not his office.'

'Right,' Tubs said giving my arm a shake. 'And that blue book he had. Where's he going to keep that? In his office?'

Tubs was talking about Sebastian's deal with my old man but after a second's thought I felt a sudden jolt. The policies Angela had written, and even the reinsurance deals, was it possible there was a paper record at Sebastian's end? Paperwork that would make it clear why someone wanted, or needed, him dead? I groaned. Days ago I'd been leaning on that desk up in Doug Aston's attic, maybe the answer to all my problems, and I'd just turned and walked away.

Letting go my arm, Tubs said, 'Light fingers Eddie Pike maybe done us a favour.'

A car parked beside us. While the couple got out I held a hand up to that side of my face. When they were gone, Tubs suggested I stayed in the car while he went to find Eddie, but there really didn't seem much point to that. The other night at the Mortlake house, and then the scene at the airport, I knew that I couldn't keep the run-and-hide game up forever. I was going to get caught sooner or later, and all that mattered now was to get hold of Pike – and maybe that desk – before it happened. If that meant showing my face at the track, then that's what it meant.

Pushing open my door, I said, 'Let's go.'

We went into the main enclosure; the crowd was building up fast, some of them going upstairs to the main stand, others around the front to the rails. Stuffing his racecard in his pocket, Tubs led me to one of the bars down below.

'Storage rooms out back,' he said. 'That's where Doug's lad said they dumped the gear.'

He had a quick word to the barman, one of his mates,

and the bloke let us through. There was a pile of beer kegs, a woman running a mop over the floor, and another one loading glasses into a washer. They looked at us but didn't say anything. Tubs nodded to the door at the back; we went on through that one, and as the door closed behind us, the noise died.

In that room there was nothing but an old commercial oven; it had been ripped out of somewhere, and now it sat there with pipes and wiring hanging out of it, waiting for the final trip to the tip. Definitely not something of Sebastian's. Tubs went across and tried the rear door; it was locked.

'Where do the stairs go?' I asked, pointing to the far corner.

He shrugged, like, Who knows? so we went on up. Upstairs a long corridor opened out in front of us; it seemed to run a good way along the back of the stand. I tried the first door off the corridor. A cupboard.

Tubs tried the second door, looked in, then came straight back out. 'Bog,' he said.

We walked further along. When Doug Aston first told us where Eddie had disappeared to, I'd thought, That's crazy. But now it made a weird kind of sense. Even guys like Tubs, who'd been coming to the Stow for donkey's years, didn't know what went on back here. The bar and restaurant staff, they came and went pretty regularly, and if anyone saw furniture being lugged down this corridor they wouldn't have batted an eye.

There was a banging and crashing behind one door, I opened it a crack and peeped in. The kitchens. And on through the kitchen you could see out to the serving counter in the main stand. I let the door fall closed, but as it did I caught a glimpse of someone out there. I pushed the door open again.

'What is it?' Tubs whispered.

I pulled my head back.

'Out at the food counter,' I said. 'To the left.'

Tubs peered through for a moment. 'Katy,' he said, turning to me. 'She could help us.'

'Leave it out, Tubs.'

He looked again, then asked, 'Who's the bloke she's got with her?'

Leaning over Tubs's shoulder I had another look myself, I hadn't seen any bloke. I did this time.

'That,' I said, 'is Mr Bill Tyler.'

Tubs caught the tone in my voice. 'Not one of your favourites?'

'Apart from him being about twenty years too old for her?'

Smiling, Tubs let the door fall to.

We went further along, poking our heads round more doors down the corridor, but we came up dry. Eddie Pike, and the desk, were elsewhere. Tubs suggested we split up so we could cover the stadium faster. He slipped a mobile into my pocket, saying, 'You cover the Pop.' The Pop, the Popular Enclosure, the cheap seats on the other side of the track. 'Any sign of Eddie, or the desk, buzz me. I'll do the same.'

Telling him not to approach Eddie without calling me first, I jogged back along the corridor and down the stairs. In the room behind the bar the dishwasher was rattling away, steam pouring out of it. As I edged by it some instinct made me look ahead through the cloud of steam and out into the bar. I stopped. It was only a glimpse I'd caught, so cautiously I eased myself to the right, getting a clearer view through the door. No mistake, it was them. Bloody Fielding and his sidekick. They were looking around the faces in the bar, but after a few seconds Fielding turned his back and stalked out, his young offsider hard on his heels.

'Fuck,' I said. 'Shit.'

'Language,' said the middle-aged barmaid, coming in from the bar with a tray of empty glasses. She put down the tray, jerking her head back. 'The two coppers not friends of yours?'

I looked at her open-mouthed.

'You're with Tubs?'

I nodded.

'Wait here,' she said, then she went out to the bar and across to the door Fielding had gone through. She looked left and right then beckoned me out. The help was so unexpected, I didn't hesitate, I didn't really have time to think. I went out through the bar, and as I stepped by the barmaid, she said, 'They went off left.'

I turned right, and she said, 'And tell Tubs he owes Mary one.' Laughing she disappeared back into the bar.

Hurrying out of the stadium, I pulled out the mobile and called Tubs. When I told him that Fielding and the offsider had arrived, he swore:

'How the fuck?'

'It doesn't matter, Tubs. They're here. I don't know, maybe it's not me they're after. Could be they've got some tip-off on Pike.'

'You believe that?'

'Christ, Tubs, it just doesn't matter.' I chopped my hand in the air. 'Listen, stop looking for Pike. If Fielding sees you charging around, he'll be all over you like a rash.'

'So I sit on my hands?'

'Go down and have a bet. See your mates. If Fielding finds you, you're just here for the dogs.'

'What about you?'

'Just do like I say, okay?' I was halfway between the main stand and the Pop. If I'd turned I would have seen the crowd in the main stand, one of them Tubs, but I kept walking. Beside me a bunch of kids clambered over the metal play-gym and swings. Tubs hadn't answered. 'Okay, Tubs?'

'All right,' he said finally. 'But you find Pike, you call me.'

I looked at the mobile. If I found Pike now there was no way I was going to risk Tubs leading Fielding right to us. 'Right,' I said, then I flicked the thing off and dropped it in my pocket.

At the gate into the Pop a gawky teenager stopped me to sign the corner of my programme so that I could cross back into the Main Enclosure later without double-paying. Years ago that gawky teenager had been me, the first paid job I ever had. Watching him now as he signed, I felt a stab in the pit of my stomach. His glance ran right past me and on to the bloke waiting behind. I was no-one. Just another mug punter.

Passing into the enclosure, I scrolled the programme in my hands. Somewhere in the recent past, it seemed, I'd crossed an invisible threshold. Life had closed in around me; maybe I'd taken some knocks that weren't going to heal. I guess it had just occurred to me that however this whole disaster ended, I'd been damaged – at Lloyd's, probably beyond repair – but not just at Lloyd's, it went deeper.

Climbing the steps onto the terraces I felt heavy. Whatever happened now, whether I lost my flat and my job, whether Fielding got me banged up in gaol or not, whatever happened, I was damaged goods. At the top of the stairs I turned and looked down to the track. The dogs were being paraded for the next race, the punters over here in the Pop studying their form guides carefully. Poor men with maybe a tenner in the kick to see them through the night. Mug punters with worries. And me. Here where I spent my childhood. I glanced across at the gawky teenager on the gate, and over to the kids on the swings. At thirty-three years of age the inevitable had happened. My future wasn't necessarily going to be better than the past, blind hope wouldn't always beat the odds, the night air was cold and I wasn't young any more.

I looked down at my watch. Lee Chan was in Dublin.

A hand clasped my shoulder and my heart jumped into my throat.

I spun round, it was Nev, I grabbed his arm.

'Easy up.' He screwed up his face, not sure if he should laugh. He tried to push my hands away. 'Guilty conscience or what?' he said.

A few heads were turning our way, the last thing I needed, so I led him up into the enclosed part of the stand.

'I'm in strife, Nev.'

'You're breakin' my fuckin' arm.'

His arm felt like a twig, so maybe I was. When I let go, he clenched his fist and worked his arm up and down. Mumbling an apology, I explained that I had Fielding on my case.

'That shit?' he said, rubbing his elbow. 'Still?'

Still, I said wearily. Looking round, I asked Nev it he'd keep a watch out for Fielding while I did a lap of the Pop.

He said, 'Then you'd still be looking for Pike.'

I lifted my head.

'You find Pike, you hand him over to Fielding?'

'I find Pike,' I said, 'and I strangle him.'

'He's not here.'

I felt like he'd just pricked my balloon. Pike wasn't there.

'Not in the stand,' Nev said, gesturing around. Then he slipped the binoculars from around his neck and handed them to me, pointing to the rear of the track. Just then the hare went zinging past, the dogs broke from the traps. On the terraces below us, the punters got to their feet.

'What am I looking at?' I asked, peering through the binoculars.

'The extension,' Nev said, 'behind the old kennels.'

I raised the binoculars slightly. Back there behind the kennels where the dogs were mustered before each race, beyond the light from the track, I could just make out a couple of concrete mixers, a pile of sand and a portable hut.

'Builders,' Nev told me. 'Been at it two months: they knock off Fridays at six, back Monday mornin'.'

I focused on the builder's hut. No lights.

Nev said, 'Pike's in the hut.'

I pulled back from the binoculars. 'You've seen him?'

'Hour or two ago.' He explained that he was pretty sure it was Pike. Anyway, he'd seen some bloke with red hair dive in there straight after the builders shot through. 'Thought if I seen Tubs later, I'd tell him.'

Lowering the glasses, I said, 'Do you still need a pass to get back there?'

Nev nodded. 'Give us two minutes.' He headed round to the bar.

I raised the glasses again, had another look at the builder's hut, then turned my attention to the main stand. The race had just finished; most of the punters on the terrace were tearing up their tickets in disgust. Halfway up on the right, I located Tubs, he was just sitting there, talking, and I thought, Good man. But the next moment I noticed who he was talking to, Katy, and I sucked on my teeth. The way he was waving his hands around, and the way she was hanging on his words, he was obviously telling her the story. I shot a look at the seat next to Katy, but it was empty; there was no sign of Bill Tyler. I suppose I should have been grateful to Tubs for that at least, but I wasn't. My hand went to the mobile in my pocket; I was rehearsing a bollocking for Tubs, then who should appear shuffling down the row of seats towards Tubs and Katy? Bloody Fielding.

'Oh, tops,' I muttered, both hands on the binoculars again. 'Join the party.'

Fielding stopped when he reached them. I couldn't make out the looks on their faces, but after a moment Katy slid into the empty seat and Fielding sat down between them.

Nev reappeared from the bar with two passes.

'Bloke needs 'em back in an hour,' he said, giving me one of the white cards.

I swung the binoculars around to the path by the kids play-gym, the way I'd crossed, searching now for Fielding's offsider. There was no sign of him.

I said, 'You don't think you're coming back there with me, Nev.'

Smiling, he said, 'You don't think I'm not.'

I handed him the binoculars. He was half-dead, wasted to the size of a stick-insect, but short of bashing him over the head with a brick there was no way I could stop him from following me. Pig-headed, like Dad. Like Tubs. Like that whole generation of crotchety old bastards, but for some reason that didn't piss me off now quite like it used to.

Besides, I had no choice.

Together we headed for the stairs.

7

Once we'd flashed our passes at the gatekeeper in the white coat we made our way back behind the kennels. The noise of the crowd in the stands was muffled back there, but you could hear the kennel-lads getting the runners in the next race set to parade. The pint-sized tractor that dragged the track sweeper was parked up, there was no sign of the driver, and when we'd walked out of the light and into the building area it felt like we were completely alone.

There was no window on the near side of the builder's hut. When we reached the sand-pile we had a clear view of the door, about ten yards away, and closed. Nev started to creep towards it. I pulled him back.

'Where are you going?' I whispered.

He grinned at me like an idiot.

Then came the pre-parade trumpet flourish over the loudspeakers, and from behind us the shout of the steward as he led the six runners out onto the track. It gave me an idea.

'The race'll start in five minutes,' I told Nev quietly. I pulled up a plastic bucket the builders had left, and flipped it over. 'Sit tight.'

He stayed on his feet for about a minute, then exhaustion seemed to hit him and he sat down on the bucket. While we waited I looked around for something heavy. The only thing I could see was a bag of cement half-hidden under a tarpaulin. I dragged it out and propped it against Nev's bucket.

'What's that for? Concrete shoes, heave-ho into the Thames?'

I told Nev, very firmly, to shut it.

Once the race started I'd have about thirty seconds to do what I planned. There was no padlock on the outside of the door; I guess that could have meant a lot of things. What I hoped it meant was that Eddie Pike had smashed the builder's lock off and thought he was safe inside. If he'd done that he would have secured the door from the inside to make sure no nosy bugger stuck his head through; he really needed his privacy just now, did Eddie. But once the race started there'd be noise, punters shouting, and everyone focused on the dogs. That would be my chance to take Eddie's privacy and knock a great big hole clean through it.

'They're loadin' them in the traps,' Nev said quietly. He wasn't even looking towards the track, he just sensed it from the noise of the crowd.

I heaved the bag of concrete onto my shoulder, the bag standing like a solid pillar up past my ear.

Getting to his feet, Nev asked, 'Whaddo I do?'

'Shut up,' I grunted. I stepped out from around the sand-pile and sighted up the door.

In the stadium the bell sounded; there was a whirr as the hare sped along the wire, then a roar from the crowd. The traps were open; the dogs were off.

I bent forward, the cement bag started to topple, and I charged the door.

Luck is a fortune. If I'd tried the stunt fifty times I couldn't have pulled it off as expertly as I did with that first unpractised effort. The cement bag was almost perfectly horizontal when it hit, and I was driving off my right leg, hard. I felt a slight check, then with a splintering crack the door flew open, smashing against something metallic inside. The cement bag kept going forward, and falling, and I went after it, stumbling over the bloody thing as it hit the floor. But somehow I stayed on my feet.

From behind me a dim light shone into the hut throwing my shadow on the far wall. To the left, on the table, there were a few mugs and magazines. To the right, from a sleeping bag on the floor, two petrified eyes bulged out at me.

'Jesus Christ,' the mouth below them said, 'Jesus Christ.'

'I'm not the cops,' I told him, patting the air with my hands, trying to sound calm. 'I'm Ian Collier, and we have to talk.'

He stared at me, then his head sank back to the floor. His sleeping bag rose and fell, his chest heaving.

Peering into the darkness, I said, 'You are Eddie Pike, yeah?'

As the crowd outside roared the winner past the finishing line, he closed his eyes and bellowed, 'Jesus fucking Christ!'

It was Eddie.

Nev stuck his head in, asking if I was all right.

'Fine,' I told him.

Eddie swore at me from the corner.

'Nev,' I said, 'stay out there and keep an eye out.'

He looked past me at Eddie, then nodded and disappeared. My legs were trembling so I pulled the door to – it didn't shut properly – then I sat down on a chair. Eddie stayed in his sleeping bag on the floor, cursing me now with everything he had. I'd scared him witless with my charge through the door. Finally he raised himself, his arms braced behind him. My eyes were getting used to the dark by then; I could see he was wearing a tracksuit top. Probably the tracksuit bottom as well; he seemed to be ready for a very fast exit. He finished swearing, and glared at me.

'What is it with you, man? You fucking crazy?'

I rested my hands on the table: they were trembling too. Eddie couldn't see that so I left them there.

'Because of you, Eddie, I'm in the shit up to my eyeballs.'

'Bollocks.'

'I need to know what happened at Sebastian Ward's place. The night it burned down.'

'Sebastian who?' he said.

'Ward,' I said.

He shuffled back, resting his shoulders against the wall. His legs were still wrapped in the sleeping bag in front of him.

'Sebastian Ward.' He stared into space. 'Who he?'

My hands balled into fists on the table.

'He,' I said, 'is the man you worked for. The guy whose valuables ended up being stored at Doug Aston's kennels for a few days after the fire. And I think you know who Doug Aston is.'

Eddie didn't answer me.

'Eddie?'

'Fuck off.'

'Not this time.'

He gave me a sideways look and I realized then that he probably hadn't known till that moment who'd paid him the late-night visit at the kennels. But he was too wary to question me about that yet.

'When you cleared out of Doug's place you left one of Ward's paintings behind.'

'Bullshit.' He made as if to stand. 'If you've had your say, piss off.'

'Ward employed you as his security guard, Eddie. The cops have been looking for you since the day they realized it wasn't you that got fried in the fire. And right now,' I said, jerking my thumb over my shoulder, 'they're here at the Stow, and still looking.'

Eddie's gaze slid past me to the door.

'All I have to do,' I said, 'is whistle.'

He turned back from the door, figuring. He figured I was lying. 'Then whistle,' he said, but he wasn't quite sure enough to sound cocky.

I went and opened the door, Nev was sitting right there on his bucket. I slipped the binoculars from around his neck, then I called Eddie over from the dark corner of the hut.

Swearing, he climbed out of the sleeping bag and came over. I handed him the glasses and pointed into the stand.

'Can you see Tubs Laszlo?'

'What is this?'

'Halfway up,' I said, still pointing.

His lip curled, but he raised the glasses and looked. After a few seconds he said, 'So I see him. So what?'

'And the bloke next to him? On his right?'

The glasses moved. Eddie let out a quiet moan when he saw Fielding. I pulled the mobile from my pocket and punched the buttons, and now Eddie looked at me curiously.

'Person to person call,' I told him. 'Me to Tubs.'

Understanding glimmered. Eddie snapped the glasses back to his eyes, looking up at the stand. In my ear the phone started ringing. Eddie saw Tubs reaching inside his jacket to answer.

'Oh for fuck's sake,' Eddie hissed at me. 'Turn it off.'

'Can we talk now?'

'Turn it off!'

In my ear Tubs said, 'Hello?'

I waited a moment, studying Eddie. He was scared out of his brain.

'False alarm,' I told Tubs, and I flicked off the phone.

Eddie swore at me again as I herded him back into the hut. Behind us, Nev closed the door.

'I wasn't there that night.'

'Nigel Chambers disagrees.'

Eddie had been making himself comfortable on the sleeping bag; now he lifted his head sharply.

'He's dropped you right in it, Eddie. He's told me, and he's told Fielding.'

'What did he say?'

'Never mind what he said; I'm after your side of the story.'

He gave me a look. 'You're bullshittin' me,' he said, but there wasn't any conviction in it. The mention of Chambers had taken him clean between the eyes.

'You were there that night, weren't you.'

He drew up his legs, and wrapped his arms around his

knees. 'So I was there,' he said finally. 'Fucking Chambers.' He looked up. 'You can't trust that bastard, what he says.'

'No?'

'No fucking way.'

'What happened, Eddie? That night.'

He went quiet. I thought he'd decided to clam up; I couldn't see his face too clearly in the darkness, but as I was about to repeat the question, he spoke.

'I had the night off.'

'You were there, Eddie.'

'That was later,' he said. 'First off I was out here.'

'Here where?' I asked, surprised. 'The Stow?'

'Listen, if ya don't wanna believe me, I don't give a shit. If ya wanna check, arks the old bugger outside. He was pencillin' for Abes Watson that night.'

'Nev saw you?'

'Doubt it. But I seen Teddy Mills sting Abes for three grand, the third race.' He flicked a hand towards the door. 'Arks him.'

I went and stuck my head out the door and checked the story with Nev. He confirmed it. Tubs was off sick so Nev had filled in for him; he remembered the three-grand payout to Teddy Mills quite clearly. The bookie, Abes Watson, was still spitting chips about it, Nev said.

Going back inside, I said to Eddie. 'All right, you were here first, then what?'

'Got jack of it after a bit so I went home.'

'Your rooms at Ward's place.'

Eddie nodded.

'What time?' I said.

'Christ knows.' He shrugged. 'I dunno, maybe nine thirty? Ten? Comin' up the drive I see there's a few lights on, no car 'cept for Sebastian's, so I park round the back like normal and go in. No big deal.'

'The door was locked?'

'Ahha.' Eddie hugged his knees tighter. It seemed like he didn't have to try to remember, that night was right there for him, like something he just couldn't forget. 'The first thing I do is, I go check in the security room. You know, all the alarms and that, they're wired up to this one main panel. The security cameras, the monitors and stuff, they're all in there, so the first thing I do when I get back is go in and check it out. Shit.' He shook his head like he couldn't quite believe this bit himself. 'You know, he even got a badge made up for me?'

I thought of that badge, the only time I'd seen it, lying next to Sebastian Ward's charred body.

I said, 'Everything in order, was it, in the security room?'

'Well, nothin' was broken.'

I looked at him. A leer spread over Eddie's face.

'Sometimes,' he said, 'Sebastian thought it was a good idea to have the security cameras turned off.' This one went right past me till he added, 'That friggin' bedroom, man, the stuff he had in there.'

'He'd turned off the security camera in his bedroom?' My mouth was working two steps ahead of my brain. 'Why?'

When Eddie laughed, I got it.

'You thought he had someone up there?'

'Hey.' Eddie raised his hands. 'Man's entitled to his privacy.'

My mind went back to that picture of Justine and Sebastian, the one Eddie had left behind when he bolted from Doug Aston's place. Suddenly I knew where it came from.

I asked, 'How hard would it be to lift a still photo from the security film?'

Eyes lowered, he said he didn't know anything about that technical shit.

What was it Nev had called him? A weasel? Way too generous. Eddie Pike was a leech. He'd been gathering a collection of Sebastian Ward's most private moments, and saving them up for a rainy day. Wanting this to be over now, I said, 'Then what?'

'Well, I come outa the security room, I was gonna turn off the lights and get some kip. Into the front room, there

397

he is, Sebastian, flat as a tack.'

'On the floor?'

'Whadaya think, swingin' from the fucking chandelier? Course on the floor. The bastard was dead.'

'Shot?'

Eddie's gaze slid away. 'Chambers give yous the story, didn' 'e?'

He still wasn't sure if I was bluffing about Nigel Chambers, and I had a feeling he was getting set to give me some complete load of bollocks. So I took the plunge and explained that Chambers had pointed the finger at him. I told Eddie exactly what Chambers had told me.

When I was done, Eddie held his head in his hands for a bit, his head moving slightly from side to side. 'Bastard,' he said in disbelief. 'The fuckin' bastard.'

'Is all that true?'

'True?' His head swung round. He looked at me like he couldn't believe the question. 'Course it's not fuckin' true, you think I'm daft?'

I didn't answer.

'Bastard,' he said again, his mind going back to Chambers.

I took a breath. 'So what is true, Eddie? What happened that night?'

He seemed to draw back into himself, figuring again, sly as a rat. Then I noticed him glancing towards the door. I took out my mobile and placed it on the table, my hand resting there lightly. His face fell.

'What happened?' I said. 'Or would you like me to just whistle?'

The steam had gone out of him now: after hearing about Chambers I think maybe he realized he was in even deeper trouble than he'd imagined. Much deeper.

'Look, Sebastian was dead. Stone cold. No mark on him, no blood, seemed like he'd just keeled over, you know, stroke or somethin'. There was a blanket beside him, an empty champagne bottle too. The way he was lyin' there, he coulda been asleep 'cept for his fuckin' lips were blue. Straight up. I went back to the security room and flipped through all the cameras.'

'On the monitor.'

'Yeah. Seein' if anyone was in the house.'

'You checked the bedroom?'

Eddie nodded. 'Nothin'. Nothin' anywhere. Then I went and done a lap of the place, doors and windows. Fuck all. Everythin' just like normal. In the end I go and take another look at him.'

'You checked his pulse?'

'Pulse? The fucker was dead. I tell you,' he said, staring at the floor of the hut like Sebastian was lying there, 'I coulda kicked him in the guts.'

I made a sound. Eddie looked over.

'Max, you know, the son? He hates me. Once he took over I knew I'd be out on my arse. Unemployed and homeless in one big hit. Terrif.'

'So you didn't call the police?'

'I was gonna.'

'When?'

He didn't answer, so I made my guess aloud.

'Once you'd helped yourself to a few of the valuables?'

He smiled at that. He seemed pretty proud of his own quick thinking. And maybe he could even have gotten away with it. In a house like Sebastian's half a dozen pieces weren't going to be missed, not unless someone did an inventory. And if Sebastian really had died from natural causes an inventory would be the last thing on anyone's mind. Max would move in, Eddie would be thrown out, and the stolen goods might not be missed for years.

'Hey,' Eddie said. 'Easy come, easy go. Sebastian was no fuckin' saint.'

'One of those valuables wasn't a diamond brooch, was it?'

'I wish,' he said.

I hadn't really held out much hope for that idea; Pike would still have had the thing in his back pocket. And he certainly wouldn't have given it to Fielding. But I had to try.

'And that's when Chambers showed up?'

He lifted his knees and lowered them, rubbing his legs. He nodded unhappily.

'Bastard come right in the house. I walk outa the study, there the bastard is, hangin' over Sebastian. He turns round and clocks me. I'm standin' there with a friggin' oil painting.'

'What did he do?'

'Nothin', just stared at me. Then he says, "He's dead," like he's arskin' me to tell him somethin' else. For a bit there I thought I was gonna have two dead fuckers on the floor, he looked chronic.'

'Did you ask him why he was there?'

'Yeah, but he pulls hisself together then. He goes, "What you got that for?" ' Here Eddie pointed into the darkness of the hut.

'The painting?'

'Yeah. Fuckin' clever dick. "What you got that for?" We give it some verbal, I'm shit scared he's gonna call the cops. I mean, I've got some gear in the van already, and there's Sebastian lyin' there, fucked.' Eddie screwed up his face. 'But he never. We go on givin' it the verbal then it kinda slides off. Next thing he's lookin' at Sebastian again. I swear, I thought the bastard was gonna cry.'

Unlike with Nigel Chambers, Eddie didn't seem to be spinning me a story; he seemed to be really remembering what happened. More than that. He couldn't forget.

'He was upset?'

'Chambers?' Eddie's eyes opened wide. 'The bastard went berserk. He starts screamin' at Sebastian; he completely lost it. "I'm ruined," he goes. "I'm fucked." He ponces around a bit – like a fuckin' kid – then he comes up with his brilliant idea.'

'Did he say why he was ruined?'

Eddie shrugged. 'Shares or somethin'. Big fuckin' kid, he was.'

Now the whole thing opened up in front of me. Nigel Chambers, in debt up to his eyeballs, the only collateral against the debt a truckload of WardSure shares and his house, had walked in on the biggest disaster in his life. Sebastian Ward was dead. From Nigel's point of view it hardly mattered how Sebastian got that way, what mattered was the drubbing the WardSure shares were going to take when the market got the news the next morning. Standing there over Sebastian's body, the awful truth must have crashed down on Nigel like a whacking great boulder. Financially, he was about to be wiped out.

'What was his brilliant idea?' I asked Eddie.

'Hide the body,' he told me glumly. 'Can you believe the berk? He wanted to use my van.'

'You wouldn't let him?'

'Why should I? Hide the body – I didn't give a shit about the body – then he threatens to dob me in, let the cops sort me.' Eddie shook his head. 'Full of it, the wanker.'

'What then?'

Outside, there was the tinny blare of taped trumpets over the loudspeakers, the signal for the dogs to parade before the next race. You couldn't hear the crowd.

'Hey,' Eddie said, looking up. 'Fielding's not seriously tryin' to do me for murder? That's bullshit!'

Ignoring that, I said, 'You torched the house. That was for what? Just another way to hide the body?'

'All part of the fuckin' masterplan,' Eddie said sarcastically, turning his face to the wall. 'Chambers. Mr Intelligence. Worked a fuckin' treat, ay?'

I opened my mouth to ask another, then I stopped. The masterplan. Clearly something Eddie had been talked into, and now regretted. But unless there was a cut in it for Eddie, he wouldn't have lifted a finger. Not Eddie Pike. So what was it? The stuff he was stealing? But that wasn't nearly enough for him to have gone along with the arson. It had to be money. Chambers had to have waved a stack of money at him. But Chambers had no money.

And then, way too late to do me any good, it clicked. I am a moron.

'It was you.'

Eddie faced me. 'You what?'

'You and Chambers.' I got up. Eddie pushed back in the corner. 'You. It was you.'

I hung over him; he looked up at me with startled eyes. If Nev hadn't banged his fist on the wall in warning, I think I might have kicked the shit out of Eddie Pike.

Instead of that, I stood there frozen, blood pounding in my ears, just dimly aware of the voices passing outside. Pike and Chambers, a pair of complete tossers, they'd had me terrified of being shot, shit scared, that night at the end of the Greenwich Tunnel. I took steady deep breaths, trying to calm down, while the voices outside moved on.

'Why'd you ask for me?' I hissed at Eddie. 'Any bastard could have been the courier, why me?'

'Who said we did?'

I thumped the wall, Pike put up his hands.

'Nobody asked for you, okay? Not Chambers or me.'

Then he seemed to realize that he'd just confessed to the kidnap, or attempted extortion, or whatever it was. He looked sick.

I said, 'Don't feed me a line.'

'It's fuckin' true.' He seemed offended that I didn't believe him. 'Chambers sent the demand, it come back like, "Okay, we want Collier as the courier." '

'Chambers told you that?'

'I seen it. I was standing right there, it come up on his screen thing.' Eddie was getting to his feet now, scared of what I might do to him. His voice was wheedling. 'The whole fuckin' thing: the arson, the bollocks kidnap, the whole thing, it was Chambers' idea. He's lying. I can prove it.'

'You can't prove anything.'

Eddie smiled nervously. Considering the position he was in, it looked completely idiotic. He said, 'I've got pictures.'

A leech, and cunning as a sewer rat. Cunning, but as he'd proved right through this whole business, a long way short of clever. Eddie Pike had pictures.

Putting two and two together, I said, 'You lifted stills from that night's security tapes?'

Five minutes earlier he'd denied he knew how it was done. Now he didn't bother.

'Chambers with Sebastian's body?' I said.

Eddie's smile became smug. And then I knew exactly what had flushed Nigel Chambers from cover. Why he was suddenly so eager to tell everyone he was at the house that night, and why he wanted to give his story to the police. Eddie Pike had pictures. And some time after the K and R went wrong, he must have decided that Nigel Chambers owed him big.

'Chambers only went to the cops last night,' I said. 'I don't suppose you happened to show him one or two of the pictures yesterday, did you? Trying on a bit of blackmail? "Give me money, or I take these to the police?" '

Eddie, you could see, was pretty pleased with himself. He still didn't see his mistake. Nigel Chambers had no money.

'Eddie, you spooked him. And now Chambers has spun a line to the cops that makes your pictures of him with Sebastian's body absolutely worthless. He's nobbled you.'

'Crap.'

'Your word against his.'

'Yeah?' He stuck out his chin. 'What if the cops see a photo of Chambers dousing the body in petrol? And another one of him setting the body alight? Ay? Reckon they'll still believe his bullshit then?'

He really was something, Eddie Pike. Maybe, just maybe, a set of photos like that might make Fielding listen to his story.

I said, 'What about the gun? The pistol found with Ward's body.'

He shrugged. He said Chambers thought they should leave it there along with the security guard name-badge to help mislead the cops. He added glumly, 'Only idea the fucker had that worked.'

So Nigel had lied to me and Clive about that too. I guess he knew he had to have a very good reason for not coming forward sooner, so he dreamt up the story about the gun. For me it didn't matter now anyway: as far as I was concerned Pike had told me what I needed to know; I'd had a gutful of the pair of them.

Pike stepped towards me but when I blocked his path to the door he didn't have the bottle to shove his way past.

'If that's it,' he said, 'I got business.'

I waited till his gaze stopped darting around, till his eyes settled on mine. Then I asked my last question.

'Did you juice Jeremiah and Lucky Lip for Sebastian?'

The strife Pike was in right now, a doping from months back probably seemed trivial. His eyes went to the door as he said, 'What if I did?'

And then I saw the change in his expression when his brain clicked into gear. He must have known Sebastian had stung one of the bookies. A second's thought, and he remembered which one.

A sound escaped from his throat. I stepped up and swung.

He ducked, my fist swiped the air, and he crashed into my side as he ploughed past me out the door. Turning, I stumbled over the cement bag. I hit the floor, then got up grabbing my mobile. When I finally got outside, Nev was pointing off towards the side of the stand. We watched Eddie Pike disappear into the dark.

Nev started to apologize – Christ knows what he thought he could have done. Over on the track, the traps opened and the crowd roared. I slumped down on the step of the hut.

'Have much to say for hisself?' Nev asked me, lifting his chin after Pike.

Plenty, I told him.

Too much, I should have said.

Pike's version of what happened at Sebastian's place that night just had to be a truer picture of things than Nigel Chambers' cock-eyed story. And the K and R disaster, Jesus, I could have strangled Pike and Chambers both for what they'd put me through. But mostly what I thought of, sitting on the step of that hut, the crowd still roaring, was Mum and Dad. It wasn't Dad that had killed them. What had killed them was a bottle of dog juice, and Sebastian Ward and Eddie Pike.

'Hello,' Nev said quietly. He nodded to the darkness near where Pike had gone.

At first I couldn't see anything, but then I noticed movement, a figure coming towards us. Not Pike, I saw that immediately, but I couldn't see the face. I quickly swung round and scanned the stand. The race had just finished, people were drifting off or retaking their seats, but Tubs was still there, and Fielding too. Katy was just going up the steps away from them. I swung back and watched the figure, thinking it might be Fielding's offsider doing the rounds while Fielding stuck by Tubs, but it wasn't. The bloke still hadn't seen us, he kept on coming, then I recognized him. Lowering the glasses, I waited till he was almost on us, then I said, 'Got your pass?'

Bill Tyler stopped like I'd brained him. I stepped into the light and when he saw who I was he didn't react for a moment. But when I said his name, he seemed to come back to himself.

'Nearly gave me a bloody heart attack.' He smiled as he came on the last little way. 'Hear you're in deep shit.'

'That's the rumour.'

He seemed about to say something more, then he shrugged as though it was none of his business. He pointed to the Pop stand. 'How do I get there?'

Behind me Nev piped up, 'Whaddya after?'

'Longer odds,' Bill told him, and the pair of them laughed.

Nev shot me a glance, like asking if I needed him to stay. I shook my head, and he offered to walk back to the Pop with Bill. That was when Bill noticed the stove-in door of the hut. He didn't say anything. I could see he wanted to, but by then Nev was up and walking. Bill followed him, looking curiously at me and the door. As Bill passed, the ride-on tractor started up, there was a faint smell of diesel, and then there I was again, alone.

I sat on my arse, on the step of the hut, thinking. After my meeting with Eddie Pike I had plenty to think about. I was still at it a few minutes later when Detective Sergeant Fielding showed up.

8

This time I didn't run. Tubs was with Fielding, talking loud from a long way off to warn me they were coming, but I didn't run. I just looked up and watched them. Fielding had Tubs's mobile in his hand. Sensing someone off on my left I glanced over that way and saw Fielding's offsider closing in. He must have spotted me sitting there and then radioed Fielding.

Hey hey, I thought dismally. Hey hey, the gang's all here.

The three of them reached me together. Tubs was giving Fielding lip, but Fielding wasn't paying the slightest bit of attention. When Tubs paused to draw breath, Fielding leant over me.

'I understand you're unemployed, Mr Collier.'

I looked up at him.

'How's it feel,' he said, 'being back where you belong?'

I didn't say anything.

He gestured at his offsider to take a look inside the hut and I got up and let the bloke go in. A few moments later he came back out with Pike's sleeping bag.

Fielding looked from the sleeping bag to me. 'Visiting a friend?'

'Sure,' I said. 'That's why I had to break the fucking door down.'

He shook his head. 'You don't learn, do you. Aiding and abetting a suspected murderer. Now that's a serious offence.'

'Bullshit,' Tubs muttered, but I signalled for him to shut up.

I said, 'Aiding and abetting?'

'You deaf?' the offsider said, but Fielding shot him a nasty look.

I said, 'I'm not in the frame for Sebastian's murder any more? What happened, you couldn't jog Max's memory on the brooch?'

Fielding handed Tubs back his mobile, and Tubs made a show of wiping it clean. Facing me again, Fielding said, 'Where's Pike?'

'Pike?' I jabbed the air in front of Fielding's face with my finger. I had to work not to bunch my hand into a fist. 'You've trashed my home, you've lost me my fucking job, you've waved your frigging handcuffs all round the Room with my name on them, and now that you know it wasn't me, what? I'm meant to help you?'

He considered a moment. Pushing my finger aside he said, 'That's right. That's what you're meant to do.'

I swayed forward, pushed my face up very close to his, and whispered, 'Go fuck yourself.'

Fielding froze. Glared at me. And that's when the alarm started sounding way up in the main stand. Tubs turned first, then Fielding's offsider. The noise pulsed loud, a wailing siren I'd never heard before. In the kennels, the dogs went wild. Finally Fielding said to me, 'You'll keep,' then he turned too.

Up in the stand the crowd was moving like a wave, rolling back from the top right-hand corner. But people down on the terraces weren't moving fast enough; a lot were turning round to gawk at what was happening behind. Those spilling down from the upper tiers just kept on coming, not waiting for a clear passage, you could see bad crushes forming in the aisles. And between the pulses of the siren now you could hear shouts and screams. A few seconds later the first people started to fall.

A track official, white coat flapping, came sprinting from the darkness, shouting for someone to back up the watertruck. The last word I heard him cry before disappearing was, Fire.

Fielding's offsider saw it first; he pointed: 'Up there.'

Then we all saw it. From the top right of the stand, the stewards and officials deck, the smoke rose in thick black clouds.

The screams from the stand got louder.

Tubs faced me.

'Where's Katy?' I said, but even as I spoke he started to run. He was heading for the stand.

The offsider grabbed me, I kicked him in the shins and he went down howling. I legged it after Tubs.

When I caught him up, he waved a hand towards the fire. 'She thought she'd seen Pike up there,' he said, wheezing. 'I couldn't stop her.'

You could have kept your big mouth shut, I thought angrily, but this wasn't the time for a debate. I sprinted past him, Fielding shouting at me from somewhere way behind.

At the bottom of the stand I hit the body of the crowd, the whole mass rolling away from the danger, shouldering and shoving. I looked over their heads, up to the tiers where people were still pouring down. There was no way I could get through the tightly packed bodies.

'Katy!' I screamed. 'Katy!' But my voice was swallowed up by other voices, everyone shouting for someone in the crush.

Jostled and spun, I looked up to the smoke and my heart seemed to seize for a moment. The first tongues of orange flame flickered behind a window. Then the window burst, and the showering glass brought another roar from the crowd. The siren wailed like some hopeless cry for help.

Tubs had said she'd gone up after Pike.

I turned and ran to the side of the stand where we'd seen Pike disappear. I tried to replay it in my mind, trying to picture if Pike had had time to get up there for Katy to see him. Maybe. Just. Free of the crowd now I sprinted along the side of the stand. About halfway along I found a door. I grabbed the handle and pulled; the door swung open. It was a concrete stairwell, the stairs leading up to my right. I dived in and started up, taking the stairs two by two.

The stairwell muted the sounds from outside, and the bare bulbs threw a sickly yellow light over everything. After two flights I slowed, put my hands on my hips and breathed. I climbed and breathed. I put my hand on the railing, taking the steps one at a time now, and it was then, in those moments of relative quiet, that I felt it creeping over me, the cold tightening in my gut and the sweat on my palms, and I knew I was back there, back to the night Mum and Dad died. I was sinking beneath a suffocating blanket of fear.

I stopped. Footsteps came clattering down the steps above me.

'Katy!'

But the next moment a steward appeared, an old man, he grabbed my arm as he went by, saying, 'Clear the stand. Everybody down.'

Yanking my arm free, I started up the stairs again. He shouted after me, 'What you playing at? There's no-one up there,' but I kept going, then I heard his footsteps clattering below me, heading down.

Five more flights, and I couldn't hear the crowd any more, only the siren, and from above me a dull roar like the wind. I was sweating freely now, my mouth wide open, sucking in air. My eyes started to itch, I rubbed them. Smoke. Then I hit the landing, saw the door, but I'd lost track of how far I'd come.

I pulled the door open and had a sudden vision of flames flaring out to engulf me. But it didn't happen. On the other side of the door there was smoke, thick smoke, but no flames and I went in there, calling Katy's name. The siren was loud again, wailing.

Ahead, to my right, something moved. A man, I saw him coming down some stairs. The smoke was thicker there, it seemed to be rolling down from the fire up on the next level. He came towards me coughing, half-choked, holding a hankie over his mouth. Another steward, his eyes were fixed on the door behind me. He hardly seemed to notice I was there.

'Is there anyone up there?' I shouted. When he didn't answer I stepped between him and the door. I put a hand on his chest as he tried to get by. I shouted my question again, in his ear.

He nodded, dazed. He was old and thin, I thought maybe he was in shock too.

'A man,' he said.

He edged his way round me.

'Just a man?'

'One man,' he said, 'and one woman. I saw them.' He pointed behind me, the way I'd come. 'Top of the stairwell, there's a fire-door.'

He pushed past. I stood staring at the steps he'd come down. The smoke there was thickening all the time, and that roar like the wind, I realized with a jolt that it was the fire blazing somewhere out of sight. Turning, I followed him back out to the concrete stairwell and up the last flight of stairs. The staircase ended on a narrow landing; in front of us was a red metal door.

'You're sure you saw them?'

He said he'd seen the man going into the storerooms, then a few minutes later, a woman. He described them briefly. It couldn't be anyone but Katy and Pike.

He reached his palm out to the door, testing the heat, but when his hand touched the metal he flinched. That seemed to finish him. Whatever reserves of courage had kept him there while everyone else had fled, they were gone now. He looked straight at me and started talking about his wife, like an apology or an excuse, I don't know what really, maybe just the ramblings of a frightened old man. Then he turned his back on me, gripped the railing with both hands and stumbled away down the stairwell.

On the other side of the door, I heard something explode. My legs were trembling; I couldn't control them; I turned and leant my back against the wall. Heat radiated off the metal fire-door, the skin prickled on the left side of my face. I almost puked then, but I just managed to choke it back.

It was happening again. Not Mum and Dad this time, but my sister. My head fell back, and I screamed like an animal, 'Katy!'

Behind the door the fire roared on like a train.

'Collier!'

The call came twice before I opened my eyes. Swinging to look down the stairwell, I answered, 'Fielding! Up here. Top of the stairs!'

When I put my hand to my face, there were tears. I wiped them away with my sleeve. Then I slung my coat on the doorhandle, grabbed the handle through the coat, and heaved. The door didn't budge. I braced my foot against the doorframe, tried again, but it wouldn't come. The fire must have warped something, or melted it, the bloody thing was stuck fast. Grabbing my coat, I ran down to the next landing where I met Fielding coming up.

'What are you,' he said, catching his breath, 'the fucking fire brigade?'

'My sister's caught up there. And Pike.'

He thought about that for a moment. 'Bully for Pike,' he said.

Our eyes locked, the bastard really didn't give a toss. I shoved past him into the room where I'd seen the old bugger coming down the stairs; it was completely filled with smoke now. Bending low, and holding my coat to my nose and mouth, I ran to the stairs and stumbled up.

The fire was enormous. Not tongues now but great surging waves of flame, they made a wall to my right. To my left, and ahead, the fire hadn't reached yet. I crawled up the last step, got down on all fours where the smoke was thinner, and shouted for Katy.

There was a tug at my ankle. I looked back and saw Fielding. He was wiping his eyes and coughing as he came up beside me from the stairs.

'What the fuck's your sister doin' up here?'

Ignoring that, I pointed to the flames. I had to shout above the roar.

'They must be trapped in there. Can't get out the fire-door, it's jammed.'

He looked at the flames, then back at me. It must have been there on my face, plain as day, the fear. More than fear, it was terror. Mum and Dad, and now Katy. She was going to die.

I stared at the fire, hypnotized by the leaping flames.

Then Fielding shouted something at me. It didn't register, so he poked me in the ribs, and I turned to him. We were lying on our bellies now; he pulled himself nearer to me, rising up on his elbows. The bastard actually grinned this time as he shouted, 'Not your sister's lucky day.'

'What?'

'I said, "Not your sister's—" '

My fist caught him on the cheek, rolling him over. I scrambled to my knees, then lashed at him with my foot as he got up. It hit him in the chest and he went over backwards, tumbling down the stairs. I looked down. He hadn't gone far, just a few steps, he was clutching the banister, trying to get himself the right way up again.

Turning, I crawled away from the stairs. The flames didn't hypnotize me now. I wasn't locked in those awful moments from the past, I was here, now, at the Stow. And it wasn't Mum and Dad, it was Katy, and I could still do something, I still had that choice.

But in front of me the fire was a wall. I shielded my face from the heat and glanced back. Fielding's face appeared at the head of the stairs. He saw me, but he saw the flames too, getting bigger, and he didn't come on. He didn't go away either, he just watched me. After a second I realized that was all he was going to do. When I faced the fire again, he shouted, 'Go on then! Go on!'

In my mind I was already way, way beyond Fielding. Way beyond me even, and Mum and Dad. I was terrified, sure, but I guess I was even more terrified of the whole thing happening again, and of losing her. I'd finally got to the only place that mattered. It was Katy in there, my kid sister, who might still be alive.

Suddenly part of the ceiling collapsed, a beam swung down, spraying plaster, and a gap opened in the wall of flame. The heat flared, then the fire fell back on itself. I didn't even think, I just pulled my coat up over my head and shoulders, bent double, and ran.

The heat raked my face and hands; I was terrified of falling; then the flames seemed to close over me. It must have been only a second but it felt like forever, and then I was through. To what? More fire, but scattered, not like the wall of flame behind me. Turning, I glimpsed Fielding back there, gaping. But then the gap closed, and the fiery wall was solid again.

I spun round. 'Katy!'

I couldn't see a bloody thing. My eyes closed up against the heat; I had to shade them with my hands. I stumbled forward a few paces hopelessly.

'Katy!'

I was too late. Too late.

And then, from the flames and the smoke, a figure rose up like a ghost. It staggered towards me, then dropped, and I caught it in my arms. It was Pike. Clutching at my shirt, he looked up at me. His face was burnt red, and the skin was peeling away from his cheeks.

'Collier?' he said, choking.

He looked over my shoulder at the flames. I hauled him up by the wrists. His hands were bleeding, and black from the ash. God knows what had happened there.

'Is it burning?' he croaked. 'Is it burning on the other side?'

I shook him. 'Where's Katy?'

He stared past me at the wall of flame, eyes bulging.

'Did you see a woman?' I screamed at him. 'A woman?'

Still staring past me he slapped his chest with a bloodied hand. He said something about pictures, he was half out of his mind with fear.

'Stay here!' I shouted, hoarse now.

He bent towards me like he hadn't heard. I cupped my hands to my mouth, and then it happened. He tore my coat off my shoulders. He tried to wrap it over himself as he stumbled towards the wall of fire; I didn't have time to react. I swung round cursing him. Then suddenly he tripped and went down on his knees in the fire. He tried to get up, but his leg was caught on the coat, and he went down again. His hands reached forward instinctively into the fire to save himself, while his body arched back, and away. When his head twisted round, I saw his face. His open mouth trying to scream, but it wouldn't come. I watched, horrified, as his hair went up in a halo of fire. And then the scream came. Mercifully, his body surrendered. He went limp and collapsed, crumpling like a broken doll into the flames.

I bent over and retched, but nothing came up, only bile. The heat was burning my skin now; I stumbled away, wiping my mouth, and praying. I prayed I still had time to reach Katy, that she might still be alive.

The next minute or so I don't really remember, not properly. I remember seeing Pike go down, and I remember stumbling around like a blind man through the smoke and flames. But I must have been dazed, I suppose, because when I came across Katy's handbag I didn't know what I was looking at, not at first. I was crouching right over it, staring at it, but not taking it in.

Then I knelt. I picked it up and turned it over. Green, with big white clasps, definitely Katy's. I reached round and tucked it under my belt at the small of my back, then I lifted my head.

'Katy!'

Dropping down under the worst of the smoke, I crawled. A few seconds later my hand touched a hand. It didn't move. I ran my hand along the limp arm, then pulled myself forward to see the face.

Katy.

'I'm here. It's Ian. Don't worry, I'm here.'

She didn't move or open her eyes. She just lay there on her side, it was like she was sleeping. Frantic now, I ran a hand over her other arm, then down over her body, and her legs. I thought maybe something had pinned her down, but there was nothing. She seemed to have just dropped. The fire had blazed all around and left her untouched: it was a bloody miracle. But why was she lying there like that?

Then I coughed, really hacking. Smoke.

I put my ear to her mouth and rested my hand behind her head. Useless. Then I slid my hand down to her chest feeling for her breathing. One second. Two seconds. Could I feel movement?

'Come on, Katy. Please.'

And then I felt it, her ribcage rising, shallow. Tears, real tears of relief welled up in my eyes. She was alive. Alive. But when I wiped my eyes, I felt something like oil on my hand. I looked, and it wasn't oil, it was blood. It was on Katy's chest too, on her pink sweater where my hand had been and, half-delirious now, I thought stupidly, I've killed her.

But her chest still rose and fell. My hand went to the back of her head again, where I'd held her. There was blood. And down the back of her neck, and on the rug underneath. I propped her up then, rested her head in my lap and parted her hair. The lump was like a golf ball. When I touched it, she moved for the first time and moaned.

More of the ceiling came crashing down in a fiery ball beside us, spraying flame. I shook my head, and flicked a burning stick off Katy's sweater. We had to move.

Putting an arm round her back, I got up on one knee, and slid my other arm under her legs. Then heaving, I staggered to my feet. I took three steps before I knew it wasn't going to work. I sank to one knee, gasping for air. I couldn't breathe, standing up like that. And I couldn't see either, not even the little I could make out from down nearer the floor.

Katy moaned again. I tried to say something, to reach her. I told her we were going to be fine, that she was safe, while all around us now the building was collapsing in flames.

Grabbing her under the arms, I hauled, sliding back on my arse. More ceiling dropped, burning beams falling like trees in a forest fire.

I thought maybe I could get us back to where Pike had

fallen. With the fire-door jammed that was the only way out, the place I'd come in. Maybe, I prayed, that wall of fire had died down and we had some kind of chance to get through. I was on my knees, hauling Katy beside me. Then I stopped and looked round. I had a moment of sheer panic, a sob came up in my throat; I think if Katy hadn't been there I might have gone off my head.

The fire wasn't dying, it was swelling, the separate fires joining into a solid blaze. I couldn't even make out the walls of the room, couldn't see where we were. Should I go forward? Back? In the middle of a roaring inferno, I was lost.

Then Katy moved in my arms.

Forward or back, it didn't matter. I had to get her away from the flames.

I grabbed her wrists, took a few quick breaths of rotten air near the floor, then I stood up and hauled her. I got half a dozen paces, then suddenly the world broke in two. One second I was on my feet, the next flat on my back, and there was this ripping, buckling sound, louder than the fire. I sat up, shaking my head, I still had hold of Katy. It felt like she was shuddering, then I realized it wasn't her, it was the whole floor. And the fire. I couldn't believe my eyes; half of it was gone. It was still roaring away on our right, and in front, but to the left it was gone. The smoke seemed to be clearing too. Then it did clear and I saw the stars, and my heart slammed against my ribs.

The top floor of the stand had collapsed. Not all of it, just the central section, and the front of the section where we were. Out to our left there was nothing but fresh air and a hundred-foot drop to the concrete tiers of the stand. Ahead of us, fire, and another drop. To the right, more fire. Behind – I turned. Now that the smoke had cleared I could see it quite clearly. I could see it, but I didn't know what to feel. The fucking fire-door.

'Katy, can you hear me?'

She didn't answer or move.

I let go of her. Bent double, I hacked up gobs of black phlegm.

Looking round me again I tried to get a grip. We were perched on a ledge. The ledge was burning, the edges crumbling as the fire ate its way towards us. From the track below, the concrete stairwell must have looked like a giant chimney-stack now, with just our ledge and the roof above us jutting out from it, suspended over air.

It was the fire-door or nothing.

I pulled my sleeve down over my hand, grabbed the handle and shouldered the door. It didn't budge. I tried a few more times, then I stepped back and kicked it. The bloody thing was jammed solid. In a frenzy I charged it again, hit hard, and felt something in my right shoulder tear. Pounding with my left fist I slumped to my knees, then I heard that ripping sound again and I turned just in time to see the front half of our ledge disappear. It dragged most of the ceiling down behind it. But the ceiling didn't collapse completely; it lodged like a cage of fire around us, around what was left of the floor.

I knelt down by Katy and held her. That was when I knew for certain we were going to die.

I wasn't scared then. Christ knows, I was angry, fucking furious, but the fear seemed to have worn itself out, become irrelevant somehow, and with my left hand I pulled Katy's legs back from the flames. I stroked her hair, I remember that. And I talked to her.

They say your whole life flashes before your eyes – well, that didn't happen to me. I just remembered things. Mum and Dad, and Katy when she was a kid. Things just kind of rose up and went by me as I breathed in the smoke. Hallucinations? I saw Lee Chan. My hand felt Katy's hair; it was softer than silk. I told her what I saw but when I looked down at her I could see she didn't hear me. When I said her name, she didn't answer. I was glad she was safe. The fire was flaring now, soon it would be burning our skin. She was sleeping, I bent down and kissed her head.

There was another ripping sound, loud and close.

Katy's sleeping, I thought. I thought, She won't feel a thing.

The flames were beautiful. Then my body jerked to one side, I held tight to Katy and out of the fire someone whispered, 'I've got you.'

'I've got you. You're okay, we've got you.'

My body rolled in slow motion. The fire-door was under me, lying flat, torn off its hinges, and someone had hold of my arms. He was dragging me. I breathed. Breathed again. There was air. Pain exploded in my shoulder and I screamed out for Katy. Tubs's face came out at me like a mask.

'She's okay. We've got her. She's okay.'

I reached out for the mask, pain ripped through my shoulder, and that's when I slid away into the dark.

9

NOW SELLING.
Sitting on the edge of my bed, head in my hands, I stared out at the sign across the way. It was morning, the sun rising into a cloudless sky, and I felt awful. Worse than awful, like death. My mouth and throat were caked with gunge, my whole body ached, and the slightest movement of my right arm sent a whiplash of pain over my shoulder and on down my back.

I looked at the clock. 7 a.m. If I started now, I could probably get myself showered and dressed in time for a taxi to get me to the hospital by nine. The start, so they'd told me the night before, of visiting hours.

God, I wanted to sleep. Just an hour. I closed my eyes but it didn't help. Groaning then, I eased myself gingerly off the bed and headed for the shower. The shower. So bloody normal. Less than twelve hours earlier, I'd been ready to die.

Katy wasn't in danger. They'd told me that the night before too. Out of danger, sir, but you can't see her now, come back in the morning. This was at 2 a.m., well after the last of the journalists had gone. The nurse had strapped up my shoulder by then, and the doctor had checked my lungs and shone his little torch in my eyes. They wanted me to stay in for observation, but I hate hospitals, so when they told me it was my choice, I checked out. I told them to make sure Katy got a private room; I signed the payment guarantee, and then Tubs took me home. He watched me get myself into bed, then he had to get back to his place to check on his mum. One last time he told me not to worry about Katy.

Showered and dressed now, I took an overnight bag and went into Katy's room to pack some fresh clothes for her. Stuff she might need in the hospital. On the way through the lounge I hit the answer machine. Three messages.

'Ian, it's Lee.' I sat down on Katy's bed and opened her dresser drawer left-handed. 'Are you all right? What was all that at the airport? I didn't know what I should do so I just got on the plane. I don't want to talk on this thing, can you call me? I'm at the Phoenix Hotel, Dublin. The number here—' There was a pause, then she read out the numbers. 'I'm in and out all day, but I'm here for a week, so call. Hope you're okay. Bye.' Another pause. 'Katy, if you get this message instead of Ian, can you call me? Bye.'

Socks, underwear, and a few hankies. Next drawer down, some shirts.

Out in the lounge a beep, then the second message came on.

'Ian, it's Pam, at the office.' She sounded embarrassed. 'Mr Mortlake asked me to call you.'

Rummaging in the drawer, I muttered, 'Tell me the worst, Pam.'

'There's some personal things of yours down on the box, and up here in the office, he wants them taken away. He says tomorrow.'

Tomorrow, I realized closing the drawer, meant today. Today I'd been invited to empty my desk. My suspension had become permanent. I was fired.

I took the bag through to the bathroom and opened the medicine cabinet. Toothbrush, toothpaste—

'Mr Collier.'

Kerry Anne Lammar; her voice cut through the air like a chainsaw. I stopped, my left hand on a brown bottle in the cabinet.

'It's Ms Lammar from Lonnigan's, about the Coopers Dock penthouse? There's no point drawing this out, Mr Collier. Under the terms of your contract, your failure to make full payment on the property, as I'm sure you remember, triggers clause seven.' To refresh my memory she read out clause seven in full, detailing the five thousand quid a week penalty. She was ringing to inform me that she'd just made the first deduction from my deposit. She was getting a real kick out of all this. 'To avoid any misunderstandings we'd prefer it if you could come down to the office. I'll be only too happy to run through it all with you in person then, Mr Collier. Thank you.'

She rang off. My hand still on the pill-bottle, I stared. Awake for just twenty minutes and my day was on an accelerating downward slide. I finished packing, then left for the hospital.

'Anyone home?'

Katy looked up. 'Hey,' she said, dropping her magazine onto the floor. She shuffled her pillows behind her back and tried to sit up.

Going into her room I said, 'I brought some clothes and stuff.'

She pointed to the chair. I put the overnight bag down there, then I perched myself on the window ledge. She seemed surprisingly normal. Her face, like mine, looked badly sunburnt, and there was a carefulness in how she fixed the pillows that wasn't like her, but apart from that, and the bandage around her head, she really seemed okay.

I said, 'They reckon you'll live.'

'You didn't see breakfast,' she told me, her voice rasping a bit.

'You feeling okay?'

She put out a hand, tilting it from side to side.

We seemed to stall then. I found myself looking at her, wondering what it was I'd expected. Tears? An emotional scene where we bawled our eyes out about how much we loved one another?

'How's the head?'

'Sore as hell.' She bent forward, running a finger down the bandage. 'No stitches but they reckon I'm lucky my skull wasn't fractured.'

'More bone than brains.'

Pulling a face, she slumped back into her pillows. She was knackered. I saw now why the nurse had only given me fifteen minutes.

I said, 'Do you remember much?'

'Nope.' She reached out to the side table and picked up a sheet of paper. 'The cops just left. That shit Fielding. I gave him a statement; he left a copy.'

She held it out to me. Taking it, I asked her what happened when Fielding came to the flat. 'Did you see him plant that brooch?'

'He didn't plant it,' she said, surprised. 'It was just sitting on the dressing table in your room.'

I frowned.

She said, 'He went straight to it, like he knew where it was. I was with him. He didn't plant it, Ian.' She looked at me curiously. 'Whose was it?'

Shaking my head, I sat down on the edge of her bed and read the statement. She watched me in silence.

Katy claimed to have gone to the Stow to watch the dogs. She'd bumped into Tubs and they'd sat together in the stand, where they'd been joined later by Fielding. She'd left them to go to the Ladies, but she found that the Ladies was full. There was a queue. Not wanting to wait, she'd gone upstairs to the staff toilets which she knew were off-limits to the public, and probably empty. They were empty. She didn't remember if she'd been hit. All she remembered after going into the staff toilets was waking in hospital with a severe headache. She didn't remember anything about a fire.

Underneath all this was her signature.

I handed the statement back to her and she replaced it on the side table.

I said, 'They swallowed that?'

She ignored the question. She said, 'Were a lot of people hurt?'

I didn't say anything: the nurse had warned me not to get Katy too stirred up.

'Ian, I'm not gonna throw myself out the window, am I? Come on. What happened?'

'There was a crush in the stand,' I said. 'When the fire started, people panicked. No-one died.' Then remembering Pike, I added. 'Not in the crush.'

On the way over in the taxi I'd seen the banner headlines at the news stands. 'Dog Stadium Blaze: 1 Dead. 27 Injured'. For the first time in fifty years the dogs had made the front pages. Around the kennels, no-one would be cheering.

'A big fire?'

'Yeah,' I said. 'Big.'

She waited for more, but when it didn't come she screwed up her face. 'You're worse than the bloody cops, you are.'

'How about I tell you then you tell me.'

'Tell you what?' she said warily.

I pointed to her statement. 'The truth?'

She mulled that one over. Finally she nodded.

I went first. I took it from me and Tubs arriving at the Stow, the edited highlights of my talk to Pike, and on to the fire. I told her that Pike died in the fire, but not the details. And I told her that I'd dragged her from nowhere-near-the-Ladies, over to the fire-door. Again I glossed the details. I really didn't feel like reliving the whole thing over, right then.

When I was done, she looked down at the blanket.

'The cops said the stadium collapsed.'

'Yeah,' I said.

'The whole thing burnt down?'

'Just the top floor,' I said. 'Last I saw, anyway.'

She lifted her head. 'The nurse said you pulled me outa there.'

Her look went right into me. Was she thinking what I was thinking, about Mum and Dad? Eventually I nodded, just the once. The reluctant hero.

'I could have died,' she said.

'Your turn,' I told her, pointing to her statement. She grabbed my arm and squeezed. The pain went zinging over my shoulder, I let out a loud yelp and pulled back.

'Sorry, Ian. Jesus.'

Wincing and rubbing my shoulder, I went back to the window ledge.

'Did you get hurt too?'

'I'm okay,' I said irritably, the heroic moment gone now. I nodded to her statement. 'Forget the bollocks, what were you doing up there?'

'I can call the nurse, she'll look at your arm.'

I gave her a look, and she pulled a face at me. The normal brother–sister relationship re-established.

Pointing with my left hand, I repeated very firmly. 'Your turn.'

She tugged at the blankets, straightening them over her legs. 'Okay. So I went to the track with Bill.'

'He didn't get a mention in your statement.'

'Why drag anyone else into it? You didn't get a mention either. I only put Tubs in because Fielding saw him. Anyway, I'm with Bill, and we bumped into Tubs. Tubs told me you and him were there looking for Eddie Pike.'

'Did he say why?'

'Why you were looking for Pike?' She shrugged. 'About Ward. Tubs said if you could find Pike, Fielding might lay off you.'

'That was all?'

Her brow wrinkled under the bandage. 'Yeah. What else?'

I told her to go on with her story.

'Bill saw some old mate or something, so he went off. Me and Tubs sat down. Then Fielding came along, God, what a dickhead. He goes, "Where's Collier?" and Tubs puts on that stupid face, and goes, "Collier?" Fielding carries on asking questions; after a while I got sick of him; I started looking around to see where Bill was. That's when I seen Pike, way back in the stand, heading upstairs. I couldn't tell Tubs, Fielding was right there. When I got up, Fielding says, "Where you going?" I go, "The loo." Then I whispered to Tubs that I seen Pike. He had to stay put because of Fielding.'

'And you followed Pike.'

Katy nodded, remembering. She grabbed a tissue and

coughed into it. 'I went up those stairs to the top floor, you know, with the red carpet? I wasn't sure which way he went, then I thought I heard something weird down on the right.'

'Weird like what?'

She frowned. 'Crackling. Popping? I went along there, thinking it was Pike, in through a couple of rooms – whoosh, there's the fire.'

'It was already going?'

'Not big,' she said, as if that was a reasonable explanation for not turning and getting straight out. 'It was like in small patches. What with Ward and all that, the first thing I thought was arson. Then I seen through the door into the next room. There was this desk, all the drawers pulled out on the floor, paper everywhere. The desk was burning. Anyway, I went in there.'

I waved my left hand. 'The place was burning? What the hell were you doing?'

Her eyes opened wide at me. She coughed again. 'You wanna hear this or not?'

I looked at her, my kid sister. Shaking my head I slumped back against the ledge.

'Tubs said something about papers Pike had, you needed. I guess that's what I was thinking. These were the papers, and Pike was trying to burn them. I couldn't see Pike; I thought he'd shot through, at least I could try to save the papers – they might help you.' She looked at me, defiant. 'Go on, say I was stupid.'

It had been right on the tip of my tongue. But now, I said, 'You went in and started sorting through the papers? What got into you? Didn't you hear the alarm?'

She nodded, vague. She said she thought the alarm started wailing sometime about then.

Sometime about then? This was the fire that had come within a whisker of killing us both; I put a hand over my eyes and dropped my head.

'Well, what was I meant to do?'

I looked up. 'What were you really looking for, Katy?'

Her eyes locked on mine for a second then the defiance

went out of her. Her head fell back into the pillows.

'Ward's blue book,' she said.

At last. Confirmation of what I'd half-suspected.

'Tubs told you about that?'

She nodded, resting an arm on the pillow behind her head.

'There at the track?' I said. 'He told you Pike had Ward's desk, and in the desk might be the blue book where he thought there was proof Dad insured the house.'

After a moment, she nodded again.

I clasped the back of my neck with my left hand and squeezed the tightening muscles. I reminded myself that Katy was still a patient in hospital, that this wasn't the time or place to blow my stack.

'Katy—'

'And I found it too,' she said.

I just stared at her.

She closed her eyes. 'There were these papers with Mortlake's name on: the blue book was right under them. I flicked through it. Dad was there. His name, B. Collier, the address and everything. I had it.' When her eyes opened they were filmed with tears. She looked at me, willing me to believe in Dad. The tears brimming in her eyes were tears of frustration. 'I had it, Ian. I shoved it in my handbag with the other papers. Then this—' She touched the bandage on her head.

'You what?'

'I had it,' she said brokenly. 'In my hands.'

I took two steps across to the chair and unzipped the overnight bag. I reached in and pulled out Katy's handbag. When I turned, and she saw it, she didn't react at first. All she did was look up from the handbag to me, stunned.

I undid the white clasp and opened it. A smell of smoke came out. I looked inside. Then I went and sat down on the bed.

'Ian?'

I placed the open handbag on the blanket, in her lap. She hesitated, afraid to look I think, but finally her glance went down. Her hand came forward slowly, dipped into the bag and came out clutching Sebastian Ward's little blue book.

I watched as she turned the pages. Neither of us spoke. After maybe a minute she found it. She turned the book round, holding it open for me to see.

B. Collier. Then Mum and Dad's address, the Insured Property, the Insured Amount, £120,000 and the premium, £400. The word PAID was scrawled across the premium, with Sebastian Ward's signature beside it.

Katy started to cry.

For her, I know, that moment marked an end. From way back at the start, from when Mum and Dad died, she'd been almost obsessed with the idea of proving to me that Dad hadn't let us down. And not just to me, either. Katy, I realized now, must have had doubts of her own. She wasn't a girl any more: I'd had plenty of proof of that this last little while. Even before Mum and Dad died, her ideas about them both must have been changing. When I got older, wasn't that what happened with me?

And now with her sitting in the hospital bed beside me weeping, it all made sense in a way it just hadn't done before. Times like way back when Katy first moved in with me, when I'd said Dad was an irresponsible bastard, and she'd gone off the deep end. Now, at last, I knew why. She'd started to look at Dad with the eyes of an adult, not a girl, and she wasn't sure she liked what she saw.

But now, with that one small page in Ward's blue book, she had him back again, the father who for most of her life she'd adored. He hadn't let her down; she still loved him like she'd loved him as a girl. Without doubts now, with a clear heart, she could lean her forehead on my shoulder and let the tears fall.

The nurse put her head in. With a stern look at me, she silently mouthed, Two minutes, then withdrew.

'Shh,' I said quietly. 'Hey.' It went on for another minute before I eased Katy off me.

That's when I noticed the other sheets of paper sticking

out of her handbag. Curious, but not really expecting anything, I pulled them out.

Katy wiped her eyes. 'I grabbed that stuff from the same drawer,' she said, sniffing. 'I saw "Mortlake Group" written on it, so I just grabbed it.'

The pages were badly crumpled: I smoothed them out on my knee. Katy tore open a box of tissues. She blew her nose a few times, then I guess she must have seen the change come over my face. I flicked forward through the pages, and back again.

'Is it important, Ian?'

Lifting my head, I gazed out the window. The trees and the clouds stood out at me like pictures; the whole world seemed too bright. Katy, and now this. It was so clear to me that I almost wished for the dark again. The pages she'd saved were important all right. So important I almost longed for someone to reach up and put out the light.

As I was walking out of the hospital, a car suddenly backed out in front of me and stopped. It was Fielding. His window went down; he was without his sidekick for a change.

He said, 'I'd offer you a lift into work, but there's nowhere to take you now, is there?'

I bent down to the window and in a few brief words I told him exactly what I thought of him. He didn't even blink.

'Don't push your luck, Collier. I'm still wonderin' whether I should do you for the assault you committed on me last night.'

I would have walked right on by, but there was something I needed to know.

I said, 'I hear Nigel Chambers solved Sebastian's murder for you.'

'Good police work solved the murder. Chambers just happened to be what the good police work turned up.'

I smiled at that one. He didn't like it, but he didn't drive off either. I got the feeling he had something to say.

For a moment, ridiculously, I thought he was ashamed of what he'd done the night before.

When I stepped away, he said, 'Collier,' and I stopped.

'I don't wanna see you down the station again.'

I took a step back and looked in at him.

'Ever,' he said, then he turned aside. 'And I don't wanna hear about you shootin' your mouth off down the Gallon or anywhere else. The case is over.'

What was he trying to tell me? It took me a few moments, but that shifty look he had; it finally occurred to me.

I said, 'You found Sebastian's murderer. You solved the case.'

He stuck out his jaw.

'Fielding,' I said, shaking my head and smiling stupidly, 'They're not promoting you?'

He turned and pointed. 'You shoot your mouth off I was doin' this, I was doin' that, I'll come down on you like a ton of bricks, son.'

'You're worried I'll file some report against you. The way you've treated me through this whole thing. That could stuff up your promotion.'

'A ton of fuckin' bricks,' he said, scowling.

I leant in close, there was a smell of whisky.

'Fielding, you ever come near me or my sister again, I'll file a report that'll have you on the carpet so fast it'll make your head spin. You stay out of our lives, I'll stay out of yours.'

He swore at me; I had to pull my head back fast as the car lurched away. Then I went to my own car and sat there a while thinking of what I was going to do. I decided my first port of call was Piers Crossland.

10

As I walked through the Room to the 486 Box, no-one nodded to me. In fact no-one, not even the brokers, acknowledged me at all – word had obviously gotten around that I'd been fired. Offers of sympathy – I kidded myself there might be some – would have to wait for a more private place than the Room. For the time being, clutching my briefcase, I passed among the boxes like the invisible man, or one of the undead, the newest addition to the market's list of untouchables.

When I reached the Mortlake boxes my colleagues weren't sure how to handle me either. There were one or two brief smiles of pity but I had to sit down at my desk and begin the shameful business of emptying my drawer before anyone actually spoke to me. And then who was it? Bloody Frazer.

'Bad night at the dogs?'

I lifted my head slowly and looked at Frazer Burnett-Adams.

'Hear about the fire?' he asked.

'I was there,' I said, 'with my sister.'

He grinned. 'Trouble and you, Ian. Like shit to a blanket.'

'My sister's in hospital. Care to join her?'

He tried to laugh but the sound died in his throat. He smiled and shook his head.

'Sad,' he said. 'Looks like you won't be here for the big announcement.'

I dug in the drawer and pulled out an old calculator and a birthday card from two years back. Opening the card, I glanced at the half a dozen signatures, one of them Frazer's. Binning the card, I dropped the calculator into my case.

Frazer came round and perched on the edge of my desk. 'Not curious?'

I really was sick of the bastard, so I said, 'Allen's going to announce the Mortlake Group–Crossland merger. The new company's going to be called Mortland Insurance. Allen thinks he'll be running it, and I guess you think you'll be the new big cheese here on Box 486. How's that?'

Frazer's look changed; I'd unsettled him. 'Allen told you?'

'No.' I lifted my briefcase and clicked it shut. 'Piers Crossland told me.'

'When?'

'Two days ago.'

Frazer was completely thrown. He'd thought this was his big opportunity to piss all over me, but it hadn't gone according to plan. When I started to close my desk drawer, Frazer's hand shot down and held it open.

'You haven't finished emptying it,' he said.

Nodding, I made a show of looking in the drawer. It was only junk. 'Bits and pieces,' I said. Then I stood and gave him a confident smile and a friendly pat on the shoulder. 'Just stuff I'll be needing when I come back.'

I had the satisfaction of seeing the doubt in his eyes turn to horror before I turned and walked away.

Pam buzzed through into Allen's office. She told him I was there, then she flicked the intercom switch and waited for a reply.

I asked her, 'Has he got someone with him?'

'Just Angela,' she said, 'and the caterers.' She started to apologize for calling me with that message the other day.

'Not your fault,' I said.

She seemed relieved. Allen's voice suddenly barked from the intercom, 'Tell him to wait,' and Pam's relief turned to blushing embarrassment.

434

I pointed to Allen's door. 'Do you mind?'

Pam rearranged the pencils. She told me to be her guest.

There were flowers all over the place. A giant bunch in the centre of a table that had been rigged up along the side wall, smaller vases along the other wall, and more again on Allen's cleared desk and the coffee table. White lilies and God knows what else. It looked like a florist's.

In one corner the caterers, three men in white shirts and black trousers, were busy arranging food onto trays. They paid no attention to me. Nor did Allen at first, he was down on his knees plugging a lead into a wall socket behind a giant vase. But Angela was on her feet. She turned, her fingers prodding at the flowers on Allen's desk. Her glance flitted to Allen, then back.

'Not the ideal moment, Ian,' she said, returning her attention to the flowers. 'Guests expected, and all that.'

Hearing my name, Allen reared up on his knees. His cheeks were flushed red. 'I told you to wait.'

I went calmly across to the sofa and sat down. I rested my left ankle on my right knee and lolled back in the cushions.

'Nice flowers,' I said. 'What's the celebration?'

'If you want an appointment,' Allen said, getting to his feet, 'Speak to Pam. I might have a window in my diary early next week, that's the best I can do.'

'I'm busy next week.'

Allen cocked his head. 'Have you cleared your desk?'

'Some of it.'

He exchanged a glance with Angela, not quite sure how to handle this.

'Ian,' she said. 'No-one expects you to be happy with the way things have turned out. But if you want to discuss severance pay, that'll have to wait.'

I smiled a crooked smile.

'Till next week,' Allen put in. 'Next week at the earliest.'

Nodding towards the caterers, I asked him, 'Do you want to keep this private?'

'Ian—' Allen jerked a thumb over his shoulder – 'get off my sofa and out of my office. Now. Right now.'

'How about you, Angela? Or shall I just come straight out with it?'

As usual, she hid her feelings brilliantly. She gave me a thoroughly bored look, like this was a ridiculous game she had to endure. Then she turned and waved the caterers out of the room.

When they were gone, she said, 'Okay, Ian. Make it brief.'

That's when I knew for sure. I said, 'You don't care, do you.'

'Care?'

'About what I say now.'

'Could I stop you?' She dropped into a chair by Allen's desk. 'But you can save your breath. Allen is—' she glanced up at him, then quickly away – 'aware,' she said.

'Happy?' Allen said to me. 'Now get out.'

I looked him straight in the eye. This was a moment I was going to savour. 'So you're aware,' I said, 'that Angela was fucking Sebastian.'

There was absolute silence. He was aware all right, and he had been for a lot longer than me, but that wasn't helping him any right now. I'd just rubbed his nose in his wife's infidelity, as crudely and as bluntly as I could. The whys and wherefores didn't matter in the least; the fury he felt came off him in waves.

'For God's sake,' Angela said, turning on me.

But she didn't say any more. Maybe she knew me better than to think I'd come up just to indulge in a moment of petty spite, I don't know. Maybe she just couldn't believe that I'd said what I'd said to Allen.

'Well.' I looked from one to the other. 'It's good to see that you've talked it through.'

Allen came at me. 'You little shit!'

Angela jumped to her feet, blocking him with her arms. 'Allen,' she said, 'Allen.'

He shrugged her arm off but then stayed where he was, in the centre of the room. He pointed at me. 'I'll fucking destroy you,' he said. 'You are nobody. Nobody.'

I bent down and picked up my briefcase. Then I placed it beside me on the sofa, popping it open. Taking out the photocopies, I said, 'Before you get too carried away—' I held the photocopies out to them.

'I want you gone,' Allen said threateningly. 'Now.'

Angela touched him on the wrist. The way she looked at the photocopies, I think she must have guessed. And her guess somehow communicated itself to Allen; he made a sound in his throat. Finally it was her that came and took them. She barely glanced at them, then pushed them into Allen's hands and went and sat down. He studied the sheets, mouth slightly open.

'How's that?' I said.

He looked up. 'So we wrote the lead on Connolly and Blythe.'

'More than that, Allen. Angela knew they were crooks, and still we wrote the lead on Connolly and Blythe.'

He read the papers again, shaking his head. The pose seemed to be that I'd got it all wrong.

I said, 'And that's not all we did.'

He turned to the next sheet. 'We reinsured it? What else is the market there for?'

'Angela reinsured all of it.' I pointed at him. 'And you knew that, Allen. It's your scratch on the confirmation to the LCO.' The stuff Lee had given me out at the airport. I faced Angela, she stared at the carpet. 'And that's not quite how the situation was explained to me the other night,' I said.

She didn't raise her eyes. Eventually she rested her elbows on her knees and buried her head in her hands.

But Allen – Allen bloody Mortlake – he just wouldn't give up. He put on his angry-face and launched into a defence of Angela that was completely beside the point. I think, even then, he really thought he could steam-roller right over me. Unbelievable. The arrogance. And what made it worse was that I'd seen him put on performances like this before, bullying his way over people to get what he wanted, and those times I'd actually admired him for it. The whole market admired him for it. Allen Mortlake, as everybody knew, was tough. But now, with him waving the evidence of his own crime over his head, shouting at me that I was an imbecile, I saw it quite clearly. Allen Mortlake didn't know the first thing about tough. Tough was Nev Logan, joking about his cancer. Tough was Tubs, looking after his mother to the bitter end. Tough was my old man, killing himself rather than bend his knee to Sebastian Ward and Allen bloody Mortlake. Tough was definitely not a rich managing director in a suit.

He finished with another order for me to get out. I stayed right where I was, on the sofa.

I said, 'Tell me that bit again, Allen, where you and Sebastian each get a share of Connolly and Blythe's claim.' He laughed at me, but I was way past worrying about that bullshit. I indicated the photocopies. 'How much was it? Four and a half million quid? That makes it – what? – a third of the claim each. That makes it one and a half for you, one and a half for Sebastian, one and a half for your friends at Connolly and Blythe.'

He raised a finger. 'Repeat that allegation outside this room, and I'll sue you till your nose bleeds.'

I reached into my briefcase and took out the final photocopy. This was the clincher. The telex Katy had saved from the fire. I didn't ponce about with it, I just read it straight out aloud.

' "Confirmation of payment. Attention Mr S. Ward. Cheque for the sum of 1,500,000.00 pounds sterling received on 3/7, and deposited to the benefit of account number 730561894, account name Mr A. Mortlake. Funds cleared 7/7." '

I glanced at Allen; he wasn't glaring any more, the colour was draining right out of him. Then I read the rest.

' "Cheque for the sum of 1,500,000.00 pounds sterling received on 3/7, and deposited to the benefit of account number 127813684, account name Connolly and Blythe.

Funds cleared 7/7. Regards, Banco della Republica (Jersey)." '

Looking up, I held the photocopy out to him. He didn't take it. I turned and waved it in Angela's direction.

'Honestly,' I said smiling. 'That's what it says.'

She couldn't face me, either. She turned and stared out through the glass wall into the atrium.

Allen finally came over and took the photocopy. He looked at it and mumbled something about how he thought we could all sort this out, that maybe there'd been a few misunderstandings, but we could resolve them. He mentioned Angela's job. When I didn't respond to that, he took another look at the photocopies.

I said, 'When did you decide to stitch me up, Allen?'

'Pardon me?' He screwed up his face. He turned to Angela for support but she wasn't having any of it; she kept her gaze fixed on the glass wall. 'Me stitching you up?' he said, turning back.

'Was it when you saw that photo of Justine and Sebastian?'

'You're on drugs.'

'You must have known back then.' I glanced at Angela. 'Both of you, given the history. If Sebastian was shafting Justine, and Justine had signed up on Ottoman, you must have put two and two together. You must have known why she'd done it.' Like mother, like daughter, Justine had fallen for Sebastian. Only Justine wasn't half the underwriter Angela was. She didn't reinsure. 'The way I see,' I said, 'you couldn't have known much earlier. If you had, you would have settled, wouldn't you? There's no way either of you would have let Justine step into court with that hanging over her.'

'You're reaching,' Allen said.

I pointed. 'You knew right from the start that the Ottoman claim was bent. That's why Bill Tyler was set loose on it from day one, wasn't it?'

Neither of them spoke.

I said, 'Sebastian must have mentioned he had Mehmet lined up. But when you went into hospital—' I pointed at

439

Angela – 'he decided not to wait. He needed the money. As Nigel Chambers explained to me, WardSure wasn't in as good a shape as people thought. So Sebastian put it through Justine. She didn't reinsure, and my guess is he meant to cut you out of your share of the claim. Am I right?'

'You're romancing,' Allen said.

But Angela's face said something quite different.

'And at first you must have thought Justine just screwed up. You didn't think it was her Sebastian had in his pocket, did you? No, at first you thought it was me. And that's why,' I said, facing Angela, 'that's why before you went into hospital you told me I'd be getting your job, and when you came out – after the Ottoman sting – you suddenly went cold on the idea. You thought I'd conspired with Sebastian to rip you off.'

She said, 'You're drawing a long bow, Ian.'

'Am I? And then the K and R.' I turned back to Allen. 'And after that the murder investigation. Whenever things got messy you made sure I was right in the middle of it. You stitched me up.'

'Ian,' Angela said. 'No-one stitched you up.'

I studied her a moment. Maybe, just maybe, she really believed that.

'I don't suppose either of you knows anything about a certain diamond brooch. Possibly Sebastian's. Shaped like a butterfly?'

Allen's gaze didn't flicker. But Angela frowned, her brow creasing.

I said to her, 'It was found in my flat by the police. Someone gave them the idea it was Sebastian's, and that maybe I'd stolen it when I murdered him and burnt his house down.'

That rocked her. Shocked, she made a sound in her throat, instinctively turning to face Allen. He wouldn't look at her.

I said to Allen, 'Bill Tyler's a handy bloke to have around, isn't he.'

He dropped the photocopies on the desk, moving away from me.

'Hard up, what with those two ex-families to pay for. And violent,' I went on, 'in a manageable kind of way. Ideal combination really.'

Allen pushed a vase of lilies to the side of his desk. 'I don't follow.'

'Well, let me put you back on track.' I leant forward. 'Bill Tyler's hard up and violent. And you, Allen, you're rich and gutless.'

His jaw clenched so tight his neck muscles stood out in cords.

'You had him plant that diamond brooch in my flat, then you or him tipped Fielding off where to find it. And you knew Fielding was out to nail me for the murder, because I – with my big fucking mouth – told you. As long as the fingers were pointing at me, they weren't pointing at Justine or you.'

He sat very still. Over near the glass wall, Angela turned and looked at him. This bit she quite obviously hadn't known. 'Allen?' she said.

'And I told Clive Wainwright, and Clive told you, that Pike had saved some of Sebastian's papers, and the desk, from the Ward fire. Christ.' I gestured to the photocopies. 'You must have died when you heard that one.'

'I don't see that any of this is relevant.'

'Relevant?' I raked my fingers up through my hair. Then I thought of Katy back in the hospital and that helped me get a grip. Very evenly, I said, 'Just tell Tyler from me, if he ever tries to see my sister again, someone's going to be up on a murder charge. Just tell him that.'

'I hardly think—'

'Just tell him!'

Allen reared back; it was probably the first time anyone had shouted at him in years. But his look, when he came forward again, was dark. As he spoke, he counted the points off on his fingers.

'The Mortlake Group wrote leads on business that turned out bad. No crime. The Mortlake Group happened to reinsure those leads. No crime. I received the repayment of a personal debt for one and a half million that Sebastian happened to owe me. No crime.' He indicated the photocopies. 'You think this is evidence of anything? It's evidence that a recently sacked employee has a very big axe to grind. No court is going to give you the time of day, son.' He rose from behind the desk. 'Piss off,' he said. 'We've got guests coming.'

'They've been delayed.'

Angela looked at me curiously. Allen cocked his head. 'What?' he said.

'There's an important meeting on upstairs.'

'Get out.'

'Piers Crossland,' I said, pointing a finger upward, 'and the Chairman.'

It took a moment for this to sink in. When it did, Angela let out a low moan. Allen looked down at the photocopies, then up at me.

I said, 'I gave Crossland his copies on the weekend.'

This time the colour didn't just drain from Allen's face, he went absolutely white. He sat down, holding the desk.

I said, 'Piers contacted the Chairman straight away. Apparently they had some senior LCO people going through the files all Sunday. They got Max Ward to open the WardSure offices too: they've been in there checking on whether full payment was made on those other claims, Kestrel and the rest. You know what? Only a third each time.'

You could see the realization of what I'd done to him take hold. Allen touched his forehead, dazed for a second. Under normal circumstances, he was right, I couldn't have blown him out of the water with what I'd discovered. But Piers Crossland was not, like me, a nobody. Maybe what I knew about the Mortlakes was useless in court, but in the hands of Piers Crossland it was dynamite. And Piers Crossland wasn't going to waste the opportunity. The merger might – probably would – still go ahead, but everything would happen on Crossland's terms now. Suddenly he wasn't the junior partner. Suddenly he was helping the Chairman of Lloyd's clear up a very messy situation. Discreetly. Nobody wanted a scandal.

'You shit,' Allen said quietly.

Gesturing around, I told him, 'Maybe you can save the flowers for another time.'

He snatched at the vase on his desk. I think he meant to hurl it at me, but he mistimed the grab. The vase went skating over the edge and smashed on the floor. A water stain spread out across the carpet.

'Fuck,' he said. And then, 'You.' He pointed, but the rage was choking him; he couldn't get any more out.

'Allen,' Angela said turning away from him. 'For God's sake.'

Then Pam's voice came over the intercom. 'Mr Mortlake? The Chairman's office just called through: they're asking if you can go up there. Now, if you can, they said.'

Allen closed his eyes. He looked sick as a dog.

After a long moment, Angela told him, 'You'll have to go.'

He stood there a few seconds more, breathing in and breathing out, then he opened his eyes. He tilted his head back, working his jaw to ease the muscles in his neck.

She said, 'Shall I come?'

He shook his head. He came round the desk, still speechless with rage, and trying, quite desperately, to think. When he got to the door, I said, 'Good luck.'

He stopped, one hand on the door. Without turning to face me, he said, 'If I ever see you again, Collier, I'll fucking kill you.' Then he opened the door and went out.

On the floor, where the vase had broken, the water stain was spreading. I bent and picked up one of the lilies and squeezed the white petals between my fingers. It smelt like sugar. Angela watched me.

At last she said, 'What did he offer you?'

I looked up.

'Crossland,' she said.

'That's not how it was, Angela.'

'Did he offer you my job? Underwriter on the 486 Box. What you wanted?'

'That's not why I did it.'

Weakly, she smiled. 'I'm not pointing the finger.'

'You lied to me, Angela.'

She seemed taken by surprise.

'You didn't tell me the whole truth,' I said. 'You told me half the truth: it was as good as a lie.'

She didn't try to justify it. After a moment she simply nodded.

I went and picked up the photocopies and looked at them. I thought of my years in the Room. Finally I put them down and faced her. 'All this,' I said. 'I don't get it. It's just not you, Angela.'

'I wish it wasn't.' Her voice was sad. Sad and old.

I said, 'Did Allen force you into it?'

She turned her head.

'Then what? Help me out here, Angela, I mean I looked up to you. I really did. And you—' I put my hand on the photocopies – 'you were pulling this shit.'

That stung her; she moved uncomfortably in her chair.

'And then I was in serious trouble, and you lied to me to protect yourself.'

'To protect Allen,' she broke in.

'Whatever.' I waved a hand. 'Him and Tyler had me hanging out there, with Fielding trying to nail me, and—'

'I didn't know about Tyler.'

'Well, does that make it all right then?'

She turned aside. 'You've made your point, Ian.'

I followed her gaze to the glass wall. Stuffing my hands in my pockets, I went over there and looked out and down to the Room. It was getting busy again, the brokers touting their slips around the boxes, the money going round. I leant forward, my forehead resting on the glass, tired to death. Was this it, all there was to my life?

'I really thought I loved him,' Angela said suddenly.

When I turned, she stared past me.

'It's not an excuse, I know that.'

'Sebastian?'

She nodded, almost to herself. 'It wasn't just an affair. Not at first. Not to me, anyway.'

'What was going on with that diamond brooch, Angela?'

'I didn't know.'

I waited.

Finally she said, 'It was something Sebastian gave me years ago. A gift.'

We were silent a while, each with our own thoughts. I didn't quite understand it, but I was sure now that the news about the brooch had taken her right out of the blue.

I said, 'What about the policies? The leads on the bad business. How did that happen?'

'Like I told you. Except that after the first time, when I reinsured the whole lead line, Allen noticed. He knew something wasn't right. I don't know, maybe he had his suspicions about Sebastian and me already.'

'What did he do?'

'He waited.'

I gave Angela a questioning look. When she turned away, I said, 'Don't you think I'm owed some kind of explanation, Angela? All I've been put through?'

Her head went down. 'The next time it happened, when I wrote the lead line through WardSure then reinsured the whole lot, Allen went and saw Sebastian. Not a word to me. First I heard of it was months later; Sebastian told me.'

I turned that one over. 'Allen cut a deal with Sebastian?'

She nodded.

'He cut a deal with him, while he knew you were having an affair with Sebastian?'

She nodded again.

Genuinely surprised, I muttered, 'Bastard must have ice in his veins.'

'You're missing the point,' Angela said. She saw, by my look, that I was still missing it. 'I found out from Sebastian,' she said. 'Not Allen. Allen never said a word. He went on treating me like a wife.' She repeated it quietly. 'Like a wife.'

After all these years, the wound was still raw. This was Allen Mortlake we were talking about: the man who schemed schemes in his sleep.

'That was his revenge?'

She dropped her head again. And then I realized something else.

'That brooch Sebastian gave you. Allen knew about that too?'

'I never wore it.' She put her hand to her mouth. 'Perhaps Sebastian told him,' she said as if speaking to herself. 'Maybe he just guessed.'

It was like panels sliding back, and me getting to finally see what was really behind them. Allen having Bill Tyler plant the brooch in my flat: that wasn't just to drop me in it. It was also a little tap on his wife's shoulder. Hey, you think I've forgotten? Well here, look at this. And Angela couldn't have spoken up and saved me without bringing the whole pack of cards down on herself and Allen and Justine. Her family. Lee Chan's thing about revenge being a dish best served cold, it hadn't been so wide of the mark. Allen Mortlake was a very twisted man.

But Angela's thoughts had moved on; she started speaking. 'I came to my senses about Sebastian pretty soon after. Allen and I stayed together. I told myself that was best for Justine. Perhaps I thought we could patch things up, that I could make it up to him somehow.' She took a moment with herself, then looked up. 'And it didn't escape my attention,' she said, 'that his business was doing very well. I knew I could do a lot worse than Allen.'

This moment of brutal honesty was a touch of the old Angela. But after all that had happened, I couldn't bring myself to cheer.

I said, 'You went on writing the rotten leads.'

'Allen asked me to.'

I waited.

'Okay, Ian. Allen asked me to, and I owed him, and I was too much of a coward not to. As the actress said to the bishop, It only hurts the first time.'

She couldn't quite hold my gaze. It wasn't just brutal honesty in her voice now: there was a definite note of shame, even self-disgust. A long time ago she'd made a mistake – with Sebastian, and with that first rotten lead she'd written – and ever since then Allen had made her pay the price. If I hadn't had my life turned inside-out getting this far, I might have felt sorrier.

Turning, I clicked my briefcase shut. I had one more question. I had to steel myself a moment before asking it, but I knew there'd never be another time.

'Angela, why was Allen going to give me your job?'

This time she didn't answer.

Still looking at my briefcase, I said, 'It wasn't because you thought I was the best candidate, was it? It wasn't because you recommended me.'

'Does it matter, Ian?'

There, if I had the guts to see it, was my answer. I made a sound. Does it matter? I'd worked my balls off for twelve years; I'd played the game, climbed the slippery pole, and I'd believed that what success I'd had was down to me. Does it matter? God. God, what an idiot.

I said, 'It wasn't just the regular duties I was meant to take over, was it? I was meant to take over this bullshit.' I pointed to the photocopies. 'Angela,' I said. 'Jesus Christ. You had me lined up to be Allen and Sebastian's new patsy.'

'It wasn't like that.'

'How far back? When Allen first took me on?'

'Ian.'

'All that crap Sebastian gave me at lunch that time.' I shook my head. He hadn't been doing what I'd guessed back then, helping Allen test my integrity. He'd been checking to make sure I'd play ball. That when Angela was gone, and he and Allen wanted a rotten lead dropped into the market, I'd be up for it. And what I'd told him over lunch hadn't been at all what he, or Allen, either expected or wanted to hear.

Quietly, I said, 'And whose bright idea was it to lean on my father?'

She faced me squarely. 'I never knew about that, Ian. Not till it came out in court.'

'But that's what happened, isn't it? Sebastian punted my father into the ground then whispered in his ear that he could help him? If I just did Sebastian a little favour, like writing a rotten lead into the market, then Sebastian would forgive my old man's debt? Isn't that what happened?'

'I don't know.'

'After it came up in court, you must have asked Allen. He must have said something.'

Her brow creased; she looked at me oddly.

'Angela?'

At last she nodded. 'I didn't know until then. But surely you, Ian.'

Tears, unexpected tears, suddenly prickled behind my eyes. I closed them, and pressed my fingertips to my eyelids.

'Oh my God,' she said softly. 'Your father never told you.'

I picked up my briefcase and stood. At that moment I felt like Katy must have felt when she got her hands on that little blue book; I thought my heart was going to burst. My father never told me. Sebastian had screwed him with the idea of getting leverage over me, but Dad hadn't spoken a word. Sebastian and Allen, my heroes in suits, the guys I once wanted to be, they'd read him all wrong, a mistake that had cost Mum and Dad their lives.

Dad was too proud, too honest, too ashamed, maybe, of the situation he'd punted himself into. A situation I'd always warned him would happen, and when it finally had – and with Sebastian – how the hell could Dad tell me? How the hell could he tell me?

Going out the door I shot one last look back at Angela. She was standing now, one hand resting on the desk for support. She looked grey and old, and I felt no pity at all.

Quietly I said, 'He'd rather have died.'

11

'What's the big secret?' Tubs asked me, coming into the kitchen. He helped himself to a sandwich, and between mouthfuls he added, 'You reckon you bought something?'

'Katy's coming over to see it. I thought you might as well too.'

He raised a brow. 'She outa hospital?'

'She's here.'

We went through to the lounge. No Katy. But coming from her bathroom was the faint swish of the shower.

Tubs smiled. 'Sounds like a full recovery.'

I went and banged on her door. 'Katy!'

'Five minutes.'

'Tubs is here. We're going out. See you downstairs in quarter of an hour.'

There was a muffled answer; I took that for an okay. I went and put on my coat, and opened the front door. Tubs stood in the middle of the lounge room stuffing the last of the sandwich into his gob.

'Going out where?'

For a walk, I told him. I told him he looked like he needed the exercise.

We didn't walk far, just partway across the paved waste-land, then Tubs found himself a bench by the canal. He lowered himself onto the bench with a sigh. It was four days since my last meeting with the Mortlakes, the big showdown, and Tubs asked me now how that whole business had panned out.

'Painfully,' I said, 'for the Mortlakes. Painfully and quickly.'

Clive Wainwright had phoned me each afternoon to give me the gossip. The Lloyd's Committee had closed ranks against Allen and Angela. As I'd thought, no-one wanted another scandal in the market, but the call I'd got from Piers Crossland that morning had put the final seal on it.

'They're out,' he'd told me bluntly.

The Mortlake Group had gone ahead with the Crossland merger, but Allen and Angela had been forced to give up their holding in the company. They'd been paid six million pounds, less than half what the Mortlake Group was really worth, and been forced to sign agreements never to return to work at Lloyd's in any capacity. Justine, apparently, had been made to sign this agreement too.

When I'd explained this to Tubs, he said, 'They got six million?'

I nodded.

'You think that's painful, Ian? They're fucking villains, those people, they walk away with six million?'

What to say? How could I explain to him what Allen must have felt to be stripped of his company like that? How Angela must have felt, given her family connection with Lloyd's, to have been elbowed out in disgrace? How could I tell Tubs that the Mortlake family, in their own circles, had taken a fall they'd never recover from? Allen would try to get back up somehow, I knew that, but judging from what Piers Crossland told me, Allen would be wasting his time. A permanent bad smell had settled on the Mortlake family name. Piers Crossland, with the information I'd given him, had sunk the knife into them about as far as it could go. In the London insurance market, the Mortlakes were finished.

But Tubs didn't understand any of that. What he understood was that a bunch of crooks had walked away from the wreckage with six million pounds.

'If I tried pullin' a stroke like that,' he said, 'I'd be

banged up in gaol in two shakes.'

And what to say to that? What to say to any poor bastard who'd struggled honestly all his life just to keep his head above water? I thought of his mother back there in the two-bedroom semi in Hackney.

'Tubs,' I said sitting down beside him. 'They're from a different world.'

'Yeah.' He stared across the canal. 'Tell me about it.' It was more sad than bitter, the way he said it, like he'd resigned himself to that kind of bullshit a very long time ago.

I looked at him. That aggressive edginess he'd had this past little while was gone. He seemed calm now, like he was at the other side of things, as if he'd come through. And seeing him like that, I realized I couldn't let it rest. I really had to know.

'Tubs, that blue book of Sebastian's, when did you tell Katy about it?'

'At the track,' he said, eyeing me curiously. 'What's the problem? Did you take it down to whatsaname, the son?'

'Max,' I said. 'Yeah. I took it down to Max.'

Tubs half-turned to me.

'Full payout,' I said. 'A hundred and twenty grand.' Rumour had it that Max Ward was trying to sell WardSure while he still had a company to offload. He needed evidence of Sebastian's dirty business practices surfacing now like he needed a hole in the head. When I explained that to Tubs, he nodded grimly.

'What's he get? Six million too, I 's'pose.'

'Almost.'

'Fuck,' Tubs said. He muttered something about the national lottery but I wasn't going to be distracted.

'Tubs, when I spoke to Pike, just before the fire, he said—' I interrupted myself then. There was no point drawing this out. 'Tubs, I checked with Abes Watson. The night Sebastian's house burnt down, you weren't at the Stow. Nev Logan pencilled for Abes that night. You were off sick.'

Tubs shrugged. So what?

'That's not what you told me, Tubs. Remember I came back from work the next day, you and Katy were there? I told you what had happened to Sebastian. You banged on about Jigsaw – he trapped like this, he got bumped at the turn – all crap, Tubs. All crap. You never saw him run that night. You weren't there.'

Tubs didn't say anything. He looked over the cans again.

'And Dad's bag,' I said, 'and his ledger. You had them for months. Are you telling me you never looked in his ledger? You looked in it, all right. And Dad dropping that stuff on you to give to me. Then him dying. Knowing what you knew about Sebastian punting Dad into the ground; don't tell me you didn't guess it might be suicide.'

Again no answer.

'When you gave me Dad's ledger, when I figured out that last bet meant he'd taken out the house insurance with Sebastian – that wasn't news to you, was it? Tubs?'

'Leave it, Ian.'

'You led me by the friggin' nose.'

'You dunno what you're getting into.'

'But I think I do, Tubs. I think I do.'

'Then leave it alone,' he said.

Why not? Why not do just that? I wasn't under suspicion any more, Fielding thought he'd found Sebastian's murderer. Eddie Pike did it. Nigel Chambers said so. And Eddie Pike, in an attempt to burn the last of the evidence against him, had died in a fire of his own making at the Stow. Everything neat and tidy.

But I couldn't leave it. None of that was true.

I said, 'When Mum and Dad died, and you got on my back about making a claim, you said you thought Dad had taken out a policy with Sebastian.' I looked at him. 'You knew he had, didn't you. From that last entry in Dad's ledger.'

Tubs stayed silent.

I reached out and touched his shoulder. 'This is just

452

you and me, Tubs. This isn't going anywhere else.'

'Okay,' he said quietly. 'So I knew.'

'And when I went and asked Sebastian, and he told me I was mistaken; there was no way Dad gave him a premium—'

'And you believed the guy,' Tubs said, accusing me suddenly. 'And when I said I thought he was lying, you told me to piss off.'

I lifted my head in surprise.

'That's what you said.' Tubs waved a hand. 'Piss off.'

I wanted to deny it, but thinking back, those weeks just after Mum and Dad died, I could have said anything. And Tubs, quite obviously, remembered. I bowed my head. I said, 'Is that when you told Katy?'

'It's history.' He was annoyed with me now. 'Forget it.'

'Why didn't you tell me?' I asked him. 'Way back then, right at the start, you told Katy everything you knew. That's why she kept on at me about Dad not letting us down. That's why she risked her damn neck at the Stow fire, trying to get her hands on Sebastian's blue book. You didn't tell her just the other night; she knew all along about Dad's ledger. Tubs, you told Katy, why the hell didn't you tell me?'

We looked at each other. He seemed to make a decision.

'You wanna know why, Ian? Because I didn't trust you.'

I swayed back on the bench like he'd smacked me in the mouth. He didn't trust me?

'Don't look so bloody surprised. You turned your back on your old man. You were just about bum-chums with Ward.'

'No, I wasn't.'

'Christ,' he said, 'look at this clown Mortlake you were working for. Now it turns out he's had his fingers in the till for years. I mean, think about it, Ian, what kind of people you got yourself tied up with there. A different world, all right. A bunch of fucking crooks.'

'I didn't know that.'

'Ward was a wrong'n, I told you that. Jesus, your old

man told you. Would you listen?' Tubs spat over the side of the bench. 'Would you fuck.'

'I was doing a job.'

He looked away. 'Yeah, well I hope it was worth it.'

Tubs. I wanted to grab the fat bastard and shake him. That's not how it was, I wanted to say. I wanted him to understand how it was being big bold Bob Collier's son. Not his penciller, or his friend, but his son. I didn't turn my back on Dad; I didn't turn my back on any of them. But Tubs had made up his mind. He thought just like Dad thought; there were two lots of people in the world, Us and Them. And Tubs believed that when I'd bust up with Dad, I'd crossed over.

'You didn't trust me,' I said. 'But you trusted Katy.'

They were her parents too, Ian. And yeah, I trusted her.'

I faced him directly now. 'That was no reason to take her to Ward's house that night, Tubs. No reason at all.'

He gave me a long, cool stare. Then he said, 'This isn't clever, Ian.'

And maybe it wasn't. Maybe if Fielding hadn't tied things up so neatly with Eddie Pike, I would have let it be. But it had cost me plenty to get this far; I'd seen my world come apart, and no-one, not even Tubs, was going to slam the door in my face now.

'When Pike got home that night, Tubs, he checked the security cameras. The ones in Ward's bedroom, and all the private areas, were switched off. Pike told me that was the usual form when Ward had female company. Like Justine Mortlake. Or Angela.' Resting an elbow on the back of the bench, I said, 'And somehow, Tubs, I'm pretty sure he wouldn't have gone to that kind of trouble on your account.'

'What good's this do anybody?' Tubs opened his hands. 'It's finished, Ian. Drop it.'

Then from way up behind us, we heard someone whistle. We both turned to look up at the balcony of my flat. Katy stood there in her white bathrobe, a towel wrapped like a turban on her head. She held out a

454

hand, fingers splayed, and called, 'Five minutes!' then he went back inside.

Facing Tubs again, I said, 'I could ask her.'

He thought it over for a while. I let him do that, and then I said, 'Tubs?'

'You're not gonna believe this, Ian.'

'Try me.'

He swore quietly. He knew I wouldn't back down. 'It wasn't just the ledger. I seen Ward and your old man at the Gallon. I seen Bob give him the money and Ward write it down in that bloody blue book he had. And yeah, after the fire, after you told me to piss off, I let Katy know.'

I nodded. I said I believed it.

'Not that,' he said. He dragged a hand over his face. 'Ian, I didn't make her go to Ward's house that night. Once she knew about the blue book it got to be like a mission, how she'd get her hands on it, prove that Bob done the right thing like, and that Ward was bent. That afternoon, I got this call from her. Cancel everything. She's got an invite to Ward's house. Just the two of them.' Tubs avoided my eyes. 'Bloody women,' he said. 'She made me go.'

I asked him if Katy said why Ward had asked her over.

He shook his head. 'But what she was wearing when I took her round there. It wasn't a business meeting, Ian, I tell ya.'

'Did you go in?'

Again he shook his head. 'I parked out in the street. I watched her go up through the gates, I was just meant to wait there.'

'The plan being what? Katy sleeps with him? While he's snoring his head off she tip-toes down, steals the blue book and does a runner?'

'It wasn't my plan, Ian, okay? I was just there.'

'And then what?'

He avoided my eyes again. 'Few hours later she comes out. She's seen the blue book, she's tricked Sebastian into getting it out for her.' For the first time

since we'd sat down, Tubs smiled. 'Know what sh[e]
done? She give him fifty quid; she told him she wante[d]
to insure Jigsaw against injury. Can you believe th[e]
greedy bastard? He goes and gets the blue book out o[f]
his desk – she seen him. He signs a slip for her, loc[ks]
the blue book back in the desk, then up and back int[o]
the champagne.'

Which explained why Tubs was so keen to help m[e]
find Pike. And the desk. He hadn't been guessing, h[e]
knew Sebastian's blue book was there. And so had Kat[y.]

I said, 'She didn't come back out of the house with th[e]
book.'

'Couldn't find the bloody key. Ward's upstairs asleep[,]
she's going nuts trying to open his desk. She thought sh[e]
heard him movin' around.'

I looked at Tubs, waiting.

He shrugged. 'She done a bunk, I took her home, en[d]
of story.'

'You were there a few hours.'

He nodded.

'So when you took her home it was what, midnight[?]
One?'

'About,' he said, pulling a face. 'Look, what's the bi[g]
quiz?' He glanced over his shoulder but there was no sig[n]
of Katy yet.

I said, 'Eddie Pike got back to Ward's place from th[e]
track at nine thirty or ten. And Ward was already dead.'

He turned back to me slowly.

'Tubs,' I said, 'don't you think you've bullshitted m[e]
enough?'

We looked at each other, me and my family's olde[st]
friend, almost there at the end of the line. I'd closed th[e]
gap but I hadn't quite reached him, and I saw that h[e]
wasn't going to speak. He wasn't going to, so if I wa[s]
going to finish this, I had to.

'Maybe I've changed, Tubs. Maybe you're even right t[o]
blame me a bit for the bust-up with Dad, but really, [I]
haven't changed that much.'

Tubs's face was like stone.

'I'm not excusing myself. I wanted something different from Dad, that's all. Mum knew that, she didn't blame me. You want the truth, if Dad was alive now I'd make an effort with him too, but he isn't, Tubs, neither of them are, and I can't change that. You think I don't lie awake some nights? You think it doesn't hurt when I think about what Dad did, and maybe why he did it? Well, it does. It hurts because they were my family. It hurts because I stood there and watched the house burn down on top of them – don't get up, Tubs, I'm not finished.'

He paused half-standing, then sat down again.

'All that stuff, I can't do one bloody thing about it now – I can't even say sorry. They're gone, Tubs. And you can put some of the blame on me for that if you want: I won't argue, but I'm not going to roll over and die. Maybe the world might be better for it if I did, but I'm not going to.' He looked out over the water; a gull cried. I'd reached the end. I said, 'She's my sister, Tubs. My sister.'

He didn't say anything to that.

'When she came back up to London after the funeral, Tubs, whose place did she come to? Yours or mine?'

I saw that one go into him. I'd reached him at last. When he faced me I took the dark brown bottle out of my coat pocket, and placed it on the bench between us. We both looked at it. A brown bottle with nothing left in it but half a dozen strong-dose sleeping pills, Tripzatol. A brown bottle from Katy's bathroom cabinet. Katy, the vegetarian, the homeopath's dream customer, who for the past five years hadn't been within shouting distance of even the lowest-dose aspirin. A brown bottle she hadn't bothered to hide even after Fielding's visits to our flat. The warning about cardiac side-effects was right there on the label.

I said, 'She doesn't know she killed him, does she?'

Tubs stared at the bottle a long while. The only piece of evidence.

'She spiked his drink, right?'

Tubs's eyes were sadder than anything. 'His fuckir heart,' he said. 'How was she meant to know?'

Suddenly I felt very cold.

'How?' I said stupidly, as if that made any differen now.

Tubs looked like he still couldn't believe how tl whole business had panned out. He folded his arms. guess he figured it was useless holding back now.

'She came back to the car, I dunno, an hour later? hasn't gone like she planned. She's slipped him tl Mickey Finn; he hasn't even made it up to tl bedroom: he's just flaked out on the bloody sofa. Sl tries the desk but it's locked; she goes through h pockets: she can't find the key, can she? She can't fin the bloody key. And all the time she's worried tl bastard's gonna wake up and spring her.' He looked me. 'Did I oughta be tellin' you this?'

'So she left?'

'Not straight off. First she goes and pours the rest the champagne down the sink, she brings the emp bottle back out and puts it on the floor next t Sebastian. Chucked a blanket over him too, she recl oned.'

An empty bottle and a blanket, just like Eddie Pik told me. But Tubs saw my puzzled look.

'Katy wasn't giving up,' he said. 'She thought if h woke up like that next mornin' he might believe happened like she was gonna tell him. You know, "Yo had too much to drink; you flaked out, so I covered yo up and left." She thought maybe she could get anothe shot at that blue book another time.'

'Didn't she notice anything wrong with him?'

Tubs didn't answer for a moment. Then turning awa from me he said, 'She reckoned he moaned a bit.'

A sound came up from deep inside me. Sebastia moaned a bit. Not, like Katy thought, in his sleep. H moaned because his dicky heart was packing it in because lying there, flaked out on the sofa, Sebastia Ward was starting to die.

I took a moment with that. 'So then she came out and you both drove off.'

Tubs nodded. I turned and faced him directly.

'How long have you known the truth?'

'For sure?' He opened a hand. 'Only the other night. When you told me Pike's story was the same as Chambers' – they both said he was already dead – well, I thought, yeah, it had to be.'

'And back when I told you about Sebastian's bad heart? The K and R business, when I told you he was on medication?'

'It started bells ringing,' Tubs conceded, fixing me with a steady look.

He knew what I was thinking: how could he not know? He'd spent days watching Fielding turn me inside-out; he'd listened to my desperate complaints against the bloody injustice of it all. Christ, he'd even helped me escape from the City airport security people and Mehmet – how could he not know what I was thinking now?

'You didn't say a word, Tubs. And if Fielding had got what he wanted, if he'd pinned Sebastian's murder on me, you wouldn't have said a word then either.'

It wasn't a question and he didn't treat it like one, he kept his gaze on me, steady. He really would have done it. If it had come to a choice, he would have looked on silently while I got sent down for a murder I didn't commit. He would have done it so Katy could stay free. Anyone but Katy, and I would have taken his head off.

'I'm not gonna apologize, Ian.'

Standing, I picked up the bottle. I turned it over in my hand a few times then I walked over to the canal and unscrewed the cap. I jerked my hand and the last of the pills shot into the air, then rained down, peppering the surface of the water. I put the bottle in my left hand, took one step back and bowled the thing overarm into the middle of the canal. It splashed down and sunk like a rock; the ripples spread. That lone gull came swooping in, crying as it dipped near the water

where the bottle had gone. Another pass, then the gu
flew on. I dropped the bottle cap and scuffed it into th
canal with the toe of my shoe. I put my hands in m
coat pockets.

What, exactly, had I expected from Tubs? Loyalty
Friendship?

'You don't owe me an apology,' I said, turning. 'Bu
Tubs—' I stepped up close to the bench and leant ove
him – 'just so there's no disappointment here, don
expect any bloody thanks.'

To my surprise, he simply nodded at that. I don
know, maybe he'd been waiting for something wors
from me – a tantrum perhaps – over what he'd bee
willing to watch me go through. I was angry with him
sure, but there was too much else as well; other feeling
like a kind of grudging admiration. He'd made hi
choice, and his choice was Katy, and I really couldn'
blame him for that.

'Ian!'

There she was, my kid sister, hurrying across th
pavement wasteland. She was huddled over, trying t
stop her coat from blowing open. She stopped an
waited for us.

I took a few steps towards her then I stopped too
Tubs sat on the bench, unmoving. Hadn't I been her
before, with Dad? Angry and nursing a grudge agains
him, him not budging an inch because he didn't thin
he'd done wrong? Dad and Tubs, they were out of th
same bloody kennel. They had their ways all right, bu
after what I'd learnt about the likes of Allen Mortlak
and Sebastian Ward, those ways didn't seem quite s
bad any more. There were plenty worse qualities tha
pig-headedness, and a lot worse men in the world tha
Tubs and Dad. A bit late in the day, but I'd learnt.

Glancing back over my shoulder I said, 'Tubs,' and h
craned round to face me. He didn't know what to expect
If I'd slammed down the shutters on him then, it woul
have been just like with Dad, a complete bust-up. Tub
knew it too, but he didn't say a word. It was my call.

I said. 'Are you coming?'

After a moment he hauled himself off the bench and came over to join me, and we fell into step side by side.

12

When I parked outside Kerry Anne's office I told Tubs and Katy I might be a while. 'Why don't you go round and see Nev?' I arranged to meet them there in twenty minutes then I watched them go off down the street. They were discussing Jigsaw. On the way over, Katy had announced that she planned to go back to college: it seemed she'd already booked herself in. It was going to be strange not having her around, and it felt strange now just watching her walk down the street with Tubs, her not even knowing what she'd done, the one single worry in her head what to do with Jigsaw the wonderdog when she checked out of London.

Katy was free. Not just free of the law, free in her head too – it was what Tubs had given her just by keeping his mouth shut. I don't know, maybe I really should have thanked him.

Sebastian unintentionally killed Dad, and Katy unintentionally killed Sebastian. It was one of those things that could have made you believe in God if you thought about it too much.

Tubs and Katy turned into Nev's shop, and I went up to see Kerry Anne Lammar.

I can't say she was pleased to see me. When the receptionist showed me into the office, Kerry Anne stood up and smiled as she said my name; she even shook my hand, but she would much rather have throttled me. She really thought she'd been going to teach me – the jumped-up East End boy – a lesson. Sure, she was happy the

penthouse was going to be paid for in full now, that sh
was going to get her full commission. But she just woul
have preferred it if my deposit had disappeared into h
boss's pocket first. After that, any alternative purchaser
brought her would have been stuffed with caviar an
champagne. As it was, Piers Crossland, sitting across th
desk from her, had nothing in front of him but papers.

'Give the man a pen,' Crossland said without lookin
up. He carried on reading, then signed the page, the
turned to the next.

I sat down next to him and Kerry Anne gave me th
papers I had to sign to relinquish my rights over th
penthouse. It was much less painful than I'd thought
was going to be. It took fifteen minutes.

Once that was done, there was a brief discussion abou
solicitors and banking details between Crossland an
Kerry Anne. Only when that was finished did Kerry Ann
finally produce the cheque for me, my deposit of on
hundred thousand pounds, less the five thousand poun
penalty, less administrative deductions, whatever tha
meant, of two thousand pounds. I slipped the cheque fo
ninety-three thousand pounds into my wallet. It coul
have been worse. A lot, lot worse.

Without the help of Tubs and Clive and Lee Chan,
knew bloody well I would never have got to the bottom o
Allen and Sebastian's scam. And without that, Pier
Crossland's enthusiasm for the property market woul
never have stretched to a penthouse on the Thames, an
my deposit would have disappeared straight down th
toilet.

Piers went out the door ahead of me. Before I followe
him, I said to Kerry Anne, 'You're glad I didn't get th
place.'

She thought about denying it, but in the end she jus
smiled. 'You bit off more than you could chew, M
Collier. Whose fault's that?'

'Thank you for keeping me so well informed on clause
seven.'

'My pleasure,' she said, beaming now.

'Go see a head doctor,' I told her as I went out the door. 'If you want a free opinion, I think it's a sexual thing.'

Her smile disappeared; her eyes blazed. Gently I closed the door. That, I sincerely hoped, was the last I ever saw of Kerry Anne Lammar.

As I followed Piers down the stairs he asked me if I'd reconsidered his offer. His offer, as I remembered it, was that I become a general dogsbody in the administrative section of the new merged company. A job for life, but not a job as an underwriter. Not a job I wanted.

'At least till things settle down,' he said now.

'How long? A year?'

He didn't answer.

'Two years?'

'These things take time,' he said.

I touched his shoulder. He stopped and looked back.

I said, 'I'm finished in the Room, aren't I.'

He started to shake his head, then his eyes met mine. He saw I wanted it straight.

'It won't be easy, but I'll try,' he said. 'Maybe after a few years—'

I made a sound.

'That's the way it is, Ian. You know you're innocent, I know it, but the market isn't you and me.' He considered a moment. 'Straight up?'

I nodded.

'I can't afford to have you underwriting for me. After everything you've been caught up in, the market doesn't trust you. I'm sorry, Ian.' He touched my arm. 'That other job's yours if you want it.'

He carried on down the stairs. I hadn't seriously expected more from him. I'd delivered him Allen Mortlake's head on a plate, and he'd taken the penthouse problem off my hands; he didn't owe me anything now. And he sure wasn't going to risk his company's reputation in a hopeless attempt to restore mine.

But down in the foyer Crossland stopped again and faced me.

'Listen, this is probably no consolation, but I wasn't going into the merger blind. I'd checked the numbers and the people. If things had been different, you'd be running the 486 box now.'

He was right; it was no consolation at all. But surprised me.

'Not Frazer?'

'Burnett-Adams?' Now he was surprised. 'Took me two years to get rid of him last time I was landed with him. This time he's got six months.'

'He's out?'

'Invited to resign.' Crossland looked at me curiously. And then, as usual too late to do me any good, I got it.

'You don't like him?'

'I had to sit next to him on the 423 box for two and half years, listening to his family history,' Crossland said. 'Never again.'

My head dropped. I even managed a wry smile. Office politics really is not my game.

Mistaking my look, Crossland asked if I thought he was making a blunder, getting rid of Frazer. I said, No, that it seemed like he knew what he was doing. I offered him my hand and when he took it, I told him, 'And I won't be changing my mind about the job.'

In his eyes I saw the realization come that I meant it.

'Well, if things don't work out for you . . .'

'Sure.'

We went out onto the pavement. He wished me luck, then I watched as he went over and got into his Roller. His chauffeur closed the door behind him. When the Roller pulled out into the traffic I saw Piers Crossland already on his mobile, absorbed in his next deal or his next problem, a million miles away.

Fielding had won half a victory. I wasn't in gaol where he would have liked to put me, but my life at Lloyd's was over. Old habits and long-held ambitions being what they are, it was going to take more than a little while to get used to that. Turning, I headed down to Nev's.

There was a Closed sign on the door, but when I went

466

nside the party was in full swing. He'd decked the place
out in streamers and there was a stack of coloured
balloons floating up near the ceiling. On the TV screens,
horses were charging over the turf, but the sound coming
from the speakers was pure Rolling Stones. Over near the
beer keg a few people had started to dance.

I was halfway to the betting counter when Clive Wainwright emerged from the crush.

'All done?'

All done, he told me. He told me now he just needed
the cheque.

We pushed on to the counter; I took out the cheque for
ninety-three thousand pounds and endorsed it. He took it
and disappeared into the crowd.

Leaning back, I ran my eyes over the room, picking out
faces. Some from the old days at the Gallon, like buck-
toothed Freddie Day, and some from the Stow, and heaps
more I didn't recognize, they must have been the staff
from Nev's other two shops and his regular punters, all
invited down for the party.

Then the crowd opened up and Tubs appeared, beer in
hand, Katy just behind.

'Seen Nev?' he asked me, scanning the room. 'First
wake I been to where the guest of honour's still on his
feet.'

Katy punched his arm. Beer sloshed out of the plastic
cup and down his sleeve, and he laughed. Then the music
went off. A few people booed, then someone said, 'Shut
up,' and after a bit everyone went quiet as the heads
turned towards the corner where Clive Wainwright was
helping Nev up onto a chair. When Nev was steady he
looked around, holding his beer close to his chest.

'Ladies,' he said, 'and fellow blockheads.' There were a
few laughing jeers; he nodded and spoke right over them.
He thanked everyone for coming, cracked a joke, then got
down to business. Logan's betting shops, he said, were
ceasing to trade. He said he wasn't in any kind of shape to
make a long speech, besides, there were people there
worried about their jobs, he wasn't going to draw out their

agony, he just wanted to tell them straight. 'First of
you'll be happy to hear, we're not turnin' into a ham
burger shop.' A lone cheer came from back near the doo
'And second off, yous haven't got rid of me yet, I'll b
helpin' out the new management for a bit.' Then Ne
glanced down at Clive and said, 'Where is 'e?'

Clive stood on tip-toe and pointed.

'Anyway,' Nev said, 'as from next Monday, the shop
have got a new owner. If anyone wants to introduc
'emselves, that's him over there, the berky-lookin' bloke
He pointed where Clive had pointed, straight at me. 'Ia
Collier. You all woulda known his father. Ian's big Bo
Collier's son.' Nev raised his glass. 'The new owner,' h
said.

Around the room the glasses went up, everyone tryin
to get a look at me. Tubs and Katy just stared. I raised m
glass to them and drank.

Someone called out, 'Speech!' but I shook my head.

I told them I didn't start till Monday. 'But feel free t
get stuck into the grog. It's on Nev.'

They cheered.

Tubs reached over, his hand closing round the lapel o
my jacket. He gave me a couple of friendly thumps on th
chest. 'Fuck me,' he said. 'You.' Then he turned to Katy
laughing, still trying to get his head round what I'd done

Katy stepped up and kissed me on the cheek. Her eye
had misted over; I think it was the mention of Dad tha
did that.

'I'm so glad,' she said. She squeezed my arm an
looked around. 'I think it's great, Ian. Really great.'

I looked around too, and I wasn't so sure it was grea
there was a hell of a lot of work to do on the place, an
even more on the other two shops. But I was glad a
right. From that moment on I never had any real doubt
about what I'd done.

People came up to me and introduced themselves, an
the music played, and the grog went down. But all th
time I was smiling and talking I was thinking to myself
Call her.

It was over an hour before I managed to pull myself away from everybody. I slipped into Nev's back room and used his phone.

'Sorry, sir,' said the receptionist at the Phoenix Hotel in Dublin. 'Miss Lee Chan's not answering.'

'Can you take a message?'

She said she could, but she couldn't guarantee Miss Lee Chan would pick it up. 'And she's checking out first thing in the morning.'

'When?' I asked.

Paper rustled. 'Four a.m.,' she said. 'Any message, sir?'

I pictured Lee wheeling her bags out the hotel door to the taxi, my message sitting there behind the reception desk until someone noticed it later in the day and chucked it in the bin. And Lee already halfway to San Fran.

'No,' I said. 'No message,' and I hung up the phone. I sat there a while staring at the clock. Outside in the shop, the noise was trailing off now, I glanced through the two-way mirror and saw people leaving.

Then Nev and Tubs came in from the back, and Freddie Day and Clive right behind them. Clive had taken off his tie; the end was dangling from his pocket. He came over and clapped me on the shoulder. He told me I was better off out of that snakepit at Lloyd's; he said he admired my guts. It might have meant more to me if I hadn't realized he was already half-cut.

The other three called him over to the table and he clapped me on the shoulder again and went. Nev pulled out a pack of cards and started to deal. When the money came out, I picked up my coat and did a round of the table, shaking hands. They all said how pleased they were.

I found Katy out by the betting counter; she was sitting on some young bloke's knee. She jumped up when I came over and introduced me to him. He seemed about Katy's age but not as tipsy as Katy. I gave him a warning look as I drew her aside.

I said, 'I might not be home tonight. Got your key?'

She checked in her purse, then nodded. I looked over her shoulder at the young bloke. Handsome, I suppose,

clean cut, and a bit sheepish when he noticed me lookin
him over. God knows, she'd picked worse.

I turned her away from the young bloke so that h
couldn't hear me say to her, 'Actually, Katy, I'm definitel
not home tonight.'

Then I made the mistake of looking her in the eye. I fel
myself blush. She laughed, surprised, and more than
little embarrassed too. Some things, for all of us I guess
take time.

She hugged me. When we stepped apart, she said
'Hey, anyway, where are you going?'

And where was I going? I'd left Lloyd's, Piers Crosslan
had the penthouse, and I was now the junior partner
alongside my bank, on both my old flat and three run
down betting shops. Looking at the balance sheet lik
that, I didn't have any right to be feeling as hopeful as
did. But I wasn't really looking at the balance sheet righ
then, I was looking ahead, at the future. It would take
time, but I knew I could turn those three shops round
make them so much better than what they were. Possibilities, that's what I saw. Possibilities to improve and grow
the business, and be part of something I was proud of. To
earn the respect of men I respected.

My old man would never have bought Nev's shops,
knew that. But I wasn't my old man: I couldn't spend the
rest of my life down on the rails at the Stow taking on all
comers, it just wasn't me. And after what I'd seen lately,
knew I couldn't go back to being a suit in the City: that
wasn't me either, not any more.

Sebastian Ward's death had moved my life on; I'd been
through the fire. And so had Tubs and Katy. And so, in
her way, had Lee.

'Wish me luck,' I said to Katy, and she kissed me, not
knowing why.

Take a punt, my old man must have told me that a
million times.

My life was starting over. Maybe not the life I'd always
thought I'd wanted, but that life had crumbled beneath
my feet. And in so many ways, Sebastian's death had set

me free. Mum and Dad were gone, and now at last I felt that I could finally let them go. And Katy was going back to college, not to gaol. And things might be awkward between Tubs and me for a while, but that would come round in the end. I didn't have a penthouse, I had Nev's shops, and I was finished with Lloyd's, but even that wasn't going to kill me. My life was starting over. The world, if I had the courage for it, was full of possibilities.

Take a punt. For the first time since my bust-up with the old man, I knew in my heart he was right. I got a taxi to the airport and booked myself a seat on the next flight out to Dublin.

I had a proposal to put to Lee Chan.

Moon Music

Faye Kellerman

Las Vegas. The Gomorrah of twentieth-century America. A city on the edge of a desert, its inhabitants living on the edge of their nerves. Amongst them is Detective Sergeant Romulus Poe, assigned to the murder of a showgirl whose mauled body, Poe realises, has echoes of a twenty-five-year-old unsolved case. But when Poe discovers his colleague, Steve Jensen, had a relationship with the murdered woman, the anxieties of the present soon overshadow the half-forgotten past.

Poe's own relationship with Jensen's wife, Alison, is far from straightforward: childhood playmate, teenage lover, adult confidante, Poe is still entangled in the emotional ties that Alison, afflicted with anorexia and a habitually unfaithful husband, exerts. But as he watches Alison's struggles with her body Poe begins to wonder if her obsessive research in to what went on in the Nevada Desert three decades earlier could hold a key to the identity of the animalistic murderer still at large in Las Vegas, the most amoral of cities . . .

'Sharply drawn . . . Kellerman's best' *Publishing News*

'It's a credit to Kellerman's storytelling abilities that long after she reveals "who done it" readers will be frantically flipping the pages to find out just how and why' *People* magazine

0 7472 5232 7

Fear Nothing

Dean Koontz

Christopher Snow is athletic, handsome enough, intelligent, romantic, funny. But his whole life has been affected by xeroderma pigmentosum, a rare genetic disorder that means his skin and eyes cannot be exposed to sunlight. Like all Xpers, Chris lives at night – and has never ventured beyond his hometown of Moonlight Bay, a place of picturesque beauty and haunting strangeness.

Despite the limitations imposed by nature, he has always been determined to lead the fullest life and, with the help of family and friends, he has on the whole succeeded. But for Chris – and all the inhabitants of Moonlight Bay – a terrible change is about to happen; a change of potentially catastrophic proportions.

'Not just a master of our dreams, but also a literary juggler' *The Times*

'Plausibly chilling . . . Koontz at his best' *Express on Sunday*

0 7472 5832 5

If you enjoyed this book here is a selection of other bestselling titles from Headline